CONFLUENCE

A GIDON ARONSON THRILLER

Stephen J. Gordon

D1502730

CONFLUENCE
A GIDON ARONSON THRILLER

Stephen J. Gordon

Apprentice House
Loyola University Maryland
Baltimore, Maryland

First Edition
Printed in the United States of America
ISBN: 978-1-934074-86-2

This is a work of fiction. Characters, places, names, and incidents are either the product of the author's imagination or are used fictitiously to facilitate the story.

Cover design by Andrew J. Peters
Author photograph by Sophie Brooks

Published by Apprentice House

Apprentice House
Loyola University Maryland
4501 N. Charles Street
Baltimore, MD 21210
410.617.5265 •410.617.2198 (fax)
www.ApprenticeHouse.com
info@ApprenticeHouse.com

To Becky, your love and support make everything possible; to AJ and Esty, Michal and Avrohom, Jeff, Alana, and Sophie, your unwavering enthusiasm always helps me stay the course.

PROLOGUE

The next man he had to kill was 70 years old, in good health (not that it mattered), and didn't know this was coming. The killing had been decided about three months ago, and it had taken him that long to track him down. Didn't matter. It had been decided, and that was that.

The target was a hundred feet away, hastily working behind a closed glass door to get his clothing shop ready for the Memorial Day weekend opening.

It was ten o'clock on a Wednesday night and his store was the only one in the strip with any activity. The mini haberdashery was located midway along Bay Street in Watch Hill, Rhode Island, basically a one street resort village near the Connecticut-Rhode Island border. Shops and condos straddled both sides of the narrow street. In one area were these quaint, tourist centered shops and eateries, and in another area was the protected harbor and yacht club. For now, though, it was a ghost town…even emptier than what you'd expect from the off-season. The owners of most of the shops would typically drift down from Boston or up from New York on weekends to get ready. But not Mr. Meyers. The season was too important to leave it for only weekend set-ups.

Across the street, the driver in a rented burgundy Infiniti took out his 9mm Beretta and verified there was a round in the chamber. This was going to be easier than he anticipated. His advance team had said it would be straightforward. They were right.

Six hours ago he had arrived on a British Air flight from London into Providence's T.F. Green Airport. Four hours ago he pulled out of the Hertz Rental facility adjacent to the airport. Three hours ago a man at a rest stop off of Route 1 near Westerly handed him a large padded envelope that contained the Beretta.

The man in the Infiniti stepped out of the car, covering his gun in the folds of his lightweight, all weather coat, and crossed the dark street. There was a slight breeze, and he could smell the salty sea air blowing in off the water. The light in Meyers' shop drew him like a beacon. As he approached the glass door, he could see Meyers taking T-shirts out of boxes and stacking them in wooden cubbies along a side wall.

The man glanced to his right and left to triple check that the street was empty, and then with the knuckles of his gloved hand knocked on the glass door.

Meyers looked up. The septuagenarian still had a full head of gray hair, though it was long and unkempt, like a crazy Russian composer's. He approached the front door.

"We're not open yet," he called. "Not for another two weeks."

The man outside shook his head and just said, "What?"

Meyers moved closer. "I said," he raised his voice, "we're not open–"

The driver raised his gun and shot the store owner in the head through the glass door. He then shot him twice more. The glass shattered and lay in varying sized pieces at the killer's feet, but hadn't touched him.

The man in the all weather coat walked back to his rental car and got in. He could now cross Meyers off his list. Next stop, Baltimore.

1

I found myself sitting in the back row of an empty Northwest Baltimore synagogue, trying not to think of anything...not my daily routine, not what I had been doing twenty minutes earlier, not what I had planned for the rest of the day. I particularly did not want to think about the past.

In the front of the modest sanctuary, maybe seventy feet away and the focal point of the entire room, was the ark. It was a rich, polished, wooden cabinet set against the wall, with a dark blue curtain covering its doors. A spotlight illuminated gold Hebrew lettering embroidered on the fabric cover. The wording, translated as "Know before whom you stand" stared at me across the empty room.

Terrific. Not the sentiment I was hoping for. "Know before whom you stand." I closed my eyes for a moment. Maybe this wasn't such a good idea. I wasn't looking for an admonition. I was seeking understanding.

Sometimes after you've killed someone – even if it's justified and righteous – a malaise settles over you like a tangible presence. It weighs you down, draining you of energy and spirit. I have a friend, who spent four years with Israel's Mossad. Today, several years later, he still has recurring dreams about the clandestine work he had done. He saved many lives by killing the right people – bad, truly evil men who planned and carried out bus and restaurant bombings, kidnappings, and murder sprees along beachfront communities – but he couldn't sleep without nightmares.

What was it that George Orwell said? Something like, "People sleep peacefully in their beds at night because rough men stand ready to do violence on their behalf."

But there is a cost. Orwell didn't mention that.

It was late in the afternoon on a Friday, but not so late that services were imminent. For now, I had the place to myself. I had not been in a sanctuary such as this one for maybe two years. But recently... recently, I had been considering coming here. Now, this visit had nothing to do with services or with prayer or sermons or people. That's not what drew me. I simply wanted to be somewhere holy.

So I sat there, alone, with a small, crocheted *kippah* on my head. It was a *kippah* I had been carrying around just in case I found myself in such a place. More than a few years ago, my soon-to-be fiancée, Tamar, had given it to me. At the time, I was still in my Israeli Army uniform, and we had been walking through Jerusalem's Jewish Quarter on a cool, spring day. We were heading down a stone staircase that led to the Western Wall Plaza when we had passed a dark complexioned man of about forty, standing to the side. He had laid out three or four stacks of crocheted *kippot* on the waist high wall next to the staircase. I didn't think the *yarmulkes* were any different than any of the ones on sale in malls or on Ben Yehudah Street, but Tamar spotted a particular azure one. She bought it – not because I typically wear one – but because the tones, she said, matched the color of my eyes.

I smiled to myself, letting the images of another time and place dissolve. As I was seated in the rear of the shul, the entire room was open before me. It was completely silent. There were rows of turquoise-cushioned seats lined up, maybe twenty-five rows in all, leading up to the slightly elevated stage where the rabbi and officers had their individual high-backed chairs. And there was the ark with its gold lettering and ancient phrase, which I wanted to ignore.

The sanctuary was fully lit beneath fluorescent fixtures. In the center of the room stood an island, a raised platform and table, for the reading of the Torah. To the rear of the table was a cushioned bench.

I turned back to the curtain covering the ark. They had to pick *that* phrase? "Know before whom you stand." This wasn't the place for me. So, Gidon, get up and leave.

I looked toward the front again. Hanging from the ceiling near the top of the ark was the "Eternal Flame." Okay, it was an ornamental light fixture with a golden bulb, but still, a decent representation.

The cell phone in my pocket vibrated for a second then stopped. After a moment, I checked the display. There was a text: "COME BACK TO SCHOOL. I NEED YOU."

I pocketed the phone and looked up again at the Eternal Light.

"You know," a man's voice called from the front of the sanctuary, "if you sit in the back row long enough, you might fall asleep."

A thin man in his late thirties was coming toward me. He must've entered from a door tucked off to the side. The man had some books in his hand, and placed them in a book holder behind one of the seats. He was wearing an open collared, seafoam-colored shirt and khakis. "At least that's what happens when I begin to speak. Well, that's not entirely true," he said moving closer, "sometimes people sleep in the front row, too."

"I would *never* do that," I said, standing up.

The man, now to my right, held out his hand. "Josh Mandel."

"Gidon Aronson." I shook his hand. He had a firm grip. "I hope it's okay that I was hanging out back here."

"If the door's open and you got past our secretary, then it's okay." He paused. "For the record, my speeches are always enlightening and stimulating. Never ponderous or esoteric."

"I don't doubt it. You don't seem like a ponderous man. Esoteric, maybe."

"Only on the first Saturday of every month. The congregation expects it."

I looked at Rabbi Mandel. He was about five foot ten, and had thinning, sandy-colored hair, and an easy smile.

"What brings you around? Services don't start for a few hours."

I smiled, "Would you believe esoteric reasons?"

"And it's not even the first of the month." He paused. "Maybe *you* want to give the sermon tomorrow."

"Another time, perhaps."

He let a moment go by. "Seriously, though, anything I can do for you?"

"No, just wanted to wrap my head around a few things."

"That's refreshing."

"What?"

"That you came to a synagogue to do that. I'm really glad."

"So all this is yours."

"Well, they seem to like me. I talk, I teach, I talk, I teach."

"And they keep coming back. Impressive." I smiled. I had never met a rabbi who was so easy to talk to. Maybe because he didn't have that professional clergy aura – and the fact that he was on the younger side and closer to my age.

He seemed about to say something, but then interrupted himself... "Wait... Gidon..." he trailed off, his mind running. "Why do you seem familiar to me? Have you been here before?"

I shook my head. It was a small lie. I was here months ago, in the social hall, as an invited guest to a fundraiser for an Israeli dignitary. There was an assassination attempt and I stopped it. I didn't want to discuss it.

"I'll get out of your way." I began to move toward the door. "I'm sure you have things to do."

"You can stay longer, if you want. Did you find what you came for?"

I looked over at the aphorism on the ark cover. "No, it's okay. Timing must not be right."

"Come to services tonight. Friday evening is really special here. Better than *Shabbat* morning, but don't tell anyone I said that."

"Thanks. It's not my thing. No offense."

"JJ?" A woman's voice called from the front of the sanctuary.

"Over here," the rabbi responded.

I turned to see a young, slim woman coming toward us, carrying a manila envelope. She had shoulder-length, dark straight hair except for the hair cut short to frame her face. She was clad in an orange Orioles T-shirt, a pair of faded jeans, and blue Teva sandals.

"Shelley, this is Gidon." He turned to me, "Gidon, this is Shelley, the *rebetzzin,*… my wife."

I looked at her again. She was a head shorter than me, maybe in her early thirties, and not what I'd have expected. She looked more hippy-ish than rabbi's wife-ish.

"Okay," she said, looking down at her T-shirt and reading my thoughts, "the congregation puts up with the way I dress because they really love my husband. They would prefer I wear a dress all the time, be demure…"

I didn't know what to say.

She patted me on the arm. "Don't worry. I know the look on a person's face when we're introduced."

"Sorry I was so obvious. I pride myself on being inscrutable."

She smiled and turned to the rabbi, handing him the manila envelope. "You forgot your notes, Einstein."

I couldn't help but smile.

She turned to me, "So, Gidon, are you from around here? Got a meal tonight? Do you want to come to us?"

The rabbi leaned in to me, "Shelley wants everyone to have a Friday night meal. I think tonight's an off night. We don't have any guests, do we?

"Nope, just the kids and us."

We began to head out of the sanctuary. Soon, we were outside the building, standing on the sidewalk at Seven Mile Lane, a quiet suburban street. We spoke in the shade of a big maple.

"So, Gidon, really," the rabbi pressed, "do you have a place for tonight?"

I thought about the text message on my phone. I hadn't responded to it.

"JJ," Shelley said to her husband, "Gidon is hesitating because he has to check with his wife or girlfriend, right?"

As I considered a response, a red Kia went by with four kids inside. I could hear rock music blasting through the open windows as the car passed us.

I turned to the rabbi. " 'JJ'?"

"Joshua Jeffrey."

Shelley explained: "We've known each other since high school. Now stop avoiding the invitation. Go talk to your friend and let me know." She didn't mention "wife" this time. She noticed I wasn't wearing a wedding ring.

The phone in my pocket vibrated again. Another text message. I ignored it.

"Okay," I smiled. "I'll ask."

A maroon, late model Buick approached from the left with three men inside. It seemed to slow as it went by, and the two passengers – one in front and one in back – were looking our way. I didn't get a good look at them, except to see that the man in front was wearing aviator-style sunglasses.

"Here's the address," the rabbi handed me a card. It said, "Shelley's Party Planning" with a phone number and address.

"If you come to dinner, I'll explain the card," Shelley said. "We're just around the corner. I'll give you directions when you call." With that, she put her arm through the rabbi's and the two of them headed back into the building.

Even before the glass entry door closed behind them, I dug the cell phone from my pocket and read the text.

"I NEED YOU – NOW."

I texted back that I was on my way.

～

By the time I pulled my Grand Cherokee into the Solomon Stein

Day School parking lot outside the Beltway, only a few cars were left. Being late in the day, students as well as most staff had gone for the weekend. The Day School was a K-8 private school, teaching both secular studies and Judaic courses. I hustled across the parking lot and over to a curved roof overhang, protecting the school entrance. I swiped in, knowing that a computer somewhere was recording my name and entry time. No sneaking in unnoticed.

The building, like the parking lot, was all but abandoned. The lobby was a two story open affair with offices to the left and a floor to roof mural ahead of me to the right. It was some modern impressionist thing that I was told represented various events in Jewish history. Most observers couldn't figure it out. The artist, rumor had it, had gotten the idea from the mural high up in the Capitol rotunda in Washington. Never mind that the Capitol mural was designed to look like a series of sculptures, or that it only went around the inside of the dome and wasn't floor to ceiling. Here at the school, I don't think anyone paid attention to this mural anymore. Around to the immediate right was a staircase, and I took the steps two at a time.

On the second floor, I followed the corridor to the left, turned right past a storage room door painted in the style of the mural, and then walked past yellow walls covered with student art. Down a silent hallway, I found the office I was looking for. The door was closed and had the name Katie Harris inscribed on a brass plate at eye level. I knocked, waited for a "Come in," and stepped inside.

Katie was sitting behind a desk with neatly stacked piles of papers and folders. I always marveled at anyone who could keep a neat desk. Katie stood up. She was a petite woman in her early thirties, with her blonde hair pulled back with a barrette. She was wearing a peach jacket over a collarless white top and green skirt.

"So where were you? I had to send a second text."

Katie came around her desk, and as she did, she took off her jacket to reveal that her white top was a tank top. I loved Katie in tank tops. They accented her tanned shoulders and her curves. And this white one was my favorite. I couldn't take my eyes off her.

"If you must know, I was actually in a synagogue, thinking."

"You were in a synagogue. Thinking."

She put her arms around me and held me close. She kissed me.

"Well," she lowered her voice, "I was here…thinking…that tonight we have no plans. I get to spend the entire evening with you." She inched her body closer until we were *very* close. We stood groin to groin.

Katie moved her hips minutely and looked into my eyes.

I peered back. "You keep doing that and I'll lose…"

"Lose what?" she whispered, as she moved her hips ever-so-slightly again.

"I don't remember." I kissed her gently. "I guess I should tell Josh and Shelley we won't be joining them for dinner."

We swayed slowly as one.

"Who are Josh and Shelley?" she asked barely audible in my ear.

"He's the rabbi of the shul. Shelley's his wife."

"Mmm."

"They're nice."

"…And they invited us to dinner. That's sweet."

I swallowed. I could feel my heart beating against her. "You'd like them."

We rested our heads on each other's shoulders. I closed my eyes.

"So, do you want to go?" Katie asked.

I kissed the side of her neck, then paused. "Go where?"

"To your new friends."

"What new friends?" I could smell her scent on the skin just below her ear. I breathed it in.

She stopped swaying. "I think you should go."

"What?"

"I think you should go."

"You do?"

Katie pulled away just enough so we could look at each other.

"Yeah. You've been looking for something lately."

"Have I?"

She smiled. "You can't hide anything from me."

"Will you come?"

She kissed me slowly. Then after a moment, "You should go by yourself."

I just looked at her.

"I'm…not ready yet." She paused. "I will…another time, just not tonight. "You go," Katie repeated. "I'll find something to do, and I'll be waiting when you get back."

We pulled away a little more.

"You don't mind? What will you do?"

"I don't know. Maybe see if someone wants to try that new restaurant on Charles Street."

We separated completely, and I took a few breaths to settle my heart, which was definitely racing. After another moment, I looked at my watch. "I better get moving, then. I want to shower and change."

With that, Katie turned off her computer, switched off the lights, and we headed out.

As we had come in our own cars, we went our separate ways. Katie drove to her place – she lived in Cedarcroft, a neighborhood just inside the City line west of York Road – and I headed for a liquor store in a small shopping area just north of the Beltway on Reisterstown Road. The upscale shop was next to a cell phone retailer, and inside, after my inquiry, was directed toward a display of kosher red wines. I bought a bottle of Merlot.

Back in my Jeep, a phone call to the Mandels confirmed that I was coming – solo. Josh gave me directions, which helped me visualize where to go.

Thirty minutes later, I was in my shower. As water poured over my head, I leaned with both hands against the front wall, and let the shower cascade over me. I thought about the afternoon…sitting in the shul, trying to find solace. I thought about Katie in my arms. And I thought about a young man in an Israeli Army uniform walking through Jerusalem's Old City with his fiancée.

By the time I got myself together, darkness had fallen over the city. Josh had said to come about 8:00. I drove northward on tree lined Roland Avenue to Northern Parkway, up out of the Jones Falls valley and over toward Northwest Baltimore. As I headed up Park Heights Avenue toward the County line, I passed several synagogues to my right and left. Men dressed in dark suits, some in shirtsleeves and pants, were walking out of services. In a matter of minutes, I found the Mandels' street. It was about four blocks from their synagogue, on a one-way street. I made the turn onto their block and parked almost immediately on the right. I grabbed the bottle of Merlot, and stepped onto the sidewalk.

Their street was a long, straight block, maybe four car widths across, with older trees lining sidewalks on each side. As I came out of the Grand Cherokee, I looked up and down the block for cars of course, but also for people. It was an old habit…know who and what is around you. Even though the rabbi's house was up the street on the left, I stepped onto the sidewalk on the right side and headed up the block.

The May evening was cool. I was dressed in an open collared white shirt, blue blazer, and khakis. I would've come without the jacket, but it was Friday night and decided to err on the side of being better dressed. Despite that, there wasn't even a thought about wearing a tie. An open collared shirt was a carryover from my Israel days.

As I walked up the block, wine bottle in hand, I noticed that virtually all the houses on both sides of the street were semi-detached, with three or four steps up to a small front porch. Most of the houses were also of the same construction. Red brick. The street itself was quiet; no traffic. While I had no idea if this were accurate, I wouldn't have been surprised if the majority of the people on the block were

Sabbath observant and wouldn't be in cars for the next 24 hours.

Josh and Shelley's house was coming up across the street on the left. It was the only one on the block different from the rest. Their house had no front porch, the brick was painted white, and there was an addition on the left side. While I was still a few houses back diagonally, movement ahead caught my attention. A car was parked directly across from the Mandels'. It was a late model Buick, the Regal, and had three figures inside. Two in the front and one in back. The car had Virginia plates. Nothing unusual about that, except that Virginia plates were common on rental cars here, particularly from BWI airport. I made a mental note of the license plate. Another old habit.

I was pretty sure this was the same car that cruised past us a few hours ago as the rabbi, Shelley, and I spoke in front of his synagogue.

A car length behind them, I stopped walking.

The driver, just a silhouette through the rear window, was moving his head, speaking first to the figure beside him and then to the figure in the back seat. After a moment, the two passengers got out, one from the front and one from the back. They looked to their right and left – they should have easily noticed me – but they weren't really looking, as their minds seemed elsewhere.

Both men appeared to be of average height, with close cut dark hair. The man who had come from the front seat was in black pants and a lightweight, dark zippered jacket. The passenger from in back was in jeans and a green windbreaker. They looked at each other, then crossed the street. What were the chances they were heading to the rabbi's house?

They walked across to the white brick house that had an addition.

What were the chances they were guests like me? Shelley and Josh had said they had no other guests tonight.

The man in the lightweight dark, zippered jacket reached inside his coat with one hand and rang the bell with the other. In a few seconds, I could see Shelley at the door. The man in the dark jacket said something and Shelley quickly stepped aside. The two men went in, and the second man closed the door behind them.

In front of me, the driver in the maroon Buick stayed where he was behind the wheel, watching his associates. For a moment I had wished I had brought my folding knife along. It was a three and half inch Benchmade combo blade, half straight edge, half serrated. Didn't matter. I put the bottle of wine down beside the sidewalk and moved into the street to come up behind the Buick on its left. I figured I would come up to the driver and see what was going on. If he made any sudden movement with his hands inside his jacket, I'd punch down at him with the crown of my first two knuckles into the corner of his eye. I'd then reach in and grab him by throat between windpipe and muscle and take it from there. If he wasn't in position for that, I'd figure something out. I wanted to know who those two men were inside the rabbi's house. If they were just asking a question or in need of other directions, no problem. The man would not reach inside his jacket, and would be spared multiple fractures to the orbit of his eye.

I passed the left rear corner of the Buick and walked forward, realizing the car was idling. How focused was the driver on the Mandels' front door? Approaching from this angle was a calculated risk. Would his peripheral vision pick me up? No other way to get close to him. Even as this went through my mind, the driver spotted me in his side mirror. All I could make out were some dark eyes beneath thick, dark eyebrows. Before I took another step, the car slipped into gear, then shot forward into the street, speeding down the block.

Shit.

I ran across to the Mandels' front door. It was a dual entryway. First there was a storm door and then an inner, solid wooden door. To the left of the door frame was a four-sectioned sidelight. I looked inside.

The foyer led straight ahead to a short hallway that ended in what looked like the right side of a kitchen. To the left of the foyer was a doorway; I couldn't make out what was beyond it. To the right, another doorway to what could have been a study. Again, I couldn't tell. Regardless, no one was in sight. I knew there were at least four adults in the house, and I didn't know how many kids. Where were they? In the kitchen? In rooms to either side? Were they all together?

Whatever was going on, I needed to interrupt it. I knocked on the door. A few seconds passed. Nothing.

I looked through the sidelights again. No Josh, no Shelley.

I knocked on the door again.

This time Shelley came from the kitchen at the end of the hall. Gone were the jeans and Orioles T-shirt from this afternoon. They had been replaced with a green dress that had yellow curving lines running diagonally from shoulder to hip. She saw me looking through the glass panel and looked straight into my eyes. The fun I had seen in them earlier was gone.

I waited, holding the storm door open. The deadbolt slid back and Shelley opened the inner door just a few inches. She was pale and unsmiling. In fact, it looked like she was clenching her teeth.

"You have to come back tomorrow," she said flatly.

She began to close the door, but I leaned into it.

I put a finger to my lips and placed my mouth to her ear. "Where are they?" I whispered.

She turned to my ear. "In the kitchen."

Josh called, "Shelley, is everything okay?" His voice sounded a little higher than I remembered.

I nodded to her.

"Yes."

I moved back to her ear. "Let me in. Everything will be fine."

She soundlessly opened the door just enough to let me slip in.

"Dear?" Josh again, from the kitchen. "Is everything okay?"

"Yes. Coming."

I whispered again: "Is there another way into the kitchen?"

She pointed to the room on the left.

"Stay right here. Don't move…and look straight ahead."

She nodded.

I moved to the open doorway to my left. The room beyond, I could now see, was a dining room with a table beautifully set for a Friday night meal. There were five place settings. I guessed they were for Shelley and Josh, me, and two kids. I could see some silver wine cups on a plate near the head of the table, a breadbasket, and some flowers. Off to the side was a sideboard with four lit Shabbat candles.

I moved into the dining room and hugged the common wall with the hallway, just to the side of the doorway.

"Dear," Josh called again, "are you coming?"

Shelley turned to me. I put my finger to my mouth and shook my head. I then pointed for her to look toward the kitchen.

A few seconds went by.

"Shelley," came Josh's voice, "are you okay?"

Shelley didn't answer.

The two men from the Buick were in the kitchen with Josh and his kids. That was my guess. I had no idea why and I didn't care right now. I was also guessing that one of them would come through the door to check on Shelley. If he came through the other door, the one through the dining room side, he would see me. Then things would start getting interesting. Maybe I should grab a table knife. It wasn't weighted for reliable throwing, but I could always throw it as a distraction. And then what? I had no idea.

He didn't come through the dining room. He came through the hallway. I could hear his footsteps. The man, I hoped, would have emerged from the kitchen to see Shelley standing, immobile at the front door. He would be walking toward her, curious. From where I stood behind the dining room entrance, I could see Shelley indeed still standing near the front door. She looked petrified, but she did as I had asked and kept her focus straight ahead. In a moment, one of the men appeared, a semi-automatic in his right hand. He was the one wearing a windbreaker and jeans. I noticed several things at once.

16

He was my height, younger than me, and his handgun was a Czech CZ 75. I knew it to be double action weapon – if there were a round in the chamber, the hammer did not have to be cocked for it to fire. I also knew that it came in both 9mm and .40 caliber – not that such a difference would matter to my chest or head at this range.

I silently stepped forward before the man was beyond my reach. The thought of being shot didn't occur to me. My hands and hips moved rapidly and in concert. With my left hand I used a *chin-na* variation, pulling him slightly off balance and locking his wrist. Simultaneously, with my right I grabbed the Czech pistol over the slide and twisted the weapon against his trigger finger, both pulling his finger away from the trigger and breaking his hold on it. I tore the gun out of his grasp before he knew I was on him. I continued the *chin-na* hold, pulling his shoulder and torso forward. He was now bent over. I raised my right arm high and brought my descending elbow straight down onto the spot where the back of his neck ran into the back of his skull. There was a nice hollow there, and I hit it – hard enough, but not with everything I had. The man crashed face down to the floor.

A moment went by, and a voice came from the kitchen, but it wasn't Josh's.

"Mazhar!"

Once again, I put my finger to my lips to indicate that Shelley should remain quiet.

"Mazhar?"

Another few seconds passed.

"Mrs. Mandel," the voice from the kitchen said, "If you do not come here I will shoot your husband, and then I will shoot your children."

The man had an accent, but I couldn't place it. Mediterranean? Slav? Romanian? And what was that name, "Mazhar?"

"Do you hear me, Mrs. Mandel? I will save your children for last."

Shelley looked at me, her eyes wide. I nodded.

"I'm coming," she said quickly.

I whispered in her ear, hopefully, one last time: "If you can, walk slowly." I didn't wait for her response.

With Mazhar's pistol in hand, I headed into the dining room for the other kitchen entrance. I stopped at the corner, just before the opening to the kitchen. Hopefully, when Shelley would walk in from the hallway, all eyes would be on her. In that moment I'd turn the corner, take in the situation, and shoot. In theory. It really all depended on where everyone was, and if the man's gun was pointing at someone.

I looked down at the CZ 75. I moved the slide back just enough to verify that there was a round in the chamber – there was – and waited.

"Here I am," I heard Shelley say. I wondered if that was for me.

I turned the corner, and leveled the gun. In that moment, I saw the second man was indeed looking at Shelley. His back was almost completely to me and had a .45 to Josh's head.

"Tell me what happened, Mrs. Mandel, or I'll shoot him. Is someone else here?"

I was essentially behind him, but the angles were horrible: Josh and the gunman; Shelley on the other side. I could shoot the intruder, but Shelley could get hit as the bullet passed through him.

"Yes, there's another guest," I said from the far doorway.

The man with the .45 on Josh turned and pulled him closer.

Positions had gotten worse. He now had the rabbi almost completely in front of him.

With a quick sweep, I took in the room: exterior wall to the left with a large window midway across. Beneath the window was a sink, then a countertop to both sides. Double oven to my left, fridge to my right. Island in the center of the room with bar stools around it. Across from me was Josh and the gunman. Shelley had moved to the left between Josh and the countertop. Two young girls, maybe 8 and 10, stood in front of her.

All eyes were now on me.

Not good at all.

I looked at the man holding Josh. He was in his forties, with an olive complexion. He had a wide nose and high cheekbones.

"Mazhar is dead," I said. I didn't know if he was. "This is his gun."

I noticed Josh's torso. He was thinner than the gunman, but I still didn't like the shot. The man needed to take his weapon off of Josh's head. I couldn't risk shooting the guy and having him inadvertently pull the trigger.

Josh's eyes darted from me to Shelley and then back to me. I relaxed, keeping my gun on the intruder, but allowing my focus to stay wide. I could see Shelley and her young girls to the left, Josh and the gunman in the center, and dishes and glasses on a small counterspace near the fridge on my right.

I really didn't have a shot, but I smiled. "You're fatter than the rabbi," I said to the man holding the .45. "I'm going to shoot you in the side and then I'm going to shoot you in the head."

I spoke to the two young girls in front of Shelley, but kept my eyes on my target. "Girls," I said, "Close your eyes and keep them closed until your mom tells you to open them, okay?"

The two girls looked at Shelley who nodded. They closed their eyes.

I lowered my gun slightly and pointed it at the gunman's side. The man behind Josh moved his head out and began to aim at me.

I raised Mazhar's gun and pulled the trigger.

2

The concussive sound of the gunshot hung in the air, but the action was over in a split second. The gunman had just moved his .45 away from Rabbi Mandel's head when I fired. The bullet hit him at the junction of his nose and his forehead. When hit, his finger didn't twitch and he didn't reflexively pull the trigger. The man's head was knocked back ever-so-slightly as he collapsed backward to the floor. Behind him a spray of blood appeared on the wall.

"Josh, Shelley, take the kids upstairs. Go out this way," I indicated the opening to the dining room behind me. "Watch out for the body in the hallway."

They ushered their kids out in front of them, the girls' eyes still tightly shut.

I looked at the Czech pistol in my hand, released the magazine, and ejected the round from the chamber, locking the slide open. I put the clip and single bullet in my jacket pocket, and placed the gun on the kitchen island in front of me. The body at the other end of the room instantly had that look of something discarded on the floor. A small pool of blood was collecting under the dead man's head.

I took a deep breath and tried to calm the sudden energy surge that my autonomic system dumped into my body.

So, who were these guys? What were they doing here? A home invasion with the family still at home? No, something else. Someone had sent them...the man who had driven off in the Buick? Maybe I should reload the gun.

I stood over the body, very much wanting to go through the man's pockets. But I didn't. Didn't want to mix my fingerprints with this guy's. The police would tell me what they found. Nate would tell me.

I pulled out my cell phone and dialed Nate D'Allesandro's number. Nate, who was not related to Baltimore's old political family – though probably if you went far enough back, there had to be some connection – was a police homicide captain. He was a friend born from the aftermath of an extremely tense situation. A few years ago, his daughter was hiking with a girlfriend in the extreme north of Israel, when late one evening – early morning really – they happened across a team of Hezbollah terrorists on their way to a nearby kibbutz to kill as many Israelis as they could. She told them she was an American. They killed her friend and took her hostage. I led the unit that went in to get her. The rescue was a success, and when I came to Baltimore later, I followed up with Nate, and we became friends. His number has resided in my phone ever since.

As soon as Nate answered his cell, I knew he was in a restaurant. I could hear the background noise. "Yeah, Gidon, hold on." My number must've been in his address book to come up on his caller ID.

For about twenty seconds there was the sound of silverware clattering, someone asking about chicken, a sizzling sound, and then quiet. He must've moved into an entry area, between inner and outer doors. Or maybe he was in the men's room.

"What's up? You should be out with Katie at dinner or something."

"Well, I *was* on my way to dinner…"

"Oh, Christ. What happened?"

I told him…the whole story from being invited over the Mandels, to spotting the Buick, to the guys going in the house, to the Buick taking off, to what happened in here.

"All right, I'll call it in. What's the address?"

I gave it to him.

"The uniform guys will be over first. Don't shoot them when they come to the door."

I laughed.

"I'll have the waiter pack up my steak, *which I just started by the way*, drop off Rachel and be over."

"Apologize to her, please."

"*You* apologize to her when you come over this week."

"Deal." I paused for a minute, looking at the body at my feet. "You *will* tell the uniform guys I'm a good guy, right?" All I needed was for them to enter this little scene, spot the guy on the floor, and draw the wrong conclusions.

He hung up without responding.

I looked around. What a mess. The guy in a heap at my feet had stopped oozing blood onto the floor. What about his partner? Hopefully, his heart was still beating. I stepped around the corpse and then into the hallway. The guy in jeans and a windbreaker – and former owner of the Czech CZ 75 – was where I had left him, facedown on the floor. The pulse in his neck, was faint, but still there. While his heart was still beating, I couldn't vouch that any of his appendages still worked after that smash to the base of his neck. There was no need to tie him up, so I headed back into the kitchen and filled two glasses with water.

I found Josh and Shelley and the two girls in what must have been the girls' bedroom. It was painted light purple with a flowery border along the ceiling, had a poster of Masada and some blond kid from a television show, a white bookcase, and a pair of matching dressers. The Mandels were spread out on two beds: Josh and the older daughter on one bed, Shelley and the younger one on the other.

"Well," I said, "the police are on their way. "They'll need to speak with you," I looked from Josh to Shelley. They appeared shell shocked. I held out the two glasses of water. Each took one, but didn't drink.

"What...?" Shelley tried to start a question, but couldn't get the words out.

"I don't know," I said. "We'll figure it out. Meanwhile, maybe the girls have friends on the block they can spend the night with?"

Shelley nodded. "Next door. The Levins." She looked at Josh. "We can take them over," she added.

Josh was just looking at me. Less than ten minutes ago he had two strangers invade his house, and one of them hold a gun to his head.

"Why don't you both go. Take them next door, explain to the neighbors there are going to be police cars all over the place in a matter of minutes. Get the kids settled, make *kiddush,* and then come back. I want to speak with both of you when there's a chance."

They nodded and threw some clothes together for the kids. Within five minutes, the four of them headed out the front door. I watched them go to the neighbor's, and then went back into the kitchen. Without looking at the body on the floor, I pulled a bar stool out from the island in the center of the room and sat down. Mazhar's semi-automatic was just a few feet from me on the counter, its grip devoid of the magazine, and the slide locked open. I took the clip and single bullet from my jacket pocket and placed both near the gun.

After a few long deep breaths, I ran the confrontation through my mind: disarming the first man, hitting him with the descending elbow, Josh held at gunpoint, baiting the other guy so he moved the gun off of Josh, and shooting the bastard through the head.

Without being conscious of it, these images were replaced with others. Sidon, Lebanon at night, and my four man *Sayeret Matkal* team hustling through a second floor apartment one block from the harbor. We were hunting a bomb maker. We called him *ha-bogair,* the Graduate, because he looked like a young Dustin Hoffman.

The bomb maker's apartment was a series of rooms off a narrow hallway. We were all dressed similarly in jeans, ratty shirts, and *kaffiyahs.* All four of us were wielding M4 carbines. We divided into two pre-arranged groups of two. Each pair took a different section of the apartment.

Asaf and I went straight ahead. Gal and Eitan went left. We knew exactly where we were going. We had been practicing in a mock-up of this apartment every day for a month. Asaf and I cleared two bedrooms and then moved to the end of the hall. Asaf was a big man – six-four and solid – but moved fluidly and assuredly. I knew the other pair was moving the same way. At the end of the passageway, Asaf and I turned left into a dining room that had dirty white walls, a low, slip-covered sofa and a wooden coffee table. As soon as we entered the room, we froze. We saw another team member backing out of a side room, slowly stepping away from the Graduate. The terrorist had his arm around the neck of our fourth man, Gal, and was pressing a pistol into his head. *Ha-bogair* saw us and started shouting, first in Arabic then in Hebrew. He ordered us to move back and drop our weapons. He was going to shoot Gal. The man was shouting quickly, almost hysterically. His eyes were wide and bloodshot. Gal was trying to stay calm, but he kept looking at me to do something.

The Graduate continued shouting at us, but the team stayed even, pointing their M4s at him. The remaining three team members to include me had fanned out in the dining room, with all of the weapons aimed at one focal point – the bomb maker. But there was no clear shot. The terrorist was using our fourth man as an effective shield. I looked over at Asaf on the far right. He caught my silent signal and started speaking. *Take it easy, take it easy. We're lowering our guns.* The three of us did so. Asaf continued: *Let him go. We'll leave. Just let him go.* As Asaf spoke and distracted the man, I drew my Glock 19, and aimed it at the Graduate's head. The bomb maker saw me and began to move his pistol off his hostage.

I fired, but so did he. He must have already been squeezing the trigger as he turned on me. His gun had just cleared his human shield. My nine millimeter hollow point blew into the center of his forehead. His hung there for a millisecond then collapsed. His hostage, Gal, stepped away from him and nodded to me. I nodded back.

There was movement to my right. We turned to see Asaf on the floor, pressing his big hand into the right side of his neck. Blood was spewing everywhere.

The doorbell rang.

I blinked a few times as the Mandels' kitchen came back into focus. "Police." The doorbell rang again.

I got up and moved to the front door. Without hesitating, I opened it to see two large Baltimore City Police officers, each easily a head taller than me. The one on the left was Caucasian, the one on the right African American. "Gentleman, come in," I said, opening the door wider and motioning for them to enter. Behind them, I saw their parked cruiser with its revolving red and blue lights.

"Step back, please," the officer on the right said.

I stepped back.

Both officers came in, their hands resting on their service automatics.

"Major Aronson?" the officer on the left asked.

I smiled. That was what the Israeli Army ID in my bottom right desk drawer said. I simply responded, "Yes." Nate must have given them my rank to help build a sense of brotherhood and authority. I would have thought that rank would not have impressed these guys. If they felt compelled, they would have drawn their weapons regardless of my rank.

They saw the body on the floor in the hallway.

"There's another in the kitchen," I offered.

They looked at me. "Have a seat," the mountain of an officer on the right said, nodding to a dining room chair.

I complied. "There's also an unloaded semi-automatic on the kitchen counter," I said to no one in particular. "It's his." I looked at the man on the hallway floor.

The Caucasian officer left his partner standing over me and went into the kitchen. He came out ten seconds later, and spoke to his partner: "Just like the report. Body on the floor. Gunshot to the head."

The African American officer addressed me. "I'm Officer Williams. This is Officer Johns." He nodded to his partner.

"The Captain specifically asked me to tell you that you're a pain in the ass."

"He's only being complimentary because I'm still alive."

They both smiled.

"And where are the homeowners, sir?" the Caucasian partner, Johns, asked.

"Rabbi and Mrs. Mandel. Next door, getting their children situated. They'll be back in a few minutes."

"Captain D'Allesandro asked us to get your statement," Williams said. "Said it would be good practice since you'll be telling it again to the detectives."

I nodded and recounted the events objectively, professionally, without embellishments. By the time I finished, there were more lights flashing through the windows, and Josh and Shelley had returned, still looking very shaken.

Within minutes the Mandel household was filled with activity: cops everywhere, both uniform and plainclothes, as well as EMT's, and forensic men and women. Josh and Shelley had parked themselves out of the way on a nearby staircase. They were huddled close to each other, with the action swirling around them in their own house.

A few minutes later, as the medical people were examining Mazhur's body on the floor, a man about fifty walked in. He was wearing a tan blazer over a navy polo shirt. He was about my height with receding close cut salt and pepper hair. It was actually hard to tell where his hair stopped and his scalp started, for his hair was cut nearly to the skin. He was followed by a thirty-something, well dressed man in a black sport coat, white shirt, gray pants, and a lavender tie.

The two men took in the room, walked into the kitchen, then came out a few seconds later. The older man came over to me.

"You couldn't have shot him in the shoulder or arm?"

"I was aiming for his leg," I said to him from my chair.

"Jesus, Gidon…"

I stood up and held out my hand. Nate D'Allesandro took it and we pulled each other into a quick one armed hug.

"And on Shabbat, too," he continued. "No one has respect for anything anymore."

The younger man, the well dressed thirty-something, stepped closer.

Nate asked: "Remember Matthew...Detective Medrano?"

The younger detective stepped in and we shook hands. I nodded to him. "We met in my dojo."

Medrano nodded, then asked simply, "What happened?"

I told them, and since I now had plenty of practice, the flow of events sounded even more straightforward than before. When I finished, Nate said to his junior, "Matthew, why don't you take Mrs. Mandel into the dining room and talk to her. We'll take the rabbi."

Medrano went over to the staircase where the Mandels were sitting and led them this way. He asked Shelley to go with him, leaving Josh with us.

I did the introductions. "Josh, this is Captain D'Allesandro. He's a friend."

They shook hands.

Nate asked, "Is there a place where we can talk?"

"My study?" He led us to a room off to the right of the main hallway. The study was about the size of the girls' bedroom upstairs. Two walls had floor-to-ceiling bookcases, filled with Hebrew texts and reference books. I recognized several of the oversized volumes as a collection from a Talmud series. There was a desktop populated with papers, a laptop, and several framed pictures. Along the right wall was a small couch, and an armchair. I sat next to Josh on the couch and Nate took the armchair.

"So," Nate began, "question number one, do you have any idea who these guys are?"

Josh shook his head. "No, never saw them before."

"They just came to the door, rang the bell," I said, "and..."

"You'd have to ask Shelley what specifically happened at the front door. I was in the dining room with the girls, setting the table. After a few seconds, Shelley comes in and there are two men with guns in their hands behind her. They told us to go into the kitchen."

"And you have no idea who they are," Nate said again.

"Not a clue."

"What did they say?" Nate followed up.

"Nothing. They just looked at us, moved us together into the kitchen, and then Gidon came to the door," he looked at me. "Do you think it was a robbery?"

Nate responded: "Don't know. They didn't have time to ask for anything," he looked at me.

"Josh," I said, "everything okay at the synagogue? No pissed off members or anything?"

"No."

"Congregation have any money trouble?" from Nate.

"No. Not that I've been told."

"What about you?"

"No."

"Witness any crimes or serve on a jury lately?"

"No."

Before we could ask another question, Officer Williams, one of the two officers first on the scene, poked his head in the room. "Captain, the EMT's are taking the unconscious man to Sinai."

I thought he probably could've used Shock Trauma, but it wasn't my call.

"Thanks, Officer."

He left and we turned back to Josh.

"Gidon told me he saw these two men drive past the synagogue earlier today when the three of you were speaking outside. Ever notice them before, hanging around?"

"No. Not that I noticed."

Nate stood up and Josh and I followed suit. "We'll figure this out. Let's see how your wife is doing."

With that, the three of us headed into the dining room. As we passed the hallway, we caught sight of a stretcher being rolled to the front door. Mazhar, the man who had wielded the Czech pistol, was on his back beneath a white sheet on the stretcher. He had been strapped in and an intravenous line was running to his right arm. The EMT's lifted the stretcher and carried him through the door.

We walked into the dining room to join Shelley and Detective Medrano at the table.

"How are you doing?" I asked Shelley.

"Better." A moment passed. "What's this all about?"

"Don't know yet," Nate said. "But we will."

As I looked at Shelley and Josh, I'm sure they felt all this was surreal. The Shabbat table set beautifully in front of us, white tablecloth, gleaming plates and silverware, the flowers, two loaves of braided *challah* set on a tray beneath an embroidered cover, two police detectives, me, uniformed officers moving about. Forensics taking photos everywhere and making notations. There was also, perhaps, the body on the floor in the kitchen. Maybe it was still there; maybe not.

Medrano asked, "Do you folks have a place to stay tonight?"

"Here," Shelley responded.

"This place is a mess," Nate said. "You don't need to stay here tonight." What Nate meant was there was blood on the floor and on the wall in the kitchen and they didn't need to see that.

"Sleep out tonight," I suggested, "and let the clean up crew straighten up." Nate looked at me knowing there was no cleanup crew. He didn't say anything. "I know it's Shabbat and you don't want anyone working here, but it's extenuating circumstances. Come back tomorrow."

"Besides," Medrano said, "your kids are next door."

Shelley and Josh both nodded.

A young Asian woman in a Baltimore Police Forensics windbreaker came out of the kitchen. She was carrying a small device not much bigger than a large cell phone. She looked at the group, "Major Aronson?"

At then mention of my rank I looked at Nate who just smiled at me, and then turned to the woman, "Over here."

She turned to me: "I need to get your fingerprints so I can isolate any others on the gun." The tech must have been processing the Czech pistol I left on the counter. She came over and I held out my right hand. She had me press each finger in turn onto her handheld device. After each digit she tapped an icon on the screen to enter the image and then clear the screen. I was not crazy about logging my fingerprints. I'd rather not be in another database, but realistically it didn't matter. My fingerprints were already on record in Israel and also here, since every teacher has to be fingerprinted and I was an active substitute where Katie worked.

"Thank you," the tech said and walked back into the kitchen.

At the thought of Katie, it occurred to me that I needed to let her know that the evening's timetable had changed.

"Excuse me," I said standing up.

I moved into the hallway, pulling out my cell phone. "Hey there," I said once she picked up. "I'm going to be later than I thought."

"Okay. You still at dinner?"

"Well," I hesitated for a moment, then gave her an abridged version of what happened...I just said I was able to stop two intruders.

"Is everyone okay?"

"Yeah, we're fine." Except for the dead guy and the unconscious guy.

"Do you want me to come by?"

That was very sweet.

"No. Thank you, though. I'll be here a few or hours yet, and then I'll come by."

"I'll wait up for you."

"Thanks. See you in a bit." I hung up.

By the time I got back to the living room, Nate, Medrano, and the Mandels were standing.

"The Mandels are going to gather a few things and go next door," Nate offered.

With that Josh and Shelley headed out of the room.

Once they were out of earshot the three of us looked at each other. "This was not a robbery," I said.

Nate nodded.

"It was a hit."

"You don't know that," Medrano said.

"It was a hit," I said again. "And I'll talk to the Mandels after tomorrow."

"Why after tomorrow?" Medrano asked.

"After Shabbat," Nate responded. "Let them relax tomorrow if they can."

"I have a license plate for you," I said. "The Buick that cruised by the synagogue this afternoon."

"And was carrying these two guys."

I nodded and gave them the Virginia plate. "I didn't get a good look at the driver."

"If this car is a rental," Nate was thinking of the Virginia license plate, "maybe the agency has a camera in their office. We may be able to get an image of the driver."

Unless it was one of these two guys who rented the car, I thought.

"Unless it was one of these two guys who rented the car," Nate said. "We'll find out."

In a few minutes, the Mandels came down the steps. Josh had a small shoulder bag, and Shelley a large knitting-type bag.

"Thank you for everything," Josh said. He shook my hand as well as Nate's and Medrano's. "There's gotta be a way to work this into my sermon tomorrow," he smiled.

Shelley came over and kissed me on the cheek. "Thanks."

"We'll walk you out," I said.

We headed to the front door. On the way over, Josh handed me a key. "To the front door. It's a spare. Just lock it when everyone's finished. If you don't mind."

I nodded, and we escorted them out.

As soon as we stepped outside, we were faced with a small crowd milling about. They must have been neighbors drawn by the three cop cars with their lights still flashing. Josh and Shelley moved down the walk and were immediately surrounded by their friends. I could hear Josh say, "Everything's okay."

Nate, Medrano, and I watched them from the stoop, trying to get next door.

I looked at Nate.

"What?" he asked.

"You know."

"Yeah."

"This was not someone's A Team."

"What do you mean?"

"The guys panicked. They should have shot the rabbi or Shelley right away. Then walked out."

Medrano said, "You surprised them."

"Maybe."

"Maybe it was something else," Nate commented.

"Maybe," I said.

We stepped inside the house. By now, the uniformed officers were filing out, and the forensics people were packing up. Medrano peeled off to speak with one of the uniformed cops, and Nate and I walked into the kitchen. The body had been removed, but there was an eight inch pool of drying blood on the floor plus splatter on the wall.

"You know there's no cleanup crew," Nate said. "You told Mrs. Mandel that a cleanup team would come."

"You're looking at it. I can't leave this for them and they wouldn't let me take care of it, if I offered."

"Let's find a mop and bucket."

With that, Nate and I looked around to see what we could find. In the back of the house there was a laundry area where we found a pail, some rags, and cleaning supplies. It wasn't a big job. After donning some vinyl gloves Nate had for handling evidence, I cleaned the splotch on the floor, and Nate took care of the spray on wall.

"By the way," he said as he finished up and looked at me, "nice job. You saved their lives. Very clean. Glad you remember all that *Sayeret* shit."

I nodded, thinking that it worked this time.

Nate had just finished with the wall when Medrano walked in. He looked at Nate, gloves on his hands and holding a rag. "Mr. Clean, I presume?"

"Medrano, if you did stuff like this for your girlfriends, you'd get laid more often."

The three of us laughed. Well, not so much Medrano.

Nate and I put the cleaning paraphernalia away, sealed the rags in a trash bag, and headed out with Medrano. We were the last to leave. On the stoop, I pulled the door shut and locked the deadbolt.

"Call you tomorrow, if I have anything," Nate offered.

"Thanks."

With that, we left. They headed off in separate vehicles, and I crossed the street toward my Jeep. On the other side, near where I had first spotted the three guys in the Buick, I saw a bottle of Merlot lying sideways on the ground. It was right where I had left it. I smiled, picked it up, and continued on.

The ride to Katie's took thirty minutes. It was now pushing 1 AM and the evening's events were beginning to finally drain me. I pulled into Katie's driveway on an old tree lined street, and parked behind her sky blue Mustang. Looking up at her two story home, I saw a dim light on in her second floor bedroom.

In a matter of seconds I was upstairs and watching her from the doorway. The overhead fixture was off, and Katie was in bed on top of the covers, reading by the light of a table lamp. She was wearing a large Kermit the Frog T-shirt that went down to mid-thigh and nothing else. Her bare legs were crossed at the ankles. My fatigue was rapidly disappearing.

"Hi there."

"Hey," she put down her book.

I went to the bed and kissed her very sweet lips. "Thanks for waiting up."

"Of course. So, it was Gidon to the rescue?"

I shrugged. "How was your dinner?"

"Excellent. You'd like the place. Had some great vegetarian dishes. But don't distract me...you saved the day."

"So who'd you go with?"

"Tammi. She says hello. Now tell me what happened. You left out the details."

"Yes, I did."

I started peeling off my clothes.

"Did you ever eat?"

"No. Now get rid of the book and turn off the light."

3

My phone rang – buzzed really – two hours later, but it didn't wake me up. In fact, once Katie's breathing had become deep and regular I got out of bed. The vibrating, lit up phone caught me practicing some internal *chi gung* exercises off to the side. I scooped up the cell from the night stand and stepped into the hallway. It was Nate.

"Hey," he said.

"Hey. What's up?"

"Something to show you. You know Pimlico Race Course?"

"Of course."

"Come up Northern Parkway toward the race course. Turn onto Preakness Way. You'll see us."

"Be there in fifteen minutes."

I quickly showered and put on a pair of jeans and a lightweight black sweatshirt that had some Chinese characters on it. They were part of a random collection of clothes that seemed to have ended up here. Six feet from where I stood, Katie was still sleeping. I went over and kissed her gently on the forehead. "Gotta go out for a little while," I whispered. "Nate has something for me."

She opened her eyes halfway. "What time is it?"

"About 3:30. Go back to sleep." I kissed her again and headed out.

∽

Pimlico Race Course was in an area that was a mix of residential

37

housing, a convalescent home, and the Sinai Hospital complex. There was a perpetual fight by the City not to let the vicinity adjacent to the Race Course spiral down into an economically depressed area. This year they seemed to be winning.

I turned onto Preakness Way, which was a short street sandwiched between a parking lot to my right and a wooded area to the left. Beyond the woods, and not far in, was the property of a convalescent home. Normally at this time of night, the street would be all but abandoned. Not tonight. About fifty feet in from the corner were four cop cars, two blocking both sides of the street, and all with their red and blue lights flashing. Beyond them were more cruisers, an EMS vehicle, and a shitload of police personnel. Somewhere above me was the sound of a helicopter circling. I pulled to the curb and got out.

As I approached the two police cars blocking the road, a woman officer stepped forward from the inner perimeter. Before she could turn me away, I said, "I'm with Captain D'Allesandro. Gidon Aronson." She nodded and waved me through.

The EMS vehicle was the center of all the excitement. Its rear doors were open, a plainclothed officer was inside, standing over a stretcher, while more detectives were over near the left side of the cab. The driver's door was open. The vehicle's headlights were still on, and I saw Nate and Medrano standing near the front left bumper in the wash of the lights. Nate was dressed just as he had been earlier but without his jacket. Medrano looked the same. I wondered if he even had made it home. I would soon find out that no matter what time of day, Medrano always looked sharp and fresh.

Nate spotted me. "Over here."

As I passed the open driver's door, I saw a scrub attired man slumped away from me. There were blotches of blood on the seatback and the windshield had two bullet holes in it.

"This was the ambulance that was taking Mazhar to the hospital," Nate said.

Sinai was literally around the corner. It never made it.

"The driver took two gunshots to the chest," Medrano added. "Based on some of the tire marks, it looks as if someone swerved in front of the ambulance, cutting it off. He – or she – stepped out and shot from about here." Medrano stepped in front of the vehicle and raised his right hand like a gun. "We found two shell casings." There were some chalk circles on the ground.

Nate began walking to the rear of the ambulance. I followed.

The two back doors were swung open. Inside the brightly lit work space was the stretcher I had seen when I had walked past. I couldn't tell who was lying supine. My guess was Mazhar. The detective I had seen inside was now climbing down. He was about forty, all gray, and like Nate, in a polo shirt, but his was black to Nate's navy. The detective's sidearm was holstered near his right side pocket, and a Baltimore City Police badge was clipped next to it. Once on the ground he saw Nate, nodded to him, and moved off, looking at some notes.

Nate picked up where Medrano had left off: "The shooter opened the back doors, shot the second EMT" – I saw another scrub clad body on the vehicle floor on the left side – "then climbed up and shot Mazhar. Twice in the head."

"No loose ends," I offered.

"I'm thinking the guy in the Buick." This from Medrano.

"What could the rabbi have done?" I asked, thinking aloud.

"Or his wife," Medrano posited.

I shook my head to myself.

Nate wasn't saying much of anything, but he was looking at me.

"You're thinking the shooter's thinking I saw him," I said.

Nate nodded. "Or is wondering if you spoke to his men."

I looked at Nate again.

"Where's that Glock I bought you?"

"In my desk in a lockbox."

He just looked at me, as if to say, "Well??" but he knew I wouldn't go for that option yet.

"Okay," I said, "I'm going home." I began to move off, but called back, "Thanks for inviting me to the scene. Much better imagery than a phone call."

"Remember, you're coming to dinner this week."

I waved to him, and headed around the police vehicles blocking the road. As I walked to my Jeep parked on the side, the night still felt pretty quiet. Baltimore would be getting up soon – maybe a little later than usual, for it was now Saturday morning – but the air was still calm.

I climbed into the Grand Cherokee and headed back to Katie's.

4

When Katie opened her eyes in the morning I was next to her. Not asleep, but next to her.

"Good morning," I said, maybe twelve inches from her eyes. "How do you feel?"

"Mmm. Pretty good," she smiled. She leaned over and gave me a kiss. "And you, did you sleep?"

"Not really."

She just smiled, knowing a sleepless night was not unusual for me. "What did Nate have for you?"

"Ah, romantic pillow talk, huh?"

She smiled. "Was it good news or bad news?"

I always debated how much to tell Katie about stuff like this. Katie had seen me defend myself, but never with the really bloody, bone crunching stuff. Ever since I broke up with Alli, who flipped out witnessing my violent side when we were once attacked, I was leery about getting too specific with Katie. She *might* have been fine with me telling her I had to shoot a guy in the head, or that I probably broke a guy's neck for instance, but I really wasn't sure.

"You're debating how much to tell me, aren't you? Just tell me, Gidon."

"Oh, you sweet talker." I paused. "Okay, so I stopped some intruders in the Mandels' house. Well, Nate and I think it's more than that. We think someone is trying to kill them…or one of them."

"Oh my God."

41

"We're not a hundred percent sure, but it's looking that way. Someone killed one of the men we caught so we couldn't interrogate him. He was in an ambulance on the way to the hospital when someone shot the driver and then shot my guy on his stretcher."

"They're dead?"

"They're dead."

"What about the other man? You said 'intruders,' plural." Katie hadn't missed that. "Can't you find out from him?"

"Nope. I shot him last night…in the head. He was holding Josh hostage."

She looked at me for a long second. I had no idea what she was thinking.

"And the Mandels don't know what's going on?" She had either processed what I had done or was ignoring it.

"They say they have no idea."

"Do you believe them?"

"I believe that on the surface they can't figure out what this is all about."

"But you'll help them?"

"They're friends. Yes." I didn't mention that the guy who sent the hit team might have gotten a look at me. The fact was, I didn't really know what was going on. The guy in the Buick was probably just a wheel man. No way of knowing yet.

"So what are you going to do now?"

"Now," I shifted a little closer to her, "I am going to invite you into the shower, and we'll see what develops."

We had a late breakfast and then I headed back to my place to change. I lived less than five miles away near the Hopkins Homewood Campus in a modest, forty year old, two story home. In a matter of minutes, I was back in my car, heading to the Mandels' *Beit Shalom* Synagogue. My interest still wasn't in prayer. I did, however, want to see how Josh, Shelley, and their kids were doing. There'd be no visit to the sanctuary.

I parked half a block from the synagogue and walked back to the building. The sky was cloudless and the air was still cool. Single family brick homes were set back on modest front lawns, and a mixture of cars and vans were parked either in driveways or at the curb. Pink, red, and lavender azalea bushes guarded several of the walkways, and blooming rhododendrons added to the peaceful, clean, suburban atmosphere.

As I approached the single floor synagogue, I could see a number of young couples hanging around in front. I had no idea if services were still underway. It was just before noon, and Saturday morning prayers could typically run from two and a half to three hours, depending on the speed of the cantor, how many times the rabbi wanted to emphasize a message, or just because the pace was slower or faster on any given day.

I crossed Seven Mile Lane to see a County Police Car blocking the driveway entrance. A uniformed officer was leaning against the side of the vehicle and watching the front of the synagogue. I walked over to him and he watched me through rectangular wire-rimmed sunglasses. The officer was about my age and half a head taller, blond, fit looking, and maintained a high and tight haircut.

"Good morning," I said.

He only nodded, arms across his chest. On his right forearm I could see part of a tattoo that had parachute wings and a scuba diver. There were also the words "Semper Fidelis." He had been a Marine.

"Recon?" I asked.

"Force Recon," he specified. "You?"

I shrugged. After a moment I said, "The guy you're looking for may not come in the Buick."

He looked at me again. "Heard some Israeli Special Operator walked into a hostage situation last night at the rabbi's house. Took a gun off of one guy and used it to put two in the other guy's head."

I looked up at him and held his gaze through his sunglasses.

"Actually…it was one round."

He grinned. "Oorah. My lieutenant said it was one shot, too." He held out his hand. "Greg Thompson. My friends call me Tuck."

"Tuck," I repeated, shaking his hand. "Gidon."

"My unit had some joint training with Israeli paratroopers on a base northwest of Jerusalem."

"Near Modi'in."

"Yep. Met some real cool dudes." He paused for a minute. "What can I do for you?"

"Services over? I want to speak to the rabbi, but don't want to go in."

"Don't think so, but folks are drifting out."

Sure enough, in a few minutes people began pouring out of the synagogue. There were older people, younger people, teens, and young couples with children. The men were dressed mostly in ties and jackets and the women in dresses. I didn't see the Mandels. My guess was they'd be among the last to leave.

I turned to Thompson. "How long have you been on duty?"

"Drove behind the rabbi about 8:00 as he walked here. Another unit followed his wife and kids later."

"Thanks."

He shrugged.

Josh and Shelley and their two girls came out the front a minute later. I turned back to the cop. "Take care." I shook his hand.

"Anything you need…" he gave me an official business card with his name on it.

"I appreciate it."

I walked over to the front of the synagogue, and hung back a few feet as a number of members engaged the Mandels in conversation. From what I could hear, it had nothing to do with last night. It was more about school and some upcoming family celebrations. In a minute, Josh spotted me, and then Shelley did as well. I waited until only one man was left speaking with them. He was about forty, with a little paunch, and dressed in an off-white suit with a pale blue shirt and yellow tie. The man seemed to be wrapping up whatever he was saying, so I stepped in.

"Shabbat shalom, Rabbi. Shelley."

"Gidon, hi. Shabbat shalom." Josh gave me a hug; I wasn't surprised by the emotion.

"Shabbat shalom," Shelley echoed and gave me a kiss on the cheek.

The man in the off-white suit lingered. "Hi," I smiled at him, but turned back to the Mandels. "Do you guys mind…I'd like to walk with you." I looked at the hanger-on. Hopefully, he picked up that it would be a private conversation.

Shelley responded: "Please," and we began to move off. The other synagogue-goer waved and walked the other way.

"Again, we can't thank you enough." Josh began. "I really don't know what to say."

"The whole thing is so unbelievable," Shelley added.

I looked at their two daughters, walking several paces ahead of us. They were dressed in similar, flowery Spring white dresses.

"Were you able to sleep?" I asked.

They both nodded. "Sort of," Josh responded.

"The kids okay?"

"I think so," Shelley said. "They have a lot of questions, but having them close their eyes was very helpful. Thank you."

"Sometimes I want to close *my* eyes," I smiled.

Without looking, I knew that Officer Thompson was in his cruiser, inching along behind us.

After a few moments of no one saying anything, I offered, "I just came by to see how you were." We stepped around a telephone pole rising out of the middle of the sidewalk. "Do you guys have someone you can talk to…to help you unwind?"

Josh responded: "Friends are coming over after lunch."

"Excellent." A thought occurred to me, and I reached into my pocket, pulling out their house key. "The cleaning crew did the best they could," I said, handing Josh the key. "The kitchen is fine; you'll need some spackle on the wall in one spot." Where the bullet hole was, but I didn't say it. "And there are some rags in a garbage bag in the back room that'll need to be put out."

"Thank you," Shelley said, probably figuring out who did the cleanup.

"That's it. Just wanted to say hi." I took out a card with my phone numbers on it. "In case you want to call me," and handed it to Josh as well. "I'll talk to you soon."

With that, I let them keep walking. I looked back at the officer in his vehicle, nodded, and headed back to my Jeep.

∽

The entire afternoon was in front of me, and so I headed to my bastion of refuge. It was an unassuming place located on North Charles Street, several miles from the center of the city. At this point, Charles Street was one-way northbound, and was a blend of businesses and residences, with the latter on the upper floors. Cars could park on both sides of the road, and often did, beneath trees planted years ago alongside the curb. All buildings were set back from the street. To enter any of them you'd either walk up a few steps or down a few. My place was a walk-up between the studios of a radio station on the right and a natural foods bistro to the left. I had never set foot in the radio station, but the natural foods place had tables and chairs set out on the sidewalk, and served great sandwiches. There was a parking spot in front of the radio station, so I pulled in there, rather than going around to a dedicated tenants' lot. Carrying my sport coat, I took the five stairs two at a time, then pulled open the glass door lined with orange paper, and stepped in.

The entryway was an open vestibule with hardwood floors. The walls were white and bare, giving no clue as to what went on here. However, it was apparent soon enough. The foyer opened onto a large square floor space, now filled with two rows of martial arts students facing each other. When I had walked in, the line to the left was standing in front stance, right foot back, while the opposing students stood ready. A moderately tall, curly-haired man in his mid-twenties wearing a red T-shirt and loose fitting black gi pants, was walking down the line, watching them. A black belt was tied around his waist and worn low on his hips.

"Ready," he said, voice projecting, "go!"

With that, the line on the left stepped forward with a straight-on middle punch. The opposing line stepped back, responding with a middle block and a counter move.

"Reset," the man said, and the class moved back into the previous position. "Go!" The attacking line stepped forward and the defending line stepped back.

As he repeated the sequence a number of times, I looked more closely at the group. All students were attired in an unconventional martial art dress code – traditional gi pants but T-shirts in the color of an individual's rank. Students were a mixture of small and tall, and of varying ages and ranks. They ranged from 13 and 14 up to late teens and early twenties. The ranks began with white and yellow belts at my end to purple belts at the other end. In the purple range there were some proficient college age men and women. Interestingly, in their small group of three, two were women. One in particular always caught my attention: a slender coed of about twenty who had her red hair cut short in that messy style of spikes on top and a mat of hair over the forehead. I knew her to be hardworking and with a stretch that always got the attention of any guy older than twelve.

The black belt instructor running the drills saw me. He let the group finish their attack-response sequence, then said, "Okay, stop. Stand. Turn to Sifu and bow."

The class stopped what they were doing and turned to me, stood feet together, and bowed with a traditional right-hand-in-a-fist/left-hand-covering-it bow. I returned the bow, and said simply, "Thank you. Continue, please."

The black belt said, "Now the attacking line will be defending. The defending line will now be attacking." With that, he had the class resume.

As I watched for a few more moments, I thought how at home I was in such a place. Before going to Israel, before all the army stuff, a place like this in New York was where I began to figure out who I was.

I nodded to the man in red and black and walked into my office off the practice hall. The room had all the essentials: desk and computer, filing cabinet, and some chairs. There were also some luxuries – an old secondhand sofa, a television, and DVD player. I draped my sport coat over the arm of the sofa and sat in the chair behind the desk.

The Saturday afternoon class was Jon's, the black belt instructor; I would certainly supervise, but the class was really his. As the sounds of the workout drifted in through the open door, my mind wandered. Last night. Josh being held by the big man with the .45. Telling the Mandels' daughters to close their eyes. Shooting the intruder in the head. The ambulance later that night, rear doors open, and the scrub suit clad EMT huddled, dead on the floor in back. Mazhar's body on the stretcher. I stared at the darkened computer monitor, not seeing it. I saw an apartment in Sidon, Lebanon and me firing at the bomb maker as he was holding a soldier captive. I fired just as he moved his weapon away. His gun went off. I turned to see my friend Asaf on the floor, blood flowing from a neck wound.

A single yell from twenty students burst in from the next room. The instructor was having them scream as they lunged forward in an attack. I looked down to the bottom right drawer of my desk and pulled it open. Nestled in the deep compartment was a lock box. Inside was a .40 Glock, a present from Nate. Next to the mini vault was my carry permit…and an ID from the IDF. I closed the drawer without removing anything.

"Sifu?" I looked up to see the curly-haired instructor poking his head through the open office door.

"Yes, Jon."

"They're ready for *katas*. Would you watch them?"

"Of course."

"Thanks. And there's one kid in particular I'd like you to watch. Charlie." He was a fourteen year old yellow belt, almost ready to be tested for green.

"Sure."

When I stepped into the main hall, I could see that Jon had set up the class in three rows with plenty of spacing between the rows and between each student. I moved to the front left corner of the room, with the students facing forward. Charlie, the student I wanted to watch, was in the middle row toward the left side. He was a slender, serious young man, whose long, straight brown hair always covered his forehead. The boy, like the entire class, was already drenched in sweat from its previous workout.

Jon started them off: "*Kata* Number One. Ready. Bow..." the class bowed first to me and then to Jon. "Begin. One..."

With that, Jon counted them through the *katas*, a series of choreographed fighting movements. Everyone performed the movements step-by-step in unison. I moved about the students, watching everyone, but always kept a clear view of Charlie. He moved proficiently; his kicks, punches, and blocks were all sharp and age-appropriately strong. But he was in pain. He wore it on his face, particularly when he punched or moved into an upper block. Based on the grimaces when he extended his arms, he had hurt his ribs.

By the time the entire class had finished their routines – the lower-ranked students dropped out as the *katas* shifted to more complicated advanced forms – a number of parents had settled in back to wait for their kids. They were a mixed bunch of moms and dads, mostly all dressed casually for this Saturday afternoon. I did see one man about forty, with neatly trimmed dark hair and dressed in a starched white dress shirt with blue pin stripes and gray pants. I knew him to be Charlie's father, an attorney.

When the *katas* were finished, Jon had all the students line up again in their rows. They were even more sopping wet than before, with hair frizzed, sweat saturating their T-shirts, and moisture running down their cheeks. The purple belts who had just finished their forms, including the red head I saw earlier, were trying to regain their breath.

I addressed the group. "Looks great, ladies and gentlemen. Keep up the good work. But, just so you keep things in perspective, I want to show you something." I paused. "Actually, I want Jon to show you something."

Jon quickly hustled over to me. "Yes, Sifu?"

"Jon, I want you to do *Kata* Number One." This was the first form students learned. It contained all the basics, and was a requirement for yellow belt. "I'll just say go, okay?"

He nodded and moved to the center of the room. The students made space for him.

"Ready..." Jon bowed in response... "and GO."

With that, he launched into a series of blocks and kicks; he punched as he walked forward...then there were more blocks, kicks, turns, elbow strikes, and knife-hand strikes. Each movement was sharp, clear, and powerful. As Jon finished, he bowed once again and then stood still.

"Nicely done," I said to him. Then to the class, "*That* is a yellow belt form done by a black belt. Doesn't look like the way you guys do it." They laughed and I scanned the students from purple belt to white. "But there's a reason for that. He's got more than a few years' practice on you...and thousands of more repetitions...and a bit of talent." I saw Charlie watching me intently. "But you can all get there. Every one of you. Just keep up the good work. See you next time. Thank you." I bowed to them, they bowed to me, and we dismissed.

As the class headed to their gym bags lining a side wall, parents went over to their children while older students meandered out the door. Charlie walked to his father and I could see the latter asking questions. In response, the boy began demonstrating an outside middle block.

Jon stepped over to me and we both moved further to the side. "So, Charlie hurt his ribs?" I asked, looking across to the young yellow belt and his parent.

"Yeah. That's my guess. But not working out here."

We watched as Charlie's father descended into his own front stance while his son stood ready. They were about to do some one-step sparring. The dad must have had some training; he moved forward, throwing a punch as he walked. Charlie put up his block, but his father overpowered him and penetrated, hitting him in the ribs. The young student grimaced.

"I've only seen the two of them do this sort of thing once or twice," Jon said, "but my guess is they do it at home, too."

"I'm sure they do."

"And Charlie's father doesn't want him using arm pads."

"Oh?" That meant the boy was taking severe hits to his forearms.

"I saw some bruises today."

That's all I needed to hear. "Charlie," I called across the room, waving him over.

The boy looked at his father who nodded, and then ran across to us.

"Yes, Sifu?"

"Spot check. Jon is going to move forward to hit you straight on. Let me see your blocks."

The two students stood in front of me, one a black belt and one a yellow. Charlie, I knew, had to be nervous, but I didn't care about that. His dad looked on from forty feet away.

"I'll count." I paused as Jon moved into a front stance with his right hand pulled back on his hip, ready to walk forward and punch. Charlie stood with his hands clenched in fists in front of him and his knees slightly bent. "Okay, Jon, take it easy. Not full speed or power. I just want to see how Charlie moves."

Jon nodded.

"And…one."

Jon moved forward. As Jon drove straight ahead, the younger student put up a middle block. I saw him wince as the edge of his forearm contacted Jon's arm. Despite obvious pain, he made the block.

"Other side, please." The pair switched in order to punch and block with their other hands. "Go."

Jon moved forward again, but the yellow belt wasn't quick enough and Jon's fist caught him on the ribs to the right of his breastbone. Charlie flinched.

"Are you okay?" I asked.

"I'm fine," he responded, but still wincing.

As Charlie said this, I looked at his forearms. On the outside of each arm, from wrist to mid-arm, was a row of amorphous, dark purple blotches.

"Do you have arm pads?" I asked, pointing to his bruises.

He nodded.

"Use them, please. Let your arms heal until you learn to position the block better. Block with the back of your wrist, not the edge of the bone. You won't get hurt that way." I held out my left arm, showing him the back of my wrist. "Now extend your right punch."

He extended his right arm. I let my left hand come around his extended punch, so that contact for me was on the back of my wrist, not on the edge of the bone. "Do you see what I mean?" I asked. "This way you won't bruise your bone, and the block remains extremely effective. Got it?"

Charlie nodded.

"Good. I'll tell your dad that you have to use your pads." I didn't raise the issue of his bruised ribs. That was for another time. The two of us crossed to where Charlie's father stood waiting. I saw that he was my height, clean-shaven, with a round face and hard, clear blue eyes. I wondered if he was a litigator.

"How's he doing, Sensei?" the parent asked, using the Japanese version of my title.

"He's doing great, but he has to use arm pads until he learns the blocks better."

"I want to toughen him up."

I shook my head. "It's not the way…not just yet."

"But to my way of thinking--"

"No. Not a good idea." I looked into his eyes and I could see he really wasn't listening.

"What about his tolerance to pain? I want to increase--"

I just shook my head.

"Okay. I guess we have a difference of opinion."

I let that pass. "More importantly, you shouldn't be working with him."

He looked at me. "What do you mean?"

"Let him do his partner work here."

This time there was no response from the dad. He just put his arm on his son's shoulder, and said, "C'mon, *Paco*, the afternoon is still ahead of us. We have a lot to do and we have to pick up Grandma at 6:00 for dinner at Frere Jacques." He looked at me again, and with that the two of them walked to the exit.

I headed back across the room to Jon, and he met me halfway.

"So?" he asked.

"He's still going to work with Charlie."

"Did you mention his ribs?"

"No."

"What are you going to do? He can't keep pounding him."

After thinking for a moment, I just looked at him. "I'll figure something out."

We moved into my office. I sat down at my desk and Jon took an upholstered seat nearby. We looked at each other. Jon was one of the few people I was fairly candid with about both my Israeli army experience and pre-army background. He was my first black belt, a hardworking kid – if he were younger than me then he was a kid – who had been into a lot of shit in earlier years…bullying, alcohol, drugs. His dad had pulled him out of a party where he was half-stoned and brought him to me. I basically presented him with some personal challenges, and he rose to my expectations. In other words, I beat the crap out of him as I worked him out.

"So, let me tell you the latest," I said. "See what you think."

I told Jon about my adventures at the rabbi's house last night and about the murders in the ambulance. He had two questions.

"What do you think the deal is with the Mandels?"

"I don't think they've consciously done something wrong...like committed a crime or anything. But someone is after either both of them or one of them for whatever reason, and it's intense enough to send assassins."

"And what are you going to do about the guy in the Buick?"

"I'm hoping he'll show up again so I can have a conversation with him."

He smiled. "Can I come?" Considering the events of last night, he knew that the hypothetical conversation would be less than polite.

"He may have taken off already. He killed the connection to him – that guy in the ambulance – or had it done, so maybe he left town." I actually didn't think he had. "Have you ever heard the name 'Mazhar'?"

He shook his head.

"Me either."

I turned on the computer at my desk, and while it booted up, went back to an earlier subject: "This issue with Charlie is troubling."

"He's a good kid. If his dad is hurting him, that's pretty messed up."

I just nodded. On the monitor meanwhile, the icons had settled in. I pulled up Google and typed in "Mazhar."

"Okay," I read to Jon, "I've got some Pakistani stuff, a tambourine used in Arabic music, and a Turkish name. I imagine Nate is in the process of getting more information from the guy's fingerprints. He'll call when he has something."

"You think this Mazhar guy was just the hired help?"

"Yep. But the nationality makes things interesting, doesn't it?"

After looking at the screen again, I felt something… almost like a pressure change or a shift in presence.

Jon caught my distraction. "What?"

"Someone just came in the front door."

We both stood up. "I didn't hear anything. How do you *do* that? Can you also tell if there's a disturbance in the Force?"

"My teacher could." I grabbed a sharpened letter opener and we headed into the practice hall.

Approaching us from the front was one of our students. She was the redheaded college girl with the short messy hair style. I moved the letter opener behind my leg, out of her line of sight. No need to show it. As the redhead came closer, she looked from Jon to me.

"I'm sorry, Sifu," she said. "I have a question for Sensei Jon." I could see her blushing slightly and I stepped away from them. "Sensei Jon, would you like to join me and some friends tonight? We're going to the Mount Vernon Tavern at about midnight?"

He smiled a smile that I knew could melt a coed's inhibitions. "Sure. I have no plans. Thanks, Angie. 12:00."

Angie beamed back, bouncing a little on her feet, then turned and headed back to the exit.

I turned to Jon: "What happened to Evy?" She was another coed Jon had met several months ago and had been hanging out with.

"We've gone our separate ways…she's off to her life and I'm off to mine."

I just looked at him.

"It was a mutual parting."

"So, when did this happen?"

"A few weeks ago."

"Where was I?" I asked, wondering how I could have missed that.

Jon just shrugged. "I gotta keep moving, ya know." He bobbed and weaved.

I shook my head and headed back into the office. "Be careful with Angie, Grasshopper. Teaching friends and lovers is very dangerous."

"You've told me. You speak from experience, Old Man?"

"I do, sonny. But that's another lesson." I plopped back down in my desk chair. "Meanwhile, I've been thinking about changing the class schedule."

He raised his eyebrows.

"I'm considering not having classes on Saturdays."

"Oh?"

"Yeah. Just an idea that's been gestating. You could still come here and work out, but maybe we'd just not teach."

After a long moment: "I think that could be cool for you. Not working on Shabbat."

I shrugged, like "I don't know."

"Did you get this idea before or after yesterday's visit to the synagogue?"

"Before." I didn't tell him that it was part of my mental state of trying to find some peace. "Anyway, just a thought."

"We'd have to figure out what to do with the classes we have today."

I nodded.

"Whatever you want, Master," he bowed, making just a little fun of me. "Meanwhile, have to take off. Have a bunch of stuff to do."

"Be gone," I waved him away, and Jon smiled, bowed seriously this time, and left.

After a moment of watching the empty doorway, I looked back at the computer screen. The Google search on "Mazhar" was still up. I ignored it and went over to the filing cabinet. In a moment I had Charlie's file in my hand. I sat at the desk and looked though his forms. On top was his Hold Harmless agreement that his dad had signed, and then under it was the application to join the dojo. His last name was Coakley. Mom's name, April, and dad's name, Robert. Their home address was in Towson, a suburb just north of the City. Mom's occupation: ultrasound technician; dad's occupation: attorney, but I knew that. His office was listed on St. Paul Street about half a mile north of the city courthouse.

I thought about the conversation with my yellow belt's father. I had said that Charlie should work with a partner here, not at home. The dad understood what I meant about not working with him. It was clear he was going to ignore me and continue hurting his son.

5

The restaurant Frere Jacques was located on West Franklin Street around the corner from Enoch Pratt Central, the main public library. The area overall was a mixture of businesses, eateries, residences, and a world class museum – the Walters – up near Mount Vernon. The late Saturday afternoon was peaceful, and I parked diagonally across from the restaurant and to the right for an unobstructed view of the canopied entryway.

I wasn't hungry, nor was I meeting anyone for dinner. I was waiting for my student and his family to arrive. At the end of my conversation with Charlie's father, he had mentioned they were coming to Frere Jacques at six o'clock to take the grandmother out.

At 5:55, a white CR-V pulled into a spot a few doors up from the restaurant. Four people got out: Charlie's mom from behind the wheel, a thin, silver haired grandmother on the passenger side, and Charlie and a young teenage girl from the back seat. The young girl, who was skinnier and taller than my student, had to be his younger sister. The four of them headed to the restaurant entrance, descended a short set of steps, and went in. After a few moments with other patrons entering, I wondered if the dad were coming – or if he had gotten here before me. Then, at 6:15 Charlie's father hustled up from the end of the block on the right, looked neither right nor left, and went into the restaurant.

Over the next hour and a half, I sat in my Grand Cherokee, I walked up and down the block, window-shopped, moved the car into another space, and then because I really *was* hungry, stopped into a corner café for a sandwich. An available table at the front window allowed a clear view of Frere Jacques' entrance. By 7:45 I was back to window-shopping when the Coakleys emerged. There was some back and forth in front of the restaurant between Mr. and Mrs., while the kids stood to the side, looking bored. The mom half turned away, shaking her head, then everyone except Charlie's dad returned to the car. Mr. Coakley headed off the way he had arrived from the end of the street.

Based on Charlie's application I knew that his father's office was within walking distance – and that was indeed where he was going. After turning a corner, he walked into a four story renovated building at the corner of St. Paul and Pleasant Streets. Fortunately, there was a small park across the street with sufficient cover, so I could watch both the St. Paul and the Pleasant Street entrances.

While waiting for Mr. Coakley to emerge, I thought about him hurting his son, plus the fact he didn't seem to care. The question was how to handle it.

The sun had already passed behind the skyscrapers, and now the orange glow from old acorn-style streetlamps illuminated the environs. While the park where I stood was well lit, there were still strong shadows, mostly caused by the leaves on ancient branches. Pedestrians came and went, as did a few joggers, but no one looked my way.

At 9:30, Robert Coakley came out a side street doorway and walked up the block away from me. No one was around. Cars were parked on both sides of the narrow one-way road, with streetlamps reflecting off of the angled windshields.

I closed the distance with silent, rapid, controlled footfalls. When I approached Coakley's back, I saw he had a cell phone to his ear – he was in a heated conversation about someone showing up late for a court date. While this distraction made it easier to come up on him, I didn't want anyone else knowing I was there. Fortunately, the attorney stopped in front of a red Lexus convertible, ended the conversation, and pulled out his keys. I was less than two feet behind him. We were completely alone on the sidewalk.

"Put your keys back in your pocket," I said simply.

He spun around, half jumping up at the same time.

"Jesus Christ! Sensei, what the hell are you doing?"

"Put your keys back in your pocket, " I repeated. "I want to see your hands." I wasn't concerned about him moving on me; I just didn't want him hitting a panic button.

The keys went in his jacket pocket and he showed me his hands. "What's going on?"

"You're never going to hit Charlie again." My voice was quiet and unemotional.

"What are you talking about? You already told me about his wrists."

"He has bruised ribs. You hit him repeatedly. I know that. And either you don't care that it hurts or you enjoy it."

The street was completely silent. There was no noise...no traffic sounds, no HVAC humming from any of the buildings around us. Nothing. It was like we were in an acoustic bubble.

"That's none of your—"

"You've got two choices. Either as your son's teacher I call the police, where I am certain you'll end up in jail, or you'll start seeing a friend of mine who is a counselor. Either way, you will never work with Charlie on karate. Ever."

I saw the anger rise in his eyes. I was simultaneously watching all of him. I saw his right arm begin to tense.

"Don't," I said calmly. "I'm faster than you, and I want to hurt you very much." I took a minute step closer.

He looked at me again, and the anger in his eyes changed. It reflected another basic emotion. Very primal. Fear.

"You will also take a martial art class. Not mine. A tai chi class. I'll tell you where. And just so we're clear, you won't stop the counseling or the tai chi before you're told it's okay to do so."

He didn't say anything.

"I'll take that as a yes. I'll give you those names tomorrow and you'll call them on Monday morning. I'll check by the afternoon."

He continued to stare at me.

"The next time I see you will be at Charlie's green belt test. I don't want to see you before that. Do you understand?"

He nodded.

"Go." I motioned to his car.

He retrieved his keys, and looked at me. I just stared at him, expressionless. He beeped his car open, climbed in, and started the engine. He pulled out of the space without looking at me again.

6

I opened my eyes at 3 AM, which was now my norm, to see Katie watching me. "Hi there," I said.

She smiled. "Hi."

"So, my dear, I know why I'm awake. What about you? Everything okay?"

"I just woke up a minute ago and there you are."

I kissed her. She moved closer and I looped my arm around the back of her head. She simultaneously leaned forward and rolled a little closer so I could put my other arm around her shoulders.

"Now that we're both awake..." I began.

"Yes?"

"I want you to tell me a story."

The light from the street washed into the room, creating a stillness.

"What about?" she looked into my eyes.

"I don't know. Tell me about your family."

"My family?"

"Back in the day. What did they do?"

"You're a little weird, you know that?"

"And proud of it. Now talk. Tell me whatever you know about... your grandparents."

"My grandparents. Okay." She thought for a moment. "I'll tell you about my grandmother on my mother's side. There was some sort of a scandal."

"Oooh. Juicy."

"My grandmother was born in Russia in a very small town about 200 miles south of St. Petersburg. From what I've been told, her father, my great-grandfather, owned a small farm, a *very* small farm. I think he had, like, two cows that he was able to milk. My grandmother was the oldest of three. She had a younger brother and a younger sister. The brother was in the middle. My grandmother, when she was about 17, fell in love with one of the boys in her village. The parents on both sides didn't get along from what I understand, but all relented and my grandmother married the boy a year later."

"So where's the scandal?"

"Patience. So my grandmother stayed at home and made babies. My grandmother's brother, the one in the middle, was sent off to the nearest big town to study and get a job."

"It's good to be a man."

"Stop." Katie poked me in the ribs. "Well, apparently, while he was there he hooked up with a peasant girl from another village and they ran off together."

"Never to be heard from again."

"Actually, from what I've been told, he came back home to get his father's blessing. The whole thing caused a big rift because his mother wanted him to get the blessing, but his father was too angry."

"What happened?"

"I don't know. I think eventually the father listened to his wife and supported them."

"What about the younger sister?"

"The younger sister was a firecracker."

"A firecracker?"

"Yeah. Don't make fun of me. She was always a rebel. After her brother went off to the city to get a job, she met a guy passing through her village. He was like a revolutionary and the younger sister was instantly attracted to him. Of course her parents forbade her from becoming involved with him."

"Okay, wait a minute." I let a second pass as I thought. "Don't tell me… she ran off with him to the city, and they became involved in protests against the Russian government."

"Yes. How did you know that?"

"Then eventually the Russian government sent the army in to throw all the people out of their homes."

"That's right."

"You're so full of crap."

Katie looked at me with innocent eyes.

"You just described *Fiddler on the Roof*."

"Did not."

"Yeah. You switched around the daughters and some other stuff… made one a guy, but that's the story."

"Okay, you got me there, *Tevye*. I stopped into a Jewish History class at school last week and they were watching the movie."

"You're so full of crap," I repeated and pulled her close. I looked up at the ceiling for a long moment. I could feel the rise and fall of her torso as she breathed. Katie had deflected my request to tell me about her family, but I let it go for now.

"Gidon?"

"Hmmm?"

"I have a question for you."

Uh oh.

"And you don't have to answer it if you don't want to."

"Yeah?" I said a little hesitantly.

"I know you've had to do really bad stuff over the years to keep people safe."

You mean like killing terrorists in Lebanon, in Syria, and even in London, I thought.

"Do you have any regrets?"

I pictured a Lebanese village and a guy I shot as he was torturing a young American girl. She was tied into a chair and he was pressing the lit end of a cigarette into her neck. I pictured more recent kills in Baltimore, outside of the IDF work. "No regrets." My voice came out softly. "Not a one. Why do you ask?"

"No reason." She let a moment go by. "You're a good man. You help people."

"You do what you can."

"I want to go to Israel," she said apropos of nothing.

"You've never been."

She propped herself up and looked into my eyes. "I want to see what you see. I want to see what you're always excited about."

"My excitement isn't what it used to be."

"Yes it is. There're just parts of it you have a problem with. Army stuff."

"Yeah."

"Next time you go, I want to come."

"Okay. But I have no idea when that will be."

"Doesn't matter. I just want to be there with you."

I didn't say anything. I looked up at the ceiling again, and closed my eyes, even though I probably wouldn't sleep.

7

"So what do a rabbi, his wife, and two guys with malice in their hearts have in common?" I looked at Shelley Mandel across her kitchen table. It was 10 AM Sunday morning. Josh wasn't home, but Shelley and their two girls were.

"I have no idea." She was back in a T-shirt and jeans – her attire when I first met her on Friday, except her Orioles shirt had been replaced by a Beatles one. Her hands were in front of her, enveloping a cup of tea. "You're sure it wasn't a mistake?"

I nodded, thinking these guys don't make that kind of a mistake, but didn't say that. "Let's start with some basics, and forgive me if you've answered these before. Anyone pissed at you?"

"No." I could see her mind running through a mental list after she answered. She was double-checking.

"You're the rabbi's wife. Your relationship with the congregation?"

"Fine. We get along really well. I guard Josh's privacy as much as I can, and maybe some people resent that, but nothing major. Comes with the job."

"What do you mean?"

"Many congregants think they should have 24 hour access to their clergy. They forget they have a family life too."

"And you do what?"

"If anyone calls here on congregation business, I tell them to call Josh. If it's during the day, he'll take the call. If it's outside of reasonable hours and not an emergency, they'll leave a message and he'll get back to them."

"That was your idea?"

She nodded. "I have to protect him."

"Seems reasonable. Everyone okay with that?"

"Pretty much."

"No crazies in the congregation?"

"There are always crazies in a congregation," she smiled. "But not like this."

"Anyone make a pass at you that might anger a jealous wife or girlfriend?"

"No. But thank you for thinking that could happen," she smiled at me.

I dipped my head in acknowledgment, then went on. "Owe anyone any money?"

"No." She took a sip of tea from her mug.

"Tell me about your folks."

"My parents? What would they have to do with this?"

"I have no idea, but it gives me context." Context to what, I wasn't sure.

"My dad was the rabbi of a congregation in St. Louis, but he died about five years ago. My mom was a classic stay-at-home mom who took care of the house and the kids. You know what I mean? She's still in St. Louis."

"I'm really sorry about all this, Shelley. I'm just trying to figure out what's going on." And what could possibly have stimulated a hit on the Mandels and killing the surviving killer? No need to be that specific. If I were in her place, I'd be pretty freaked out about all this. Maybe she thought it was over. I looked to the wall that had stood opposite me the other night. A white dot of spackle and a small "X" of the filling compound marked where the bullet had gone in.

"To say that we're grateful for your help seems really lame," she said.

"Just goes to show how important it is to invite guests for Friday night dinner."

Shelley laughed. "We'll have to get you back so we can actually feed you."

"Deal." I let a moment go by and fished her business card from my pocket. I put it between us. It said *Shelley's Party Planning.* "Tell me about this."

"It's just a little business I have with a friend. I used to be a speech therapist before the kids. Right now, I'm focusing on the girls, but I have to do something to stay sane. In a few years I'll go back to the speech therapy...or I may just grow the party planning business."

"Everything's okay with that? No problems with customers or suppliers or anything."

"Nope."

"Two more questions and I'm out of here. Have you and Josh traveled recently, maybe to Turkey?" I was thinking of Mazhar's name.

"No. Just to Israel a couple of months ago. Both Josh and I have siblings in Jerusalem, Efrat, and Nahariya up north."

I had been to all three cities; my last visit to Nahariya was to the hospital to see one of my soldiers. "So," I put those thoughts away, "any unusual interactions during your visit?"

"Aside from the Israelis' way of handling customer service?"

This time I laughed. The Israelis, particularly in banks and in government offices, had their own way of dispensing help. It often meant that after standing in a long line, you find you need to come back the next day to speak with "Sarit." You come back the following day as instructed, only to discover that "Sarit" doesn't work that day. It's not unusual to hear customers screaming at the people behind the counter. "Yeah, aside from the Israelis' way of handling customer service."

"Nothing unusual. It was a great trip. We always look forward to going back and seeing family."

"Great." I paused. I was zero for ...how many questions had I asked? "Finally," I said, "where can I find Josh?"

8

I found the rabbi sitting at a table at Benson's Bagels up on Reisterstown Road, speaking with a man I recognized from the after-services crowd in front of the synagogue on Saturday. He was the 40 year old congregant dressed in an off-white suit, socializing with the Mandels as everyone was leaving. At the moment, he and Josh were sitting opposite each other, across a square table along the side wall of the eatery. A paper plate with a smattering of crumbs was in front of each. They must have just finished. The man opposite Josh had a Styrofoam cup of coffee in his hand.

"Josh, hi," I said, stepping up to them.

He looked up. "Gidon, hi."

I turned to the man opposite him. He held out his hand: "Henry Sakolsky." I shook it. "What you did the other night was truly heroic. You saved their lives."

Obviously, Josh had spoken with this guy. "Glad I was there."

"Have a seat," Josh leaned over and tugged at the chair at the side of the table. I pulled it the rest of the way and sat down, Josh to my right, Sakolsky to the left.

The bagel place was packed with customers, both young and old, and the noise level made an intimate conversation difficult. On the other hand, everyone was engaged in their own dialogue, so they wouldn't be conscious of anyone else's. Josh inched forward a little. "Henry is the president of the congregation and a friend."

"I have some questions for you, rabbi, and I hate to interrupt, but…" I turned to Sakolsky.

"You'd like to ask them privately," Sakolsky put in.

"Yeah, sorry," I said.

A young girl, probably a high school student, wearing an apron and carrying two plates of scrambled eggs, edged past me and set the plates on the table next to us, in front of a twenty-something couple.

"No problem. Rabbi, I'll talk to you later." He stood up and turned to me. "Gidon, while you're here, can I ask you a question? I didn't know who you were at *shul*."

I stood up too, so we could speak more comfortably. "What can I do for you?" I hoped he wasn't inquiring about Friday night.

"You obviously know how to handle yourself. IDF, I was told?"

"Yes and no."

He didn't know what to make of my answer, but proceeded anyway. "You wouldn't by chance teach self-defense or anything? I would love for my 12 year old to learn karate."

I looked at him, wondering if he were legit, or if he wanted something else. "I do have a class, down on Charles Street, below 25th."

"Can we come by sometime?"

"Sure."

He reached into his pocket and pulled out a business card and a pen. "Can you write down your address and phone number? If you don't mind."

"Not a problem." I took the card, reading the front – *Sakolsky & Levin – Business Equipment* – and then flipped it over and printed the information he requested.

"Thanks." He took back the card and pen, patted my shoulder, and left.

After a moment, Josh commented: "Henry is a good guy. He's at *shul* more than I am, if that's possible."

I sat down, but didn't respond.

"He's the go-to guy."

I nodded.

"Again, I can't thank you en—"

"Stop it."

"Okay." He let a moment go by and I was conscious of all the chatter and clatter in the room. "You want to ask more questions, right?"

"We have to figure this out."

He nodded.

"I'm going to ask you the same thing I asked Shelley thirty minutes ago. What do a rabbi, his wife, and two guys with malice in their hearts have in common?"

"I really have no idea. Gidon, really, Shelley does her thing, I do my thing."

"You've never rubbed anyone the wrong way?"

"Who am I going to upset?"

"Josh, two men came to your house Friday night. One of them had a gun to your head. Somebody's upset."

He just looked at me and held his palms up.

"Your relationship with the congregation?"

"Beautiful."

"No one is angry with you."

"No."

"Do you offer couple's counseling?"

"Some."

"Any pissed off husbands, wives, or lovers?"

"At each other yes. At me, no."

"Any women make a pass at you…jealous husbands?"

He shook his head.

"Josh, I gotta say, you don't seem worried about this."

"*Ye'hiyeh b'seder.*" He had given me the classic, Israeli response to everything: "It will be okay."

He saw my exasperation.

"Gidon, I trust you."

"You don't even know me."

"I know you. Last year you stopped an assassination during our banquet. That was you, right?"

I nodded. So he knew.

"You did what you had to Friday night. I trust you."

"Tell me about your parents. They're not bookies or arms smugglers, are they?"

"Dad's a principal of a private school in Boston. Mom's a social worker for the Brookline schools. No one is going after us because of them."

"Have you ever been to Turkey?" Again, I was thinking of Mazhar's name.

"No."

"Have you traveled lately?"

"I had some rabbinical business in Charleston and in Rhode Island not too long ago, and the family went to Israel three months ago."

I nodded. Shelley had said they both had family there.

"Gidon," he looked at me, but I didn't say anything. *"Ye'hiyeh b'seder.* It will be okay."

9

I walked into the dojo an hour later with two quarterstaffs resting on my right shoulder. I was dressed in black military BDU pants and a red and white IDF paratroop T-shirt. As I stepped through the door I saw that the workout area was empty, except for Jonathan, who was in the middle of the room, working on one of the more aggressive tai chi forms. He moved fluidly and strongly; the *chen*-style form had some of the more common circular hand movements, but it also had less familiar jumps, spins, punches, and strikes. I waited on the edge of the room for him to finish. In another minute he stood quietly, letting his thoughts and energy settle down to his center. Eventually, he looked over at me.

"Nicely done," I said, moving toward him. "I liked the last section."

"Thanks." He walked forward, meeting me halfway. "How ya doin'?"

"I'm frustrated."

"And you have a pair of bos in your hand. Uh oh."

"I'm going to put all this other stuff out my head, and we're going to work on your bo technique."

"Like I said, uh oh. The last time you were frustrated you beat the shit out of me."

"I did not. Stop exaggerating. Besides, I'm going off to the side to meditate and work on my own stuff. While I do that, you'll practice the bo form." With that, I tossed him one of the bos.

"Oh, you're going to relax first. That's *much* better for me. I hurt

75

already."

I laughed and moved off to the far side of the room, while Jon pretty much stayed where he was. After leaning my bo against a wall, I moved back onto the floor, picked a spot, and closed my eyes. Too much stuff was bouncing around my head and I needed to not think of anything except my breathing right now. Before I did that, however, I thought of Katie. At this moment she was at school, even though it was Sunday, to work on some of her reports. She said she'd come by later, and I was looking forward to that. We really hadn't been connecting lately, except late at night in bed. We needed more. Everything in balance.

My breathing settled down, and the next twenty minutes I couldn't account for, as I my mind went both deep inside and outward as well. When I opened my eyes I grabbed my bo and walked over to Jon. He stopped what he was doing and we stood about four feet from each other. Then we started playing, with attacks and defensive movements.

As an Asian weapon, the bo traditionally is not handled in the Robin Hood/Friar Tuck style with two hands along the center section of the staff. Instead, one hand goes toward the very end, and the other hand is held, perhaps, two feet in. The forward hand can whip the bo into position while the back hand anchors it and locks movements into place.

Jon and I worked for the next thirty minutes on both attacks and defense. When we took a break, I asked, "What is the number one question a karate student asks?"

"I see Captain Random is back."

I poked him with the bo. "Answer the question."

"How long does it take to get black belt?"

"Okay, more specific. What is the most common question an *advanced* student asks. Think bo, sword, tun-fa, knife…"

Jon paused, then, "What is Sifu's favorite weapon?"

"And the answer?"

"Whatever's in his hand."

"Correct." With that, I went into my office, put my bo to the side, and came back with a pair of Chinese broadswords. "With that in mind, Number One, work on these." I held the swords out, handles first.

"Yes, Sifu."

Taking the weapons, Jon moved to the side and began working on a double sword form. I went back to my corner and started practicing a series of circular fighting moves. Ten minutes into this, I caught sight of the door opening and Katie walking in. I finished the routine and went to greet her. In her hand was one of those plastic bags with handholds cut into them.

"Hey there, sweaty man."

"Hey there, gorgeous." I kissed her. She was wearing faded jeans and a white cotton top with a frilly lace neckline and cap sleeves. "How'd it go this morning, wrestling those reports?"

"They're all subdued until tomorrow. Meanwhile, I have a present for you gentlemen. I brought you lunch."

"Lunch?" Jon heard the magic word and stopped his sword form.

"So much for concentration," I commented, not really seriously.

"I stopped into Baum's Deli in Pikesville, and picked up sandwiches," Katie elaborated. "You guys hungry?"

"Yes!" Jon responded before I had chance to even think about it.

Katie pulled out a foil-wrapped sandwich, looked at some scribbles on the top, and handed it to me. "Corned beef for you." She pulled out another wrapped sandwich, "bologna for Jon," she handed him the second one, "and a hot dog with everything on it for me." We moved over to the front wall, and the three of us sat on the floor. Not to leave anything undone, Katie pulled out a cream soda, a bottle of lemonade, and a bottle of sparkling peach juice for me, Jon, and herself respectively. For a minute there was silence as we each took our initial bites.

"You can always bring me lunch," Jon said. "What do I owe you?"

Katie waved him off. "Next time."

The business of eating was serious, and we conducted it mostly without talking. In a few minutes we were relaxing with our backs against the wall when there was a knock at the door. I was on my feet before it had opened all the way. Henry Sakolsky, Josh's friend who I had just seen at the bagel place, walked in.

"Hi." He looked at the three of us and at the drinks and food wrappers nearby. "Bad time?"

"No, come in." He stepped into the room and I introduced everyone: "Katie, Jon, this is Henry Sakolsky, a friend of Josh Mandel's."

They nodded to each other and then there was silence. Sakolsky had something to say, but he was hesitating. He was just standing there.

"This has nothing to do with your son wanting to take karate, does it?" I offered.

"No." He was still hesitating.

"Katie and Jon know everything," I added.

Sakolsky turned to me. "You're trying to find a reason for what happened Friday night, right?"

"Yes."

"I know Josh...Rabbi Mandel. He's really low key about some of the things he does. He didn't tell you about his *special* work, did he?"

"What special work?"

"He rescues Torahs. A couple of times a year he goes around the world and retrieves Torahs that were confiscated or desecrated by the Nazis or by anti-Semitic communities. He brings them back, has them repaired, and finds congregations who can use them."

"He never mentioned it," I said.

"Like I said, he likes to keep this low key. He looks at it as holy work and doesn't seek publicity. It's truly an amazing thing he does, and the congregation supports it. The work is mind boggling, if you think about it...tracking down these lost holy documents, investigating their history, retrieving them, having them fixed."

I nodded.

"The thing is, I know he runs into bad people sometimes…really bad people who give him a hard time. A few years ago he was beaten up in a barn in Poland after he paid an exorbitant amount for a panel of a Torah that had been discarded in a stable."

"Why?" Katie asked as she and Jon began to walk closer. "Did they want more money?"

"They beat him because he's Jewish. Because they wanted to show their contempt for what he does. But that hasn't stopped him. So far, I think he has a 100 percent recovery record."

"And he didn't think that incident was significant?" I asked.

"He's crazy like that. He doesn't like calling attention to himself."

Jon responded incredulously: "He doesn't like calling attention to himself!? I'd say he got someone's attention."

I waved Jon off, but I was thinking the same thing. I was also very disappointed in both Shelley and Josh for not mentioning this, though I couldn't have imagined what Josh could have done to warrant two guys coming to kill him. "I'll follow up with Rabbi Mandel later and get some details."

"By the way, for what it's worth," Sakolsky added, "Shelley doesn't know about the beating… well at least not all the details. Josh didn't want to worry her."

"Gidon," Katie offered, "a beating is one thing…"

"Yeah, I had the same reaction. There has to be more to this."

"That's also why I'm here," Sakolsky said.

He had our attention.

"We'd like to hire you."

"*We?*" I asked, and then, "I'm not for hire."

" 'We' is my partner and me. Robert Levin. I'm President of the congregation and Bob is Chairman of the Board. We're both very good friends of the Mandels. We think they're terrific people and they're in danger. You're investigating it anyway, right? Let us pay your expenses, whatever they are."

I shook my head. "No."

"You don't have to report to anyone, you don't have to answer to anyone. Just do what you're going to do anyway. We want the Mandels safe and don't want you to hesitate to do whatever's necessary because of an expense. We're not going to miss the money."

"If you're looking to get rid of some cash…" Jon offered.

He ignored my student. "The Mandels are good people. You know that. They did something they're probably not even aware of and now they need help."

I still didn't say anything.

He reached into a jacket pocket and pulled out a thick business envelope. The imprint on the top left said *Sakolsky & Levin* with an address. "Just return what you don't use. If you want, you can even take out a daily fee. That's up to you. If you need more, just call." He handed me the envelope.

I looked at Katie who just looked back with eyebrows raised.

"I trust you," Sakolsky said. "*We* trust you…Shelley and Josh trust you.

"You don't know me," was all I could say.

"We know what you did Friday night. You also stopped by to see the Mandels after *shul*. You care. You're not going to let this go. Do whatever you need to do," he said once again. "Call us, don't call us, update us, don't update us. It doesn't matter. Just come to us when this is over and say the Mandels are safe."

"I don't know if I'm going to use this," I said holding up the envelope.

"That's up to you, but it's there just in case."

I tucked the envelope into one of my BDU pockets and buttoned the flap. I wasn't sure I liked this.

My cell phone in one of my other cargo pockets vibrated. I dug it out and saw it was Nate, my cop friend.

"Hi." I answered, turning to the side. "What's up?" I felt a little dazed.

"News. We found the home of those two guys from Friday night.

You need to see something."

"More bodies?"

"No, just some interesting items in their basement."

"You're there now?"

"Yup."

"Let me get a pen and paper and I'll write down the address."

Before the words were barely out, Sakolsky pulled out a pen and a tri-folded letter from his pocket. He nodded, indicating it was okay to write on the back of paper.

"Go ahead, Nate." He gave me an address on the edge of Patterson Park in East Baltimore. When I had finished writing, I said into the phone but looked at Sakolsky, "And I have some news about Josh Mandel, maybe an avenue to explore." I was thinking of his Torah rescues.

"Okay."

"I'll tell you when I see you."

"I'll be here." We hung up.

I looked at Katie, Jon, and Sakolsky. "I gotta go."

Before anyone could answer, the phone which was still in my hand, vibrated again. I had a new voice mail message. I checked to find a seventh grade American History teacher at Katie's school wanted me to substitute tomorrow.

"What is it?" Katie asked.

"Carol Cayhan wants me to sub tomorrow."

"Timing is always interesting, isn't it?" All of a sudden it felt like there was a lot going on. "Can you do it?" she asked.

"Yeah. I like seeing the kids. It'll keep me balanced. I'll call her back in a few minutes. Meanwhile, Nate wants me to look at something. He found the house of the two guys from Friday night. I have to check it out. Sorry."

"I'll walk out with you," Katie said.

"Me, too." This from Sakolsky.

I turned to Jon. "You staying?"

"Maybe another half hour. Want to work out some more and straighten up."

"Okay, we'll see you later."

Katie and I went back to clean up our lunch wrappers, and then headed for the door. I said *"Lehitraot"* – see you later in Hebrew – to Jon, Katie kissed him on the cheek, and Sakolsky, Katie, and I walked out.

At the top of the entry steps, I stopped and looked at Katie while Sakolsky continued down ahead of us.

"What?" she looked back at me.

"I was going to ask you out tonight."

"And you're changing your mind?"

"Maybe."

"Ask me out."

"Let's go out tonight."

"That's not asking."

Sakolsky spoke up from the foot of the steps, "Have you been to Canton?"

Why was he still there? I didn't know whether I should have felt annoyed by his eavesdropping or not.

"There's a great promenade," he continued, "that runs from Canton to Fells Point and then to the Inner Harbor. Great place to walk."

Katie looked at me. "We can eat down in Canton and then go for a walk."

"Sounds nice."

We set a time, thanked Sakolsky for the idea, and then went our separate ways. Actually, Sakolsky stayed where he was, but I escorted Katie to her Mustang. We said goodbye and I turned to see my potential benefactor waiting for me. "What's up?" I looked at him.

"I can't tell you how much we appreciate your help."

Not knowing what to say, I just nodded and walked to my Jeep.

10

Patterson Park is a large, square shaped area of green – 137 acres – just northeast of Fells Point. Within its setting are a boat lake, tennis courts, a swimming pool, an ice rink, and a four story pagoda that dates back to the late 1800s. For a long period, the neighborhood of classic Baltimore row houses adjacent to the Park had become depressed, but now it was an up and coming area, with many of its units being bought and remodeled by young professionals.

The address Nate had given was toward the middle of a run of row houses near the southwest corner of the Park. Due to a dearth of parking spaces, I had to leave the Grand Cherokee around the corner and walk back. As I came up the block, the row houses stood wall-like on either side of the narrow street, with some second story windows blistered out in a bay construction. In general, the exteriors were well kept, and mainly faced in brick, however a number had the Baltimore kitschy formstone façades. Three police cars parked near a door halfway down the block left no doubt where to go.

"Major Aronson for Captain D'Allesandro," I said approaching two officers.

They nodded and told me he was probably still downstairs. I pulled open a screen door near them and stepped inside.

The house was deep, but narrow – maybe nine feet across – and the walls were painted a gray-blue. To the left was a mismatched, old yellow and green floral sofa and to the right a small chest and a television. Further back in the house were two sets of steps. The first led downstairs, and then almost immediately beyond it was a set of steps heading to the second floor. Voices drifted up from below and I followed them down to the basement.

The lower level matched the narrow dimensions of the main floor, but was more claustrophobic due to a seven foot plastered ceiling and unpainted gypsum board walls. I saw Nate and Detective Medrano immediately. They were huddled over a long white resin plastic folding table; a uniformed officer stood nearby. As I approached, the officer spoke to Nate: "Captain?" and nodded to me.

Nate looked over. Without a greeting, he simply said, "Gidon, take a look at this."

I stepped over to see what they were examining. In front of them was a laptop with a photo of Josh and Shelley's house pulled up, plus a series of papers and printed photographs spread out beside it. The photos were all of the Mandels: Josh and Shelley walking into their house, Josh and Shelley in front of the synagogue, Josh next to his car, Shelley with their girls in front of a school.

"And there are these," Medrano said. He was wearing latex gloves and pointed to a set of lined legal sheets. They were a list of times and events – when Josh left the house in the morning, when he went the synagogue, where he had lunch. There was also a sheet detailing Shelley's daily schedule.

"How far back does this go?" I asked.

"Almost two weeks," Medrano answered.

"So who are these guys?"

Nate looked at me. "The guy you single tapped flew into Kennedy two weeks ago, traveling on an Algerian passport. His buddy, Mazhar, was Turkish and also came into Kennedy two weeks ago. And guess what?"

"They were on the same flight."

Nate nodded.

"So who are these guys?" I repeated.

Nate shook his head. "Not a clue. That's all we got on them so far. We'll take the laptop in and check the hard drive. See what we can find."

"I tried to go through the e-mails," Medrano said, "but they were all encrypted."

"How big a problem is that?"

"Don't know. We'll see."

"We do have another piece," Nate said. "You gave me the license plate of the guy in the Buick...the guy who dropped off these guys."

I nodded.

"It was a rental from BWI. Hertz. Its most recent driver rented it this past Thursday. We got this..." he took out a folded photo print of a man standing at a Hertz service counter. He was photographed straight on from a slightly high angle; the camera must have been at ceiling height behind the clerk. The customer was broad shouldered and was wearing what looked like an all weather coat, sunglasses and a baseball cap. It was impossible to clearly see his face.

"We have guys who can play with the picture to get an idea what he looks like without the sunglasses," Medrano said. "You saw him Friday night, right?"

I shrugged. "He was a pair of eyes reflected in a side-view mirror."

Nate continued: "We ran his name. Joseph Belard. Immigration says he came in on a British Air flight last week."

"Into Kennedy?"

Nate shook his head. "Providence, Rhode Island. Flew in on Wednesday, and then took a US Air flight here on Thursday. He returned the car on Saturday, yesterday, but there's no record of him taking a flight out."

Medrano added, "The desk clerk at Hertz said that there were two men with him. No description worth anything, but his impression is that the men were picking him up after he dropped off the rental."

"So," I said, "Belard returned the car, but he could still be here."

"Ain't life grand?" Nate said. "And while you may not have seen him, he could've gotten a look at you. You, my friend, need to watch your back."

"I will."

Nate nodded.

"By the way, thanks for having officers watch the Mandels."

"Don't know how long we can do that, but we'll see. Be nice to wrap this up soon."

"Be nice to know what the hell is going on," I said. "Meanwhile, just found out that our rabbi has another side to him."

Both Nate and Medrano looked at me. I explained what Sakolsky had told me about Josh, the Torah rescues, and the conflict he once had.

"It may be nothing," Nate said.

"I'll talk to him about it tonight."

"Anyone notice the collection of people so far?" Medrano asked. "A dead guy with a Turkish name, a dead guy with an Algerian passport, and a live guy with a French name. You guys notice that?"

"Yeah," Nate said.

"Yeah," I said.

"So, you and Katie coming to dinner Monday night?" Nate asked, apparently moving onto the next topic.

"Looking forward to it." I let a moment pass. "If that's it for now, gentleman, I need to take off. I have a hot date tonight."

"You?" Nate asked. "With who? Katie?"

"With *whom*," Medrano corrected.

Nate just looked at him.

"Yes, with Katie, of course," I answered. "Every date with Katie is a hot date."

❧

Two hours later, I was freshly dressed in khaki chinos and a short sleeve black Henley. Interestingly, Katie had changed into something similar: a black knit top and white capris. Without having to search too hard, we parked in a spot near the Square in Canton, actually a rectangular series of streets encompassing a small park. On the outside of the rectangle were rows of shops and restaurants. The Patterson Park neighborhood where I had met Nate was not far away, and I felt as if I had just left the area – which I had.

Our parking spot was next to an old, beautiful Lutheran church – its stone structure easily could have gone back to the early 1900s – and we walked to a restaurant-tavern on O'Donnell Street called The Magnificent Seven. The owner must have been an aficionado of the classic western, for lining the interior walls were posters and stills from the movie. As we entered, a curvy, raven haired, twenty year old in a long flowing maroon dress slid off a stool to greet us. The front of her dress had a plunging neckline and revealed plenty of cleavage. Katie jabbed me in the side with her elbow. I looked at her, then turned to the hostess. "Two for dinner, please."

"The restaurant is upstairs. Just seat yourself and a server will be right with you."

"Thank you." We headed to the rear of the tavern and to a flight of old wooden stairs. Before we walked up I said to Katie, "Why'd you poke me?"

"I was helping you focus."

"I was focusing just fine."

The upstairs restaurant was of modest size, but filled with perhaps fifteen small tables. The room was relatively dark; the walls were paneled in a dark wood, and the floorboards were black-brown six-inch wide planks. They must have been original to the building and refinished. Half the tables were occupied, so we moved over to an available one near the front window. Within a few minutes a server came over. She was also about twenty and wearing the same flowing maroon style dress as the woman downstairs, but our server was more modestly endowed. She showed us a pair of menus and took our drink order. By the time she returned, we were ready to order. Katie chose a chicken fajita wrap and a garden salad; I ordered a salad as well and an entrée of pistachio encrusted grouper and a baked potato.

"So," I said once we were alone, "how's life?"

Katie smiled. "We haven't talked in a while."

I shook my head.

"Life is great, I suppose. Not as crazy as yours."

"Doesn't matter. I need to apologize to you."

"Why?"

"Because we've only been connecting at night and mostly rolling in the sack."

She reached for my hand. "I *like* rolling in the sack with you."

"Ah, but is it enough?"

"You've got a lot going on."

"Don't apologize for me." I let a moment pass. "Okay, I accept your apology."

Katie smiled again. After a second she asked, "Do you think we're good together?"

"Do you mean like Laurel and Hardy good, or like the Princess Bride and Westley good, because I'm partial to Westley."

She laughed.

I lifted her hand to my lips and kissed it. "We'll see."

"As you wish," she smiled.

Our meal came, and we ate over small talk, staying away from the intensity of the last few days, at least for me. We passed on dessert, and instead headed out to take up Sakolsky's suggestion of the promenade walk. I moved the Jeep closer to the Canton marina, and after locking up we meandered toward the waterfront. We cut between a pair of three tiered condos, and walked around a seafood restaurant at the edge of the marina.

As we turned right onto the promenade, we could see the walkway winding along the water's edge off toward Fells Point in the distance. Harborwalk, as the signs named it, was paved with bricks, and was bordered on the left by a fully berthed marina and on the right by the townhouse units. At the property line some homes had short hedges separating the public and private space.

Overall, the area was calm and peaceful. The sun had already set off to the left and city lights had taken over. As we strolled, we were far from alone. Joggers, both men and women, ran past us, some coming up from behind, others approaching on the left. Almost universally, all joggers, whether male or female, had white wires running down their torsos from ear buds.

"Sakolsky was right," I said as a couple passed us going the other way. "This is pretty cool."

Katie took my hand. After a few strides she looked at me. "Do you think you'll take his offer?"

"The money?"

She nodded.

"I don't know."

"You're investigating anyway."

"I know, but I don't want to be beholden to him."

"He said you won't be."

I nodded. "It would be nice not to have to worry about certain things. Like the cost of bullets."

She looked at me.

"Just kidding. I have plenty of ammo."

"Gidon!"

I smiled and we walked for a while, just taking in the atmosphere. We sauntered along the edge of a waterside hotel where the brick walkway broadened and changed to wooden planks. The first floor of the guest rooms were at promenade level, and all of the rooms had shutters for privacy in addition to curtains.

We turned another corner, following the promenade around a bend. After the turn, the walkway became narrower. The water was still to our left, and the condos were back on the right. I shifted my position with Katie, putting myself on the inside next to the townhouses. It was another old habit, putting myself between those I was walking with and any potential hiding spot to the right.

"So, I'd like to ask you a question," Katie said.

"Personal and professional? Apparently, I can be hired."

"Personal."

"Can I charge you?"

She just smiled. "Does it bother you that you can't sleep?"

After a second, "I can sleep. I just can't stay asleep."

"Gidon."

"No, it doesn't bother me. It is what it is."

"Do you have any idea why?"

I nodded. "Pretty much."

"Maybe you should speak with someone." I noticed she didn't ask what was keeping me awake, but then she could probably guess.

"No. It'll work itself out. I'm not worried."

A moment went by.

"Can I ask you about Tamar?"

Tamar, my fiancée in Israel, who had been killed in a Jerusalem café bombing. "What would you like to know?"

"How much did she know about what you did?"

I could see where this was going. "Depends." The thoughts gathered. "First, please understand that I was in the army, and in Israel there is a certain level of acceptance from family and friends that you sometimes undertake dangerous work. And there are things you can talk about and things you can't." I watched a jogger go by. "When I was training for a particular mission, I would be out of touch for weeks. Then, I'd come back and collapse. And Tamar knew I couldn't say anything. If it were after the mission itself, she could always tell if it went well. There were a few times we had casualties. I'd explain that a particular soldier was shot or killed. I would mention circumstances, maybe, but not context."

Katie was watching me as we walked.

"Tamar and I would go together to visit the men in the hospital or to pay *shiva* calls. We were all family. Israel is like that. One big family."

Katie didn't say anything.

I looked at her and continued. "I don't think I can be more explicit on what goes through my mind. Like I said, I can always tell you circumstances, but I don't know if I want to discuss context. I don't know if you know what I mean."

"I just want you to be okay."

I smiled. "I'm great. You should know what's going through my mind lately is that Josh and Shelley got into something, and while we have a few leads, we really don't know what it's all about. Our biggest clue is the collection of people we have from Algiers to Turkey…and we have no idea what that means. I'll speak with Josh in the morning and maybe he can point us in a direction."

Katie leaned over and gave me a kiss. "And now *I* have an apology."

"Is it related to the kiss?"

"No. The kiss was just because. Now for my apology. It's really a thank you for not pushing me to explain why I didn't come Friday night."

"Good thing you didn't."

"I know, but I didn't want to come and you were okay with that."

"You'll let me know when you're ready."

"I will. I promise."

I leaned over and kissed *her*.

We continued walking. The promenade had widened again. On the right now were two-story townhouses that seemed lifted from New Orleans or Charleston. Each was set back from the walkway, and had a second floor balcony with vines draped over iron railings. Additionally, gracing the backyards were drooping mimosa trees, reminiscent of Southern Oaks with hanging Spanish moss. The overall effect was quite antebellum.

To our left the water was calm, and white hulled yachts of varying sizes were moored in parallel slips. There was no breeze; at the moment there were no other pedestrians on the promenade. It was just Katie and me.

As we passed the row of Southern-style homes, we went by a small passageway on the right, between one set of homes and the next. In the passageway I caught a glint of metal and movement. I took another step forward and then simultaneously pushed Katie to the side and spun around. Two men had stepped from the shadows. Both were dressed in medium blue suits and open collar white shirts. Both were in their thirties, both were six foot, and both had dark, expressionless eyes. They each had shaved heads. The man on the right was wielding a six inch knife in his right hand. My guess was he had planned to stab me in the back. He took a step forward and swung his arm to slash me from left to right.

I saw the knife swing almost before he initiated the movement, and leaned back a few critical inches before it reached my torso. Missing me, the knife in his right hand had now crossed in front of his own body. I looked coldly into his eyes. I was the last person he was ever going to see. I slightly spread the fingers of my right hand and bent my thumb to tighten my palm and fingers. Before he could move, I stepped forward and drove my fingers into his eyes. He screamed.

I turned to his partner. The rule is take out the first man in a multiple attack, instantly and bloodily. The partner just witnessed that up close – and was totally stunned. I stepped toward him and lifted my right knee high, and then kicked down with my heel, almost stamping onto where the top of his left thigh met his knee. His leg shattered. He collapsed to the ground.

I went back to the first man. He had dropped his knife and had both hands to his eyes. Blood and fluid were running down his face. He was slightly stooped as he held his head. I stepped to his side, and moving into a front stance, horizontally swung my right elbow into the back of his head, just behind his ear, throwing my elbow solidly from my hips. There was a distinctive crack upon contact and he was propelled facedown into the brick walkway.

I stood and looked over to where I had pushed Katie. She was watching me, expressionless. "Are you okay?" I asked.

She nodded.

Nate and his team would want a look at the contents of this guy's pockets, but I wasn't waiting. Not this time. I bent over the first man, wiped my right hand on the back of his jacket, and went through his back pockets. They were empty. No wallet, no papers, nothing. I rolled him over and immediately saw a holstered semiautomatic clipped to his belt. It looked like a 9mm Beretta. Interesting that he wanted to use the knife and not the gun. Maybe he enjoyed it more. In any event, I left it untouched as a present for Nate.

I checked his side pockets. Again, nothing. Not even an "Inspected by" paper. I checked his jacket. All the pockets were empty, except for the inside breast. In it he had a folded 8 x 10 photo...of me. It was a telephoto shot, and it looked like it had been taken in front of the bagel shop where I had met Josh earlier today. I put it back in his pocket. I then looked over at the man's partner. He was on the ground, unconscious; he must have passed out.

Katie came over: "Gidon, are you all right?"

I stood up and turned to her. She was right next to me and pulled back slightly when she caught my eyes. There was a lot of energy and adrenaline running through me, and I knew they had an intense, hard expression in them. "I'm fine."

The next hours were all too familiar. After a phone call to Nate, uniformed officers arrived and then the detectives. At some point, the EMT crews showed up. As the action began to swirl, Katie and I sat on the ground, against a low brick wall out of the way. Neither of us said anything. The EMT guys started working on immobilizing the second guy, the one whose leg I shattered.

About fifteen minutes in, Nate showed up – just Nate without Medrano – followed by a forensics team. I spotted the Asian woman from Friday night at the Mandels. The team shot photos of the scene and went over the body of the first guy.

"So, Gidon," Nate said approaching us, "you really know how to show a date a good time."

I looked up at him. "Always my plan." I leaned over to kiss Katie on the head, said I'll be right back, and stood to join my friend. "One dead and one injured. I'm consistent."

We headed toward the first guy who was still being gone over by forensics. Off to the side, the EMT guys were still working on his buddy.

"How's Katie holding up? The last one didn't do so well."

"She'll be fine. I hope." After a moment, "So, what do you think?" I nodded to the body.

"Somebody doesn't like you." He took out the photo of me, found in the guy's inner breast pocket. "Amazing what the new lenses can do."

"Yeah. I had no clue someone was out there."

"No ID in their pockets – neither one of these guys. No papers, no money, no keys. Someone wasn't taking any chances leaving a trail. We'll get this one back to the lab, do our shit on him, and see what turns up. We've already started going international."

"Include the *Shin Bet*. You never know what they have."

Nate nodded.

"Where's Medrano? He's got good instincts."

"On another call."

"I'll talk to the Mandels in the morning," I said. "Get a more complete picture with this Torah rescue stuff. See where he's visited."

Katie stood up and came over. "Anything I can do?"

Nate responded: "Go home. Take him with you."

Katie smiled weakly.

"You know," I said to Nate, "there is only one person who knew we'd be here, besides my student, Jon."

"Mr. Sakolsky," Katie put in.

"Henry Sakolsky. This place was his idea."

Nate responded: "I'll check him out. Now go home."

I took Katie's hand and we headed back the way we had originally come. "You know, I think I'm going to pass on teaching the 7th grade tomorrow." I was supposed to substitute in the morning.

"Not in the mood?"

I shook my head. "And why don't you come home with me tonight? I just want to chill."

She nodded and put her arm around me.

We had only walked a few feet when she stopped. "By the way, for the record, I'm fine."

She must've heard Nate's comment about my previous girlfriend not holding up well under similar conditions.

"What you did tonight, you had to do. Don't worry about me."

"Okay."

"But that look in your eyes, that cold, hard stare, I never want to see that coming my way."

"Not a chance, Katie, not a chance."

With arms around each other we continued walking.

"Gidon, wait!" It was Nate coming toward us, carrying his cell phone. "The man who told you about this place…Henry Sakolsky?"

"Yeah."

"Medrano just called. Sakolsky's body was found in the parking lot of his office next to his car. He was shot in both hands and both legs. He was also shot in the head." Nate looked from Katie to me. "Gidon, Sakolsky was tortured and then killed."

11

A phone call to the Mandel home the next morning revealed that Josh wasn't there, but Shelley was. Neither of us felt particularly conversational, and she simply reported that her husband was in his congregation office. At 8:00, then, I walked in the front entrance of *Beit Shalom* Synagogue. The main office was just inside the entryway of two pairs of glass doors, and immediately to the right. I stepped in to see a small septuagenarian woman sitting at a desk, shuffling papers. She had silver hair and was wearing two pairs of glasses – reading glasses on her nose and a second pair resting above her forehead at her hairline. She looked up.

"Hi. Rabbi Mandel, please," I said.

"He's in his office across the sanctuary, but he's very busy. We've had a loss in the congregation."

"I know. That's why I'm here."

I didn't know if she were going to call him and ask if he were available, or just send me through – or not. In any event, her phone rang, and when she picked it up I exited. Coming out of the office, I turned right and walked down a dark paneled hallway until I found the door to the sanctuary.

The interior of the congregation was just the way I had seen it on Friday with a platformed Torah Reader's table in the center and rows of turquoise seats around it, facing forward. Josh's office was up front on the left, inset along the front wall. His door was open and he was working at his computer. Across from the office, there was a man in the first row just sitting there. As I came up the side aisle I could tell he was about fifty, balding, in a rumpled button-down yellow shirt and dark pants. The man had a round, cherubic face, but his eyes were watery. He looked deflated. An open prayer book was resting on his lap.

I nodded to him and he just looked at me blankly.

"Gidon," Josh's voice came from the office, "I don't have time right now."

I stepped into his office. "Yeah, you do." I closed the door.

"We had a congregant who was murdered last night." He continued typing and barely looked at me.

"I know."

"Henry Sakolsky. You met him with me."

"I know. He died trying to protect me and ultimately you."

"What are you talking about?" Josh stopped and stood up.

"Associates of the men after you came after me. Henry knew where I was but didn't want to tell them." No need to go into more detail, if he didn't already know.

"I have to work on his eulogy," he said. "I'm conducting the service." Josh sat down and resumed typing. In a moment, he stopped and looked up at me. He had tears in his eyes. "What's going on?"

Someone is trying to kill you, I wanted to say. *And they wanted me out of the way.*

"He was such a good man. Who would do this?"

"Some very bad people." After a moment, "Josh, do you know any very bad people?"

He shook his head, unconvincingly.

"What about your Torah rescue adventures?"

He looked at me.

"Yeah, I know about that. Anyone in that world want you dead?"

He looked bewildered, like "Who would want that?"

Maybe his mind had shut down because of Sakolsky's murder. Maybe he really had no idea.

"Someone is not happy with you," I said. "What about the incident in Poland?"

"There's nothing there. They had their fun. That's all." Josh turned away.

"Josh, either you're really naïve, or you're hiding something."

"I'm not hiding anything."

"Okay. So, you think what's going on has nothing to do with that."

"No, that's over."

"All right," I said, "if it has nothing to do with Poland, what about your other projects? Yesterday, you said you had business in Charleston and in Rhode Island. Was that Torah rescue business?"

He nodded.

"Any problems there?"

"No. The congregations had hired me to find Torahs that had survived the Holocaust. I located two damaged ones in Europe and brought them back for repair. When that was done I presented one to Beth Elohim in Charleston and one to Congregation Sharah Zedek in Westerly, Rhode Island."

I thought for a moment. "Is there a lot of money in this?"

"Well, congregations use it as a fundraiser. For me, I just ask for expenses. I don't charge anything. It's my *tzedekah*." His charity work.

"Do other people do what you do, but for profit?"

Josh nodded. "Sure. It can be big business…in the tens of thousands of dollars. I only know one person who makes this his living. There are others, I'm sure."

"So there's competition."

"I guess." He let a moment go by. Then, "You don't think…" he trailed off.

"…that someone is angry because you take these jobs and he loses out on the money? I don't know." I looked past Josh to a floor-to-ceiling bookcase filled with Biblical texts and prayer books. He had a similar one in his house. "Where do these other people live? Are any French or Algerian or Turkish?" Again, I was thinking of the nationalities of the men who had come after us.

"Not that I know of. The fellow I'm familiar with is American…
from Charleston."

"Charleston? You said you just delivered a Torah to Charleston."

He nodded again.

"Okay, write down the name of those two congregations you dealt
with, the one in Charleston and the one in Rhode Island, plus your
contacts there. Also, give me the name of the other rescue person and
his address, if you have it."

"Okay."

Josh went into his e-mail manager and began to copy and paste
names, addresses, and phone numbers. In a minute he printed out the
list and handed it to me. There were two names in Charleston and one
in Rhode Island.

The rabbi looked at me: "You're going to call them?"

"We'll see. Don't contact them, okay?"

"I won't."

He exited the e-mail program and was left with Sakolsky's eulogy
up on the screen. Josh stared at the words.

"I'm sorry about Henry."

"He was a really good man. When Shelley and I planned to come
to Baltimore, he helped us find housing and schools for the kids. We
stayed with his family when we were in transition. He had a great
sense of humor and real sense of responsibility. A real *mentsch*."

I nodded to the eulogy on the screen. "Be sure you say that…that
he took care of people. That it was important to him."

"Yeah."

We sort of nodded to each other, and I left his office, closing the
door behind me.

Back in the sanctuary, I paused for a moment to let the conversation
about Charleston and Josh's competition coalesce.

"You're Gidon."

I turned to see the balding man in the rumpled clothes sitting in the front row. He stood and came over.

"I'm Bob Levin, Henry Sakolsky's partner."

He was the Levin of *Sakolsky & Levin* on the former's business cards. I shook his hand. "I'm sorry about Henry."

"His offer still stands...whatever money you need to see this through. No questions asked."

He made it sound like payment for a hit.

"Henry had a wife and three kids. The oldest is in middle school, two in elementary. I don't want anything happening to anyone else... not to the Mandels, no one."

"I'm working on it, but I still don't know if I'm taking the money. Just so you know."

He ignored what I said, but handed me a business card. It was the same as Henry's but with his phone numbers on it. "Call me if you need anything."

I nodded.

He softened. "There has to be a reason for this, right?"

I wasn't sure if he meant philosophically or practically, and I didn't have an answer for either.

When I came out of the synagogue I saw two vehicles at the curb. One was a Baltimore County Police patrol car and one was Nate's dark green Grand Cherokee that was an earlier version of mine. Nate was over at the patrol car speaking with the County police officer, the former Marine, I had seen on Saturday. They both saw me, Nate said something to him, then walked toward me as I approached him.

"What's up?" I asked as he got close.

"Last night and the Code."

"The Code?"

"The 'Don't Fuck with Me' Code."

"You're talking about what I did to the guy with the knife." My mind replayed the attack. The Harborwalk promenade...the two men stepping out of the shadows…the man on the right trying to slice my torso open…my intense response…the strike to his eyes and the blow to the back of his head.

He nodded. "All of us get it, and you were pissed. I know you. You had Friday night tucked in the back of your mind and the hit on the ambulance. And there's the 'Don't' Fuck with Me' Code." He thought my response was too much. "Don't forget that a true master first masters himself."

I looked at him and considered what he was saying. "Noted. Thank you, Obi-Wan."

"Obi-wan?"

"You prefer Yoda? You're ears are a little pointy like his."

"Now you're embarrassing me."

"What else?" Nate was here for another reason.

"We pulled two sets of bullets from the Sakolsky crime scene. Actually, four matched one gun, a fifth matched another. The first set, the ones used on the victim's legs and hands, came from the Beretta your knife friend was carrying. The second bullet, the kill shot to the head, came from his partner. He had a forty caliber HK on him. Nice, expensive piece."

"So what does he have to say? Anything?" I knew the guy with the knife was only talking to Otherworld creatures.

"Actually, he's pretty sedated since his leg somehow got all messed up. But in his clear moments he doesn't speak English. Only French."

"Interesting. The guy from the Buick has a French name."

"Belard," Nate said.

"And neither of them had ID."

Nate just shook his head. "And one more thing we noticed…your two attackers didn't have car keys."

"Someone dropped those boys off and planned to pick them up, huh. Belard?"

Nate shrugged. Maybe. Belard was looking more and more like a key player. He dropped off the two guys at the Mandels Friday night, and he was probably connected to the two from last night who also tortured and killed Sakolsky. Maybe he was the guy who killed the EMT guy and Mazhar.

"What's up here?" Nate asked, nodding to the synagogue.

"The rabbi and I had a heart to heart. Got a few leads. May go to Charleston today. Down and back."

"You'll be back for dinner?"

"I'll try. You're really looking forward to my company, aren't you?"

"Not me. Rachel. I think she wants to speak with you about Laurie." Rachel was Nate's wife and Laurie was his daughter, currently living in Israel.

"Everything okay?"

"Not sure. We'll talk tonight."

"Okay. I'll keep you posted."

We each headed to our Jeeps. He pulled away, but I needed to make some phone calls and plane reservations. So, I sat behind the wheel, took out Josh's list and made my first call – the rabbi in Charleston Josh had been dealing with. He was the man Josh had worked with in placing his latest recovered Torah.

Rabbi Beiner answered on the second ring. I explained that I was moving to Charleston and would like to speak with him this afternoon about the community. I'd be in Charleston for a few hours and could come by his office...No sense in detailing the real reason. I wanted to see his reaction when I explained what was going on here. Rabbi Beiner said he would be in all day and to just come by. He'd be happy to help. We verified the address, and then hung up.

The next call was to Josh's Torah recovery competition in Charleston, Allan Samuels. I was hoping he'd be in. I *really* wanted to see his reaction when I told him that someone was trying to kill Josh.

"Mr. Samuel's office," a woman's voice answered.

I had already thought of my cover story. "Hi. My name is Jerry Horwitz from Temple B'nai Torah outside of Los Angeles. We would like to undertake a major fundraising campaign centered around a

Torah project, and I'd like to speak to Mr. Samuels."

"I'm sorry, but Mr. Samuels is out of town."

Not the response I was hoping for. "That's too bad. I'm planning on being in Charleston today, and I was hoping to stop by. Is there anyone else in the office I could speak with?" If there were, I didn't know what that would accomplish, but it was better than nothing.

"No, I'm afraid Mr. Samuels is the man you'd need to speak with and he's in London right now. "

"When will he return?"

"Not for two weeks. After London he's going to Israel. I can give you his cell phone number. He's taking calls if you'd like."

"Sure."

She gave me the number, then, "Just remember the time difference."

"Seven hours ahead to Israel."

"That's right, you'd be surprised how many people forget."

"Thanks. You don't happen to know where in Israel he'll be?" Maybe I could have someone check on him.

"No, I don't. I'm sorry. Jerusalem, maybe?"

"That's okay."

"Do you want me to take a message and he'll call you when he returns?"

"No, I'll probably reach him in Israel and we'll set something up. Thanks."

"You're welcome."

We hung up.

Well, that was one for two…the rabbi but not Josh's competition. I looked out the windshield at the front of the shul. A maintenance worker in jeans and a dirty gray sleeveless sweatshirt had come out and had started cleaning the glass entry doors. It wasn't optimal speaking only with the Charleston rabbi, but it was still worth making the trip. Using my phone I found some non-stop round trip flights and booked them. A quick look at the time revealed there were still two hours before check-in, so there was time for a fast visit with Katie.

As I drove over to the Solomon Stein School I knew that Katie would be in class. She was teaching a 6th Grade Study Skills at this hour, but all I needed was to tell her what was happening today. That, and to grab a kiss.

Unlike Friday afternoon, the school was fully up and running. The parking lot was filled with cars, and the building was busy with adults, and some students, walking the hallways. As before, I walked down a second floor hallway lined with student art, but instead of turning right to Katie's office, I headed left to the Middle School HQ.

The office was of moderate size, with the hive of teacher mailboxes and a copying machine to the right, and the secretary to the left. Diane, essentially the Middle School office manager, sat behind a chest high partition and shelf. She had a Jodi Foster look of swept back hair and a wide, strong jawline, great eyes that sparkled, and a playful yet dry sense of humor, though she was all business when she needed to be. Her posture was military straight, and if you were on her good side, you were set for life. I was on her good side.

She looked up as I walked into the office.

"Hey, babe," she said, simultaneously jotting notes on a list. I hadn't substituted in a few weeks, but I always got that welcome.

"Hey, gorgeous." I always responded.

"Does Katie know you call me that, or do you say that just to have your way with women?"

"No, there's only you."

"I've heard *that* before. Works every time, too."

I laughed. "You know if I didn't have to see Katie I'd just hang out here."

"Wish you would. Then we could start some rumors."

"Alas."

"Alas," she repeated. "What can I do for you?"

"Katie's teaching a Studies Skills class. Any idea—"

"261."

I knew the room. It was at the end of the hall on the left. "Thanks."

The corridor outside the office was one of several Middle School hallways, and had tall, thin lockers lining each side. Unlike public schools with their endless corridors, this one was relatively narrow and short; there were only five classrooms on each side. The hallway was empty except for a young girl kneeling in front of an open locker on the left, stuffing in her backpack. As I approached, she looked up, said, "Hi," and then returned to her backpack challenge.

Room 261 was just beyond her, set back in a small alcove. The wooden classroom door was closed, though an eight inch square window at head level allowed visitors to see what was happening inside. I peered in to see the lights off and Katie at a smart board, remotely interacting with a computer and an LCD projector. The room was set up with two rows of chair-desk combinations running the width of the classroom. Most everyone was paying attention to the front. I knocked and stepped in.

Katie looked over.

"Hi, I said. "Got a minute?"

"Mr. Aronson!" came a girl's excited voice from the middle of the back row. She had long, straight blonde hair, a blue headband, oval glasses, and lots of energy. "Will you be subbing today?" She jumped out of her seat, barely able to contain herself. "Please, please, please for Mrs. Schwartz. You can teach us more meditation."

Katie looked over at her. "Becca, sit down, please."

"Yeah, Becca," came a girl's voice from the side.

Becca sat down.

"Sorry, guys, I'm not subbing." There was an audible moan from the class. Always good for the ego, but I felt sorry for Mrs. Schwartz.

I turned to Katie and gave her an apologetic expression for interrupting.

A shaggy haired kid in a green polo blurted out, "He's here to see Mrs. Harris. C'mon."

Katie fixed him with a teacher stare and the boy lowered his eyes.

"Give me a minute," Katie said to me, as she was in the middle of a lesson. She had a half page of a geography text on the board, and was using the Smart Board to highlight a paragraph's main thoughts. The lesson was on identifying essential phrases in a section of text. A few more taps over some icons on the board and a new text selection came up.

"Okay," Katie said to them, "write down the key phrases in each of these paragraphs." The class got to work and Katie came over to me. "What's up?"

"Sorry 'bout barging in."

"No problem."

"I'm taking a quick trip to Charleston to follow some leads Josh gave me. Should be back in time to go to Nate and Rachel's...maybe by 7:00 or 7:30. I'll let you – and the D'Allesandros – know."

"Charleston, huh? Something you can't do by phone?"

"I want to see the person's reaction when I speak to him."

"Makes sense. And that's fine. I'm actually going to meet Rachel after work. We'll grab a light snack and then check out a new dance class."

"Oh? Didn't know about that."

"How is that possible?" she asked sarcastically.

I smiled.

"I'll tell you about it when you get back." She leaned in and gave me a kiss.

I was conscious of many pairs of eyes on us. I turned to the class. "She did that just for you guys. Thanks." I waved to them, winked at Katie, and headed out.

12

There was no problem finding a taxi at the Charleston airport, and while riding into the city on I-26, I followed up on two promised phone calls. One was to a tai chi teacher and one was to a friend who was a psychologist and counselor. I wanted to see if my abused karate student's father had placed the calls I had urged him to make. He had…which was good, because not only did he need to get professional help, I really didn't want to pay him a return visit. With that task done, I could now pay attention to the cab ride.

The trip into town took between thirty and forty minutes. The taxi swung off the interstate onto Meeting Street, and followed it roughly a dozen blocks. As requested, the cab pulled over at the corner of Meeting and Hasell Streets, just north of the historic area. I paid the driver, exited the cab, and looked around, disappointed. No two and three story white houses with verandas and dripping Spanish moss. There were, however, quite a few palm trees, but the intersection was more commercial than I expected…an open lot on one corner, some restaurants on others, a motel on a fourth. Interestingly, no buildings were taller than three stories. I began walking west on Hassel Street.

The midday sky was clear blue, and the air temperature felt in the eighties. Thanks to the humidity, sweat almost immediately began forming on my forehead and in the center of my back. More palm trees lined the narrow street, but they soon gave way to an opening near a beautiful, old white building on the right. The structure had six columns supporting a grand cornice and triangular pediment. The

Greek Revival style building with its Doric style columns straddling the entryway, looked very temple-like, which was appropriate, considering the building *was* a temple, although not a pagan one. This was the Kahal Kadosh Beth Elohim, the Holy Congregation House of God...or colloquially, the Reform Jewish Congregation of Charleston. I climbed the five cement stairs and stepped inside.

Immediately, there air was cooler, compliments of a retrofitted air conditioning system. The hallway I was now in was more of an anteroom, with the main sanctuary beyond another set of wooden doors. Off to the right, a small group of middle aged and elderly tourists were listening to a young female docent.

"This house of worship was founded in 1749 as a Sephardic Orthodox congregation. There were numerous Jewish pioneers who came to South Carolina, attracted by the civil and religious liberties here and by business opportunities. The congregation today consists of the second oldest synagogue building in the United States and the oldest in continuous use. Now, if you just follow me, I'd like to show you an interesting architectural feature unique to this building."

Before the group could move down the hallway, I hurried over to the docent, asking where I might find Rabbi Beiner.

"I saw him a few minutes ago in the sanctuary," she pointed to a pair of center entry doors, "but I don't know if he's still there."

"Thanks."

She moved on and I stepped through the doors into the main prayer area.

The large sanctuary was all but empty of people, but still emanated vibrancy. The white walls to the right and left were interspersed with a series of waist-to-ceiling stained glass panels, and rows of pews that led one's focus to the front raised *bima*. This mini stage was flanked by more stained glass and was set beneath a Corinthian columned overhang. Along the midpoint of this mini stage was an updated, modernized ark with curved glass doors. Upholstered armchairs sat to either side of the ark, and a center wooden lectern with intricate carvings stood in front, awaiting a rabbi with a sermon. Up high on the front of the overhang, and emblazoned in gold against flat white molding, was a phrase I had seen in Josh's synagogue: "Know Before Whom Thou Standest." Again, not the phrase I would have picked to entice the penitent. Too imposing. I'd have to ask Josh his opinion.

As the thought nagged at me, a tall, thin man entered from the back left, carrying a Torah crown. He walked onto the *bima*, opened the ark doors and set it inside. I moved toward the front.

"Rabbi Beiner?"

The man turned slightly, still with one hand inside the ark.

"Yes?"

"I'm Gidon Aronson. We spoke earlier today."

"Right. Give me a moment." The rabbi resituated the crown he had been carrying onto a shelf, then closed the ark cover doors. He came off the small stage to meet me next to the first pew. "You were moving here and wanted some information." He held out his hand and I shook it.

"First, I owe you an apology," I offered. "I'm not here for information on Charleston. I'm here about Josh Mandel."

"What? I don't understand. Is he all right?"

Rabbi Beiner was Josh's age, a little older than me, tall and thin. He'd make a great player up front on a volleyball team. Unlike Josh though, he was bald on top, and had a neatly trimmed beard that followed his jaw line. It gave him a Sigmund Freud look, though he had bright, cheery eyes that I doubted Freud had.

I took a breath and laid out the circumstances: "This past Friday night two men entered the Mandel home and tried to kill Josh and his family."

"Oh my God." He took a slight step back, as if struck.

"They're okay, but we need to find out what's going on."

"He's okay?" he repeated.

"Yes."

"Shelley and the kids?"

"All fine."

"What happened, do you know?"

I smiled before I realized I had done so.

"What?" Rabbi Beiner asked. "Why are you smiling?" He looked at me intensely.

"I'm sorry. It was your question. I know what happened because I was there."

He stared at me for a long few seconds. "You were there." It was a statement.

I nodded.

"What happened?"

"Doesn't matter. They weren't successful, that's all. Now I just want to find out why."

"Of course." Another few moments went by. He was weighing his thoughts. "Are you a police officer?"

"No, just a friend, but I'm working with the police. Like I said, I was there and I want to be sure that the Mandels remain safe. For that, I need more information."

"Mr. Aronson, excuse me, but I don't know you." He paused again. "You didn't tell me this over the phone because you wanted to see my reaction."

I nodded.

Rabbi Beiner let another moment go by. He was doing a lot of that. "Do you know the origin of your first name?"

"Yes."

Despite the affirmative answer, he went on: "Gidon was a leader mentioned in the Book of Judges. He reconnoitered the enemy Midianite camp at night to determine their strength and then used strategy and psychology to frighten them."

"Today, we call it field intelligence. He later gave every soldier a *shofar* and a clay vessel containing a torch. He divided his army into three companies, and on his signal had his men blow their *shofars*, smash the clay vessels and grab their torches. All this was at night."

Rabbi Beiner finished the story: "The Midianites were so scared, in their panic they began to kill each other."

"I guess you could say that we both served in the Israeli army."

He continued his visual evaluation of me, but didn't say anything.

"I understand your apprehension," I said, "but if it makes you feel better, call Josh. Ask about me." I held out my cell phone, but he didn't take it.

"What unit were you in...in the IDF?"

I shrugged, "An eclectic group."

"I spent 18 months in Machal." He named an army program for volunteers, who were frequently college-aged students, joining the IDF for a limited time, up to a year and a half. If he really served in the IDF, he knew not to ask further questions about my unit. He didn't.

"How can I help you?"

I leaned back on the end of one of the pews. This wasn't going to be my first question, but now it was: "You reacted pretty strongly when I said the Mandels were almost killed."

"We're not just colleagues; we're pretty close. We were roommates in college. We talk maybe once a week."

"But he didn't tell you about this?"

He shook his head. "Maybe he didn't want me to worry."

"Maybe," I said. "He worked on a Torah project for you?"

"Yes. The congregation wanted a major fundraiser. An idea was raised at a board meeting to center it around rescuing a Holocaust Torah and bringing it back to us for use. It would be like giving that Torah a new life. That would be pretty significant. I mentioned Josh and what he could do for us."

"Any obstacles to hiring him?"

"There's a local man who also rescues Torahs, but...let's just say Josh was the better choice."

"As opposed to Allan Samuels?" That was the name Josh had given me of his competition.

"Yes."

"And why was Josh the better choice?"

Rabbi Beiner hesitated. "Maybe you should just Google Mr. Samuels."

He didn't want to say anything bad about the man. A noble attribute, but I wasn't in the mood, not with all that's happened. "Let me put this in perspective for you and then you can decide whether telling me qualifies as *loshen harah*." I used the Hebrew term for gossiping. "There was a killer who put a gun to Josh Mandel's head. One of his congregants was tortured and then killed. Someone tried to put a knife in my back. Maybe you should just tell me what you know."

He looked at me for a few seconds. Then, "There have been some accusations about how Mr. Samuels obtains the Torahs he rescues. Black market dealings, mafia kind of guys. Kickbacks. It's not the type of relationship the congregation can sanction by hiring him."

"Has anything been proven?"

"I think there's only circumstantial evidence at this point. But still…"

"And Mr. Samuels knows about Josh?"

"Sure. Their relationship is not friendly. Never was. When Josh got the job here in Mr. Samuel's back yard…"

"It didn't sit well."

"No."

For a few moments neither of us said anything.

"Well, that's more information than I had before. I'll follow up," I said. "Anything else? Any other ideas who might have a problem with Josh? Some of the guys we're following up on are French and Turkish."

He looked at me.

"What?"

"Not Josh."

"Shelley?"

He nodded. "Ask Shelley about her pregnancies. That's all I'm going to say. It has to come from her."

"Okay." That was unexpected.

"That it?" the rabbi asked.

"Yup. Originally I had hoped to speak with Mr. Samuels, but his secretary said he was overseas."

"So you just came down to see me."

"It was important."

"And now you'll head back to Baltimore?"

"I have a little bit of time. I thought I'd try to catch a tour of the historic areas."

"I can do better than that. I'll show you around. Just tell me how much time you have. We can't get to Fort Sumter – it's out in the harbor – but I can give you a quick, decent look around."

"That's not necessary. Thank you, though."

"I want to. I love showing off this city. There's so much here. Maybe you *will* move here one day."

❧

By the evening I had traded Charleston for suburban Baltimore, and Katie and I were driving up to Nate and Rachel's home north of the city near the Loch Raven reservoir. Their house, a large, two story white home sat on almost three acres of land, most of it an expanse of level grass in the back yard. It was a relatively new house, built about fifteen years ago, wrapped in aluminum siding and brick. On the top floor, five windows were spread across the front, each flanked by red shutters. The driveway, to the left of the house, led to a two-car garage. We parked in front of the garage and exited carrying a bottle of wine and flowers.

Rachel greeted us at the door, graciously accepted our offerings, and led us into the house. "It's so beautiful today, we thought we'd eat out on the deck. Nate set the table. So, if the fork is on the wrong side, be sure to give him a hard time."

"My pleasure," I smiled.

We passed through a gleaming kitchen of stone countertops and stainless steel faced appliances and onto their deck. A large table had been set for four, complete with cloth napkins, candles, and flowers. As it was already mid-evening, we immediately got started on dinner. Rachel had prepared appetizers of Middle Eastern salads – pita, hummus, and baba ganoush – plus Israeli style salad, and miscellaneous cut up vegetables. It took only about ten seconds before wine glasses were filled and the four of us toasted friendship. Nate and Rachel sat on one side of the table, Katie and I on the other.

"I understand you were in Charleston today," Rachel said, passing a glass tray of cucumber slices, strips of celery and mini carrots.

Rachel was a striking woman in the Sela Ward mold. She was statuesque and dark-haired. She had a clear complexion and dark eyes highlighted by long lashes and neatly shaped eyebrows that she arched easily during conversation. She had great laugh lines around her mouth and a self-assured smile. Rachel turned heads wherever she went.

"Bastion of the Confederacy," I acknowledged. "Location of the first shots of the Civil War. Rhett Butler's hometown."

"God save us," Nate mumbled.

"It was a quick trip. Wish I could have spent more time. The rabbi I saw gave me a short, but grand tour."

"We were there about ten years ago," Rachel noted. "We stayed in a bed and breakfast at the southern end of town."

"You should go back…the two of you," Nate added, as he dipped a carrot slice in the hummus.

"That would be nice," Katie said. "I can be a Southern Belle."

"You're from Sharon, Massachusetts," I said.

"Details, details."

The meal and the light conversation continued. A cheese lasagna, Green Beans Almondine, and a garden salad followed the appetizers. At some point I brought up the topic that I knew was on Rachel's mind: "What do you hear from Laurie?"

"She's okay, I guess. Still living on that kibbutz and working in a kindergarten…but she broke up with her boyfriend. I don't know what happened. He seemed nice, from what Laurie said. I didn't even know there was a problem, but I think she's doing okay."

I wondered if she were still having nightmares from her abduction.

"It's hard when your daughter's halfway around the world and you don't *really* know what's going on with her," Rachel looked at me. "I wish she would come home."

"She's where she wants to be, Rachel," Nate said.

"Have you been to Israel?" Katie asked.

"Only when Gidon brought her back from Lebanon," Nate responded.

"Maybe it's time for a visit," this from me. "Hang out with her. See what her life is like."

"And what if I don't like what I see?" Rachel asked.

"*She* has to like it," Nate said. I had the sense that they'd had this conversation before.

Rachel turned to me. "Would you speak with her?"

"Sure."

"Just find out how she's doing. She may tell you more than she tells us."

And there are things I can ask her that you can't, I thought. "I'll call her tomorrow. It's already the middle of the night there."

Rachel reached over and squeezed my hand. "Thanks."

We finished the meal discussing Katie's school work, national politics – Nate and Rachel were a house divided – and places where we'd all like to vacation. It didn't seem long before we all got up to clear the table. The four of us each grabbed our plates and silverware. The ladies went in first, but Nate caught my eye so we hung back.

"Rachel's really worried about Laurie's state of mind. We think breaking up with this guy took a toll on her."

"Who initiated it?"

"Laurie, I think, but I'm not sure why."

"I'll speak with her."

"I'd appreciate it." As we headed inside, he switched subjects, "What did you turn up in Charleston?" He asked as he scraped the plates into a trashcan and stacked them in the sink. Rachel was putting items back in the fridge.

"A more clear picture on Josh's competition. The guy sounds like a piece of work with some dangerous friends. At the moment, though, he's in England, according to his secretary, and then he's off to Israel."

"You told me the Mandels were in Israel a few months ago."

"That's what Josh said. Business and pleasure. Maybe you and Rachel should go. Make the trip, see Laurie, and while you're there, connect with the police and see what you can find out about this guy."

"Yeah, I can barely say *shalom* as it is."

I smiled.

"We'll see Laurie when we can. Meanwhile, *you* talk to the police. You know people."

I nodded.

"Anything else in the bastion of secession, besides Rhett Butler's home?"

"Ooh, listen to you."

He smiled.

I told him what Rabbi Beiner said about Shelley's pregnancies.

"Cryptic."

"I'll have to speak with Shelley."

We went back out for more dishes. By now it was fully dark out, and the candles on the table cast a yellow light onto the tablecloth. Partially filled wine glasses looked abandoned, yet still invited consumption. We left them there. Beyond the deck, the sprawling yard was an expansive presence, and if you looked hard enough you could make out Nate's shed along the back property line.

"So, what's the latest with you and Katie?" Nate tried to make the question matter-of-fact.

"Impressive that you've lasted this long without asking me."

"Rachel wants to know."

"Uh huh. Rachel and Katie went out after work today. My guess is that topic was the first thing to come up. But if you want to compare notes, you can tell her nothing's doing. We're just enjoying each other's company."

"Neither of you is seeing other people."

"Nope."

"So you're going steady."

"I don't think anyone calls it that anymore. You'll have to ask a kid under the age of twenty for the proper term."

"I'll text my niece."

"You know how to do that, Captain?"

"Yeah, Rachel showed me."

I laughed. "Katie showed me."

"We're pathetic."

"But we're pretty good with semi-automatics."

"Amen."

We stepped back into the kitchen. Rachel was assembling the dessert, which could only be described as a chocolate pizza concoction. It looked like a large disk of chocolate meringue covered in a layer of whipped cream, topped with blueberries, strawberries, and chocolate curls.

"You've got all the essential food groups there," I said to Rachel.

"All the important ones," she responded.

Katie grabbed some extra napkins, Rachel the decadent chocolate thing, and Nate handed me dessert plates. On the way outside, I turned to him: "I'm heading up to Rhode Island tomorrow to check on the other lead Josh gave me. He did another Torah project for a synagogue in a small town there. Maybe somebody knows something."

"Welcome to detective work. Lots of questions, hoping that one leads somewhere. You driving or flying?"

"I'll fly into Providence, rent a car, and drive wherever that town is."

"Providence?"

We looked at each other.

"Your guy in the Buick flew into the United States through Providence."

"He did, didn't he."

"Take a copy of the rental car photo with you, the one the Hertz office camera recorded. We've got a cleaned-up copy for you that shows more of his face."

"Will do."

With that, we joined the ladies and essentially polished off the chocolate meringue pizza. Afterward, we sat around to make sure the wine was finished, and then we cleaned up. It was 11:00 by the time we headed out.

The route to Katie's place from Nate's didn't take me past the dojo, but with her permission I wanted to drive by, just to check that everything was okay. I took the Jones Falls Expressway, I-83, down to 28th Street then looped around onto Charles below the dojo. There wasn't much traffic; city streets only had a few cars traversing them. Mainly, vehicles were parked for the night. On Charles Street, that meant both sides of the one-way street were lined with cars. The sidewalks, too, were fairly empty, though there were a few individuals and some couples walking about, more than I would have expected.

As I came even with the dojo entrance, I stayed in the left lane next to the row of parked cars. The businesses in the block were all closed and dark, with two exceptions – the radio station, which I expected to have a light on inside, and my dojo, which I did not. The front door, made of glass and lined with orange paper on the inside for privacy, was clearly being illuminated from inside.

"Did you leave a light on?" Katie asked.

"No."

"Could it be Jon?"

"I don't see his car. Maybe he parked in the tenant's space around the corner, or up the block."

"Call him," Katie suggested.

I took out my phone and dialed his number. After four rings his voice mail came on. "No answer."

I pulled forward and found a spot at the end of the block just before the corner. It was probably too short for a legal space, but I didn't care. We got out of the Jeep and stopped at the curb.

"Déjà vu," Katie said.

Last year, she and I came to the dojo when it was supposed to be locked to discover someone had come in and killed a young man staying there.

"Yeah." I said, looking up at the door.

"I'll stay here," Katie said.

We looked at each other for a brief moment, then I started walking down the block. I passed the radio station, and came to the foot of the cement stairs leading up to my door. As I had done so many times in the past, I breathed to relax and to heighten my senses. The breath also began to bring my energy level up. Before taking another step, I looked around. Katie was at the upper end of the block near my Grand Cherokee, a couple was approaching us from down on the right, and a short man was on the other side of the street, sauntering along the sidewalk away from us. As for traffic, only a white Cadillac came up the street and drove by without slowing.

I walked up the five cement stairs and paused at the door. Maybe it was unlocked; maybe it wasn't. If someone were on the other side waiting to do me harm, he was doing a good job luring me in. There was a light switch just inside the front door, and flipping it off would be my first move, depending on the situation. If a gun were pointing at me, I'd drop and roll out of the way as quickly and as suddenly as possible. I'd probably still get shot.

Had I left any weapons near the front door? Possibly a bo, but Jon said earlier he was cleaning up; he most likely had moved it to my office. Maybe I should have listened to Nate and been carrying the Glock.

I pulled on the handle. The door opened easily.

Slowly, silently, I swung the glass door just wide enough for me to step inside.

No one was waiting for me. No one was pointing a gun at my chest or head, however, there were definitely people inside. Two muffled voices floated over from the main hall, out of my line of sight. I walked forward using the same silent walking technique I had used the other night when I had come up behind my karate student's father. The closer I got to the end of the hall, the more distinct the voices became. I could now make out a man's and a woman's voice. The man's was familiar. I stepped into the practice area to see Jon working with his new girlfriend, the redheaded college girl with the short messy hair style. Their backs were to me, and Jon had his arms wrapped around her from behind.

"Now look down where my feet are. You want to stamp down with everything you have on the attacker's instep. Not his toes." He was explaining an early move in breaking out of the hold.

I spoke up: "Angie, just grab him in the groin."

Jon simultaneously let go of her and spun around. "Jeezus, Sifu!"

"Nothing like a little adrenaline in the system, Jon. Angie, hi."

Angie turned to me. Her cheeks colored a bit.

"Jon?" I began to ask.

"We thought we'd come here and work out."

"It's okay with me, but you guys should lock the door. Angie..." I turned to her... "Could you poke your head outside and look up the block. Katie's next to my Jeep. Just wave for her to come in."

"Yes, Sifu." She trotted to the front door.

"Your car isn't here," I said to Jon.

"We took Angie's. And you tried calling, didn't you."

I nodded.

"Sorry. I emptied my pockets. Left everything on your desk, including my phone."

"It's okay." I moved closer to him. "Meanwhile, how did Saturday night go?" I had forgotten to ask about his rendezvous with Angie.

"Excellent. We discovered we have a lot in common."

"Uh huh."

"And this was her idea, by the way, to work on grabs."

"Uh huh."

Before I could follow up, Angie returned with Katie next to her. "Hi, Jon," she said.

"Katie. And how is your evening? I see you've met Angie."

"Yes."

"This was Angie's idea," he said for Katie's benefit.

The redhead shot him a look.

"Don't worry," Katie said to her, "we both know Jon too well."

"While you guys discuss Jon's dating habits," I said, "I'm going to check flights for tomorrow." Then to Katie: "Want to go to Providence? Up and back?"

Katie knew I wasn't serious, because she'd have to make arrangements for her classes. She looked at me, shaking her head at what she considered a stupid question.

I headed toward my office. "Jon, can you take the dojo classes tomorrow?"

Jon and the two ladies followed me into the office.

"Of course. You'll be back tomorrow night?"

"Late, probably." I sat at my desk. The computer was already on, but "asleep." I moved the mouse to bring it back. "Have you already worked on breaking out of arm holds?"

"Just the basic stuff."

"Angie's a purple belt. Show her some take-downs. Use the mats, if you'd like."

Jon turned to his new protege: "That's Sifu's way of saying if you want to be a wimp, use the mats."

She just smiled. "We don't need the mats."

"Good attitu—" I never finished the thought. Something distracted me. Almost like a pressure change in the room, or a shift in presence.

"Gidon?" Katie saw my attention move off somewhere.

I said calmly, "There's a disturbance in the Force." I looked at Jon. Katie looked from me over to Jon and back. "What?"

My student lowered his voice. "Someone just came in the front door."

I thought for a few seconds, then motioned for Jon to come over to the side wall. At eye level there was an electrical panel. I swung the narrow metal cover open. "When I tell you, flip the first two circuit breakers on each column."

He nodded. While he and the two women watched, I pulled off my light-colored polo. Good thing my pants were dark. I reach for my bo, which was right where I had left it the other day, leaning against the wall.

"Maybe it's Nate," Katie whispered.

"It's not. Whoever it is, left the door open." I looked at Katie, Jon, and Angie. "Stay here." I nodded to Jon and he cut the lights in the entire dojo.

13

Before my pupils could fully adjust, I moved into the practice hall. If my eyes were acclimating so were those of whoever was out there. His image of the room would be exactly what it was before the lights went out, and that was to my advantage. I silently and invisibly crossed the room to the far wall carrying the bo in my right hand, and crouched. My eyes adapted quickly, and in a minute I could see the intruder. He was tall, six-four perhaps, and was backlit by the wash of streetlights coming in the front door. I had been right; he had left the door fully open, blocking it with a rock. In his right hand he held a semi-automatic pistol that had the unmistakable attachment of a silencer. The door must have been left open for a quick get-away. The assassin stepped slowly into the room.

I moved soundlessly around him, flanking the man and stepping to his rear, maybe fifteen feet back. The luminescence of the streetlights traveled only five feet into the dojo, but as snipers could tell you, seeing at night is enhanced by the sense of sound. I had been trained to embrace patience… to relax, listen, and feel.

If I were in his place, I'd have put my back to the wall and moved secure in the knowledge that an enemy couldn't come up behind me. But we hadn't attended the same schools.

Who was this guy? I couldn't get a look at his face. The man in the Buick? He seemed to have some authority in all this. The silencer bothered me, for it spoke of a new level of professionalism. The figure in front of me, whoever he was, was walking toward the office, scanning and moving his head in concert, looking for prey. He was still beyond reach of my bo. All he needed to do was turn around, spot me, and pull the trigger. At this range, any hit would cause a lot of damage. Depending on the caliber, even an impact in my arm would knock me down.

I moved forward…and he began to turn around. I had no idea why. Maybe I was entering his personal space and he sensed me. Maybe he was better than I had thought. In another moment we'd look at each other. I'd see who he is and he'd see me standing too far away for the quarterstaff. Then he'd pull the trigger. Around the corner in the office, all Katie and the group would hear would be a focused cough of air and the sound of me hitting the ground in a terminal fall…the last fall I'd ever make.

He was now three-quarters turned toward me; his peripheral vision would soon pick me up, if it hadn't already.

In a single motion I dropped to the floor, put the bo out in front of me, and rolled forward like a ball, taking the staff with me. I sprang up just a few feet in front of him and snapped the bo up, ignoring his gun – it wasn't pointed my way yet – and hit him with the last six inches of the quarterstaff just above the bridge of his nose. Without hesitation, I whipped the bo back down to the floor and arced it up behind him, smashing him in the back of his head. Maybe a second passed between the strikes. Reversing the motion, I struck the back of his right knee. He flew backward to the floor and didn't move.

"Jon," I called. "Lights."

A moment later all the fluorescents in the room came on, illuminating me standing over the inert man. I peered down at him. It wasn't the fellow from the Buick, at least that I could tell. His gun, it looked like an HK P30, was by my feet. I kicked it to the side.

Katie, Jon, and Angie came out of the office. All three of them were staring at the guy.

"He's not dead," I commented. "Just gave him a couple of love taps."

"Who is he?" Katie asked.

"I'm going to find out. Jon, take my bo. If he comes to and tries to get up, poke him on the forehead. Not too hard."

I passed my student the quarterstaff, and without looking at Katie or Angie, went back to my office. I went over to my desk and opened the bottom right drawer. My lock box. I tilted it up, dialed the combination, and opened the hinged door. Inside was a .40 Glock 23 and a fully loaded magazine. I took both out and inserted the magazine into the grip. There was no need to chamber a round – not for what I had in mind.

The man on the floor was still unmoving and Jon was still standing next to him, ready to klunk him, if necessary. Jon saw me approaching, gun in hand. "Sifu?"

"Let's see what our friend has to say."

Katie look at me, saw the fixed expression on my face, and turned to Angie: "Come with me, dear." She took Angie by the arm and led her back into the office.

She really didn't need to. I was just going to threaten the man and he would recognize the power of the gun more readily than the bo's. Using my foot, I nudged him in the side. "Time to get up." I nudged him again.

Nothing. I could see the rise and fall of his chest. He was still alive. Nate would be happy.

Maybe he didn't speak English. We had a number of players not native to the U.S. "*Levez-vous.*" Nothing. I turned to Jon. "Tap him gently on the head with the bo."

Jon poked him as directed.

"*Levez-vous,*" I repeated. "Time to get up."

He moaned. Definitely alive.

There were many questions to ask. What was their interest in Rabbi Mandel? Who sent them? Who were *they*? Why were they targeting me – though I could guess the answer to that.

The dojo was completely quiet except for a humming fluorescent fixture near the entrance. There was the guy on the floor, Jon, and me. There was no other noise… and then I mentally confirmed something I already knew. Sound often makes itself known before its cause. Ahead of me, I heard a new stranger come into the room before I saw him – a young man in a black windbreaker entered the dojo, semi-automatic in his left hand.

A number of things went through my mind, mainly about how stupid I was. The guy at my feet hadn't left the door open for a quick get-away. He had left it open for his partner. This man was going to be the follow-up, like a second terrorist bombing after everyone relaxed from the first blast.

The figure at the door was surprised to see me standing over his associate. It was supposed to be me on the floor. In that second's hesitation, I raised my gun, simultaneously pulling back the slide with the other hand. By the time the Glock was level, I was pulling the trigger. I fired three times, hitting him square in the chest.

The powerful .40 caliber impacts blew him off his feet, and the sound of the multiple gunshots bounced off the walls.

After another second, Jon reacted. "Shit!" All he had seen was me raising the gun and firing…and the result.

"Gidon!" Katie and Angie came running out of the office.

"It's okay," I said.

They looked at the man on his back near the doorway, blood seeping into his shirt. I knew there wouldn't be a huge amount, as his heart was already gone and there was nothing left to do the circulating.

Jon walked over to him and let a few seconds go by. "Well, he's not going anywhere."

I turned to see how the ladies were doing. Katie seemed fine, but Angie had gone pale. I caught Katie's eye and nodded to Jon's new girlfriend.

"Angie, you don't need to look at this," Katie said, taking her arm. She led her to the other side of the dojo where they sat on the floor.

The guy at my feet, the first guy, moaned. There was no time to deal with him just yet.

"Jon, you know where the duct tape is?"

"Yes, Sifu."

He ran off toward a closet in the back of the room and returned less than thirty seconds later with the silver tape. I rolled the semi-conscious man onto his side, taped his wrists behind him, plus wrapped his ankles.

Standing up, I took out my cell phone and called Nate for a now too-familiar purpose.

He picked up on the third ring.

"Nate, hi. You'll never believe what happened," I said without an intro.

"Don't tell me."

"One dead, one still alive. Probably with a concussion, but still alive."

"Where?"

"My dojo."

"I'd ask you not to touch the bodies, but you will."

I smiled. "You still have someone watching the Mandels?" If someone were trying to get to me, they might also go to Josh and Shelley's.

"Yeah, but I'll send another two units."

"Thanks." We hung up.

"So, what do we do about him?" Jon asked.

"Go through his pockets."

"Wait." Katie came over, holding the polo shirt I had taken off earlier. "You don't want to distract anyone else walking in the door with that manly chest."

"Thanks." I put on the shirt. "You okay?"

She nodded. "You?"

"Getting tired of this."

She leaned over and kissed me on the cheek.

I went through the man's pockets. Unlike the team from the

Harborwalk promenade, this guy had a wallet and a cell phone. I left the wallet for Nate, but checked the phone for recent calls. There were a number of them, but two caught my attention. They were overseas numbers. One was to France – I recognized the "33" country code – and one I truly wasn't expecting: a 970 code. The Gaza Strip. I wrote down the numbers on a pad from my office, tucked the paper away, and returned the cell phone to the man lying on the middle of my dojo floor.

∽

As twice before, the uniformed police officers arrived first. They in turn were followed by forensics and then by Nate and Medrano. After getting everyone's statements, the detectives released Angie and Jon. Angie had not really seen anything, and Jon verified that I shot the second guy in self-defense. After asking my permission, Jon left with Angie to take her home. Technically, she was taking him home, since it was her car outside.

Nate, Medrano, Katie and I moved against the front wall.

"Don't you have any goddamn chairs in this place?" Nate asked.

"Can't stay on your feet the way you used to?" I responded.

"You're making me older every day, Gidon."

"I'm getting out of town tomorrow."

"Good. Kill someone in another jurisdiction, would you?"

"See what I can do."

He nodded. Then, "Glad you finally had the Glock."

"Me, too. Need it for forensics?"

"What, to match the bullets that we know came from your gun?"

"Just asking."

"You think about how they found you here?" Nate continued.

"Maybe Sakolsky told them. I don't know."

"Maybe they followed you," Medrano postulated.

"Possibly."

After a quiet moment, "What now?" Katie asked no one in

particular.

Medrano turned to me. "You go through his pockets?"

"Yeah, but just looked at his cell phone. You have my prints on file, right, to separate them from any others?"

Medrano nodded.

"Check the contact list?" This from Nate.

"No. Recent calls."

Medrano looked at me. "I recognized France."

"The other one was the Gaza Strip."

"Oh, great," Nate commented. After a moment: "You going to call your Shin Bet friend?"

"I suppose." I also knew someone in the Palestinian areas, but couldn't get ahold of him from here. Wasn't sure I could reach him even if I were in Israel.

"Suck it up and call Amit," Nate said, naming my Shin Bet contact. He turned to Katie. "Make sure he calls, okay?"

She smiled.

"You were in Charleston today?" Medrano asked me.

"Yup."

"Notice how these two guys came for you after the trip," he put out.

"You saying Rabbi Beiner down there put a hit on me?"

"*Post hoc ergo propter hoc.*"

"What the hell is that?" Nate asked.

"Latin for 'After this, therefore because of this.' One thing follows the other." He smiled. "Got that from *West Wing*."

We just looked at him.

"Of course it's not usually true."

"Gidon, you have my permission to hurt Detective Medrano."

I turned to the younger man. "You'll never see it coming." Back to Nate: "I'll call Amit after you've processed these guys. Maybe we can also give Shin Bet some more names to check on."

Nate nodded.

"How are the Mandels?" Katie asked.

"They're fine, based on the last report," Nate said.

"There've been no moves on them, have there?" I inquired.

"Nope," this from Medrano.

"Interesting. Since Friday night, guys have come for me twice."

"Plus they killed Mr. Sakolsky," Katie noted.

"To get to me. But the Mandels have been left alone."

"Maybe they want to get you first?" Medrano offered. "Maybe they don't want to go through the cops minding them."

"If they really wanted Josh and Shelley, there are ways. Something's changed."

Nate said, "Don't know how long that will last. Be nice to get them out of town."

"Definitely," I said. "I'll stop by their place tonight. Won't give them a choice."

"You can't force them," Katie said.

"No. But they'll leave to protect their family and friends."

It was almost 2 AM when I stepped solo into the foyer to face both Josh and Shelley. For a moment I wished I were with Katie at her place.

"Sorry about the hour," I apologized, somewhat sheepishly.

Shelley was in a pair of black scrubs and a signature T-shirt – this one from the Tower of Terror at Disney World – and Josh was in jeans and a polo. Both of them were barefoot and looked bleary-eyed. They probably had been sleeping.

"What's going on?" Shelley asked. "There're two more police cars out front."

"I had visitors tonight."

"Everything okay?" Josh asked.

"For me." I pointed to the kitchen. "Can we sit down?"

They led me into the kitchen and we sat at the island.

"What happened?" Shelley asked.

Always an interesting question. How to respond... "Someone wants me out of the way. Probably because I've started poking around."

"And you're all right?" Josh needed verification.

I nodded.

Shelley continued:"And the extra police are here because...".

"We don't want anything happening to you."

"You think that if someone came for you they'll come for us."

"Maybe...but I don't really think so. The police are here just in case. A deterrence."

Josh asked, "Any progress on what this is all about?" He looked at Shelley. "We really can't imagine a reason."

"My guess is you know something, but you don't realize what that is, or what you did."

The three of us looked at each other.

"This is crazy," Shelley said.

"What can we do?" This from Josh.

I had some questions about Shelley's pregnancies – the lead Rabbi Beiner had given me in Charleston – but now wasn't the time. That conversation would derail the reason for my visit.

"Primarily," I began, "I want you safe. I'd like you to take a vacation for a little while."

They didn't respond.

"I know there's the synagogue, there's school for the kids, your work, Shelley, but it really isn't safe here. This is getting worse, not better."

"We've actually been thinking about this," Shelley admitted. "We're putting our kids in danger, us, our friends, and you."

"And the police," Josh added. "So, we've been talking about getting away from Baltimore. I guess now's the time."

This was not what I expected, yet knowing the Mandels for a short time, their sensitivity was in character.

"So, what did you come up with?"

"Well, we could go to my mom in St. Louis," Shelley said.

Josh shook his head. "No. I love your mother, but no. There're my folks are in Boston."

"No," Shelley's turn. "Not that they're not great. I just wouldn't want to worry them." A moment went by. "There's Israel."

"My turn," I said. "Too far."

"You sure?" she asked.

I nodded.

"We've friends in Miami and cousins in Williamsport, Pennsylvania," Josh proposed.

"They're away in California," Shelley looked at him.

"Who?"

"The Shuchmans in Williamsport."

"Perfect," I said. "How far is it by car?"

"About three hours," Josh said.

"Their house is empty?"

Shelley took this one, "I think. And I have their cell number. Maybe a neighbor has a key."

I looked at my watch. California, where the cousins were at the moment, was three hours behind us, and it wasn't the middle of the night yet. "Call them. Ask if you can get into their house tomorrow."

"Tomorrow?" Shelley and Josh reacted in concert.

I nodded. "You wouldn't hesitate if you saw what walked into my dojo tonight. Make the call."

"It has to be tomorrow?" Shelley asked.

"Two men with guns came for me. One of them had a silencer. You need to be out of harm's way *now*. Knowing you're safe will also let us fully focus on the problem at hand."

Shelley pulled out a small spiral address book from a drawer and Josh reached for a wireless phone. He looked at me. "What do I say to them? We need a place to hide out?"

I responded, "Why not? Tell them some crazy people are after you. You don't know why, but the police think it's a good idea not to be in Baltimore for a while until they catch the guys." A moment went by as that sunk in. "Reassure them that you're not concerned."

They both looked at me.

"Or not. Up to you."

A long moment passed while no one said anything. Finally, Josh nodded and Shelley read him the phone number. Josh made the call, and after he got through, apologized for calling so late, and then got to the point. He pretty much followed my suggestion about a crazy person stalking them, and the police advising they go away for a few days. He even made a joke about how it must be a congregant unhappy with his sermons. From our end, we could tell that the cousins said it was fine to stay in their house, and gave Josh miscellaneous instructions. He put Shelley on to confirm they were okay. They chatted for another minute, then hung up.

"Done," Shelley said. "I think they're worried for us."

"Naturally. Call them every few days to reassure them. Now, what time can you be ready in the morning?"

"You're coming?" Shelley looked at me.

"Right behind you. I want to see where you'll be. From there, I'll probably drive to Rhode Island to follow up on that name you gave me...about your Torah project there."

"You really think it's related?" Josh asked.

"Maybe. Maybe not." It occurred to me that Nate should contact the Williamsport Police to give them a heads-up...let them know the Mandels would be coming. "Can you and the girls be ready by 10:00?"

Shelley and Josh looked at each other. "We'll stay up and do some packing," Shelley said. "We can be ready by 10:00. We'll have to make some phone calls...to the girls' school, to the synagogue office..."

"Just say something's come up with out of town family, and you'll be back after next weekend. No need to be more specific. The more you offer, the more complicated, and the more difficult, it gets. In general, don't tell anyone where you'll be."

They nodded.

"I'll see you in the morning, then. Call me if you need anything. I'm sure I'll be up."

⚉

When I got home I didn't go straight to bed. That would have been smart. Instead, I went to my first floor office, passing the overhead light switch, and walked over to my desk. I sat in an old wooden chair, turned on a small table lamp, and looked around. The warm glow of the bulb filtered through the shade, painting the room in a muted yellow luminescence. I liked my décor, though it was a little Spartan: an oversized upholstered chair on one side, a floor to ceiling bookcase on another, and a Chinese poem on parchment hanging beside it. The poem, written with flowing brush strokes, was reminiscent of the *Tao Te Ching,* and spoke of the winds of creation. To my right was a relatively new acquisition, a framed gold leaf papercut of the word "Jerusalem" that I had placed on the room's eastern wall.

"Enough procrastinating," I said aloud. There were phone messages and e-mails to check. That took forty-five seconds. I shook my head at my dawdling, turned off the light and finally went upstairs.

My get ready for bed routine proceeded on autopilot, and eventually I got into bed. My eyes, however, did not close. It had been a long day, but the ceiling looked back at me. Katie would be fast asleep by now. She was really great for me; even-tempered, smart, funny, sexy, and not freaked out by certain aspects of my personality, like overwhelming violence when called for. She was guarding something, though. She dropped little clues, like not wanting to go to the Mandels this past Friday night, or not telling me about her grandparents. We'd visit all that at some point, no doubt.

I followed a small crack in the ceiling as it scribed a line across my line of sight and off to the left.

These really had been a crazy few days. No need to close my eyes to see Josh at gunpoint in his kitchen. Or to see me shooting the guy threatening him. Or me pounding the first guy with my descending elbow to the base of his skull. Or me thrusting my fingers into the eyes of the man wielding a knife, or smashing his partner's knee. There were my bo moves tonight, smacking the guy at the dojo in the forehead and then in the back of his head. I had absolutely no feeling of remorse shooting the man who came in after him. Three .40 caliber shots to the chest. These were bad men.

I had no feeling one way or the other about shooting that bomb maker in Sidon, Lebanon, the one we called the Graduate. I did remember his eyes, the moment I shot him in the head. But he had gotten off a round. And Asaf, the big soldier who could move fluidly and silently, was on the floor, hemorrhaging from the right side of his neck. I should have pulled the trigger a split second sooner. I guess I did have feelings about my actions. I closed my eyes, but that didn't stop the images.

14

We unceremoniously pulled out of Baltimore under a cloudless blue sky after the morning rush hour. The Mandels led the way in their silver Volvo station wagon, packed with the four of them, three large suitcases, a cooler for snacks and food, plus several backpacks like the ones kids use for school. We headed up I-83, almost due north on a stretch of highway that, once out of the urban area, became a pleasurable tract of road with lush trees on either side. The Pennsylvania line changed some of that, particularly between York and Harrisburg, with increased congestion and industry visible just off the road. As we approached Harrisburg, the Mandels' route had us turn onto city streets, without crossing the Susquehanna River, to follow U.S. Route 11 which virtually hugged the western bank of the river as it wound its way northward.

State roads came and went on the left leading to various townships, and the drive was a leisurely one. Off on the right from time to time I'd see pairs of kayaks navigating down the Susquehanna. About two and a quarter hours into the drive, the Mandels pulled into a small restaurant parking lot just off the road in the town of Selinsgrove. They stretched their legs and everyone headed in to use the facilities. While they were inside, I got out of the car, walked around, and placed a phone call to Nate.

"Just wanted you to know I've gone 12 hours without needing the police."

"So why are you calling me?" he asked.

"I'm escorting the Mandels to Williamsport. They'll stay in a cousin's empty house."

"That'll work."

"Could you tell the Williamsport cops about the Mandels? Maybe have a patrol car stop by every so often to see how they're doing."

"You're a control freak, you know that?"

"Yeah. Sometimes."

"Medrano will call them. Give him the address. What else."

"The two guys from last night?"

"Both are from Boston. Refreshing, isn't it. Americans. Not much in their pockets. The dead guy had the same phone numbers in his cell phone as his buddy. By the way, you should know that his buddy, the one you clocked, claims he was just coming to rob you. Denied anything about a hit."

"Right. And he was using an HK with a silencer in a robbery."

"It didn't escape us that the guy who killed Sakolsky also used an HK, a P30."

"Maybe whoever's behind this got a bulk discount."

"You still heading to Rhode Island?"

"If I can connect with the rabbi there. That'll be my next call."

"Let me know."

We hung up just as Josh and Shelley and the girls came out. They got settled in the Volvo and our mini-caravan pulled back onto the road. The Mandels seemed to know where they were going. On the outskirts of South Williamsport, houses and businesses began sprouting up. They took us over the Susquehanna and onto Market Street through downtown. We passed several construction sites as a number of hotels were expanding. It was soon clear we were essentially driving in one side of Williamsport and out the other. In a matter of minutes we were climbing out of the valley and onto rural roads. With the town behind us, we drove up another hill toward a street in a relatively new development. A final right turn brought us into a court. We headed to the end, parking toward the left curve of the cul de sac.

The Mandels got out, and I did the same.

The clear blue sky had turned overcast, and despite the midday sun, the air temperature had easily dropped ten degrees. Josh went over to a ranch style brick house and rang the bell. From where I stood I could see a middle-aged woman answer the door. She and Josh spoke for a minute, the woman smiled, then handed him something. Josh came back over to us.

"All set," he held up a key.

I helped the Mandels unload the car and carry everything inside. For now, we left the suitcases in the foyer, as Shelley and Josh helped the girls get situated in their rooms off to the right somewhere. The house was magnificent, with a large open area that ran from a dining room on the left and into an expansive family room. There were bookcases, an entertainment center with a large flatscreen television, a stereo component system, and a computer all nearby. Despite the furniture and the accoutrements, what commanded everyone's attention was the view. Beyond sliding glass doors, a deck overlooked a row of rolling green mountains that ran across the full landscape.

"Not bad, huh," Josh said, following my gaze.

"I could tolerate this view for a little while," I smiled.

As the Mandels unpacked, a laptop went onto the dining room table, school books came out of backpacks, and the cooler was brought into the kitchen. While Josh and Shelley continued getting acclimated, I stepped outside to call the lead in Rhode Island Josh had given me. He had named a Rabbi Seidman as the person he worked with a few months ago. Leaning against the passenger side door of the Grand Cherokee, I made the call.

"Nancy Seidman," a woman's voice of indeterminate age answered.

I wasn't expecting a woman rabbi. I didn't know why, and it didn't matter. "Rabbi Seidman, my name is Gidon Aronson. Rabbi Josh Mandel in Baltimore suggested I call you. I'd like to speak with you about your recent Torah rescue project."

"The one in Westerly?"

"Yes."

"Sure. What can I help you with?"

"If you don't mind, I'd like to speak with you in person. Perhaps take a look at the Torah. That sort of thing. I just have a few questions."

"You'll be in the area?"

"Yes."

"Well, I'm in New London right now, but I'll be in Westerly tomorrow."

"Perfect."

"Do you know where the Congregation is?"

"No."

"Can I e-mail you directions? I can do it right now."

"Sure." I gave her my e-mail and we set a time.

"See you then."

I headed back inside.

The Mandels were all in the kitchen off to the left, with Josh and Shelley putting out cold cuts, salad, some tuna salad, bread, and side dishes. They must have brought it all from home.

"Lunch?" Shelley offered.

"Sure. In a minute. Thanks.

While the Mandels began lunch, I checked my e-mail on my phone. Rabbi Seidman had been prompt, the directions were waiting for me. Westerly was just over the Connecticut-Rhode Island line. Traffic permitting, it should take about six hours. Realistically, my body would shut down at some point, so I'd spend the night somewhere, and then head into Westerly in the morning.

Over lunch with the Josh, Shelley, and the girls we talked about everything except what was going on. It was the first time I really saw the girls for more than just a few minutes. They both were younger versions of Shelley. They had dark, wavy hair and dark eyes, plus shared Shelley's angular jawline. In front of me, the younger one, the eight year old, had folded a disk of bologna and was taking a bite out of the center. The older one, maybe ten, had opened the tuna salad sandwich

Josh had made for her, and was re-sculpting the tuna spread.

Afterward, I helped clean up and then told them I'd be heading out. "You've been terrific with all this," I acknowledged.

Josh said, "It helps to know we have friends who are watching out for us."

"I asked Captain D'Allesandro to have the Williamsport Police check on you from time to time."

Shelley started to protest.

"It's not up for discussion. So, don't be surprised if someone stops by."

"So, what happens now?" This from Josh.

"We follow leads, ask questions, poke around a bit."

"Be careful," Shelley said.

I nodded. After a moment, I looked around to be sure the girls were occupied elsewhere. I heard the television in the other room. "There is one thing, Shelley, I need to ask you, and I apologize in advance."

"What?"

"Was there something unusual about your pregnancies that might have anything to do with all this?"

She and Josh exchanged glances.

"This is what happens when you poke around," I said. "Stuff comes out."

"It's not a secret…Just something we haven't discussed for years," she said. "I'm sure it's not related." She waited another moment. "Without going into details, I wasn't able to carry a baby, so we hired a gestational surrogate."

"For both pregnancies?"

"Yes," Josh said. "Shelley had a number of miscarriages…"

"Good thing you had an option. Same host each time?"

They nodded.

"Was there a problem?"

"At the time, yes." Shelley said. "After giving birth to Leah, the surrogate didn't want to give her up."

"She was actually pretty hysterical," Josh added. "Her husband got involved. A really volatile guy."

"What did he do?"

Shelley shook her head, stopping that discussion. "No. That was eight years ago, and we haven't heard from them since. End of story."

"I don't suppose you'd give me their name and address?"

"Gidon, I don't want you going there. It was pretty terrible."

"I understand and I'm sorry, but the situation here is pretty intense, to say the least."

They nodded.

"I'll make you a deal. I won't pursue it unless something else leads me in that direction, okay?"

"Okay," Shelley said softly. Josh nodded.

"You just have to give me a last name so I'll recognize it if I come across it."

Neither Josh nor Shelley said anything.

"No address, no first names. I won't pursue it without checking with you first."

The Mandels looked at each other. Then Shelley relented: "Ben-Susa."

I looked at her. It was a Sephardic name, with origins in Persia. Susa, according to the *Book of Esther*, was the capital of the Persian Empire. The Bible called it Shushan. A number of questions immediately came to mind, but I said I wouldn't follow up on it. I looked from Josh to Shelley. "Thank you."

A moment passed.

"Well, I need to get moving. Miles to go before I sleep." I headed for the door. "You guys'll be okay?"

"The kids have schoolwork to do, and I have sermons to write," Josh said.

"We'll explore the town, watch DVD's," Shelley added. "Call friends."

"From your cell phones," I said. "And don't tell them where you are."

"We know."

I kissed Shelley on the cheek and gave Josh a hug. "I'll give you daily updates." And with that, I went out the front door. As I walked away from the house and heard the door close behind me, I tried to clear my mind and not feel like I was abandoning them.

15

Rhode Island was about 330 miles ahead of me to the east. Travelling toward New York was pretty straightforward – I-80 for the most part – but instead of continuing eastward across the George Washington Bridge and dealing with the Cross Bronx, I opted for I-287 up to the Tappan Zee, then over the Hudson, and down to I-95 just west of the Connecticut line. After two rest stops, several cups of coffee and two candy bars, I finally pooped out approaching New Haven. A perfectly timed motel just off the highway caught my attention, and that's where I turned in. There was a ten o'clock phone call to Katie, then my traditional attempt at sleep, followed by meditation, work-out, and some wandering.

By 8:00 the next morning I was back on the road. Almost an hour later I crossed the Gold Star Memorial Bridge over the Thames River, connecting New London and Groton. As I drove over the bridge, I craned my neck to catch a glimpse of the submarine base far below on the east bank to my left. Interestingly, while the title of the famous sub base is "Naval Submarine Base New London," it's physically in Groton across the river from New London. The Coast Guard Academy was also located along the Thames as well, but closer to the bridge. I managed to catch sight of the tall ship *Eagle* as it was putting to sea.

About ten minutes later, I-95 crossed yet another bridge, much smaller and lower, over the Mystic River with a view of Mystic Seaport not far away. Soon, I was turning off the last exit in Connecticut and heading south toward Westerly. The road brought me almost directly into downtown. I could see that Westerly was one of those small, New England towns with a series of streets built around a main drag, with one-way and two-way roads branching off in varying directions. The hub of downtown seemed to radiate away from the main post office at the junction of Broad and High Streets.

I followed the directions Rabbi Seidman had given me, and in a matter of minutes – and a few short turns later – I was parked beside a steeply pitched, apex roofed, white building. A free-standing sign on the front lawn identified this as Congregation Sharah Zedek. The synagogue itself was up on a small bluff, with a long line of rising steps leading to the front doors. I climbed the steps, pulled open the right wooden door and stepped inside.

The vestibule, not unlike the one in Charleston, was essentially a hall in front of the sanctuary, which was beyond a set of double doors. To the right, a corridor led to some rooms, only one of which had a light on and a walnut nameplate that read Rabbi Nancy Seidman. There were the sounds of a keyboard in use, and I stepped into the doorway.

Rabbi Seidman was indeed at the computer. While her desk faced the door, her computer workstation was at right angles to it, so she was facing away from me toward the monitor near the adjacent wall. I knocked. "Rabbi Seidman?"

She turned around. "Mr. Aronson. Hi."

"Gidon." I moved over to her as she stood up. We shook hands.

"Nancy," she offered.

Nancy Seidman was in her early forties, just a little shorter than me, large boned and solid...not fat in any way, just sturdy, like a physical presence. She had shoulder length straight blonde hair and oval, wire rimmed glasses.

"So, were you really in the neighborhood," she began to ask, "or was this a special trip? Not a lot of people in the Jewish community know about Westerly. We're like a great secret." She laughed a hearty laugh. Before I could say anything, she continued. "I know, you wanted to talk about the Torah project. Where'd you have to come in from?"

"Baltimore, actually."

"Baltimore? You *really* must want to see this Torah."

"Actually, I want to speak with you more about Josh Mandel."

"Rabbi Mandel? You said he referred you."

"He did. Sort of." Before she had a chance to object to any projected subterfuge or gossip about Josh, I pre-empted my comments. "He's a friend…and he's in trouble."

"What's going on?" She waved me over to a pair of black padded metal armchairs in front of her desk. I took one chair, while she took the other.

"This past Friday night, two men tried to kill him after he got back from services."

"Oh my God," her eyes went wide.

"Actually, it's not clear who they were after…Josh or Shelley. It didn't matter because their intent was to first kill their target and then murder whoever else was in the house."

"Oh my God," she repeated. "Everyone okay?"

"They're fine. I'm just trying to find out what's going on. He told me about the Torah project for this congregation, and I'm just following up to see if there's a connection."

Rabbi Seidman's eyes drifted off of me for a moment, and she visibly blanched.

"What is it? What are you thinking about?"

"Last Wednesday night one of our members, Mr. Meyers, was murdered."

"What happened?"

"He has…had… a clothing shop down at Watch Hill and someone just shot him. He was in the store late one night." She looked away from me again. "We have no idea why. It's hard to believe…It wasn't a robbery. Nothing was taken."

"I'm sorry." I let a second pass. "Do the police have any theories that you know of?"

"No. Not as far as I know."

"Were you close with him?"

"He was a great man. Always had a joke, a *clean* joke. He was just a sweet, sweet man."

I didn't say anything.

"We're really a small community. In fact, we only have services once a month usually, and on the High Holidays, so when something like this happens, it's pretty devastating. We don't have violent crimes like this."

I let a few more seconds go by. Then, "Was he on the Torah project committee?"

"Peripherally. He was just on the organizing board. You think there's connection to Rabbi Mandel?"

"Maybe. So he only knew Josh from the project?"

She nodded.

"Does the name Allan Samuels mean anything to you?" Samuels was Josh's competition, the man I wanted to see in Charleston besides the rabbi.

She shook her head.

"How did you find out about Josh to begin with?"

"Rabbinical grapevine. He has a great reputation for finding lost Torahs."

"Do you know his wife, Shelley?"

Again, she shook her head. "No."

"Okay," I thought about where to go next. "About Mr. Meyers. What can you tell me about him? Again, I'm just trying to see if there *is* a link."

"He was about 70, married, with three children, all married and with kids of their own. He was from Boston, had a clothing store in Brookline and kept one here for the summer season. Owned a cottage near the beach. They'd come down every May to prepare for the Memorial Day opening. The police said he was setting up his store when he was killed."

Now it was my turn to follow a thought. He was from Boston… Nate had said the two killers who came to my dojo were from Boston. My mind shifted again. I wondered if anyone here came across a man who liked renting Buicks.

"Mr. Aronson?" the rabbi brought me back to our conversation.

"Rabbi Seidman, you don't happen to know the name of the detective on this case?"

"I do. He interviewed me, and I have his card."

"Call him, please, and ask if I could meet with him."

"Sure. But if you don't mind, I'd like to be part of the conversation. Mr. Meyers was a friend."

"Not at all. I didn't want to presume."

"Thanks. Let me get his card."

The Westerly Police Department was located on Airport Road, about ten minutes south of town, in a modern, two story building designed to look like a giant hut. Rabbi Seidman and I had been sitting in the waiting area in the first floor lobby for ten minutes – desk sergeant off to one side, humongous map of the Westerly area on a nearby wall – when a tall, lean, sharply dressed man in a solid blue shirt, yellow and black tie and black pants walked over to us. The half windsor knot on his tie was perfect, his full head of medium length salt and pepper hair was neatly brushed, his shirt was devoid of wrinkles, and shirtsleeves were cuffed and buttoned neatly at his wrists. He was probably in his early forties, and given his natty appearance, could have been Detective Medrano's older brother or uncle. Attached to his belt near his right pants pocket was a clipped-on gold badge and a holstered Glock 23, the same model as mine. The rabbi and I stood as he approached.

"Rabbi," the detective said as he came closer, holding out his hand.

She shook it and then introduced me, "Gidon Aronson, Detective Holden."

"Hi," I nodded slightly, but still maintaining eye contact.

"Mr. Aronson, the rabbi said on the phone you had some information about Mr. Meyers' homicide." As he waited for my answer, he quickly assessed me…no doubt a well-polished habit that was now second nature.

"Not so much information, more a series of events and some observations."

Detective Holden continued to evaluate me. "Mr. Aronson…" I saw it coming… Maybe it was the way I looked him directly in the eye. Maybe it was my handshake. Perhaps it was my posture. I knew he was going to say it… "Are you in law enforcement?"

I smiled, innocently. "No, I'm not. However, if you listen to my story and need verification, I can give you the name of a homicide captain in Baltimore."

He just nodded, and I related pretty much everything, beginning with Friday night. I told him about the two men in the Mandel's house, the murders in the ambulance, the attack on me at Harborwalk, Mr. Sakolsky's murder, and the two men in my dojo.

He didn't ask for Nate's number.

"So you were there when this whole thing in Baltimore started."

"Yes."

"Good thing you were, apparently."

I didn't say anything.

"And maybe now they want you because you stopped the first two guys."

I nodded. "They're pissed. And I'm asking questions."

"And you think what's happening in Baltimore is connected to Mr. Meyers?"

I looked at Holden. In his starched, pressed shirt and fastened cuffs, he looked like nothing ruffled him. He seemed like one of those guys, who even in the middle of the summer heat, would stay cool and sharp looking. I'd be sweating like crazy. "There was a man," I said, "outside the Mandel house that Friday night who dropped off the two killers. We know he flew into Providence the previous Wednesday. That was the day Mr. Meyers was killed, right?"

"Uh huh. And it's just over an hour's drive from Providence to Watch Hill where Mr. Meyers was shot – depending on traffic." He had made the connection.

"If he had flown just into BWI and not here—"

"We wouldn't be talking. Do you have a name or a picture?"

I pulled out the photo of the Buick guy that Medrano had cleaned up from the Hertz office camera. Nate had thought I should take it with me. "His name is Joseph Belard, and if you check Providence Airport security cameras I'll bet you'll see him."

"Can I keep this?"

"It's the only one I have. Can you copy it and I'll also ask Captain D'Allesandro to e-mail you one. You should check Hertz, too…maybe he rented a car from them up here like he did in Baltimore."

"If we can get a make and a model, we can check traffic cameras around town."

Rabbi Seidman was listening silently and watched us go back-and-forth.

"Something else," I began. "Send Nate, Captain D'Allesandro, your ballistics report. His forensics people have a collection of bullets already. Maybe there's a match somewhere."

"That would be nice."

"And just so you know, they seem to like HKs… 9mm and .40's. I think one guy had a Beretta."

Detective Holden was looking at me again. I saw this one coming, too. "You're ex-military, aren't you?"

"Not so 'ex' if you ask some people."

He looked at me and ever-so-slightly nodded. The people I meant, of course, were in Israel, but I wasn't going to explain that. It was too complicated anyway.

"We still don't know why." Nancy Seidman spoke up for the first time since introducing me.

"We have to talk with Mr. Meyers' wife," I responded. "There has to be a connection to Josh or Shelley."

"Your Torah project?" Detective Holden looked at Rabbi Seidman.

"There has to be something in common," I offered. "Maybe it's the Torah project, maybe it's something else." I wondered if Mrs. Meyers had heard the name Allan Samuels, Josh's competitor. I was also debating whether I should ask her about "Ben Susa," the name Shelley had given me of the crazy surrogate's husband. "Any idea where Mrs. Meyers is?"

Rabbi Seidman knew. "She's probably down at their shop in Watch Hill. She sat *shiva* for just a few days. Then she told me she had to get out of the house and finish what her husband had started."

I looked at the rabbi. "My Jeep's at the synagogue. Can you give me a ride?"

"Of course. I'd like to be there anyway for Mrs. Meyers."

Detective Holden added, "I'll follow you. Just let me copy this picture you brought, and get someone to check the airport cameras against this photo. I'll also have someone forward the ballistics report. I'll meet you outside."

✑

Ten minutes later I was sitting next to Rabbi Seidman in her gunmetal Civic coupe as we drove down scenic Route 1A toward the shore. We rode with our windows fully open, and I enjoyed the breeze whipping through the car. Holden, in an unmarked blue Crown Vic, followed several car lengths behind.

As we headed south under a cloudless, bright sky, I turned to Rabbi Seidman behind the wheel. "Tell me a little about this area."

"Okay." She paused to gather some thoughts. "Westerly, as far as I know, goes back to the mid-1600s. At one point over the years there was a large granite and stone-cutting industry here. There was a strong Italian presence then...maybe it had something to do with all the stone-cutting. That's a stereotype, I know. Sorry. On the other hand, I knew there was a kosher butcher shop here eons ago... but that's a non-sequitur, isn't it?" She laughed that hearty laugh I had heard before. "More recently, there was a major stapler manufacturer not far from here, but the plant closed, putting a lot of people out of work. But that was also before my time."

I looked out the window as she spoke. Route 1A was one lane of traffic each way, and as we went around curves and moved further west, we would parallel a small river on our right for a short distance, then we'd move away again. We'd pass houses to either side, though it seemed most homes were off the main road, hidden behind shrubbery.

"As far as the Jewish community, there definitely was a presence here. Like I said, there was a kosher butcher shop, but over time the community sort of died out. That was decades ago."

"Yet you have a shul."

"We still have members here and there, so we meet only once a month."

"And on the High Holidays. I listened to you back in your office," I smiled.

"I bet you hear every word."

"Depends who you ask." Out the window, some single story and two story houses went by. "So, with only monthly services, do you have enough rabbinical work here?"

"Actually, I'm sort of a circuit rabbi. I travel between Norwich, Worcester, and here. I received my ordination from the Jewish Theological Seminary, and while most of my classmates wanted to be part of big city congregations, I prefer the small towns. When you only have one congregation in a community, it's really awesome when people of varying Jewish traditions come to one place and participate in services together." We went along a left hand curve, hugging the center line. "What about you? You live in Baltimore..."

"I substitute at a Day School there...and do other stuff. Generally, I keep to myself."

"You spent time in Israel."

I nodded. "Some college and beyond."

"IDF?"

"Do you think Detective Holden picked up on that?"

"Probably."

"What brought you back, or was that the plan all along?"

I hesitated.

"Sorry. That was too personal. I do that sometimes."

"Don't worry about it," I said, watching the landscape go by.

"Sorry," she said again. "So what part of Israel do you like the most?"

"You've been?"

She nodded. "A year at Hebrew U."

"The north. The Golan and the Galil. "You? Jerusalem, probably. Right?"

"Yeah, but also the south. Give me the heat, baby," she smiled.

Route 1A peeled off to the left and we continued south onto Watch Hill Road. The street narrowed, and to either side the houses had become larger, more mansion-like. Most had gray, weathered shingles, three stories, angled roofs and multiple gables. In half a minute, the road split at the foot of another large house. We took the left-hand fork and began a slight climb. In a short while, from our higher elevation we had a great view of the entire area, with the ocean ahead of us, and large homes occupying hilltops to either side. We passed a large yellow and white Victorian-style hotel, identified as the Ocean House, and soon descended toward water level and Bay Street.

"You'll see that Bay Street, where Mr. Meyers had his shop, is just one block long." The road curved to the right and we passed an old carousel on the other side of the road. "That's the oldest, continuously operated carousel in the United States," Rabbi Seidman said, "though it doesn't look like it's open for the season just yet."

To our right and left were a strip of street level stores and second story apartments. In a short bit, the stores on the left gave way to a marina, while small shops continued to line the street on our right.

We passed a bookstore, a ladies' clothing store, a restaurant, an antique store, and a gift shop with nautical-themed items in the window. Most stores were dark and had "Closed" signs hanging on the inside of their doors. We parked midway up the block in front of a clothing store called "The Brass Buckle." In the side view mirror, I saw Detective Holden pull in behind us. The rabbi and I got out, and Holden joined us near the store front.

"This looks like a great place to vacation," I observed, looking from the shops to the marina across the way.

"Imagine the sun beating down and the sidewalks filled with tourists...but not overly crowded," Holden said. "Not like Cape Cod on a summer weekend."

"You'd hear the music from the carousel," Nancy added, "smell suntan lotion, see cars riding by, and parents walking up and down the street, holding their children's hands."

"The children are all blond, of course," I said, "and with rosy cheeks."

"That would be from too much sun," Holden interjected.

"Any crime?"

The detective shook his head. "Not really. Some shop-lifting maybe, but nothing like last Wednesday night."

"Mr. Meyers."

He nodded.

"So what happened?"

"Best we can figure, some time after nine o'clock Mr. Meyers was working in his store." He nodded to the Brass Buckle to our right. Inside, I could see two women moving about, carrying boxes or armloads of clothing. "Mr. Meyers was inside the shop. Someone came up to the door, but didn't go inside. From where we found the body, he must have called Mr. Meyers over and then shot him in the head through the door. Broken glass was scattered near the entrance."

"How many rounds?" I asked.

"Three. The first one was pretty straight on. The other two were from a little distance, based on the angles and the forensics. The killer didn't step inside."

He didn't say it, but we both knew that two shots would have been sufficient. Three were unnecessary. To my side, I was aware of Rabbi Seidman being very still. "Anyone hear anything?" I asked.

"No. No one was around. The owner of the restaurant down the block drove by about two hours later, just because he likes to do that, and saw the light on here. He called us."

I looked at the women inside the shop. "How much does Mrs. Meyers know?"

"No details. Just that her husband was shot. She was in Boston."

"How is she?" I looked at Nancy.

"I don't think she's processed all of this yet. But she seems pretty adamant about opening the shop. Told me it will be good for her."

I nodded, then after a second, "Shall we?"

The three of us stepped up to the newly replaced glass door. On the other side, we could see two women working diligently. An older woman who had a stylish, short feathered haircut, was sitting in front of a rack of men's shorts near the front, arranging a shelf. The second woman, maybe in her thirties and dressed in a denim workshirt and black capris, was unloading a box of clothes onto a table. Both women had their backs to us. Detective Holden knocked on the glass pane.

The two women looked over and both Rabbi Seidman and Detective Holden waved to them. The older woman, pulled off a pair of reading glasses, and came closer. She waved back, rotated a key in the lock, and pulled the door open.

"Good afternoon, Mrs. Meyers," Holden said.

"Detective, Rabbi...come in." She stepped to the side and the three of us came in.

"How are you doing today, Barbara?" Rabbi Seidman asked.

Mrs. Meyers looked at her and smiled weakly. Before we could say anything, the younger woman approached from where she was unloading the box of clothes. She was petite and had features similar to Mrs. Meyers…similar shape to her face and eyes. "Hi." she said, looking at all three of us.

"Susie, how are you holding up?" the rabbi asked her.

"Still in shock." She turned to me, the stranger in the group.

Holden made the introduction. "This is Gidon Aronson from Baltimore."

"Hi," I said, shaking Mrs. Meyers' hand and then Susie's.

"I'm her daughter," Susie said.

I smiled. "Family resemblance." After a moment: "I'm sorry for your loss."

They both said thank you, and then Mrs. Meyers looked between the detective and the rabbi. "What can we do for you?"

I spoke up. "I'm a friend of Josh Mandel."

"The rabbi who worked with us on the Torah project?" Mrs. Meyers asked.

"Yes. Someone tried to kill him last week – he's okay – and we think that it's related to what happened to your husband."

"You think it has to do with the project?" This from Susie Meyers.

"Possibly," Detective Holden responded. "We're all trying to find a reason for this."

Rabbi Seidman added, "The project is certainly something the two had in common."

"But what possibly could they have done to lead to murder?" Mrs. Meyers asked.

"We don't know," I looked at her. "That's still the question," I said. "Right now, we're working on who."

I took out the picture I had brought with me from Baltimore and handed it to Mrs. Meyers. She held it so her daughter could also see it.

I explained, "We think this man is responsible. His name is Joseph Belard. Does he look familiar?"

They both shook their heads. "No," Mrs. Meyers said. She handed it back to me.

"Have you heard the name Allan Samuels?" I asked.

Mrs. Meyers and Susie thought for a moment, then Mrs. Meyers' eyes opened a bit more. "Yes. I remember him. He called Jack and said that Rabbi Mandel was a thief and couldn't be trusted. He really made my husband angry."

I looked at Rabbi Seidman. She hadn't heard the name. She turned to Mrs. Meyers. "Barbara, why didn't you or Jack didn't say anything to me?"

"What for? It was slander. We checked on the computer. It was Mr. Samuels who's the criminal."

"How did your husband respond?" Detective Holden asked.

"As soon as Jack heard those kinds of comments from a total stranger, he was just not interested. He pretty much hung up on him."

"And that was it?" Holden followed up.

"No. Samuels called back one more time. Jack heard who it was, and said if he called again, he'd call the police. And then Jack hung up."

"Did he ever call back?"

"No."

Holden looked at me. "Do you know where Samuels is?"

"Either London or Israel."

Holden caught my eye as if to say, *We have to talk more.*

"Is there anything else about the Torah project that stands out? Any sort of conflict?" I asked.

"No," Mrs. Meyers answered simply.

Holden turned to her daughter. "Anything strike you in terms of your father's business or anything else?"

Susie shook her head.

Wrapping up, Holden said, "Well, thank you for your time,"

Nancy Seidman kissed both women. "I'll call later. Are you heading back to Boston tonight, or will you be staying here?"

"We'll be at the cottage," Susie said.

As the rabbi continued the small talk, I scanned the shop. It was a nice little place... not really a boutique, but trendy. It had some funky

knick-knacks on shelves and some pop culture posters on the walls…
mostly shots of various rock bands I didn't recognize. The shelves and
clothing carousels were all in the midst of being re-stocked. There
were men's bathing suits on some of the racks, women's one and two
piece swimsuits draped over a chair, a box of Hawaiian shirts yet to be
unpacked, and a half filled rack with miscellaneous T-shirts waiting to
be shelved. A few of the shirts caught my attention. I wandered over
to a partially filled rack and saw a red T-shirt with a white Coca-Cola
logo on it – in Hebrew. Next to it was a T-shirt with an American
flag and an Israeli flag intertwined. A third had a graphic of an Uzi
submachine gun and the words "Uzi does it." Kids would really love
that one; parents not so much. These were T-shirts you'd find in tourist
shops all over Israel.

I picked up the Coca-Cola one and showed it to Mrs. Meyers.
Before I could ask, she explained, "Jack loved those. You never know
with these customers, but he thought the logo in a foreign language
would sell. The others, too."

I asked, but already knew the answer. "Where did he get them?"

"From a vendor on Ben Yehuda when we were in Israel three
months ago. He worked out a deal."

Holden saw the light bulb go off in my head. "What is it?"

"The Mandels were in Israel three months ago."

"What does that mean?" Rabbi Seidman looked at us.

"It's another commonality," the detective explained.

I put the T-shirt down and went over to Mrs. Meyers. "I need you
to do something."

"Of course."

"I need you put together a list of everything you and your husband
did when you were in Israel. Where you stayed, where you ate, what
tours you took. Anything and everything. As detailed as you can.
Hour-by-hour, if possible." I turned to her daughter. "Rabbi Seidman
mentioned to me that you have siblings. Any of you on the trip?"

"No," Susie said. "It was just my folks."

Detective Holden looked at me. "What're you thinking?"

"I'll ask the Mandels to do the same thing. Maybe they both ran into Allan Samuels. Maybe it has nothing to do with him. Maybe it's something else, but when we compare their notes, it might point to something or someone."

"I still have all our receipts," Mrs. Meyers said. "That will help me remember."

"I'll go through them with you, Mom," Susie said.

"Excellent. Can you e-mail me the list as soon as you're done?" I asked. "Or in sections, if you want."

"Sure," Mrs. Meyers said.

"Mom's pretty tech savvy," Susie smiled.

"Have to be when you run a business."

"Perfect. Thanks." I gave her my e-mail address.

"You just get these bastards," Mrs. Meyers said.

"I will." I leaned over and gave Mrs. Meyers a kiss on the cheek, did the same for her daughter, and then headed out with the rabbi and the Westerly detective.

16

Once back on I-95, with the Rhode Island line behind me and a stretch of highway in front, I began the first in a series of phone calls. The first was to my student, Jon.

"Hey, how you doing?" I asked. I hadn't spoken to him since the evening in the dojo when we had the unwelcome guests. "Sorry I haven't called. You okay?"

"Two guys with guns come into the dojo. One with a silencer. We could have all been killed. You know what kind of effect that has on a person? I've been waiting by the phone for you to call out of concern, but no, my teacher, who I've invested all this time with, not a word, not a text, not a voice mail message. Nothing."

"So you're fine."

"Of course. You have to show me that raise-the-gun, chamber-a-round, aim-and-fire thing you did."

I smiled. "Sure. It's really just practice."

"And we have to talk about the bo moves you used."

"Basic stuff. You know the moves, but we can run some scenarios."

"Awesome."

"How's Angie?"

"She's fine. Some initial freak-out stuff, but now she wants to learn more."

"Good for her. You going to continue private lessons?"

"You bet your ass." He paused, afraid he was being disrespectful. "Sorry. I meant, 'You bet your ass, *Sifu*.'"

I laughed. "You be fine, laddie. Listen, need you to do some things for me. Where are you?"

"The office."

He meant *his* office, not mine. He worked in his father's real estate firm on St. Paul Street. "First of all, I won't be back in time for classes tonight. Can you take them? I'll owe you."

"I think you owe me a vacation in Barbados at this point, Sifu."

"Don't get cocky. Maybe Vegas." I let a second pass. "When you go to the dojo tonight, I need you to go to the pencil drawer of my desk…"

"Pencil drawer?"

"That thin drawer in the middle above your lap when you sit down."

"That's a 'pencil drawer'? Never knew it had a name. Don't I feel stupid."

"If it makes you feel any better, I didn't know it was called that either until Katie told me a few weeks ago."

He laughed.

"Guffaw at my expense. Thanks, sonny. Anyway, in that drawer is a small white card with only a phone number on it. It probably begins with an 057 or something similar. Let me know what it is."

The number belonged to David Amit, my Shin Bet contact. That was a call I didn't necessarily want to make, but should. Between Allan Samuels being in Israel, the Gaza number I found on the killer in my dojo, plus the Mandels and Mr. and Mrs. Meyers being in Israel at the same time, it was reason enough to call him.

"I'll call you, Sifu, soon as I can."

"Thanks."

"You won't be back tonight?"

"No, I'm stopping off to see Sammi."

"Really? Wow. How long has it been?"

"A while."

"You're actually going to visit her?

"That's the plan. If she's home."

"Nervous?"

"Me, nervous? I'm excited."

"Yeah, you're nervous." He paused. "You'll tell me all about it?"

"Probably not."

"Probably will. That it?"

"No. Charlie Coakley should be back tonight." He was the kid whose father was using excessive force on him. "Let me know what you see."

"Roger."

"And please take it easy with Angie. She's got a lot of potential and I don't want any drama. My heart can't take it."

"I can't help it if women want me all the time."

"Really…no emotional scars, Jon. Okay?"

"Okay." He paused for a second. "That it?"

"Yup. Call me later." We hung up.

I passed over the long Thames River Bridge and continued through New London toward the Connecticut Turnpike. The sky had turned overcast, but not dark enough to anticipate rain. Traffic was still light, with plenty of space between each vehicle. I settled behind a maroon Passat.

My next call was to Nate. I was prepared with a quip in case he wanted to know who I had eviscerated or something this time, but his voice mail came on. I left him a detailed message about a possible Meyers-Mandel conection, and what Mrs. Meyers had said about Allen Samuels phoning her husband. I told him I'd be back in town tomorrow.

The third call was to Josh and Shelley, and immediately from the background noise, I knew I had reached them in the car. Interestingly, while I had dialed Josh's number, Shelley answered. "Hello?"

"Hi. It's Gidon."

"Hi."

"Just wanted to see how you're doing."

"We're fine. Let me give you Josh," she said immediately.

My eyebrows went up. That was a little weird. Unlike Shelley to be so abrupt. She was ever cheerful. Was she pissed at me, and didn't want to talk? Was Shelley annoyed at my insistence they get out of Baltimore? Maybe she was just busy.

In a moment, Josh came on. "Hi, Gidon. How are you?" The road noise over the phone was unmistakable. There was also that vacuous presence that made his voice slightly unclear. "Back in Baltimore?" he asked. "Sounds like you're in the car." The road noise over the phone worked both ways, of course.

"Nope. On my way back from Rhode Island. Sounds like *you're* on the road, too." I was fishing. Just wanted to be sure everything was copacetic.

"Yeah." That's all he said. He didn't offer where they were going.

"So, not trying to be nosy here, but just out of curiosity, where you headed?"

"Oh, just driving around. It's beautiful country up here." He let a moment pass. "We're getting antsy."

"I understand. Just don't wander too far. There are plenty of attractions around there."

"I know. We'll check them out."

"Good. Meanwhile, I need you to do something."

"Okay. What is it?"

"I need you and Shelley to put together a list of everything you guys did when you were in Israel three months ago."

"Okay," he voice went up, sounding unsure.

"It has to be a detailed list. When I say 'everything,' I mean everything. Where you went and when...stores, shops, little pizza kiosks, synagogues, relatives, friends. *Everything* and every place. And who you saw...relatives, friends. Even anyone you bumped into you weren't expecting to see."

"That always happens in Israel."

"I know. And I'm serious about it. Anyone. No gaps okay, Josh?"

"I understand. We'll do our best." There was a horn in the background. His attention wandered for a moment. "What's all this for?"

"Just trying to make connections. How soon can you get to it?"

"Soon as we can. I'll call you when it's done. May take a while, but Shelley's good at details."

"Great. I'll call later just to check in. Make sure you're okay."

"Look forward to it."

After we hung up, I just watched the road for a few minutes. Exit 75, Waterford came and went. For a moment I considered going back to Williamsport to help direct them in putting together a daily list of their Israel activities. That would definitely be too much of a control freak thing to do. It was just important. Would there be any match with Mrs. Meyers' list?

Another green exit sign went by, and I realized, of course, I had another call to make. Sammi.

As I anticipated speaking with her, my heart rate picked up slightly. I hadn't contacted Sammi in more than three years. She was truly special; one-of-a-kind, but I had no idea how the call would be received. I hoped she'd be forgiving...hopefully, she'd blow off my feeble excuse and we'd pick up where we left off. That would be great.

More cars had begun to fill the highway, and I told myself to pay attention to the road. I also told myself the proper thing to have done was to have stayed in touch with her more. Sometimes months go by, in this case it was even longer, and then it becomes awkward. Well, nothing to be done about that now, except make the call and apologize.

I merged onto the Connecticut Turnpike, waited for the traffic to let up, and then re-activated the phone display on the dashboard. Her phone number went from my brain to my fingertips as if no time had passed. Two rings. Nothing. Maybe she wasn't home. The third ring sounded. She picked up.

"Hello?" Her voice sounded no different than I had remembered.

"Hi. It's Gidon."

A long second went by. "Gidon Aronson. Well, what d'you know? What a surprise," she said calmly. Then in an equally calm voice said, "If you're anywhere within two hundred miles, Gidon, you better stop by."

"How's an hour and a half or so?"

"See you then."

I hung up, and though I wouldn't admit it, let out a breath.

My final call, before I pushed my luck phoning while in the car, was to Katie. It was possible she was still at school, so I tried her office line. She answered right away: "Katie Harris."

"Hi. It's Gidon. Didn't know if you'd still be in."

"Working on lesson plans. Where are you?"

I read a sign. "East Lyme, Connecticut. That doesn't help, does it?

"No," she laughed.

"About 40 miles up from New Haven." A huge tractor trailer suddenly blew past me on the left. "Whoa."

"What?"

"The biggest truck you ever saw. Anyway, how was your day?"

"The kids in the Study Skills class want to see you again. They like seeing us together."

"*I* like seeing us together."

"How 'bout tonight?"

"Can't, my luscious one…won't be back. Sorry. I'm stopping off to see Sammi. Tomorrow will work."

"Sammy?"

"I never told you about her, did I?"

"Ah, Sammi with an 'i'."

"She's an old friend. I knew Sammi in my pre-Israel days."

"'An old friend.'"

"She's not what you think. She's…" I paused, ready to explain, but instead said, "I'll tell you all about her over dinner tomorrow night."

"Deal. I'm looking forward to a good story."

"You just want to hear about me in the old days."

"You bet. And bring pictures. So," she shifted subjects, "how'd it go in Rhode Island?"

"A man in the community was killed here last week. He had worked with Josh on a Torah project, and the man who pulled the trigger was probably the guy in the Buick. Also, there may be another connection between the victim and Josh. Both were in Israel at the same.

"You think something happened to both of them over there?"

"I do…and we need to find out what."

"Did you call Josh?"

"Yup. Asked him to make a list of what they did in Israel and who they saw."

"Maybe give you a lead."

"It'd be nice." I let a moment pass. "Sorry 'bout tonight. I really had expected to make it home, but I can't drive past Sammi's house without stopping by."

"When was the last time you saw her?"

I told her.

"And you haven't spoken with her since?"

"No."

"I'm looking forward to your story tomorrow night even more."

"As long as I'm looking into your eyes, I'll tell you anything."

"If only that were true." There was a wistful, playful tone in her voice.

"It *is* true. Sort of."

"We should talk about that, too, tomorrow night."

"Deal. I'll call you from the road tomorrow."

We hung up, and I relaxed a bit more, now that all the phone calls were done. In three-quarters of an hour I was closer to New York than Rhode Island, and the road became more crowded as I entered the environs of Bridgeport and Norwalk. No one lane seemed to be the best in terms of traffic flow, so for the most part I stayed in the center as much as possible. A little more than thirty minutes later, I passed

Greenwich and shortly after that into the Empire State. The exit for Port Chester and Rye came up, and I moved off the highway onto local streets. It had been quite a while since I had traveled these roads, so I looked for familiar landmarks...a park, a fire station, an old castle-like home. I drove through a retail area – really a quaint, upscale, suburban strip of stores and boutiques on both sides of the road – and caught sight of a florist shop that was still open. I swung over to the curb and ran in for a bouquet. In a matter of minutes, I was back in the car.

Sammi's home was tucked away past several small, winding streets off a main road. The houses throughout the community all had generous yards by New York standards, with sufficient buffer between neighbors. Large, old trees provided property delineation and plenty of shade. I pulled into the driveway of an old, beautifully kept, three story stone house and parked behind a medium blue Prius. Scooping up the bouquet of lilies, Gerber daisies, and more, I walked to the front portico, trying to look casual. As I approached the large maroon wooden door, it opened.

In the doorway stood a woman just a few inches shorter than me, dressed in a flowing, mid-calf length green and yellow flowery dress. She was probably in her late forties – I never knew for sure – and she still had her straight auburn hair grown long. I remember she frequently wore it either pulled back with a barrette or braided and put up somehow. Her face was round, with large dark eyes that were always full of excitement. Sammi never wore eye make-up, or any other kind for that matter, and never needed to. Her skin, as ever, was clear and glowing.

"Well, you're still alive. Far out."

"Okay," I bowed my head, "let me have it."

"No. Don't need to do that. You feel bad enough already. Come in."

I took a step closer and we gave each other a hug. I handed her the flowers as we stepped into the foyer.

"Good move, Gidon. They're beautiful. Thank you."

"You're welcome. Of course."

"So it's been a lifetime." She looked into my eyes. "Looks like it's been several lifetimes."

"It has."

"Come," she put her arm through mine, "I haven't eaten dinner and I know you haven't either."

I just smiled, remembering how she just knew things. We walked toward the kitchen, past a living room on the left, decorated with miscellaneous Chinese themed items...a hand-painted lacquered chest, antique end tables, a painted wooden screen of cranes against a gold background, and more. On the way into the kitchen we passed a vertical length of parchment with beautiful Chinese calligraphy flowing up and down. It hadn't been there before; Sammi must have painted it since I saw her last.

"So, how're the kids?" I asked.

"They're great. Carol's just wrapping up her graduate work in England, and Danny's finishing his junior year at University of Vermont."

"Oh my God, they're grown up."

"Yeah. It's pretty cool." We stepped into the kitchen.

"Dinner's ready. I just need to put the salad together. Why don't you set the table?"

We both washed our hands and then I began to take out plates and silverware. Sammi pulled from the refrigerator a bag of baby spinach leaves and containers of strawberries, goat cheese, blueberries and walnuts. In a matter of minutes, the salad was on the table, along with a selection of quiches, a dish of olive oil with herbs, home baked bread and white wine.

"So, I do have to ask," she said, as we began to eat. "What's going on? You have a few lifetimes to tell me about. Oh, before you do, just know that I have kids coming for a meditation and massage class in about an hour and a half."

"A great class," I smiled.

"So tell me. Start after Max died… after you left."

I smiled wryly. "I don't know if we have enough time."

"Just start, Gidon." She looked right into my eyes.

I took a sip of the wine and began to tell Sammi what I'd been doing since the last time we saw each other. I told her about leaving the States, going into the IDF, the sort of work I did, living in Israel, returning here, and my new life since then. It really wasn't what she was asking me to tell her, and I didn't know why I hadn't spoken of the impact of the missions, Tamar's death, the killings, and more. She understood there was something deeper than what I had related, but didn't say anything.

In a little while, after we had enough to eat, we took our glasses of wine into the living room. Sammi told me about raising their two children, about their accomplishments and challenges, about some of their life decisions, and what she was doing now, teaching at Columbia.

When she finished, I looked around the room. I remembered helping Sammi and Max, her husband and my mentor, move into this house. I remembered the many trips back and forth from their apartment near Riverside Drive and 98th Street. On one of the trips it had begun to rain as we brought in some furniture. I also remembered finishing a work-out at two in the morning with her husband, and then driving here to set up the bedrooms. That's what you did when your teacher and his family needed help.

A number of dojo stories came to mind about her husband… funny incidents that happened in work-outs, confrontations and how he handled them, teaching stories…and I debated about bringing them up.

Sammi put down her wine glass on an end table and turned to me. "You were his heir. Do you know that? You were the one he wanted to take over."

I nodded almost imperceptibly. I let a second pass. I said softly, "I had to leave."

Sammi didn't say anything.

"How angry was he?"

She smiled. "He was pretty angry. He loved you and he respected you…and he wanted you close. But…he knew you. He knew you had to do that. His emotions went back and forth."

"I'm sorry."

A moment of silence went by.

"Why didn't you come to the funeral?" She was looking deep into my eyes now.

My voice became even more quiet. "I couldn't. I was on a mission."

She moved back ever-so-slightly and she seemed to see my whole face.

"Something happened, didn't it?"

I didn't say anything. I just nodded.

Sammi searched my face…and the doorbell rang. Her meditation students were beginning to arrive. She looked at me for another second and then walked to the door.

Over the next five minutes, six young couples came in. Some of them looked like they could still be in college; others looked more post-graduate. Regardless, they were young. They all appeared clean-cut, dressed casually in jeans or shorts with loose-fitting tops, and excited to be here. I moved into the background as Sammi welcomed them into the living room. Without being told, they all sat in a circle, Sammi included, along the perimeter of a sage, ivory, violet, and light blue Persian rug. After some greetings and catching up, they got started. They began with a measured breath exercise that led to guided imagery. I picked up Sammi's wine glass from an end table and drifted back into the hallway.

As Sammi's calm directions filtered in from the other room, I looked at a series of diplomas hanging along a wall. Some belonged to Sammi; some to my teacher. I couldn't help but smile. There was so much more to Sammi than met the eye. I knew she had been an Asian Studies major and had gone to China during her junior year. There she had met Professor Tan who was lecturing on Chinese antiquities and became one of his most dedicated students. Not only was Professor Tan an expert in Chinese history and ancient artifacts, he was a grand master in various internal martial arts. Sammi soon became his trusted student and friend. It was clear that despite a fifteen year difference in their ages, they were kindred spirits.

As the class continued in the next room, I went into the kitchen, and cleaned up, mindful of being as quiet as possible. Dishes and silverware were washed, dried, and put back into cabinets and drawers, food items were returned to the fridge or cupboards, and I re-corked the almost empty bottle of wine. Finally, when everything was put away and counters cleaned, I walked out a door to the back porch, only then realizing that night had already descended. The backyard past the porch was in two sections. The first, closer to the house, was a modest brick patio with a few lawn chairs and a table, and then beyond it, a beautiful flower garden. I took off my shoes and socks, along with my watch, cell phone, and wallet, and placed them all near the backdoor threshold. Feeling less encumbered, I stepped across the patio and into the flower garden. There was a small clearing between plum flowers and chrysanthemums that was perfect. I sat down on grass that was exceedingly soft.

The air was calm, filled with the scent of many types of flora, but up in the heavens, clouds had moved across the sky, and bursts of white light lit their interior like a series of ethereal strobes. I observed the light show for half a minute, then closed my eyes to pay attention to my breathing. At first there was blackness behind my eyes and the awareness of breath entering and collecting down near my waist, but soon, as the breath began to expand my awareness, there was no garden...no sound... no sense of self...

༄

Sometime later I opened my eyes. Sammi was sitting directly opposite me, eyes closed in a mirror image of my sitting posture. She was totally, completely calm, placid and still. As I looked at her, I slowly become aware that it was raining. The drops came down in straight, thin lines, joining us to both heaven and earth. I watched Sammi for a minute through the veil of precipitation, and she opened her eyes to see me gazing at her. I could see the change in her eyes as her presence came back into focus.

After a moment, I spoke quietly, "When I was in Israel I lost men on several missions." I told her about the soldiers who had died in my arms. I told her about carrying their bodies back from Syria and Lebanon. I told her about their wives, their mothers, and fathers who listened to me give them the news. I told her about Tamar and the suicide bombing in Jerusalem...and how I looked into her eyes as her life ebbed away. I told her everything.

When I had finished, Sammi wordlessly rose and held out her hand. As the rain continued, I stood and took it. She led me over to the brick patio, and without a word, stepped closer and placed her hands on the backs of mine. I understood. We began moving our arms and then our torsos in the circular Push Hands practice. She'd push forward, I would move back. I'd swing toward her, she'd retreat and then shift in another direction. We became sensitive to each other's energy and intent. We'd move one way and another, up and down, around and back, always in motion, shifting, rotating, trying to instinctively feel where the other was open, to press an opportunity. The give and take was fluid and smooth, with each of us constantly adjusting to the direction and press of the other's arms and hands. We accelerated and decelerated; our motions became large, then small, and large again. Our bodies moved, always trying to keep our hands in contact with our partner's. We would rise and we'd drop, we would extend and we would roll back. We'd separate the other's arms and we'd twist; we'd bring them together and we'd shift.

Finally, after an unknown length of time, we stood quietly, facing one another. We bowed, smiled to each other, and then made our way back into the house. We stood in the kitchen, clothes soaked, and dripping onto the floor.

"Not bad," she smiled.

"Thank you."

"You know where the guest bedroom is. Why don't you grab your change of clothes, go upstairs, change – leave your wet clothes in the bathroom – and then come down. I want to work on your body. It's been a while."

I was speechless. I went out the back door, around to my car, and grabbed my overnight bag. A few short minutes later, I had returned to the vacated living room, a little drier, and wearing only a pair of boxers. Sammi was waiting for me. She, too, had changed, but into a beautiful black, purple, and turquoise floral patterned shift.

She nodded to the floor. "On your front, please."

Sammi had set out a light blue sheet over the Persian rug. I lay down as instructed, putting my arms to my sides. She tucked her shins under her and sat next to me. I knew that one of Sammi's areas of expertise was chi massage, and I thoroughly welcomed her practiced touch. She began with my scalp and neck, massaging both the chi meridians and nearby muscles. She used small circular motions with the tips of her fingers in some areas and her entire hand in others.

Over the next thirty minutes her warm hands became even warmer as she moved in sections from my head to my toes. Frequently, she would start massaging in one location and I would feel chi move into another. When she massaged the back of my neck along the center line, I could feel a rush over the top of my head and down to my brow. When she moved her hands along the inside of my biceps, I felt my hands grow warm. Sammi was a master. I knew that wherever she touched me, red marks blossomed on my skin.

After flipping onto my back, she continued, and paid attention to almost everything. Sammi pulled down the front of my boxers slightly so she could massage my lower abdomen. My eyes were closed, and at some point she said, "You can get your hui-yin." She was referring to the chi center just behind my scrotum.

Sammi moved down to my legs, massaging the energy lines in my thighs, and then down to my calves. She followed the chi route to the bottom of each foot, and then finished with massaging the joints on each toe. When she was done, I was tingling all over. I allowed myself to revel in the pervasive energized sensations for another minute before sitting up.

Sammy leaned back on her tucked-under shins, and was smiling. "You need to get here more often."

"Yeah, I do."

I looked down at her hands resting in her lap. They were both turned palm up, with the back of her right hand resting in the palm and fingers of her left. Her hands were bright red.

She continued to look at me. "But I think that's enough for one visit."

"Thank you."

"I'm really glad you came. Don't wait another few lifetimes."

"I won't. I promise."

I looked at her for another moment, knowing we were finished for the night. I said thanks one more time, and walked upstairs. In the bathroom, still tingling from her touch, I uselessly checked my wet clothes hanging over the shower rod, and went through my bedtime regimen. Once done, I walked back down the hallway toward the guest bedroom. To my left was a polished, dark wooden banister and beyond it I could see down to the foyer. The lights were still on and I could hear Sammi moving about, opening and closing cabinets and moving dishes.

For a moment I debated about going back down, but then shuffled into the guest bedroom and turned off the lights. Above the foot of the bed, rain smacked against a window, and in the ambient light, I walked over to the bed, and pulled down the blanket. A digital LED clock read 4:08. I really had no clue that hours had passed. I slid between the soft sheets, nestled into the pillow, and closed my eyes. After a few breaths I was asleep.

17

When I opened my eyes, the first thing I realized was how bright the room was. From the intensity and angle of the sunlight pouring in at the foot of the bed, the night – and the rain – had long passed. I turned to the digital clock near my head. 10:07. I blinked a few times. 10:07? I hadn't slept past 7:00 since basic training; stayed in bed, of course, but not slept until this hour.

I stood up, rotated my head slowly, then ambled across to the bathroom, peering over the banister. Sammi was not in view and no sounds came up from below. Considering the hour, I hoped she was still home. Stepping into the bathroom the first thing I noticed was that my clothes were no longer hanging on the shower rod. Instead, they had been dried, neatly folded and placed on top of a stand-alone wooden chest of drawers. I smiled at how thoughtful that was, and then got moving.

Less than five minutes later I was stepping into the kitchen, freshly showered and carrying my overnight mini-duffle. Sammi, dressed for work in a black dress with gold swirly things on it, was standing at the counter writing a note.

"Good morning," I said, coming into the room.

She turned around, "Gidon, hi. I hope I didn't wake you."

"Not at all. I can't believe I slept this late. Thanks for drying the clothes, by the way. You didn't have to do that."

She just smiled. A second went by. "I was just writing you a note. I have to go into the City…have to teach in a few hours. Sorry I can't do breakfast with you."

"Bummer," I smiled.

Sammi smiled back. As yesterday, she wore no make-up, however today her hair was partially wound and put up...somehow. "You're welcome to stay. There's cereal and stuff in the cabinet, if you want."

"That's okay, thanks. I'll head out also. I've got something to do, I think. It's all sort of a fog right now."

"That's what you get for sleeping so late. Re-entry will hit in about five minutes." She smiled yet once again, and scooped up a leather shoulder bag, placing it over her head so the long loop sat diagonally across her torso.

We exited through the back door – the same one that led to the patio and garden – and ambled around to the driveway. As we strolled over a row of slate stepping stones, I lamented: "Now that I'm leaving, I can't believe I didn't come back before this."

"You were busy."

I didn't respond.

We continued into the driveway. Her Prius was parked close to the house, my Grand Cherokee in front of it. We stopped beside the driver's door of her hybrid. She turned to me, but didn't say anything. I didn't know what to say either. I thought of last night...of working with her, of our conversation, of just being here and catching up.

Sammi stepped closer. "Two things," she said looked into my eyes. "Because of your missions, did you save lives?"

I nodded.

"Were the Israeli people safer because of what you did?"

"Yes."

"Did you have missions where you brought your men back safely?"

I nodded again.

"How many missions...a few? Some?"

"Most of them."

"I want you to remember that, Gidon. Think of those times. Think of the lives you've saved and think of all the good you've done."

I nodded slightly.

"That's the first thing. The second thing is you must get back here more often, that's all."

Without waiting for me to reply, Sammi turned around, opened the door to her car, and slid in. I walked to the Grand Cherokee and did the same. Easing down the driveway, I pulled out to the right and Sammi turned left. As I watched in my rearview mirror, she drove straight for a short block, then disappeared onto a side street. I sat there for a few seconds, smiled, and continued on my way.

There were a few routes back to I-95, but I drove through town to a coffee shop I had remembered from a similar stop six years ago. Inside the rustic, polished wood shop, I paid way too much for a muffin and a bottle of orange juice, and then sat at an outside patio table to check my phone and eat. There was only one message, a text from Jonathan, containing the number of my Shin Bet contact in Israel. The call to Israel was necessary, of course, but I procrastinated. Jon, instead, went first.

"Good morning, Jon Boy."

"Oh my God, it's you," he said in mock dislike.

"So how's Angie?"

"Never better, she tells me. But you know that because you know all and see all."

"That's the legend. All's well?"

"Yup. You?"

"Fine."

"Did Sammi beat the crap out of you?"

"I'm not telling. Got your text with the phone number. Thanks. Meanwhile, I'll be back in town before 4:00. You up for a work-out? Just you and me?"

"How good do you feel?"

"Excellent. Rested."

"That means I'll need all our ice packs for the bruises and contusions I'm gonna get."

"So you *don't* want to work with me?"

"I didn't say that. I always look forward to working out with you, Sifu." He let a second go by. "Call me when you get to the Beltway. That way I'll have a better sense of when I should take the ibuprofen. You know, in anticipation."

I laughed. "Will do. Thanks, again, Jon."

"My pleasure."

After we hung up, I broke off a piece of muffin and had a few swallows of orange juice.

The day was turning out to be quite beautiful with a bright, clear sky. I closed my eyes for a moment to listen to my breath and to feel the slight wind on my face. When I reopened them, I took in the block. This side was pretty much empty which surprised me. The other side across the street wasn't much better; just a lone, tall brunette pushing a jogging stroller. After a few feet, she turned right, and disappeared down an alley lined with boutiques.

I returned to my phone. I really did need to call Israel...but instead dialed Katie. She was in her office.

"Hey there, gorgeous," I said as soon as I heard her voice.

"How do you know I'm gorgeous this morning?"

"You're gorgeous *all* the time. You can't *help* but being gorgeous."

"Okay, stop. You should have left that last line out. It works better without it."

"Less is more?"

"Uh huh."

The door to the coffee shop opened behind me, and for a moment the smell of warm cinnamon pastry drifted over to me. "So if less is more, then when I see you at home this afternoon..."

"Yes?"

An image of me slowly pulling off her blouse flashed through my head. "Nothing, nothing."

"Hmm."

"So, I'll be back about four. I want to work out with Jon, and then how 'bout I come by, shower, and then we go to dinner?"

"Great. There's a new place in Clipper Mill off the Jones Falls I'd like to try."

"Sounds good."

"So how was Sammi?"

"Great. Like no time had gone by...sort of. She was very supportive."

"We'll add that to the topics for tonight's conversation. I want to hear all about her."

"Okay."

"So, you try Josh and Shelley again?"

"I will." She knew I had spoken with them yesterday, and she also knew that for me, yesterday was a long time ago. I thought of my last conversation with Josh and Shelley. "They were on the road."

"Doesn't mean anything nefarious."

"I know."

"They were just out for a ride."

"I know."

"They're antsy. Away from home, unfamiliar town, routine not what they're used to."

"I know, I get it. I just hope they're not foolish and tell someone where they are. If word gets out, there's no one there to help them."

"I'm sure they're fine, Gidon."

"Yeah."

"You're going to check on them anyway, aren't you?"

"Yup."

She laughed. "Okay."

"I'm paranoid. What can I tell you." I let a moment pass. "So, I'll see you at your place about five or five thirty?"

"Sounds good."

"Great. See you later."

After another piece of muffin and another look across the street for the tall brunette – she hadn't reappeared – I called Josh's cell phone.

The rabbi didn't answer. There were four long rings, and then his voice mail came on. Maybe he couldn't get to the phone. I waited ten seconds and tried again. Same four long rings, same away message.

Shit.

Okay, maybe they were in a movie theater. Maybe the phone was in the car and they were shopping or something. Maybe someone found out where they were and he couldn't get to the phone because he was dead.

I *was* paranoid. Not a bad thing, usually, but a real pain sometimes.

I texted him: CALL ME, and then let out a long breath. I finished the orange juice, but no longer had any interest in what was left of the muffin. I tossed it along with the empty juice bottle into a stainless steel trash can, and then headed across the street to my Jeep. On the way over, I checked my text inbox for David Amit's phone number. It was late afternoon in Israel, almost evening, and the Shin Bet man could be anywhere. After sliding into the Grand Cherokee's driver's seat, I placed the overseas call.

Twenty seconds later, after a series of what sounded like short busy signals – but were actually Israeli phone rings – Amit's voice told me to leave a message. No surprise. His caller ID wouldn't have shown my number.

"Shalom, David," I said. "This is Gidon in Baltimore. Something's come up here that you might find interesting." I gave him a quick overview of what was happening, and ended with finding the Gaza phone number on the assassin at my dojo. I didn't leave the number itself on his voice mail. Instead, just "Call me," and left my cell number. Amit was a pro, of course, and despite how he and I parted, if there was a Gaza connection to an international crime, Shin Bet should be interested.

It was time to leave.

Out through the windshield to the right, an overweight, gray-haired man in an orange polo and plaid shorts walked by. He was holding a leash and leading a fluffy, white dog that was rapidly moving its short little legs trying to keep up. I turned on the engine and pulled away.

In less than ten minutes I was on I-95 south. Five minutes after that, I was back in the center lane and mentally reviewing the last 24 hours. The trip to Westerly...speaking with Mrs. Meyers... reaching Josh while he was on the road...being with Sammi. It wasn't difficult pulling up the images of our tai chi in the rain, or the massage, or her last sentiment about how I shouldn't feel guilty over the men I had lost. Sammi's voice was still in my head when my cell phone rang unknown minutes later, pushing her out. "Unknown Number." On the highway, the Mamaroneck exit sign came and went. The phone rang a second time and I answered it.

"Gidon, *ma ha'inyanim,*" the male voice said in Hebrew, asking "What's up." It was David Amit of the Shin Bet. The connection was almost perfect. You'd never know he was halfway around the world.

"Shalom, David. Thanks for calling me back."

"No problem. What can I do for you?"

Without hesitation, I gave him a more complete version of what's been going on, to include the name of the man in Buick, Belard, who was probably Mr. Meyers' killer, and who seemed to be directing the situation here. I also gave him the Gaza phone number I had turned up.

"I'll check on Belard and the phone number. May take a while."

A navy blue Odyssey van with New York plates passed me on the left.

"What's your feeling about the rabbi?"

I responded honestly: "Generally pretty good. I believe he doesn't know what this is all about, but there is something he's not connecting."

"Sounds like it." He let another second pass. "So, thinking of coming this way?"

"Depends on what you find and what I find. No plans at this point."

"*B'seder.*" Okay. "I'll call you later."

We hung up. Amit got me thinking about Josh again. I didn't like that I couldn't reach him, so I called Nate. He picked up almost immediately.

"Hi," I said. "How are you?"

"My wife wants to know if you've called Laurie yet." Laurie, their daughter in Israel, who they thought was not doing well.

"Rachel's right next to you, isn't she, and she didn't ask. You just want to ask me before she asks you to ask me."

"Don't mess with me, Gidon."

"No, I haven't called her yet. I will. I promise."

I could hear Nate speak slightly away from the phone. "He said he would call." Rachel *was* next to him. Back to me. "I got your message about Mr. Meyers in Rhode Island and the possible connection to the Mandels."

"Yeah."

"How are the Mandels?"

"Don't know."

"You can't reach them."

"Not today. Spoke with them yesterday and they were in the car, going for a ride."

"Maybe they were heading to Hershey Park."

"Maybe. But that was yesterday."

"I'll call Williamsport PD and see if they can send a patrol car by. Check out the house. Make sure there was no home invasion and they're okay."

"That'll work." I gave him the address so it was handy, and then hung up.

I didn't like not knowing, but there was nothing to be done about it right now.

Baltimore was a good four to five hours ahead, so I watched the road for a while, and tried listening to a CD, a recording of an old Mystery Theater radio program. I couldn't follow the story, but then I really wasn't listening. The fact that Josh hadn't returned my phone message, or my text, was troubling.

The sky had turned gray and the Jeep found its way onto the Cross Bronx and eventually over the George Washington Bridge. Sometime later on the Jersey Turnpike, I set up a breathing pattern, and essentially put myself on auto-pilot, not that I wasn't there already. I changed lanes and reacted to traffic, accelerating and braking mostly without concrete awareness.

At some point I began to refocus. What day was this? For a while I peered at the length of highway ahead of me, and the sun off to the right. It was Thursday. Last Friday night was the attempted hit at the rabbi's house, Saturday night I threatened my student's father, Sunday night Katie and I were attacked along the Harborwalk and Mr. Sakolsky was killed uptown. Monday was the trip to Charleston and the midnight incident at my dojo...three shots into the intruder's chest...and the discovery of the Gaza phone number. Tuesday was the move to Williamsport, and Wednesday was meeting Rabbi Seidman, Detective Holden, and Mrs. Meyers in Westerly. Wednesday night was Sammi.

With that last memory, my palms, forehead, low-to-mid abdomen, and parts of my spine began to tingle. That was Sammi and her energy. My body was still reacting. It would be interesting to convey to Katie.

Before I could dwell on that line of thought, my phone rang. Nate. About three hours had passed since we spoke.

"You can relax, Gidon."

"I *am* relaxed."

"Yeah, sure. Anyway, one of the Williamsport officers went by the house and everything checked out."

"He went inside?"

"Looked inside...in all accessible windows. No one was home, but the place appeared nice and neat. No forced entry, nothing disrupted... like they'd gone out for the day and would be back later."

"That's the report?"

"That's the report."

"You're okay with that?"

"For now. Like I said, they're probably on the 'Sooperdooperlooper' throwing up or something."

"And there's no phone service?"

"I have no idea," the Baltimore cop said.

"I guess it doesn't mean anything nefarious."

"'Nefarious?' You sound like Medrano."

"It's Katie. Both you and I hang out with smart people."

"Where would we be if it weren't for smart people? Talk to you later." He hung up.

I let a few moments go by. Last time I spoke with Josh he did sound fine. No sense of duress in his voice, or anything out of the normal. Maybe I *was* too paranoid.

Out in front of me, a green and white sign announced a junction with the Baltimore Beltway.

Time to call Jonathan. I gave him the news that I would be at the dojo in about thirty minutes. He said he'd be waiting. With tomorrow being Friday, maybe I could talk Katie into taking off and going to Williamsport with me. She could help me assist Josh and Shelley recall their stops in Israel. Then perhaps we'd be able to make a connection to Mrs. Meyers' list, whenever she finished hers.

I was looking forward to seeing Katie. A trip to Williamsport would give us some time together. The case permitting, maybe we could spend a day or two there.

The Beltway junction appeared, providing a number of choices. I headed west on I-695, eventually past Towson, and then south on the Jones Falls Expressway. Rush-hour traffic was in full swing, but while the roads were crowded, everything kept moving, though in some areas at a much slower pace. My thirty minute estimate was optimistic; it was closer to an hour before pulling off the highway and onto Charles Street, as cars and trucks had come to a stop along one length of I-83.

There was no available parking in front of the dojo, so I pulled into a spot on a nearby cross street. The gray sky had dissipated, allowing the sun to come out again. It felt good stretching my legs and walking the two blocks under its warming rays.

Jon was working out when I walked in. He hadn't turned on the lights, and the natural, warm afternoon tones seeping in from the windows set a halcyon atmosphere. Jon, standing alone in the center of the work-out area, had a pair of Chinese broadswords in hand, and was working on the routine from a few days ago. His fluid, arcing slices and his posture rising and falling, fit perfectly in the calm ambiance of the room.

"Sorry about being late," I apologized during a break.

"No problem. Plenty to do." We approached each other. I could see sweat running down both sides of his face.

"So, what are you up for?"

"Sifu, I am but your humble, if not sweaty, servant. Before I choose," he paused, "tell me how you feel. Still pretty good from New York? No ill effects from the drive?"

"I feel excellent."

He looked at me and put the pair of broadswords down out of the way. "Okay," he turned back to me, and then I could see him mock a half wince as he formulated a request: "What about three offense/three defense?"

This was a game we sometimes played. Basically, one person moves in and the other person gets three defensive moves, one of which can be a counter-move. In the karate world of linear techniques this would be rather segmented, but what he proposed was the more fluid, Chinese ebb and flow of circular motions. It was similar to push-hands, and sometimes it was difficult to see where one technique left off and another started. For our version, there was an added catch; the defender could not retreat.

"Okay," I said, "who attacks first, you or me?"

He thought for a moment. "If you attack me, I'll be thrown all over the place, have joints twisted, arms locked, lose feeling in my hands. I'll end up on the floor, like one of those cartoon characters who's been in a fight and what's left is a jumbled pile of arms and legs.

"On the other hand," he went on, " If I go first, I'll still be thrown all over the place, have joints twisted and all that stuff, and still end up in a jumbled pile of arms and legs."

"Stop whining. You attack; I'll defend."

By letting Jon attack first, he could learn from my defensive moves. He'd move in with either a punch or a kick and I'd rotate to the side, or wrap up an extended leg for a split second before tossing him in the opposite direction…or I'd move in a circular motion, taking him to a corner. I'd move into him before he had a chance to fully realize his move. I'd spin, take him off axis, move high, drop low, pull him one way, switch and move to the other. More often than not, as he predicted, he ended up on the floor. However, each time I would throw him, he'd spring back to his feet for more. In a real encounter, he wouldn't be getting up…and he knew that. But this wasn't about me; it was about him learning from my reactions.

In a few minutes we switched…I began to attack and he'd work off of me. I was always taught that a good teacher stayed just ahead of his – or her – student. When I moved on Jon, I allowed him to experiment and mimic what he'd seen. He'd also throw his own combinations. It was a pleasure working with him. Every few moves I would point out a hand position or a motion that would be to his benefit.

At miscellaneous intervals, he'd stepped back to allow himself a smile as he caught a mistake, acknowledging learning something new. Soon, it was my turn again, and we began to accelerate the pace. My energy picked up, and my hand motions became faster and he ended up not being able to touch or grab me. A fist would move in and I'd reflect off of it and move around him, simultaneously wrapping my arm around his head or his arm or his leg or his body.

After five minutes of being thrown all over the place, Jon hustled back and said, huffing and puffing, "You know you're past your prime, don't you?" He paused to catch his breath. "I mean it, Sifu. I got one or two moves in there."

190

I laughed. "Perhaps, but look in a mirror."

He ran over to a full-length mirror on a nearby wall. As he looked at his reflection, he turned his head to see a red, partial hand-print across his right cheek and jaw from where my hand had made momentary contact.

"That is so awesome," he said.

Sammi's husband, my teacher, used to do the same thing to his students. He'd leave these chi marks all over our arms and typically on our faces. We'd wear the blotches like our own Red Badges of Courage. We also knew that it meant he could beat the crap out of us at any point.

Jon came back over: "More?"

"Definitely." I loved Jon. He was always eager, very talented, and he worked incredibly hard. Jon had discipline as well as smarts. "Pick up the broadswords," I motioned to his pair of polished steel weapons off to the side.

He picked up each by its handle and came at me.

Once you get past the fear of being cut, and once you understand body motion and weapon movement, and once you've trained under a master teacher for, say, ten-to-fifteen years at least, your entire body knows what to do instinctively. As he attacked, I watched his timing for a millisecond and side-stepped his arms. In completely fluid motions and without hesitation, I grabbed both his wrists, tied him up, moving against his center of balance. He was on the floor again, before he could figure what happened.

He got up and we went at it again, but this time he slowed down, so he could see what I was doing. He would move on me and I'd side-step and parry at the same time…or rotate into him and grab his wrists…or just move out his way entirely to frustrate his movements.

We switched just as we had before, and it became his turn again…

An hour went by somewhere beyond our own sense of temporal speed. Finally, I caught a glimpse of the wall clock. It was five-thirty.

"I have to go," I smiled, backing away from him slightly. "Sorry."

"Now? Just as I'm about to cut you to pieces?"

"Patience, my young apprentice. It'll have to wait."

"You've got a hot date, don't you?"

"You know it. Do you have enough to work on?"

"You kidding? I need another lifetime."

I smiled. "Thank you, Jon." Teachers always thanked their students.

"Thank you, Sifu," and he bowed to me. "I'll lock up. Say 'Hi' for me."

Fifteen minutes later I was pulling up to Katie's house in Cedarcroft, not that there was a place to park. Her street, draped with old maple and oak trees, was fairly narrow and had cars lining both sides. Most people were already home from work, and every spot seemed taken. It was a little frustrating. I drove to the end of the block and circled to the left. When that didn't prove successful, I drove past Katie's a second time and into the next block. Halfway up were two spaces, one across from the other. I parked on the right, locked the Jeep, and headed back down the block.

I had just passed an old oak whose roots had displaced large, irregular blocks of sidewalk, when my phone rang. "Unknown Number." Amit?

"Hello?"

"*Shalom*, Gidon," the Israeli said, cheerfully.

"*Shalom*, David. You're working late." It was past midnight in Israel. "You have something?"

"Just a progress report. The cell number you gave me was indeed from Gaza. Unfortunately, it's from a rechargeable, disposable phone. We don't know who bought it, of course, but we're tracking the calls. Maybe if you get me the model and serial number we can do something."

"Okay. Nate D'Allesandro has it."

"Your police captain friend."

"*Nachon*." Correct.

"And the name you gave me, 'Belard?' Nothing under that name here. Interpol has nothing either, but your captain friend probably checked that. Maybe the phone numbers we're tracking will help. Do you have a picture of Belard?"

"Nate does. From a rental car agency here. Call him directly and ask for both the cell phone information and for the picture. He'll be happy to help, since it means I'll stop calling him about another body or something."

Amit laughed and I gave him Nate's number. As we were speaking, a thirty-something man in a button-down blue shirt and khakis got into a Volvo beside me and pulled out. Katie's house was half a block away.

"That's all for now," Amit said. A moment went by. "It's good to hear your voice, Gidon. I hope you are well."

"I am. Thanks. And, it's good to hear your voice, too." *Despite what happened the last time I saw you.* It was true, though. I did like Amit.

"Call me if you need anything. Even in middle of the night. I don't sleep anymore. If I find anything I'll call you."

"*Toda.* Bye."

We hung up and I continued toward Katie's. Her shingled, two story home came up on the left. My heart rate picked up slightly. Only a few days had passed, and speaking on the phone to her just wasn't the same, obviously. I had a lot to share. Without thinking about it, my hands began to get warmer. Hmm. The energy was flowing.

Once inside, I had the notion of silently coming up behind Katie to surprise her, but that usually caused a sudden scream, and the involuntary throwing of whatever was in her hand up toward the ceiling.

"Katie?" I called as I entered the foyer.

"Upstairs..."

I took the steps two at a time and walked into the bedroom. Katie wasn't there, but there was rustling in a nearby walk-in closet. On the way over to it, I saw an open photo album on her dresser, and caught sight of an aging black and white snapshot of a blond-haired young man, maybe 20, pasted in the center of a gray page. The photo of the young man was about three by five inches with scalloped edges on all four sides. The young fellow was posing in front of some ruins. It looked like an ancient amphitheater, maybe Greek, maybe Roman. While it was impossible to tell how old the picture was, I'd have guessed it was from the 30's or '40's.

"I'm in here," Katie called.

I walked to the entrance of the walk-in closet to see Katie standing with her back to me. She was dressed only in a black bra and panties and was holding up a dress, evaluating it. She began to turn around.

"Don't turn around."

She didn't.

"Hang up the dress."

"Gidon…"

"Hang up the dress and close your eyes."

She looped the hanger hook through the bend of another hanger and closed her eyes. Her face was still turned to the left.

"Take a deep breath and then let it out."

She did.

"And another."

I could see her back expand a little and then contract. It was a beautiful back. I loved the slope of her shoulders and the curve of her neck. I stepped over to her and placed a hand under each of her elbows.

"Your hands are so warm," she said softly.

I leaned over and kissed her gently where the base of her neck met her right shoulder. She dropped her head and swayed slightly.

"That went right down to my…"

"Shhh."

I kissed her again, this time on the other side of her neck. I slid my hands back from her elbows and placed the palm of each hand on her back, one on each side of her spine. Barely touching her skin, I moved my hands, parallel to each other, up her back until they rested lightly on her shoulders. My hands left behind slight red marks where they touched her skin. I kissed her neck again and let my hands trace back down the outside of her arms until they were opposite her breasts. I moved my fingers slightly forward so they came around her front. I could feel the rise and fall of her chest. I moved my hands back, tracing the side of each breast through the sheer fabric covering her curves and moved my hands forward again, glancing past each nipple.

Katie moaned slightly and leaned back into me. I moved my right hand down her flat, belly to let it stop in front of her pubic triangle. Her warmth came through her underwear. I moved my hands up her torso to stroke her through the silky covering.

"Take it off," she breathed.

I reached up, unclasped her bra, let it drop, then brought both my hands up to her front to feel the undersides of her breasts and then, very lightly, each nipple. Katie reached behind her to the front of my pants and began to lightly make circles of her own with the palm of her hand. After a moment, she pulled away her hand, backed fully into me and gently swayed her hips over my groin.

I gently turned her around and kissed her on her partially opened mouth. Her lips were sweet and I touched the tip of her tongue with mine. There was a definite tingle at the moment of contact. I pulled down her panties so she could step out of them. Katie unclasped my belt and pants, and stripped me from the waist down. We stepped away from the fallen clothes. She hopped up, wrapping both legs around me. She arched her back to press her torso into me. I held her there for a moment and then slowly lowered her to the floor. Katie looked into my eyes and smiled. She moved her hips upward and I lowered mine.

18

"So what did Sammi do to you?"

We were sitting at a relatively new restaurant in Clipper Mill off the Jones Falls Expressway called The Kitchen in the Castle. It was a casual place, pub-like with brass railings, a bar off to one side, and table and chairs filling the main area. The lighting was subdued, courtesy of a series of low, stained glass chandeliers. Our small, square table was off to the right near a wall with a fireplace set in the painted white brick façade. In colder weather it would have been a prime location for a cozy dinner. It wasn't bad in the spring either. Katie and I sat four feet from each other, across an immaculately pressed white tablecloth. Silverware was in place and water had been poured into stemmed glasses. I leaned forward, looked into Katie's beautiful eyes. "What do you mean?"

"What I mean, as if you don't know," Katie lowered her voice slightly, "is that every time you touched me," she paused for a moment, "I felt this rush all over that got more and more intense as you ran your hands ran over me." She closed her eyes briefly. "I can still feel it."

I looked down at my butter dish and when I looked back up, I could have sworn Katie had colored slightly.

"Okay, so what was that?" she went on. "Everything was...like these waves flowing over my head and down my front and then radiating outward through my body."

"Ah, that."

"What did Sammi do to you?"

197

"What makes you think it just wasn't me?"

"Because it was never like that before. No offense."

I smiled. "None taken." I looked around the room and came back to her. "We worked on energy stuff...circulating, improving flow. I know that sounds bizarre, but I don't know how else to explain it. What you felt was a side benefit to what we did."

"Whatever it was, you keep working on that."

I laughed.

"Tell me more about Sammi. She must be really something."

"She is. She's unbelievably talented and the most open person I know. She's really at peace with herself, and when she works with you, you come alive. Like I said, it's hard to explain."

I looked past Katie to see a waiter moving toward a nearby table.

"The first time I saw Sammi, I didn't know who she was. This was, maybe, ten years ago. We were in the dojo working out, and in walked this hippie woman who looked like she was in her twenties. The entire class just stopped whatever it was doing...the students sparring in back, the black belts working with the newer students, those talking to Sifu...we all just stopped and looked at her. Men and women. Didn't matter. With all of us watching – mostly with our mouths open – Sammi happily walked over to Max, my teacher, threw her arms around him, and kissed him. He then introduced us to his wife."

"Everyone fell in love with her, right?"

"Yup...and all it took were those ten seconds for her to cross the room. Then, after that kiss, I think we were all crushed."

"What was your relationship with her?"

"I was senior student, and she was my teacher's wife. She was a master in her own rite. She taught classes on meditation and tai chi chuan. She could basically beat the crap out of anyone, though she never did. But we all knew she could."

"Even you?"

"Of course. Sammi always let me think we were equals, but I knew the truth. She'd never admit it, though. She's incredibly sweet.

A real flower child."

"Who can kick your ass."

"You betcha."

Before Katie could ask additional questions, our waiter, a college-aged young man in a white shirt and black pants, came by to take our order. Katie went with a Shepherd's Pie and I ordered a pasta dish – ziti with three cheeses, Roma tomatoes, broccoli, all in a light red sauce.

As we waited for the food to arrive we chatted about schoolwork, the students who were particularly challenging because of executive function issues, and about some of the kids who were real success stories. I recognized many of the students' names, as she had mentioned them over the course of the school year. By the time the waiter brought our dinners, the conversation had shifted to the Mandels.

"So, how worried are you?" Katie asked.

"You mean that I can't reach them?"

"Uh huh." She took a sip of her iced tea.

"Despite Nate's belief that they're at Hershey Park or somewhere, eating more junk food than they should, I'll feel better when I speak with them. I don't entirely buy that their phone died or that they're out of cell range or something."

"Any reason to think otherwise, that something has happened?"

"No."

"So?"

"Still. They're being hunted and something's not right about this whole thing."

"What do you mean? What are you uncomfortable about?"

"I don't know. I'm conflicted. I really like Josh and Shelley, but Josh got involved in something, probably while rescuing a Torah, and he pissed off someone."

"You think he knows more than he's telling?"

"I want to completely believe him, but…"

"Something's not right, as you said."

A moment went by. "Maybe. He seems like an up-front guy, and Shelley, I really like. She's a hippie in her own way. You should meet them. I'd like to get your impression."

Another moment went by.

"About that," she said.

I looked at Katie, who had put down her fork and looked back at me, suddenly reserved.

"You know how you invited me to dinner with them last Friday when you first met the Mandels?"

I nodded.

"And how you never asked for an explanation about why I didn't want to go?"

"You'd tell me when you wanted to." There were several things about Katie that we had never discussed. Her strong reaction to the Mandel's Friday night Shabbat dinner invitation was the most recent. Mainly, it was about her family background. She frequently used humor to avoid talking about it. I never wanted to press.

"I didn't go to dinner with you and the Mandels, because I was afraid."

I didn't say anything.

"I knew we'd start playing that game of who you know and who you're connected to."

"Jewish Geography."

She nodded. "I know you saw that picture on my dresser of a man standing in front of Greek ruins. You see everything."

Not everything, I thought. However, I did notice that photo in the open album.

"That was my grandfather in 1941. My family is from a small farming village in the north of Italy, just on the southern side of the mountains from France."

" 'Harris' is an old Italian name?"

"You can thank Ellis Island and family members who wanted to Americanize their name. Anyway, we had a dairy farm. My grandfather was one of five children, three boys and two girls. In the spring of 1941, when my grandfather was 19, he was in Crete. I'm not sure why he was there, or how long he had been gone from home, but I know he worked at different jobs, mainly as a farm hand in the olive groves up in the western mountains. He was there when the Nazis invaded."

"From what I've read, in addition to the Greeks, there were British troops on Crete, as well as some New Zealanders and Australians. They were really hammered by the Nazis as time went on."

Katie seemed not to hear me. She continued: "You know how you pray that people will do the right thing? Between the Germans and the corrupt government, as time went on and the Nazis exerted more control, there was little food in the cities to go around. Thousands of people starved to death...unless you were rich and could afford to buy food on the black market."

I watched Katie. She was steeling herself for what was to come. Her eyes had lost their expressiveness and she looked at me, almost blankly: "My grandfather became a smuggler, bringing fruits and vegetables, flour, and meat to the wealthy people in the cities. Poor people were starving to death on the island and my grandfather made a great deal of money smuggling food to people who could afford it. *That's* how he spent those years."

"My grandfather deserted from the Russian army."

She either hadn't heard my attempt at lightening the moment, or she ignored me. "The rest of my family was trying to deal with Fascists and the Nazis, and my grandfather was feeding people who were probably working with the Germans. I even heard stories from older cousins about how my grandfather became an informant on the whereabouts of Greek or British troops."

Katie's eyes came back into focus. She looked at me. "How do you live with yourself? How do you justify that...that you contributed to starving people to death or provided information that would directly kill others?"

I reached across the table and took her hand. "I don't know."

"I've been over friends' homes for meals, maybe a student's family, and sometimes the topic of family history comes up. You know, 'Where did you grow up, where are your parents from, where are your grandparents from?' It does come up – not often, but it does – depending on who's there. You know what I say?"

I shook my head.

"When it comes to my grandparents, I tell them about my grandfather's brother, Ronaldo. He also smuggled food, but he used the family's wagons and milk containers to hide morsels of grain and fruit for the local villagers, not for the wealthy who could afford it. He was caught by the Nazis, thrown in jail, and never seen again. But I don't tell them it was Ronaldo. I say it was my grandfather."

And with that, Katie began to cry. Her eyes just welled up and overflowed, sending a stream of tears down each cheek.

She went on: "And I didn't want to do that anymore...lie to my friends. So I just avoided the whole thing by saying 'no' to invitations, not even knowing if the issue would ever come up."

I got up to move over to her, but Katie stopped me. "Oh sit down. I'll be fine." She wiped the tears away with her napkin. A moment went by with neither of us talking, and then she said, "Say something."

"Sammi taught me some stuff I didn't use before. You know, keeping it in reserve for the next time I catch you partially clothed."

She laughed. "Well you better show them to me."

"Looking forward to it," I smiled.

Katie dabbed her eyes again, and then in a matter of minutes our meals came. Either the waiter didn't notice that Katie had been crying, or he was polite enough not to give her undue attention.

"*B'tayavone*," I said.

"*Buon appetito.*"

After a few moments, with Katie having broached the subject, I continued: "Is your grandfather still alive?"

"No. He died in his village in 1949. I've never been able to get a clear answer or whether it was from natural causes or not. I've heard everything from he died of a heart attack to a car accident that maybe wasn't an accident."

"I guess that's something to look into if you're interested."

Katie shrugged, "Why?"

Because if he didn't die of natural causes, I thought, *it might lead to more of an understanding of the man...or on the other hand, maybe to events that would raise more intense feelings.* I could understand why Katie might not want to go there. "So you've not been able to get closure one way or the other."

"No. If he were alive, at least I could look into his eyes and see if he felt any remorse. That would be nice. And if not, maybe after talking to him and hearing his side of the story, I could somehow understand what was going through his head."

"How long have you known this about your grandfather?"

"Since high school." Katie skewered a small piece of meat and some green beans and put it in her mouth. She swallowed and looked back at me. "I had a family history project and when I started asking my parents questions, they told me the unsanitized version of his life. Ever since then I knew I wanted to do something to help people. When I was in college, I took some Ed classes, focusing on learning disabilities and the brain. I found it fascinating and began moving in that direction."

"...to becoming a learning specialist."

She nodded.

"And if you hadn't, you wouldn't have been at Solomon Stein Day School and we would never have met."

She smiled. "Fate...Kismet."

"And good karma." I looked around the restaurant and watched two couples who were sitting at a corner table across the room. "Ronaldo sounds like he was quite a man. Someone to be proud of."

"He was supposed to be really something. Bold, daring. He always looked out for everyone."

"You know, if we ever go to Israel, you may want to stop at Yad

Vashem, the Holocaust Museum. I know someone in the research department. There may be information on him as a Righteous Gentile."

Katie looked at me. "You've assumed I'm not Jewish."

I didn't say anything.

"You never asked me."

"I know."

"Why not?"

"You noticed that, didn't you."

"Sometimes *I* notice everything."

I smiled. Then after a second, "I don't know…maybe it doesn't matter to me."

"It matters to you. You just don't know it…or maybe you just pushed that part away for now."

"Because of what happened to Tamar?" My fiancée who was killed in a terrorist attack in Israel.

Katie nodded.

"So," I smiled weakly, "are you?" For some reason my heart rate had picked up.

"I don't know. I don't think so. We never really celebrated anything. Not even Christmas. When I asked my parents about our religion or belief in God, all they said is, 'We're not one thing or another.' They said I could decide later." She let a few moments pass. "And now I work at a Jewish Day School and really love it. I love the values. I love the sense of history and place in the world."

"But you don't know if your Jewish or not."

"My family is from a village in northern in Italy."

"So, probably not."

"But you never know. There are Jews all over, you know."

"A mystery."

"Maybe you'll help me solve it."

I smiled. "Maybe I will."

The waiter came over and refilled our water glasses.

"So, really, no family discussion of religion or God or the meaning of life?"

"Nope."

"Like no thoughts on a creative life force or reasons why things happen?"

She shook her head and laughed. "No. We believed in neatness."

"Neatness?"

"We do things like clean the house before the cleaning lady comes."

"That's not cleanliness. That's fear. Fear of pissing off your housekeeper."

"We clean the house before we go away on vacations. Can't come home to a pile of laundry or unmade beds."

"Okay."

"I have an aunt who arranges the linen closet so that all the sheets and towels are facing with the fold out."

"She's just efficient. That way you know what you're grabbing."

"You're very forgiving. My mom arranges the spices in the rack alphabetically."

"*I* do that."

"No you don't."

"The spice drawer started out that way. I just haven't had a chance to re-arrange it. See, we're not that different."

She ignored my comment and went on. "Some people like to be neat. Other people are prone to being slobs."

"True. I had some friends in the army who were off the scale sloppy."

"And who do you know who is habitually neat?"

"Well, I understand your family is OCD about it."

"Besides them?"

"I don't know. I don't notice those things."

"If it matters to you, it does. Give me a first impression of someone you recently met."

"The Mandels," I said. "They're pretty neat. They have kids, so there are toys and stuff all over, but despite potential kid mess, their place is pretty neat. Of course when they came to Williamsport they began to spread out."

I visualized their cousin's house when we walked in…the kitchen, the terrific view off the living room…and then…

"What?" Katie saw my mind drift and then lock on. "Gidon?"

My mind had gone back to an earlier conversation with Nate. "Nate said that when the Willamsport cop looked in the house to see if the Mandels were there, he said that all looked neat and clean."

"So?"

"The last time I saw the place, there was a cooler out and the kids' stuff was everywhere."

"So?"

"I can't reach them. They're not out of cell range, or out of batteries. It's not that they've just straightened up the toys. They're not home. They've cleaned up because they've left."

"Beds stripped?"

"I don't know. The report didn't say, but I wouldn't be surprised."

I stood up, reached for my phone, and headed toward a secluded part of the restaurant. Katie followed.

I called Nate and told him what I thought. He was going to ask the Williamsport cops to do a more thorough look at the house…see if they could get in. He was also going to check airports.

"Check Philadelphia," I suggested. "They have a direct flight to Israel."

"Call you back soon."

We returned to our table, but I had lost my appetite. Katie, too, seemed to suddenly not be hungry.

"You think Josh and Shelley went to Israel?" Katie asked.

"They wouldn't go to either parents. Not safe and they didn't want to impose. They both have family in Israel and Shelley had suggested it as a place to go. I bet that's it."

Katie looked at me, considering the supposition.

I went on: "The last time I spoke with them, they were in the car. Shelley answered the phone, and quickly passed it to Josh. She's usually very friendly with me."

"She didn't want to lie in case you asked something specific."

"And all Josh said was that they were out for a ride. They were antsy."

"Maybe you're wrong. Maybe they're just spending the night away and didn't want to tell you."

I shook my head. "They're gone. The questions are where and when did they arrive?"

"If it *is* Israel, then what?"

"Then I go and get them."

"Maybe they're safer in Israel."

"Maybe, but they may have just put themselves closer to whoever is trying to kill them. There's a phone number in Gaza that we need to check out, and there's also Belard."

"The guy in the Buick who you think arranged the hit."

I nodded. "And who probably killed the shopkeeper in Rhode Island. There's also Samuels, Josh's competition for rescuing Torahs. He's supposed to be pretty sketchy."

"'Sketchy'?"

"I've been hanging around Jon too long."

My phone vibrated in my pants pocket. It was Nate. "The Mandels are gone. They took a flight yesterday afternoon. Arrived in Tel Aviv this morning."

"Shit."

"And it gets better."

"What?"

"Belard popped up…on a flight to London."

"And he's being tracked, right?"

"Agents at the other end lost him."

"Great. He could be on his way to Gaza, or anywhere else."

"What are you going to do?"

"Call Amit and tell the Shin Bet that I'm coming."

19

Katie and I were standing on the cement steps outside the restaurant. We were just standing there, thinking what to do next. Well, I was thinking about it; I didn't know what was in Katie's mind. I soon found out.

"When will you leave?"

"Tomorrow, I guess, though I need to talk to some people in the congregation who know about the Mandels' family in Israel."

"Like the man who hired you?"

I nodded and looked up the street, though my mind was already considering contacts to make, booking a flight, and getting Jon to cover my classes – again. The street came back into focus. This was an old, remodeled industrial area with retail shops up and down the avenue. Cars had to park a few blocks away. My Grand Cherokee was up the street to the left. As a young couple dressed in business attire moved to the restaurant entrance, I called David Amit in Jerusalem. He answered on the first ring.

After I had filled him in, he simply said, "Send me pictures of the rabbi and his wife."

"I will. Any more information on the Gaza number?"

"Not yet."

"Or Belard?"

"No. I'll let you know when we find something."

"Thanks." After a moment, "Are you still available to give me a package similar to the one you gave me last time?" He had a gun, cash, and appropriate documents waiting for me on my previous visit. It would make life easier.

"If you need it."

"Thanks. Don't worry about the papers and the cash."

"*Heyvanti.*" I understand. "Call me when you know your flight information."

"I will."

We hung up and began walking to the car.

"So, should I pack a bag, too?" Katie looked at me.

"You up for an Israel trip?"

"What do you think?"

"Then one suitcase and a carry-on."

"I can do that," she smiled.

"You can take the time from work?"

"As long as I'm back the last week of school."

"No way of telling."

"I know."

We started walking to the left toward the Jeep. "Couple of things," I took Katie's arm.

"You'll be off doing Gidon things," Katie posited.

"Uh huh."

"And they could be dangerous."

"Probably at some point."

She nodded. "I know."

"I want to take two rooms at a hotel. We'll get them next to each other, but you'll sleep there."

"Alone?"

I smiled back. "Didn't say that. I just want you out of harm's way in case someone comes looking for me." We stepped up to the Jeep. "I have a friend who's a tour guide. Kiffi. Maybe she can take you around while I'm hunting for the Mandels and hanging out with manly men."

"Oooh, you'll have to introduce me."

"Get in the Jeep." I grinned, opening the door.

She smiled and climbed in. I moved around to the other side, looking both ways, checking traffic. A white BMW pulled out of a space several cars up and headed away.

When I settled in behind the wheel, Katie turned and put her hand on my arm. "Are you sure about this...about me coming along?"

"I am. But I also want you to be safe. When I can, I'll take you around, but probably not as much as I'd like. Kiffi's a pro.... an amazing tour guide. And she's spunky. You'll like her."

"Okay."

"'Kiffi' is short for *kiffirah*, the feminine form of 'young lion'."

"I knew you'd tell me."

"God, I've become predictable."

We pulled out of the spot, making a U-turn to head back toward the main road.

"How do you know her...Kiffi?"

"From the army. She was a world class sniper instructor."

Katie just looked at me.

I laughed. "Hey, it's Israel." I let a moment pass. "Now she's a professional guide. She's married and has four kids. Husband's a pediatrician."

"Okay."

"Just don't piss her off. She can shoot you from a mile out; you'll never see it coming."

Katie's mouth dropped open about an inch.

"Just kidding...sort of."

We headed across 41st Street toward University Parkway, a beautiful two-lane road in a park-like residential setting, with large houses on either side. After a few minutes, when I pulled up to the University Parkway intersection to turn right, I noticed a white BMW, a blue Ford, and a rust colored Suzuki pick-up ahead of me, turning right. In another block or so the three vehicles had all gone their separate ways down tree-lined side streets. After a few more blocks, and a lazy half mile, a white BMW appeared ahead of me again.

"Now isn't that interesting," I said.

"What?"

I turned to Katie and then back to the road. "See that white BMW two cars up?"

"Yes."

"I'm pretty sure that car pulled out ahead of us when we were leaving the restaurant."

"He's going the same way we are?"

"Watch."

I headed down Charles Street, past Johns Hopkins University. At Art Museum Drive, the BMW continued straight, but I turned right and pulled to a stop near the Baltimore Museum of Art. We waited in an illegal space, reserved for museum vehicles. If I were correct, he'd reappear in a few minutes. I absent-mindedly scanned the museum's front. A humongous banner was hanging over the modern front façade. "Will you look at that," I said. "They're showing *The Seven Samurai* as part of a Japanese artifacts month."

"You really are ADD, you know that?"

"I've heard that. Just occupying my mind until what I think will happen will happen."

After watching several couples walk by, and three men walking and talking on cell phones, and after cars of varying types and colors passed us, a familiar white BMW drove by. A balding man in a dark jacket was behind the wheel.

"Okay," Katie asked following the car with her eyes, "what does this mean?"

"I probably have a tracking device on the Jeep and this guy is doing a front tail."

Katie raised her eyebrows.

"Following from in front. It's really tricky, but a tracking unit helps. The 'tail' is typically harder to spot, but this guy's car is too noticeable and he's staying too close."

"So now what? Follow him?"

"I'm going with Phone-a-Friend." As Katie watched, I pulled a Baltimore County Police Officer's card from my wallet. "Officer Thompson. Met him on Saturday in front of the synagogue. He was assigned to keep an eye on Josh and Shelley, and we established a nice, professional rapport."

"Talk about rappelling and guns and stuff?"

"We didn't talk about rappelling." As she shook her head – she was doing a lot of that lately – I dialed his number. "Officer Thompson, Gidon Aronson."

That's all I needed to say. Instantly, he asked how he could help. I pictured the blond, former Force Recon Marine with a high and tight haircut, and filled him in. Toward the end of my conversation, the words "off-book work" were spoken. There was no hesitation on his part; no consideration of Constitutional rights or other County or State codes. Just a very workable plan of action.

After I hung up: "What are you going to do?" Katie asked.

"Head out into the county, and let the BMW follow us."

"And then what?"

"Get some answers."

We turned around out of our parking space and headed back toward Charles Street and up University Parkway, essentially reversing our earlier route. We moved over to I-83 and headed north out of town.

In fifteen minutes we had left the city behind. In another five we were in the northwest suburbs, moving along a much wider York Road. At this point the main boulevard was several lanes wide, with an occasional gas station poised as an essential monument at busy intersections. Mid-block on either side were small strip malls, occupied by chain restaurants, banks, and cell phone stores. After passing a Lexus dealership we turned onto side streets. I circled back to the main road twice, and then pulled into a parking lot in front of a fireplace and home goods store.

Following Thompson's instructions, we waited five minutes, and then drove to an industrial park tucked away, half a mile from an isolated mega hardware store. As we approached the open gate of the warehouse facility, we saw overgrown fields to either side. I drove through the entrance and to the left, then after fifteen seconds turned right along the periphery fence to the far end. The combination of still night air and absence of any human presence, created a setting that more resembled 3:00 in the morning than late evening. The Jeep with its headlights cutting through the dead air only emphasized that we were completely isolated.

We turned right and then right again. I couldn't help but look into the eaves of the faceless buildings for the prying eyes of surveillance cameras, but as Thompson had promised, there were none.

We slowly cruised along a wide strip of asphalt that was the no man's land between two parallel rows of warehouse blocks. To our right and left were loading docks, each about five feet off the ground and shuttered by wide, vertical steel doors. Signs were posted next to each access door, declaring the business within: Ace Plumbing Supply... Maryland Electrical... Sadie's Pool Contractors... Kalish Dental Supplies. All the back entrances were recessed and blackened by shadows thrown by sparsely placed floodlights. Occasionally, there was a weak yellow light over an entryway, but mainly the face of each warehouse was in the dark.

About halfway down the row of warehouses my headlights illuminated a car parked across our path and two figures to its left against a rusty loading platform. Officer Thompson, dressed in jeans and a black windbreaker, was on his feet. The other fellow was on the ground, arms pinned behind him. I stopped the Grand Cherokee, put it in park, and left it idling with the headlights on.

Katie turned to me but didn't say anything. Her breathing had gotten shallow. I stepped out from behind the wheel, looked at the figures fifty feet ahead of me, but didn't approach them. Instead, I began walking around the Jeep. The guy on the ground next to Thompson must have placed a GPS transmitter somewhere on the vehicle. He didn't have access under the hood or to the storage hatch, so I felt along the inside of the driver's side wheel well, moved down to the fender, and then across the front bumper to the other wheel well. In another minute I found a square-ish protrusion along the recessed curved metal surface, inches from the tire. The object was about two inches long, and held in place by a magnet. I gave it a yank, pulling it loose. In the wash of the headlights it looked like a simple unmarked black metal box, but there was no doubt what it was. Without giving it another thought, I walked over to the two figures watching me.

Thompson was still leaning against the wall with his guest still sitting on his butt, arms pulled back to either side. His wrists were probably lashed behind him, maybe with plastic restraints. The man looked to be in his early forties, balding, in a black leather jacket and decent looking black pants. He had a welt over his left eye. The fellow had probably made the mistake of moving on Thompson when the officer had stopped him.

"Good evening," I said, approaching them.

"And to you," the former Marine special operator said.

"Any trouble?"

"I cut him off to stop him from turning onto a street, and he got out of his car. Wanted me to move my vehicle. Tried pulling a gun."

I shook my head and tossed Thompson the GPS transmitter in my hand.

He looked at it. "Eighteen dollars in an electronics store. Ten online."

"Does he speak English?" It was a logical question, considering the men we've been running into.

Thompson nudged the man on the ground with his boot. He looked up. "Piss off."

So that was an affirmative. "I.D.?" I asked Thompson.

The officer held up a weathered, fabric wallet.

I turned to the man sitting at our feet. My sense was this was not a guy like the others we had dealt with. "I'm going to jump right into this," I said calmly, "since none of us wants to be here. Especially you."

Aside from the Jeep's engine running behind me, there was no other sound. There wasn't even road noise from nearby streets. There were no nearby streets.

"I'm going to ask you a question, and before you choose a response, some things to consider." I looked into the bald man's eyes. They had a fair amount of indignation in them, but there was also some resignation in the way he sat slumped. "You can answer and we'll let you go. If you don't, we're going to link you to a guy who has contacts in the Gaza Strip. Considering Gaza is run by Hamas, you know, the terrorist group, that means you've been associating with international terrorists. Maybe you're an enemy combatant living amongst us. We'll arrest you and drop you off at the local FBI office. At that point, you'll end up as a guest of the Federal government, and I don't even know what your rights would be at that point, with all the new anti-terrorism laws."

I looked over at Thompson who shrugged. I turned back to the bald man, and pulled out my folding knife but kept it blade still concealed. "The other option is that I'll ask you a question and then I'll take this…" I opened the knife with my thumb, revealing a three and a half inch half serrated-half straight edged blade, "…and stick the point in the side of your neck. You'll scream of course, but no one will hear you since we're in the middle of nowhere and these buildings trap all sound." I moved the polished steel blade over toward his neck. "I'll fish around between the muscles in your neck until I hit something good, like your jugular vein or carotid artery, and then if you answer my question we'll stop the bleeding – if we can. If not, we'll just leave you. And around here when the cops find your body, they'll think it was a gang killing."

He looked up at Thompson, who nodded.

"Eventually, we'll find out what we want, if not from you then from someone else, and all that poking and bleeding will be for naught. So, there are your options: answer, go to prison, or knife. Got that?"

He just looked at me.

"Now, who told you to follow me?"

The man tracked from me to Thompson and back. Despite his silent posturing, the color drained from his face. This was not a guy like the others we had run into. He wasn't part of their inner circle and felt no loyalty. There wasn't even a sigh of resignation. "Don't know his name," he said in a low voice. "He just gave me 500 bucks to follow you around."

"That it?" Thompson asked.

"Just wanted to know where you went and who you spoke to."

I reached into a pocket and pulled out the picture of Belard that was taken at the Hertz rental office last week. Belard, the man who probably shot Mr. Meyers up in Rhode Island. The man who had organized the hit on Josh down here, and probably on me. Belard, who could very well be in Gaza by now. I had shown the same photo to the cop in the small Rhode Island town. "Is this the guy?"

The man on the ground looked the picture I held in front of him. It took a moment in the dim lighting. "Yeah."

"You're bullshitting us," Thompson said. "You'd say anything."

I moved the knife back toward his neck and touched his skin with the razor sharp point.

"No, it's him," the man tried to move away, but I locked my other hand on the back of his neck and held him fast. The point stayed in place and began to draw blood. He didn't know that, but he surely felt the pain. "He was all business," he said quickly. "And he spoke with an accent. Not German, not Russian, not Spanish. I know those."

I backed off. *French*, I thought, but didn't say. Belard for sure. "How did you know where to find me?"

"He told me what kind of car you drove and where you worked. Gave me the GPS thing. Told where to hide it on your Jeep."

Thompson effortlessly picked him off the ground by the front of his jacket. "When did this start?"

"He paid me yesterday and I waited for you on Charles Street."

"Uh huh," Thompson muttered doubtfully.

If that were true, he followed me to Katie's after my work-out with Jon. Terrific.

"When did you last report?" I asked evenly.

He didn't answer right away. Thompson pushed him back into the brick facade of the building. It was good having a guy playing the heavy, though, not knowing him well enough, I didn't know how much Thompson was playing.

The man continued: "Left a message on his voice mail when you were in the restaurant."

After a long moment, I looked at Thompson. "Cut him loose." The former Marine, now cop, spun the man around, and with a dedicated cutting tool snipped off the plastic restraints.

"Go," I said to the bald-headed man.

"My wallet." Thompson still had it.

I shook my head. The man looked at me, knowing he wouldn't get it back, and began walking in the direction of the Grand Cherokee.

"Other way," I said, not wanting him getting closer to Katie.

As we watched him do an about face, Thompson said softly, "So, we're letting him go?"

"Did you Mirandize him?"

He shook his head.

"Not worth the trouble it'd put you in."

"Appreciate that." He paused. "So what'd this do for you?"

"Confirmation of what I already assumed. And I don't like being followed. Don't like the fact that this guy knows where Katie lives. I should've spotted him."

"A front tail and a GPS..."

"I know."

"You couldn't have known. Impressed that you spotted him when you did." He let a moment pass. "What now?"

"Belard is out of the country. The rabbi and his wife are in Israel."

"You're making a trip then."

"Looks that way."

"Give my regards to the Western Wall."

I smiled.

"What about this?" he held up the bald man's wallet.

"Let me have his driver's license...in case we need to find him again."

Thompson opened the wallet, pulled out the driver's license and passed it to me. I looked at it – it was a Maryland issue, with his picture in the lower left and a crab image in the upper right – then made a mental note of his name, and pocketed the plastic card.

"Thanks for your help, Tuck." I remembered his appellation from when we first met.

"Anytime... Major." He grinned.

So he knew my rank in the IDF. "Oh, God, I hope I'm not on Google."

"Not yet." He laughed and moved silently into the darkness beyond the wash of my headlights. For a moment I watched where he had disappeared and then headed back to the Grand Cherokee.

Katie looked at me as I settled in beside her.

"So, still want to come to Israel with me?" It wasn't an invitation; it was more *Still want to be with me?* She had seen the way I threatened the guy with my knife. She had seen other stuff, too, over time. What was going through her mind? The thought lingered in my head that she was finally appalled at my very deliberate violent actions.

Except for the sound of the running engine, the Jeep was silent.

"Was your conversation fruitful?" she quietly asked.

"He told me who hired him. Belard. He would've been my guess anyway."

"And he's on his way to Israel or Gaza."

"Maybe. Probably."

"The Mandels are in Israel," Katie said.

I nodded.

"The other Torah rescue guy is in Israel."

I nodded again. Then, "I know you have your reasons for wanting to come..." I began.

A few seconds passed with no one saying anything. Finally, Katie spoke: "You're worried about me getting in the way...getting hurt."

"Yes."

"Then don't think about it, if that's possible. I'll do whatever you say...stay wherever you want. You'll take care of me."

"I will."

"Then, you bet your ass I want to come."

20

Katie fell asleep somewhere over Newfoundland. The low rumble of the A330's engines at 37,000 feet hadn't kept her awake. Not me. There was plenty to think about, and that set my mind running. While Katie had her legs folded under her, and was fast asleep against the window bulkhead, I was reviewing what happened in the last 48 hours.

I wanted to leave Friday night, the day after we discovered the Mandels were in Israel, but that wasn't practical. Primarily, I needed information on where Josh may have gone. That meant speaking with people who knew of his family and friends in the Holy Land. The best source was Bob Levin, the partner of the man who had hired me; the partner of the man who had been shot to death in the parking lot of his Northwest Baltimore office.

At midday after discovering the Mandels' flight, I met Levin at a restaurant at the Greenspring Shopping Center off of Smith Avenue. He was picking at a Waldorf salad as we spoke. Essentially, he told me that both Josh and Shelley had family in Israel; Josh's relatives were up north near the city of Karmiel, and Shelley's were in Efrat, a community twenty minutes south of Jerusalem by car, just beyond Bethlehem. That was the good news. The complication was that in each case, the families' names were not Mandel. Shelley's relative was her brother, and we didn't know his last name. Josh's relatives were on his sister's side, and again we didn't have the family surname. At least we had two communities in which to begin our search.

The next opportunity to leave Baltimore was Saturday, but there was personal business I had to set straight – my martial art classes. I had asked Jon to cover for me too often in the last week, and it wasn't fair to him or the other students.

"So what is it this time?" Jon had asked over the phone, half mocking me, when I told him about Israel.

I explained of course, and he didn't object. To make it up to him, we had a long, private session early on Sunday morning, followed later by a general martial arts class for eighteen students. For two hours I worked the older group extra hard, with endless repetitions of kicks, punches, combination moves, and forms. I looked at every student one-by-one in the latter half of the session, and spontaneously awarded promotions to deserving individuals. By the end of the morning, I had a class dripping with sweat, but everyone was satisfied with the work-out and instruction. I promised the students a month free of charge to assuage my guilt at running out on them again.

"Eileen, did you see the bathroom? It's unbelievable."

The voice from the man across the aisle to my left brought me back to the present. We were in the rear section of an almost full U.S. Airways flight from Philadelphia to Jerusalem. The late booking didn't leave us much in the choice of seats, however there was a pair together on the aft starboard side and that was perfect – an aisle for me and a window for Katie. The aircraft looked new with personal LED lighting overhead, and touch-screen monitors in the back of every seat. Plus, as I just overheard from my neighbor, the bathrooms were impressive.

The man to my left, a gentleman in his early forties with long legs and salt and pepper hair, continued speaking to his wife in an excited voice that I could clearly hear: "Everything is spotless. The fixtures are sleek, they have great lines and soft action on the touch handles, and the paper towels are a decent quality and fully stocked."

"Howard, you're getting excited over the bathroom? What did you expect? Of course everything is clean and fresh and full. It's still the beginning of the flight. Later on it'll get gross." Howard's wife on the other side of him – he had called her Eileen – was on the petite side, wearing a pair of small oval glasses, and blue jeans and a feminine black T-shirt with modest lace along the neckline and sleeves.

I actually had recognized the couple as soon as they had sat down adjacent to me. We shared a table at a banquet for an Israeli dignitary a number of months ago. It was an odd coincidence we were on the same flight, and if they didn't recognize me, that was fine, considering what happened that evening. Putting those particular images away, I turned to see Katie still sleeping next to me. Despite her excitement for the trip, Katie had passed out almost immediately when she had started reading a paperback. It was still clutched in her lap.

Howard, the man across the aisle leaned toward me, "Hey, do you have grandkids? No, of course you don't. You're too young. Well, they're the best. We have a son and daughter-in-law outside of Tel Aviv who had a kid about 6 months ago, and he's the best. I have pictures on my phone. Let me show you."

"Howard," his wife smacked him on the arm, "leave him alone." Eileen leaned forward and looked at me. "You have to forgive him. He's such a jerk sometimes. He doesn't know when to stop talking."

"It's okay," I smiled. "Enthusiasm is good."

The husband caught my eye again. He had put down his phone, but was now just staring at me at me with an intense gaze. His eyes were bright and intelligent, and behind them, I knew his mind was running a search. I could tell. After another moment it came: "Hey, I know you. I've seen you before." An additional second passed and then, "You sat at our table at that banquet for Eitan Lev, that Israeli running for Prime Minister."

I nodded but didn't say anything.

"Eileen, look who it is."

"I know, Howard, I recognized him before."

"Well, why didn't you say anything?"

"Because he probably doesn't want to be bothered."

Eileen remembered what had happened that night and what I did, but must not have wanted to say anything.

Now it all clicked for Howard, whose eyes lit up as he looked at me. "You're that guy who—"

I raised my eyebrows.

"Leave him alone, Howard."

The man looked at me again, then dropped his voice, slightly, "*Kol ha-kavod*, great job."

I just nodded.

Howard turned away and pulled a golf magazine from a backpack under the seat in front of him. He looked at me again, nodded a final time, then turned to his magazine.

"Nice of him not to mention you were with another woman." Katie still had her head against the bulkhead and her eyes closed. She obviously had heard the entire exchange. Without opening her eyes, she slid her arm through mine. I leaned over and kissed her on the side of the head.

I settled back. There was still much to think about. Mainly, what the hell had Josh gotten into and why did someone want to kill him? With the help of the Shin Bet we'd work on all the various pieces. On the personal side, there was Katie and her own demons. Maybe she'd check out the archives at Yad Vashem; maybe not.

Besides the Josh business, I wanted to see Nate and Rachel D'Allesandro's daughter who was living up north. She had been through a great deal, and had bounced back magnificently. Or so I thought. When I saw her a few months ago, she looked terrific. Apparently, according to the D'Allesandros, something had changed. A visit to see her was also a priority.

All this would have to wait more than the eight hours of air travel ahead of us. For now, the A330 was our home; two narrow aisles dividing three columns of high-backed blue cushioned seats, totaling 96 in our rear cabin alone, all packed with people sleeping, reading, and walking around restlessly.

Finally, after ten and a half hours in the air, we banked over the

Israel coastline. Katie had a magnificent view of greater Tel Aviv, as well as of the less dense areas to the northeast. When we touched down, the cabin erupted in applause, and ten minutes later we were making our way along the top level of the circular terminal.

We soon headed down to ground level along a wide, brightly lit, very long ramp. Katie, who had a blue backpack over her shoulder, turned to me: "Why do all these walks from the plane have to be so long? I mean, I know the planes can't pull up to the baggage area."

"Are you grumpy? You sound grumpy."

"No, I'm happy to be here. I'm *ecstatic* to be here. I just need a shower and a change of clothes."

"You're a whiner. Had I known you were a whiner, I would have re-thought this whole thing." I looked through the windows on our left, which showed a manicured lawn and some access roads. "I don't know about other airports, but one reason the walk here is so long is to give Israeli security the opportunity to run you through recognition software and scans."

"Scans?"

"They check your facial bone structure. Want to make sure you're not in their database of terrorists."

She just looked at me and I nodded.

When we entered Passport Control, we had to split up. "This is where I leave you." In front of us were a row of booths, set up in staggered pairs. Some were marked for citizens; others for guests. "I enter and leave the country on an Israeli passport. I made *aliyah* to serve in the army, remember?"

She took out her American passport, and stood nearby in the line for visitors. Katie's Passport Control officer was a well-groomed, twenty-something man wearing a small, black knitted *kippah*, while mine was a young woman, blonde, wearing narrow framed glasses. She looked up at me when I approached, then once more after checking her screen. In Hebrew she welcomed me back.

Baggage claim went smoothly, we passed through customs without a problem, and found ourselves deposited into the arrivals hall. As we came through the sliding doors we were greeted with a mass of people awaiting friends and relatives. I paused for a moment, scanning the faces.

"Expecting someone?" Katie inquired.

"Last time Amit sent a friend with a package. Papers and stuff." The *stuff* was a 9mm Glock and ammo. After another moment, "Nope, no welcoming committee. Let's get our rental."

Everything continued smoothly. Outside the terminal and across the street was the parking garage and shuttle for the rental car agencies. Fifteen minutes after pulling into the off-site office we were driving southeast toward Jerusalem along Highway 1 in a graphite colored Mazda3. Overhead, the sky was bright with the still-high May sun.

As we passed the interchange for the town of Lod I heard myself speak in an announcer voice: "Israel is a country the size of New Jersey, but much more narrow. From north to south it's about 260 miles. You can drive the entire country from top to bottom in under 6 hours."

Katie just looked at me.

"It's width, well, that varies on whose definition of borders you choose. Excluding the West Bank, it's about 9 miles wide at one point."

"You can stop now, Mr. I'm-Going-to-Teach-the-Geography-Impaired-Woman. I've done my homework. We're driving along the coastal plain." Katie put on her own announcer voice, totally making fun of me: "Coastal plains run along the Mediterranean. Then, moving east is a mountainous ridge that runs north to south."

"From top to bottom, like a spine." I supplemented. "To its east of the ridge is the Jordan Valley in the north and the Arava Valley in the south."

Katie glared at me.

"Okay, I'm going to stop talking now."

She laughed, and we continued driving up into the Judean Hills. The coastal plains as Katie had described, had given way to more rugged, rolling land, with hills and valleys to either side. Additionally, the hills became covered with forested areas of Cyprus and pine trees. We continued to climb, driving along a curving highway that centuries ago must have been a trade route through a pass in the mountains. At one point we had tall walls of rock to either side.

Fifty minutes after leaving the airport, we wound our way up into Jerusalem proper. The incline crested, revealing streets crowded with rush hour traffic. Cars were backed up at every stoplight, and streets seemingly went in every direction. The god of urban planning had passed over this city. One neighborhood abutted the next, and street names changed at every intersection. Fortunately, all this was familiar.

Our hotel, the Prima Kings, was located in the city center at a major crossroads along King George Street. There was no parking on King George, but fortunately I found a spot a few blocks away down Agron Street, next to Independence Park.

I began to parallel park into a legitimate space on the sidewalk. "Are we here?" Katie asked.

"Our hotel is up the street, but I want to do some shopping first. We'll come back for the suitcases."

After locking the car, I led Katie down Agron, past the American Consulate, and then onto a small road that cut through the park. The far end brought us to alleyways and narrow streets lined with restaurants, jewelry shops, and clothing stores. Eventually, we wound our way onto Yafo Street.

One of the busiest streets in town, Yafo had a sleek light rail system running through its middle, with sidewalks and shops set back to either side. In this stretch, not far from Ben Yehuda, Yafo Street was a shoe lover's paradise. There was shop after shop of shoe stores, carrying everything from name brand shoes to knock-offs. Owners' wares spilled out onto the sidewalk beside each entryway. I held Katie's hand as we moved down the sidewalk, which at this hour – still the afternoon rush – was jammed with people walking and shopping. Any number of times we had to step off the curb to move around men and women who had stopped to examine a display.

Finally, between a store selling flip-flops and one selling women's pumps, we found a small clothing store. I knew exactly what I wanted. In a matter of minutes, I had tried on and bought two pairs of black jeans and five button down shirts, some solid and some pin stripes. We were out the door in what must have been record time.

I handed Katie a bag of shirts while I carried the bag of pants. "So what's the deal?" Katie asked as we headed back up Yafo. "I know you brought clothes with you."

"I did, but I wanted something local. The clothes here are similar to ours, but the cut and styles are slightly different."

"And you don't want to look American."

"Something like that. It has to do with blending in."

"And how far down does this dressing like an Israeli go? Don't you need Israeli style underwear, too?" she asked playfully. "Are those cut differently?"

"I'll never tell, and, besides, I'm completely covered in that department."

"We'll have to see about that."

"I take that as a statement of intent of something yet to be explored."

I pulled Katie closer as we moved along with the stream of commuters and shoppers on the sidewalk. Consistent with any metropolitan area, men and women were dressed in shorts, jeans, T-shirts, tank-tops, dresses, halters, and tight-fitting tops. Juxtaposed with this, and seemingly out of place, were religious men dressed in black suits and white shirts, chasids with long black coats, and Arab women with scarf covered heads and faces.

I slowed, spotting an electronics store. "One more stop." I pulled Katie into the store, where I bought two rechargeable, disposable phones, new SIM cards, and more minutes than I could use in a month.

We continued walking. Fifty feet later, "One more stop," I said again.

We were approaching a small kiosk with the sign "CHANGE"

next to various symbols for currency – the dollar, the Euro, the pound. I stepped in and converted a wad of cash into shekels. The cash had come from the man who had hired me – the one dead in a parking lot – plus his partner, and I felt slightly unethical about using it, because I wasn't doing all this for them, per se.

We headed back up Agron Street to our car, collected our luggage, and up the hill to the Prima Kings. Located on a busy corner, we stepped up the hotel's Jerusalem stone steps, past an ever-present armed security person – in this instance a young, blond haired man – and into the air-conditioned lobby.

The reception desk was straight ahead, across a white marble floor. To our right was a large, L-shaped carpeted lounge area, filled with upholstered chairs and couches. For the most part the room was empty, but there were a few casually dressed guests relaxing. We approached the reception desk, but didn't make it.

"Major Aronson?"

A young, auburn haired woman got out of a cushioned armchair to our right. She was carrying a small black gym bag.

"Gidon," I corrected as she approached.

"I'm Officer Malkiely." No handshake was offered.

She was in her late twenties, small, at five-four, but not slight. She was dressed in black slacks, and a light blue cotton top. On her right hip was a holstered automatic. It looked like a SIG. She walked with confidence. "Regards from David Amit." She handed me the gym bag.

As I took it from her, I could feel that it had something solid inside, something with a little weight to it. "Thank you." I introduced Katie: "Katie Harris, Officer Malkiely."

They shook hands.

Malkiely smiled. "Call me Ronit."

She hadn't offered *me* her first name. As she and Katie exchanged pleasantries, I looked at the Shin Bet officer who was petite but solid. Her shoulders had a slope to them like an athlete's, someone who uses her upper body muscles. Women lacrosse players had a build like that, strong shoulders and arms. Boxers too. Malkiely's brown eyes certainly had an energy to them; they were large and bright. She had freckles on each cheek, and with her red-brown hair, her face and coloring were quite striking. She probably had a dynamite smile when she laughed.

Officer Malkiely handed me another item, a folded manila envelope. "Mr. Amit wanted you to also have this."

I unfolded the envelope and peered inside to see an item any law enforcement officer in the world would recognize. It was a folded I.D. wallet.

"Shin Bet credentials," she said.

"They're not necessary."

"Mr. Amit thought they could help in the investigation."

"I don't think so." I held out the envelope, not wanting it.

"He insisted that you accept the gift. He worked very hard on his computer to get the look correct."

"I see," I nodded.

Katie turned to me, "What? I don't understand."

"Amit wants me to keep an eye on me. Make it sort of official, like I'm one of his own. Yet, these aren't real." I held up the envelope with the fake ID. "That way if I screw up, he can disown me...can say I forged the ID."

Officer Malkiely didn't say anything.

"I guess Mr. Amit and I will be talking."

Again, no response from Officer Malkiely.

"By the way," I offered, moving on, "I think it's cool that you were waiting for us here when I never told Amit when we'd be arriving."

"Thank you. We try."

"Good recon."

Katie turned to me. "What do you mean?"

"They checked flight manifests and then followed us coming out of the car rental office. Three teams?"

Ronit Malkiely nodded.

"They had eyes on us the entire time...the drive here, on Yafo Street, on Agron. Good training exercise. Whose idea?"

"Mine."

"Nice. It's a good team."

"But you spotted them."

"I have more experience than they do."

"They need more practice."

"Still, you should compliment them."

Officer Malkiely probably didn't expect that reaction from me. She smiled. I was right. She had a terrific smile. "You're very kind."

"But give them more practice."

She nodded. "Of course."

Katie and I headed back toward the reception desk. "Major," Ronit called.

"Gidon," I corrected again.

"Mr. Amit wants to see us at 9:00 tomorrow morning."

"Us?"

"I'll pick you up at 8:40. Shouldn't take long to get there. It's around the corner from the Supreme Court building."

"*Us?* What do you mean?"

She smiled again, and this time I didn't like it as much. "We're partners."

21

"You should have seen the look on your face."

We were in our room, in the shower actually. I was rinsing my hair. "Partners. That's not going to happen." I let the water run down my face. "It's Amit playing games."

"Why would he do that?"

"I don't know. Why did he want me to have Shin Bet credentials?"

"Thinks it'll make your job easier?"

"No. It'll make my investigation official. Why should he care? And the partner idea? Not good."

"You won her over – Ronit – you know that?" Katie had been soaping her torso and turned away from me to wash off. "She came in not liking you, but you changed that."

"What do you mean?"

"When you complimented her team. That caught her by surprise."

"Didn't really think about it."

Katie turned to face me. "She's very good looking." Katie's face was less than a foot from mine, and the water on her eyelashes made her eyes sparkle.

"Yes, she is," I threaded my finger through her wet hair.

Katie moved closer, wrapping her arms around me. "Just don't charm her too much." She moved her hips to touch mine.

"Charm who?" I smiled, dropped my hands to the curve of her back, and pulled her closer, if that were possible.

∽

Katie had her own room on the 6th floor, just down the hall from mine. That was part of the deal. For her safety it was non-negotiable. It was a small buffer that helped me feel more comfortable if someone came looking for me. At the moment, Katie was in her room, drying her hair and getting dressed for the evening, while I was in my room, charging and setting up the newly purchased cell phones. I was stripped to the waist, clad only in my new black jeans and a pair of well-worn black Reeboks. Though the air-conditioner was on, the room was still warm – or maybe it was just me.

With the phones still plugged in, I made two calls. The first was to Kiffi, my tour guide friend. After a brief conversation, she invited us for dinner.

For the next call, I switched to the second phone. This number, dialed from memory, went right to the beep of voice mail; no outgoing message. The receiver's mailbox wasn't full, the service wasn't screwed up, or anything as simple as that. To me, it meant the owner didn't want his voice heard. Ibrahim was a very cautious man. In the past when I made these calls, I never knew whether he had been compromised, and I didn't want to give anyone an excuse for any distrust. These calls always worried me, but there was no other way to contact my friend.

"Zahir," I spoke enthusiastically, "it's Kevin. I'm in from London and I'm ready for that amazing dinner you promised. Where was it, Ramallah? Anyway, you've got the number. Call me when you're available."

I hung up, feeling even warmer than I had a few minutes ago. The wrong number performance was pretty lame, but that's all there was. I truly didn't know if Ibrahim were alive or dead, or if I just placed him at risk. Hopefully, he'd call back soon.

Tucking away the negative thoughts, I went to my backpack and pulled out my laptop to check e-mail. Nothing of consequence; just a note from Jon, checking to make sure the trip went smoothly. It was very considerate of him.

Finally, turning to the bed, I looked at the two items that had been dropped next to the pillows: the envelope with the Shin Bet ID and the small black gym bag Officer Ronit Malkiely had brought me. Ignoring the ID packet, I opened the gym bag. Sitting in the bottom was an unloaded .40 Glock 23 in a holster and three filled magazines. I smiled to myself. The gun was the same model I had at home. How did Amit know? Last time he had given me a 9mm, not the .40. It was Amit winking at me, that's for sure.

The holster was black molded carbon fiber with an open top, automatic locking system. I clipped the gun and holster to the belt over my back right pants pocket, then drew the weapon, pulling on the grip while counter-pressing on the holster with my thumb for leverage. Done confidently and with experience, the gun came out freely and smoothly. As was my habit, I inserted a clip, and then ran all 13 rounds through the chamber and ejection port. With the gun empty, I dry fired it a few times, then reloaded the magazine and inserted it into the grip. That done, I pulled out a gray pin-stripe button down shirt from a shopping bag, and put it on, leaving the shirttail out. There was a slight bulge in back, but as this was Israel it wouldn't be – fortunately or unfortunately – an unfamiliar sight.

I looked back at the envelope containing the Shin Bet ID, questioning whether to take it along. Before I had a chance to decide, there was a vibration coming from one of the phones on an end table. It was the second phone, the one that I used to call Ibrahim. Without disconnecting the charger, I checked the screen. There was a single word text message: BAKLAVA. I smiled, grabbed both phones, and headed out, purposefully leaving the Shin Bet ID on the bed.

∽

Kiffi's place was off of trendy, Emek Refaim, a street popular with American émigrés and tourists. Lined with cafes and restaurants of every sort, from pizza shops and ice cream parlors to upscale dining establishments, the dominant language was probably English, no doubt to the consternation of long-time Israeli residents. The location itself belied that it was in an urban area, for Emek Refaim was a relatively narrow, tree-lined street, with the ambiance of seclusion from the heat and intensity of downtown Jerusalem, a few miles away. Residential streets in this neighborhood were immediately off of the main road, weaving right and left with no apparent pre-conceived design. Kiffi's apartment, for instance, was tucked off a side road no wider than a large car. Fortunately, her building was set back in a landscaped cul-de-sac with enviable parking spaces in front.

After locking up, we walked to a break in a vine covered fence and down a shaded path to a small courtyard. Kiffi's front door was on the ground level of a three story, old Jerusalem stone building. At eye level an engraved glass plaque announced, "Kiffi & Tal; Merav & Noam." I knocked.

Three seconds later the door swung open to reveal a thirty-something woman, a head shorter than me, dressed in a modest scooped neck teal top, a jean skirt, and sandals. The ends of her wavy, dark hair partially hid a necklace of small silver, filigreed squares inset with red stones.

"Gidon!" she unhesitatingly threw her arms around me and kissed me on the cheek.

"Kiffi, *shalom*." I hugged and kissed her back.

Behind her a man, a good head taller than me, with close cut dark hair and wearing a sky blue shirt, came over, holding out his hand. "Gidon, *shalom*."

"Tal, *ma nishma*." I said. How are you? I gave him a hug, too, and then introduced Katie. There were kisses all around and we moved inside.

The foyer opened onto a spacious living room and dining room. Straight ahead was the living room, framed by two small couches on the left and at right angles to each other. On the right, sitting on a low black wood console against the wall, was a large screen television

– turned on to the news. To our left was the dining room table, set for six. In its center was an empty space – probably for the main course – while miscellaneous spreads, such as hummus, babaganoush, and matboucha were on small plates about the table. There were loaves of pita stacked on plates at either end.

"So what's going on?" Kiffi asked.

"It's a long story."

"We should sit down," Kiffi's husband Tal proposed, pointing to a couch.

"I wish I could." Everyone looked me. "I have a meeting. It just came up before we left the hotel."

"Gidon!" Kiffi said.

"I'm sorry. Really."

"We're grilling chicken and hot dogs."

"I wish I could stay. Katie can fill you in. I really do need to go. It's important."

Kiffi turned to Katie. "Does he do this to you at home?"

Katie didn't say anything.

"Of course he does," Kiffi answered for her. "Take something before you go. Grab a piece of chicken from the grill."

"Don't have time," I said, but I did take a piece of pita, scooped out some babaganoush, and stuffed it into my mouth. "Thanks."

Kiffi saw me to the door. "You could have warned me."

"Really, I just found out fifteen minutes ago."

"Where's the meeting?" Katie was standing behind her, watching me.

"Near Ma'ale Adumim." I mentioned a community east of Jerusalem.

She just looked at me, like "Really?" She knew me too well. I was heading a little further east into a Palestinian area, but didn't want to say it.

"I'll be a couple of hours at least. Can you take Katie back to the hotel if it gets too late?"

"Of course."

I looked over Kiffi's shoulder to Katie. "I'm really sorry."

"It's part of the deal," she smiled.

I went back and kissed Katie and then kissed Kiffi. As Kiffi kissed me on the cheek, she innocuously put her put arm around my waist and felt the gun holstered in back. Our eyes met for a quick second and I saw her nod ever-so-slightly.

"I'll call when I'm on my way back."

Ma'ale Adumim, the community I had mentioned to Kiffi, was on the outskirts of Jerusalem, but as she had guessed, I kept going... for another ten minutes or so. Highway 1, the highway we had taken from the airport, continued on the eastern side of Jerusalem as well. And, just as it wound its way up to Jerusalem, on this side it descended into the rift valley toward the Dead Sea. It was a different planet on this side of Jerusalem. As green and forested as some hills were on the other side of Jerusalem, here there was mostly desolation. Just rolling, empty sandy hills, some animals clustered in herds, but not a person to be seen, even though there were the occasional huts and tents of Bedouin shepherds. In baffling contrast to the squalor, in some cases there were small satellite dishes on the roofs and late modern vehicles in the yards. Mixed in were rusting, discarded older vehicles as well.

Five minutes beyond Ma'ale Adumim I descended past a sign declaring "Sea Level."

The sun was low on the horizon behind me, but its golden rays shone into my eyes off the rear-view mirror. Finally, after having dropped close to three thousand feet in altitude, the road flattened and a gas station appeared over on the right. A nearby sign said "Jericho" with an arrow to the left. I took the turn.

The northbound, dual lane road cut through flat land to either side. With the mountains in the distance to the right, and closer ones on my left, this was the parched bottom of seemingly lifeless valley. There were some low scrubs, but not much else. The outside temperature gauge on my dash read 35ºC/95ºF. I believed it.

As the road continued, a large yellow sign announced I'd soon be entering the Palestinian Authority jurisdiction. To the left, an Israeli army patrol of about 15 soldiers in full gear – packs, helmets, assault rifles – were walking northward in two columns beside the road. I hoped they had plenty of water.

In a matter of minutes, I approached an Israeli checkpoint – it looked like a turnpike toll – checking vehicles coming out of Jericho. I slowed as I went by, observing a line of about ten vehicles divided between two lanes. On my side of the road, I came up to a Palestinian checkpoint with a pair of Palestinian Authority policemen, one on each side of the narrow lane. I slowed, but they waved me on. Within another few minutes I was heading into town.

Despite the Biblical references to Jericho, there were no city walls, or remains of walls, to be seen. This wasn't *that* Jericho. The Jericho of antiquity, the city that Joshua had marched around seven times, was about a mile and a quarter from the northwestern outskirts of this more contemporary town, and was an archeological site. The Jericho I was driving through was laid out like spokes on a wheel, with all roads pretty much leading to central hub with a small park as its focus.

I pulled into the center of town via one of the spokes, and circled the small park that doubled as the area's focal point. The central square was exactly that: a modest rectangle with a circular fountain at its heart and tall palm trees standing, giant-like in the corners, peering down on everything below. Back along the hub, were two and three story boxy, square buildings. One building was a bank with huge metal plate declaring, "Established in 1880." There was also a large restaurant winding around a corner with a red neon marquee against a black background. Lettering was in English and Arabic, with Coca-Cola logos streaming across the awning. Yellow taxi cabs were everywhere, with their distinctive green on white license plates. Israeli plates were black on orange – as was mine. A minaret poked up behind the buildings behind another street.

As I drove slowly through town, no one took notice. Jericho was a sleepy town and drivers with Israeli plates were not uncommon. Not long ago there was a casino in town popular with Israelis…until radicals used its roof to shoot at Israeli soldiers. The army closed it down.

I drove along a street lined with clothing shops, small restaurants, green grocers, and electronics stores…stores that in other cities would take up long avenues, but here were all crammed into narrow stands. Traffic was bumper-to-bumper and pedestrians walked in between stopped vehicles. It had been a while since I was here, but neither the streets nor the traffic had changed. Finally, after a few blocks of creeping headway, I turned down a narrow road, then left onto another side street. A small plaza with a few outdoor cafés loomed ahead. I parked, and then headed out on foot.

The plaza, like everywhere else, was lined with one story old shops. On my left I passed a shwarma stand, a housewares store, a candy store, a pizza shop, a shoe store, and a hardware store. On the far side of the hardware store was a small café that had two roundtables set up on the sidewalk. I threaded my way between the two tables and stopped in front of the shop. In the entryway was a glass display case with baked goods – breads, rolls, pastries, and cakes. On the left at right angles to the display, and heading into the shop was a waist high, well-used white counter. I stepped up to it. A clean shaven man in a plaid shirt and black trousers stood on the other side with his back partially to me. He was hovering over a wooden counter, broad spatula in hand, with a glob of chocolate spread on it. He was applying a thin layer to sheet of filo dough. Next to the dough was a small mound of chopped nuts. He looked up as I appeared in the doorway.

"Hi," I said in English. "Good evening. Glad you're still open."

"Hello," he responded also in English. "Yes, for another hour. One moment, please." He finished spreading the chocolate on the filo, put the spatula down, and came over.

"You're Youssef, right?"

"I am."

"I was here several years ago, and I had the most amazing baklava. Do you still make it?"

His face lit up. "I have a tray cooling right now."

"*Sababa.* Can I get some and a glass of your delicious tea as well?"

"My pleasure. Would you like to sit here," he pointed to a small, round table with a single cane chair, "or outside?"

"Outside. If I eat here and look at all the desserts, I'll want everything."

"That wouldn't be so bad," he smiled.

I stepped outside and sat at the closer outdoor table, facing the open square in front of me.

As I looked around, I noted that a few stores had changed since my last visit. There was a new clothing store over on the left, and where a video store had been now stood a store selling scarfs and dresses. To my right, I noted the hardware store looked pretty much the same, except it now also carried additional housewares: there was a display of dishes, flanked by two metal rotating racks of kitchen utensils…ladles, timers, bottle openers, measuring cups. Brooms were leaning against the storefront, next to plastic storage bins. Across from the entry door I could see several pallets of six-pack, two-liter bottles of water.

Youssef brought out a plate with four pieces of baklava and a small glass of red-golden hot tea. He even gave me two small napkins.

"Thank you."

He nodded and walked back into his shop. I took a bite of the baklava, and it melted in my mouth. The nuts and honey were amazing. The honey was not overpowering, as they sometimes are, and there were just enough nuts. They must have been soaked in something. Youssef was an artist.

I picked up the glass of tea and blew lightly across the top. As I did so, I watched four young men, all in their early twenties, sit in front of a café across the square, perhaps a hundred feet away. At some point a waiter came over them, but they waved him off.

Off to my right along the narrow road, an ancient man in a dirty white *kaffiyah*, dirty white shirt and dark pants was pushing a cart of melons. The old man was so slight I was impressed he could even budge the thing.

"Is everything okay?" Youssef came out.

"Perfect. *Achlah*."

He smiled and went back inside. I sipped some tea. It was just slightly sweet and a perfect balance to the baklava. To my right, a teenager came out of the hardware store and began moving one of the rotating racks inside. I looked at my watch. 7:45. I had hoped that Ibrahim would be sitting down with me by now, but that wasn't happening.

The sun had dropped enough to lay long shadows across the plaza in front of me. At the café on the other side, the man on the extreme right – he was wearing urban camouflage pants and a T-shirt in the Palestinian colors – stood and walked into the shop behind him. The entryway was dark and he disappeared inside.

Ibrahim was overdue. He was never late. If anything, he was early to get the lay of the land. His life was a dangerous game, and I wasn't making it easier, that's for sure. For a moment, I wondered if he were the person who had texted me to come to this spot. Who else would have known that a few years ago we had met here multiple times over several months? Unless – under extreme duress – he had given up his contacts. If that were the case, he was long dead, and all that awaited me was a lot of trouble.

The young man in the camouflage pants came out of the café, leaned over his three buddies and looked my way. He said something, and they all stood up and stared at me.

Okay, what was this all about? They didn't have the look of Palestinian Security, and they didn't look like punks, either. Palestinian areas were typically filled with roving bands of thugs, but not here in Jericho. The city was usually calm. This was something else.

They began to walk toward me. Above my right back pocket I could feel the .40 Glock in its holster.

Shit. I could just see the headlines: "AMERICAN TEACHER ARRESTED FOR INCITING RIOT IN JERICHO." Or, more likely, "FORMER IDF OFFICER KILLS FOUR PALESTINIAN MEN. SHOT RESISTING ARREST." I was glad I left the Shin Bet ID in the hotel room.

As the group approached, I could see that, indeed, all were in their early twenties. Two of the three were more swarthy than their friends, but all had short haircuts, and each walked with a bit of attitude. The question was, did any have guns?

They came straight toward me, looking neither right nor left. The two young men on the left wore shirts with Nike logos, one wore an Italian football team jersey, and the fourth had his nationalist colors.

When they were ten feet away, I took another bite of the baklava and another sip of tea. At the same time, I leaned slightly forward to be sure I had solid footing on the ground.

My guess was the man in the Palestinian T-shirt and camouflage pants would be the one speaking.

I was right. "You need to leave." That's all he said.

Unlike those guys in the movies, I did not continue drinking my tea. I set it down away from me. How to react? Humor was the universal language. Maybe simple conversation would ease the conflict. "Your English is pretty good. How'd you know I spoke English? Can't be my clothes."

The one on the extreme left was tense; not in the mood. "Leave! Now!" He had the back of his right hand facing me down by his pants leg and cupped slightly. He was attempting to conceal a knife.

Youssef, the owner of the bakery, came out with a length of pipe. He yelled at the men in Arabic, but they didn't move.

"Youssef," I turned to him. "Thank you. It will be fine."

He looked at me.

"Really, I'll be fine. I'm not going to get hurt."

He hesitantly backed into his shop but stood near the display case, laying the pipe on the counter within reach. If he got to swinging, it would be a definite problem for the person on the other end.

"Leave!" the man on the left shouted again. He flavored his command with several colorful Arabic epithets.

I dropped my hands so they were under the table and braced my feet on the ground. If any one of them reached for a gun, I'd stand, flipping the table at the same time. Before the table would be halfway up, I'd move on them.

The boy working at the hardware shop to my right came out, looked at the quartet, and moved another rack inside the shop. Business as usual? Behind me, Youssef remained still.

"Go!" the young man on the left said yet again. He flicked his right wrist and brought his knife forward. He was still too far away to do anything. If I were to deal with these guys, they had to come closer.

"Threatening me from there is not a good tactic, you know. It's not really a threat."

A muezzin began the call to prayer, and the man on the left yelled something from the bottom of his throat and ran toward me with his knife pointing my way.

I sprung up from the table grabbing his wrist, simultaneously straightening and twisting his arm so the inside of his elbow faced up. Pivoting on the balls of my feet, I scooped my left arm and shoulder under the now-locked arm. Then, in one swift motion, I yanked down on the locked arm. There was a distinctive crack as his arm broke out of the shoulder joint.

Without slowing, I raised my right knee and kicked out fluidly with my heel square into the second man's sternum. He went sprawling back and down. The third man tried taking advantage of my involvement with his friend by coming behind me and punching me in the head. I turned and parried the blow six inches away, and then punched him twice in rapid succession just below the orbit of his right eye. I felt his cheek bones crack on the second punch. The fourth man, the one in camouflage pants, was probably the most trained. He tried throwing a spinning back kick, but I moved forward, stifling it. With a front kick to the side of his knee, I broke his supporting leg. He collapsed to the ground.

I went around to where he had fallen. He was the leader. Someone else had sent him my way, but this man led this group. I raised my foot to stamp on his temple.

"*Waqefuh!*" a voice bellowed.

I looked up. A tall, husky man with salt and pepper hair, round face, and mustache was approaching. "*Waqefuh?*" I said to him. "'Halt'?"

"I thought that would get your attention."

The tall man with the mustache moved past me and continued toward Youssef, who was still at the entryway to his shop. As the man walked, I noticed he had a slight limp; he was favoring his left leg. He said something in rapid Arabic to Youssef, and then gave him some cash. Youssef responded and they both nodded to each other. The big man came back over to me. "Let's leave before the PA police get here."

"What did you say to Youssef?"

"I told him you were a crazy CIA agent, but to say to the police you were Mossad."

"Jesus, Ibrahim."

I walked back to Youssof, who just looked at me.

"I'm neither CIA nor Mossad, please know that. I teach karate, that's all."

He looked at the bodies sprawled on the ground. "It works. Still, go. Quickly."

"Thank you."

I went back to Ibrahim, and we began walking away at a fast pace. He turned to me. "Feel better?"

"Yes. What if we want to come back for more baklava?"

My friend smiled at me and we hustled across the small plaza.

22

"You can't seem to stay away, my friend," Ibrahim said, as we climbed into his white Subaru. More than half of it was covered with a clingy sandy residue. He pulled away from the curb and turned down a narrow alleyway.

"Last time I was here I was working. It was personal."

"And this time?"

"Someone's trying to kill a rabbi friend. There's a Gaza connection."

"So you're here again. You can't really leave this country it seems." He pulled onto a dimly lit two-lane road, with houses on either side.

"Two guys tried to kill me. Came into my dojo. Actually, another two guys tried to kill me as I was walking with a lady friend in downtown Baltimore."

"A lady friend? Is this the one you mentioned last time?"

"Yes. I think so."

His mind went back to what I said earlier: "Someone from Gaza—"

"I think."

"Someone from Gaza tries to kill you and here you are."

"It's personal."

"And now you don't trust the Israeli Police or the Shin Bet to work on this?" He turned to me. "As I said, you can't stay away from this country, can you?"

"It's personal," I repeated.

"This whole country is personal for us. That's our problem."

"Maybe so. Can we talk about this Gaza thing?"

He pulled to a stop next to the fence of a car repair shop. "What makes you think Gaza has anything to do with this?"

I summed up what's been going on…Friday night at the rabbi's, the attack on me at Harborwalk, the attempted hit at my dojo.

"And you know they were from Gaza because…?"

"I don't know they were from Gaza. Just that they had a Gaza phone number in their cell phone." I gave him the number. There was no need for him to write it down. Ibrahim remembered everything.

"What else?"

"The guy who's probably running all this is French. His name is Belard." I took out a copy of his picture and gave it to him.

"There are a number of French businessmen in Gaza. I don't know the name 'Belard,' though. But then this may not be his real name either."

I nodded.

"And if he was in charge of the assassination team, he's not the chief."

I nodded again.

"There are always international investors in Gaza," Ibrahim commented. "French, German, Russian, Iranian, Saudi. Money is being poured in. There are some beautiful homes and hotels…"

"But…?"

"As you know, there is great unevenness in the population."

"Keep the masses poor and unhappy and focus their problems outside."

"It's worked for centuries. I'll see what I can find out."

We let a moment go by. In those seconds, I looked at my friend in the wash of a white street light. He had put on a few pounds since I saw him last – his face was a little more round – but other than that, he looked pretty good.

"Yes, I put on more kilos."

"It's the baklava."

He laughed.

"So the four guys at the café…"

"My men."

I raised my eyebrows.

"Four men who wanted to be my men. I told them if they could make you leave I would consider letting them work for me."

"You didn't let them have guns."

"I didn't want you to kill them. Too complicated to explain to the Palestinian Authority."

"But you *are* the PA."

"My friend, I am still alive because I float above the Palestinian Authority. I am friends to everyone."

"Bullshit. Everyone's afraid of you."

"You and I both know that is not accurate. No one is immune in my world. Alliances are like smoke. They shift with the wind. The only certainty is that religious fanatics are getting stronger all the time. Even I am questioned sometimes because I don't have a beard."

"It's time for you to leave, I keep telling you this. Move up north at least. There are plenty of beautiful places in the north."

"That's what Amira wants me to do. She grew up in the north. She still has family there."

"You should do it."

"I tell you what, my friend. I'll move up north if you'll join me. You don't have to even be my neighbor, if you don't want to be."

"I'm not ready to come back yet."

"Your new lady friend?"

I laughed. "She'd probably *want* to come."

"So?"

"I can't. This isn't the place for me anymore."

"Yet here you are."

"Yup."

Ibrahim only smiled.

"Your men at the café didn't have to push so hard."

"What do you mean?"

"They didn't all have to come over. One of them could have offered me something to drink, try a little charm. Invite me to just leave for a little while…maybe go for a walk. Would that have satisfied your criteria?"

"Criteria?"

"Your requirements to get me to leave."

"Yes. Would not have mattered. Before they started I knew what they were going to do," he commented. "All they know here is push, shove, get angry."

"Not everyone is like that. We both have met brave people in our travels."

"It's true. And we need to protect them."

"We do," I agreed softly. A car came up on our left and kept going. "How are your kids doing?"

"They are in England with Amira. We have relatives there. Had to get them away from the brainwashing. That's what I worry about the most. The children are being taught to hate."

He absent-mindedly rubbed his left thigh just underneath the steering wheel.

"I'm sorry I had to shoot you." There was a moment a few months ago when I needed to put Ibrahim in my crosshairs – literally.

"It was necessary to save my life."

"We save each other's lives again and again." A moment passed. "It was a helluva shot, though, missing the bone and the artery."

He smiled. "I always liked your modesty."

Another car passed us, though this one came from in front, and passed us without slowing down. Its headlights lit the interior of our car. We each covered our faces. After it had disappeared: "So, who are the French investors you know in Gaza?"

"I know of three. Barbier, Gagnon, and Leveque. Don't know them personally and haven't heard anything about them. Just know they are businessmen. One's involved with natural gas production, one is in construction, and one is an importer."

"Who is who?"

"Barbier is gas production, Gagnon construction, and Leveque is the importer."

"Maybe Belard works for one of them."

"Maybe."

"Barbier, Gagnon, and Leveque," I repeated. "Guess I can look them up on the internet."

"Do that. And ask your friends in the Shin Bet."

"I have a meeting in the morning."

"Good." He let a moment pass. "Now tell me about your lady friend."

23

On the way back to Jerusalem I had a lot to think about. Mainly, about a possible connection between Belard and one of the businessmen Ibrahim had mentioned. This seemed to expand the breadth of what's been going on, though of course, all it did was add more names to all of this. What could Josh have possibly done to a French businessman to warrant a kill order? I had no idea. The only thing I could come up with was that his Torah rescue business had somehow intersected with one of those guys. Maybe he pissed off an investor, though I couldn't see Josh doing that. There was also Josh's competitor in the mix. Maybe.

The route back into Jerusalem was simply the other side of Highway 1, just heading west instead of east. I was soon back above sea level, and now the darkness was hiding the desolate landscape I had seen earlier to either side. The closer I got to Jerusalem, the more populated the area had become. Housing communities appeared where a few years ago there were none. Israel always impressed me with its ever-present construction activities. Israelis were always building, widening, creating, much to the consternation of their enemies.

While Highway 1 was still climbing out of the rift valley, I passed through a checkpoint on the outskirts of the city. Katie would be back at the hotel by now. When I had called Kiffi to say I was on my way back, she told me that she had taken Katie to the hotel. As this was the end of a marathon two days of preparing to leave Baltimore, the eleven hour flight, and the time here, Katie had to have been exhausted. It would hit me, too, if I let it.

Right now another concern crept into my head. With the idea that Josh was involved with something beyond Belard, I knew that as I poked around, someone would poke back. It's already happened. Not only that, Katie was now exposed, too, thanks to the guy following us back in Baltimore. Was Katie safer here with me, or at home? "I don't know. I don't know," I said to myself out loud.

One highway merged into another, but traffic always kept moving. The ebb and flow was more manageable now that it was past midnight, and in a few minutes I was in the City Center. I pulled up Agron just as I had earlier today toward the Prima Kings, but there were no spaces. Instead, I crossed the always busy King George Street, past a fountain near the crossroads, and drove through the sleepy area of Rehavia. Cars were parked bumper-to-bumper, lining both sides of the street, with old trees providing a canopy up and down the road. Busy, but calm outdoor cafés lent an air of peaceful city night life. As I turned onto a tucked-away side street, a cavity between two parked cars stared at me unexpectedly. It was a gift, waiting to be taken advantage of. I accepted the invitation and parked comfortably in the wide space. After locking up, I headed back to the hotel, enjoying the walk through the peaceful neighborhood.

By now, the entry doors to the Kings were locked; neither the sliding door nor the revolving one was operating. Instead, a dark haired female guard let me in. Across the empty lobby, the elevators were to the right. In less than a minute I was walking down the gold carpeted floor past my room to Katie's. I listened before inserting my key card. There wasn't a sound. She must have been dead asleep. I really liked the idea of separate rooms. It was the smart thing to do.

I quietly entered the dark room, and waited just inside the door to allow my eyes and other senses to adjust. Katie's bed was around the corner to the left.

There was no sound in the room. Nothing. Just dead air. No breathing sounds, no rustling of sheets…just total…nothing. Katie should have been here. She was falling asleep and so Kiffi had dropped her off. Before stepping forward, I listened and felt the room. There was no one here. I walked forward to see that the bed was still made: bedspread still untouched and pillows undisturbed. I didn't need to turn on the lights to see there were no notes. Katie's suitcase was where she had left it on a stand next to the dresser. Nothing had been touched. This was where she was supposed to be.

I closed her door and walked back down the hall to my room. If she weren't there, I'd check the lobby and then head into the street. I should have bought Katie a phone. Maybe she went for a walk. I guess that was okay. This was her first time in Jerusalem. I could understand wanting to walk around to take in this unique, historical city. On the other hand, back home we definitely had been followed. The guy we had cornered in the industrial park could have taken our pictures somewhere along the way. I never checked his cell phone. If he had forwarded Katie's photo to Belard, Belard could have forwarded them to his boss. But so what? They didn't know we were here. Not yet, right?

I stopped in front of my door. There was a pinpoint of light in the peephole, but no sound came from inside. With my right hand moving on its own toward the holstered Glock, I slipped in the key card with my left, pulled it from the lock, and opened the door. Katie was lying on my bed. It looked like she had just opened her eyes. They had a bloodshot, fuzzy look to them.

"Hi." She came off the bed toward me.

"Hi."

She gave me a hug, then took a step back. "What's wrong?"

I smiled at her, and tried not to blow what was going through my mind out of proportion.

"I met with a friend who gave me some ideas to think about."

"And?"

"And there's a lot to think about." I waited for a moment before going on. I said softly, "I need you to be in your room."

"I know. That's the deal. I came in here to get something I left in your suitcase, I lay down on your bed for a second, and I conked out. I just woke up. Are you okay?"

"Yeah."

"You're pissed at me, aren't you?"

"I just want you to be safe."

"No, you're pissed. I shouldn't be in here. That was our agreement. Let's go back to my room."

We didn't say anything as we walked back to Katie's room. She turned on the light and then went over and sat on the bed.

"So how was the rest of your evening?" I asked, trying to move on.

"Great." Katie responded matter-of-factly. She had just disengaged from my reaction and was simply answering the question. "Kiffi's got a wonderful family. She gave me a phone – it belongs to her son – and she's taking me through the Old City tomorrow. I'll be out of your way."

I moved closer to her. "You're not in my way. I was just a little worried."

"You don't have a handle on this, do you?"

"Not as much as I'd like. Getting there, though."

"Getting there is good."

I reached out and she took my hand. I pulled her up off the bed. Katie moved closer.

"You know, you sleeping in my room probably won't fool anyone."

"Maybe. Maybe not. I just need a few seconds if someone comes a-lookin'."

"All right. You can stay."

"Thank you."

"On one condition. You can't be pissed at me."

"No deal."

"Well then, sleep in your own room."

☙

We fell asleep in Katie's bed, next to each other, but I awoke at five. I had a meeting scheduled in a few hours with David Amit and Officer Malkiely at the local Shin Bet office, and I wanted to be ready. Without disturbing Katie – she was really out – I went back to my room, sat at a small round table in a corner, and turned on my laptop. If we were going to track down Josh and Shelley, I needed their pictures. Fortunately, the shul's website had a picture of him, and Shelley's Facebook page had plenty of both of them. I copied a sampling to a USB drive.

Next I looked up the three Frenchmen Ibrahim had mentioned, Barbier, Gagnon, and Leveque. Each had a substantial write-up and I copied their photos, as well some basic information. Finally, I checked e-mail. The most recent had a return address of Susie Meyers, a subject line stating "Israel itinerary," and an attachment.

It had been five days since I had made the trip to Rhode Island, and had spoken to Mrs. Meyers, the wife of the shop owner who was killed by Belard. She was going to send me a day-by-day log of what she and her husband had done while in Israel. The idea was to check for commonalities with the Mandels when *they* were in Israel. This must have been it. I opened the attachment. That's exactly what it was: a daily breakdown of where they went, where they ate, and who they saw. It was impressive. I saved the document to the same USB drive that had the Mandel pictures.

Now we just needed to find Josh and Shelley and have them do the same thing. I shut down the laptop and went back to Katie's room for another hour or so of sleep.

⚶

The Shin Bet office where I was meeting Amit and Ronit Malkiely was not part of the main Security Services complex in another part of town, but at a satellite building just north of the Supreme Court. It was mid-block on a new side street, one of those access roads that city traffic had turned into a shortcut to avoid other traffic. As in most

Israeli cities, housing space here was also at a premium, so this small street had an equal number of low-rise apartments as well as office buildings. Fortunately, there was a dedicated parking lot around the corner, and all I had to do was show my new ID – which I had the foresight to bring – for access. I backed into a space, locked up, then headed back around to the main point of entry. As I stepped onto the sidewalk toward the entrance, I looked up into an azure sky that had only a few white clouds toward the east. It was just before 9 AM, but the sun was already hot. The rainy season was over and the climate would be like this through the fall.

The government building was set back from the road behind a security fence, so access for pedestrians was through a modest guardhouse. Typical of Israeli security style, entry guards were in a separate screening area away from sensitive buildings. This not only gave guards time to intervene if someone ran their barrier, but also provided a buffer in the event a bomber set off a device at a gate.

I stepped into the air-conditioned guard room that had floor to ceiling glass on all four sides. Straight ahead was a revolving door that led onto a plaza in front of the building itself. Between where I stood and the door were two armed guards standing away from each other, plus an X-ray machine and a walk-through magnetometer. A well-dressed man in a navy blue suit – very unusual for Israel – was ahead of me. Before he even had a chance to put his briefcase on the conveyer for the screening, the guard asked his business, who he was seeing, and whether he was expected. The guard then asked for the man's identification. The well-dressed visitor pulled out his driver's license and handed it over. The security man checked it, and then put the ID in a drawer. He directed the man to step to the side and wait for an escort.

As he turned to me, Officer Malkiely entered through the revolving door. I showed my "official" ID as she spoke with the guard, simultaneously signing the log for me. I nodded to the second guard and Ronit and I headed through the door. We crossed the short courtyard and I had to squint to compensate for the sun reflecting off of the white stone walkway.

"We're on the third floor," Ronit said, entering the building.

As we walked to a stairwell, I asked how her evening was, and she asked the same. Then, more on topic, I turned to her: "So, when did David speak to you about all this?"

"A few days ago. Wanted me to check some of the information you mentioned to him."

"Like…?"

"Like the Gaza phone number."

"Still no results on that?"

She shook her head.

"And here you are chaperoning me."

She smiled a smile that meant she knew something I didn't. Or maybe it was just a look of, "I have better things to do." Either way, it was a nice smile.

We exited onto the third floor and down the hall past open offices to one marked only with a three digit number. This door was closed, but she indicated we should enter. We stepped into a small, brightly lit conference room. Mainly, the room was dominated by a six-foot conference table. Four unopened file folders had been placed in the center. A PC was off to the side at its own workstation, and a flat screen monitor was mounted on the far wall. Only two other people were present, and I knew them both.

Sitting at mid-table on the right was David Amit. I had met him a number of months ago in Baltimore, actually. He was of average height, perhaps in his late thirties. His face was round beneath thinning, dark hair, and he wore black wire rim glasses. I saw that he had some deep wrinkles around the corners of his eyes.

"Gidon, *shalom*. Welcome back." He came over and gave me a firm handshake.

"*Toda rabbah*. Seems like I was just here."

"You remember Commander Dror," he looked across the table to the other man in the room.

"Of course. Commander." Dror wore a police Commander's uniform, which was appropriate because he was Chief of the Jerusalem police.

"Ilan," he corrected the formality. "Welcome back to Jerusalem, Gidon."

I smiled, "*Le shana ha-ba-ah...*" I began to say the classic "Next year in Jerusalem."

"Not what you expected, though," Dror smiled.

Dror was of average height and weight, but I knew his hazel eyes had seen almost everything. He wore reading glasses, but at the moment they were pushed back, resting on top of his shaved head.

"So, what brings you back to us?" Dror asked. Everyone sat. "David told me some things, but I want to hear from you. He may have missed something," he smiled at Amit.

"A little more than a week ago," I began, "two men tried to kill Rabbi Josh Mandel in Baltimore. It was to be a pre-meditated hit that I believed was directed by a man named Belard." I took out my copy of Belard's photo – the one taken at the Hertz office – and showed it around. "The police and I believe that Belard also killed a man in Rhode Island, an elderly businessman. A few days after the rabbi was attacked, two of Belard's men paid me a visit because I was checking into the attack. One of them was carrying a phone with a Gaza number in it. I gave the number to David to check it out."

Amit and Dror nodded at each other.

"What does the rabbi say about all this?" Officer Malkiely asked.

I turned to Ronit. Her eyes had changed. The fun expression she had in them earlier was gone now. She had become quite serious.

"He says he has no idea what's going on. He says he has no enemies, except for some board members at his shul," I smiled. "He was joking about that, of course...the board members."

From Amit: "He has a side business." Amit opened a nearby file folder. "Torah rescue."

I nodded. "He goes all over the world. Not everyone is cooperative. I was told he has had his share of conflicts. One time he was beaten pretty severely."

Amit nodded. "What else?"

"He also has competition. A man named Allan Samuels who doesn't seem to have Josh's moral compass. He's in Israel right now. I'll call his secretary to find out where."

Amit, Dror, and Ronit all made a note of the name, each writing it in a folder.

"And this brought you here?" Dror asked.

"The Gaza number, plus Belard, who is French, and the fact that there are a number of French businessmen in Gaza." I didn't mention that I had just learned that fact last night.

"There *are* a number of French businessmen in Gaza," Amit confirmed. "Are any of them connected to a man named Belard? We don't know."

"What about the Gaza phone number?"

"We're working on tapping it."

From Dror: "Anything else?"

"The man who was killed in Rhode Island spent a few weeks in Israel at the same time as the Mandels. It's the only thing the two have in common that I know of. I have a day-by-day account of when Mr. Meyers was here." I pulled out the USB drive from my pocket and held it up. "I want to match it up with what the Mandels did when they were here."

"The Mandels are now here, correct, trying to escape all of this?" Amit asked.

"They have family here. In Efrat and up north."

"We'll find them," Ronit said and I nodded.

"I have pictures of the family," I held up the USB again.

"We also have photographs," Amit said, pointing to the folders.

I opened the folder closest to me to see a stack of pictures of Josh, Shelley, and their kids. They were mostly the same images I had found online, but there were some additional ones. The others were photos shot at the airport, time stamped at the end of last week. They were taken as Josh and Shelley were in line at passport control.

It was my turn to ask questions: "What's the deal with these French investors in Gaza?"

"Gaza is one of the most corrupt places on the Earth," Dror took this one. "Many foreign countries throw money into Gaza to help them build an economy and infrastructure. The money, however, goes into the hands of a select few."

"Usually the few are Hezbullah," Amit added.

Dror went on, "There is building going on in Gaza…hotels, some very expensive homes. Some of the French investors even have places along the beach. Often their companies are the ones contracted to do all the work. It's big business."

I didn't need to ask; it was clear that the Shin Bet kept an eye on things over there.

"So you know who these French guys are?"

Amit nodded. "We'll see if there's a connection to Belard."

I noticed he wasn't passing along any names.

From Ronit: "The question is are these foreign investors actively involved in smuggling, or digging tunnels, any sort of terrorist activities?"

"We don't have any evidence of that, but it may be happening."

"Back to the Mandels," I said.

"We'll go to Efrat where he has relatives nearby," Ronit answered. "I know the community. There are some central areas where people come and go and shop. Maybe someone has seen the family."

℘

The community of Efrat is about eight miles south of Jerusalem, on the southern side of Bethlehem. We left central Jerusalem in Officer Malkiely's Renault, driving first to the neighborhood of Gilo and then onto the Tunnel Road. Originally the road to Efrat went through Bethlehem and some Arab villages, but when Israeli residents and commuters came under Arab sniper fire a number of years ago, the government built a by-pass road around and under trouble spots. As clashes with Palestinians continued, bulletproof barriers were expanded in some locations. Along the road, we passed through a short tunnel, a bridge over a deep valley, and then through a longer tunnel beneath Har Gilo and Beit Jala. Unlike the landscape on the way to Jericho, the land here was a series of hills and valleys, with steppe farming a typical sight. Through my window I could see scrub and scruffy, low-lying foliage, as well as a number of well-tended vineyards. After we passed through the second tunnel, the road widened and fed into a large checkpoint. Similar to when I was driving out of the Jerusalem environs last night, the stop was not meant for us, but rather for vehicles on the other side heading into Jerusalem.

In another five minutes we turned left off the main road onto a curving access road toward the northern end of Efrat. We slowed as we approached a guardhouse and its lowered gate. As with so many communities in Israel, barriers across entry roads were not uncommon for security reasons. The guard remained inside and looked at us through his closed window. Before Ronit held up her ID, he raised the gate. If we had Palestinian license plates – green and white, unlike our black on orange – or were more "Arab-like" in clothing styles or appearance, the gate would have stayed down and there would have been queries. The guard, though, had seen us approach and had profiled us.

"Pull over," I said once on the other side of the barrier. "Let's talk to him."

Ronit nodded and we parked on the graveled shoulder. As we walked back to the guardhouse, I noticed that the gate across the road was only on the entry side. On the exit side there were only rumble strips and spikes that depressed if you went over them on the way out. Ronit pulled out her ID as we came up to the guardbooth, while I took out pictures of the Mandels. She held up her identification to the window, and the young guard stepped out.

"Shalom," Ronit said to him. The young man was tall and skinny, had a day's growth of stubble, and was wearing a Baltimore Orioles baseball cap.

"Nice cap," I commented.

He smiled and Ronit went on: "We're looking for this man and his family. Have you seen them?"

I gave him the photos that Amit had prepared.

The man shook his head. "Maybe? I don't know."

"The man's not dangerous. We just need to speak with him," I mentioned.

Ronit added, "He's here with relatives, so if you see him in a car, make a note of the license plate and call me." She handed him a business card.

"Don't stop him," I said.

"I understand."

"Good. Now is there another way into Efrat?"

Ronit answered. "There's another entrance like this one on the other side of town." She turned back to the guard. "Keep the pictures. Be sure you tell whoever comes on duty after you."

"I will."

"Thank you."

We went back to the car, climbed in, and drove into town. Efrat's main road ran two to three miles from one end of the community to the other, with various neighborhoods branching off in either direction. The road climbed in altitude and we soon had a view of the entire valley and of the hills beyond. In a matter of minutes we were in a small, central shopping area. Ronit pulled into a space across the street, and we got out.

"This is one of the main areas of Efrat," she said. The town was essentially built along the sides of a hill, and the shopping area and offices were two stories, with the lower level dropping down along with the slope of a hill. "Go, show the pictures. I'll check with the town security office." I nodded and off she went toward the upper level off the shopping plaza.

I crossed the street and made my way over to the lower level. To the left was an open square and to the right were the shops. My first stop was a pizza parlor. The Mandels were a family with young kids. They'd come here sooner or later, if they hadn't already.

I walked into the air-conditioned shop. The counter was straight ahead with a lanky, sandy haired teenager in an apron behind it. Using a ladle, he was spreading sauce on a large disk of dough. To my right were four or five small, round tables. Along the far wall sat a young father and a boy of about ten. The boy was eating a slice of pizza, while the man played on his iPhone. Pulling out my ID, I went over to the boy behind the counter.

We had virtually the same conversation that Ronit and I had with the man at the guardhouse. Similarly, this young man might have seen the Mandels, but couldn't swear to it. I left him with a set of photos and the clear instructions to call us.

I subsequently stopped into every store and office in the shopping area – an optician's office, a green grocer, a burger place, a gift shop, and more. Not one person I spoke with could positively say that he or she had seen the Mandels. I wrapped up back at the pizza shop where I bought two ice coffees, which were more like ice coffee slushies, and then headed out toward the promenade. Across the street, Ronit's Renault was in a different space than it was earlier. As I approached a bench, she came over from the car.

"For you," I handed Ronit the ice coffee.

"*Toda*," she smiled.

"You're welcome. So what did you find at the security office?"

"Amit had already e-mailed the pictures and instructions. I also went to the other guardhouse and gave the guard a set of pictures since he hadn't gotten them yet. What about you? Any positives?" She pulled off the top of her slushie cup and used the straw to stir the thick drink.

"Only several maybes."

We watched the traffic for a few seconds.

"The Mandels will come here at some point," I said. "And now people will be watching for them."

"Hopefully, they won't warn the rabbi or his wife."

"Hopefully. I want to walk up to Josh and Shelley and ask them a few, very specific questions. If I have to sit with them as they recount their daily activities from their last trip here, I will."

"You're angry with them."

"A little. They should have trusted me."

"They're afraid."

"I know. And they think they're safe here. They may have walked into a worse situation. They just don't know it."

"You're...*matmid*."

"Tenacious? Yeah, I am."

"I heard that about you."

"From Amit?"

She nodded and I shook my head, not surprised.

"What else did he say?" I stared at Officer Malkiely. In the sunlight her auburn hair showed more than few red streaks. As I looked into her dark eyes she looked back into mine.

"He told me about some of your missions when you were in the army."

"Oh?"

"He mentioned the rescue."

I turned away, watching pedestrians getting into their cars.

"You should be proud of that."

"I am. I wish they all would have gone so well."

A large garbage truck lumbered down the main street a block away from us.

"So tell me about you. It's only fair."

"Okay," she smiled, noting the change in subject. "I was in *Modi'in* in the army."

"Intelligence."

She nodded.

"And that brought you to Shabak?" I used the formal name for the Shin Bet.

She nodded.

"Making it a career?"

"I don't know." She looked away, staring off. "We'll see what happens."

"Be careful… or it'll consume you. Do you have a boyfriend?" I looked down at her left hand where there was no wedding ring.

"No."

That's all she said on the subject. After a very long moment passed, I turned to her. "Be careful of Amit."

She looked at me.

"You don't know him very well. Don't trust him completely. What he told us in the conference room? He's full of crap. He said he's in the process of tapping the phone number I gave him. That's bullshit. He's already listening in."

Ronit didn't say anything.

"And he already knows about the connection between Belard and the French investors. He may not know which one of them is the boss, but he's got names."

"Why wouldn't he tell us?"

I shrugged. "He has reasons. Maybe they're political, maybe they have to do with security. Maybe he wants us to find out on our own? I don't know."

I looked up and down the street again. The father and son customers from the pizza shop crossed the street to their car.

"I've run into this before. He doesn't give you the full picture. I like him, but I don't totally trust him. I don't think he'd put us at risk, but he knows more than he's telling."

I got up and took my mostly unfinished cup of ice coffee and threw it away in a nearby green metal trashcan.

"Ready to go? There's nothing else we can do here. I'd like to get back to Katie. She's in the Old City and I want to see her."

Ronit looked up at me. Her mind had moved elsewhere. "I was married…for six months."

I didn't say anything at first. Then, "It's none of my business. I shouldn't have asked."

She ignored the apology. "Yoav was a paratrooper. He was on patrol with two other soldiers in the West Bank one night. They made a wrong turn into an Arab village."

A chill ran across my shoulders and down my back. I knew where this was going, and I sat back down next to her.

"They ended up near a Palestinian police station. They were quickly surrounded, dragged into a building and beaten to death. All three of them."

I had no come-back. In Israel most families had horror stories about family members or friends who had been killed. No one was immune. I had my own story. "Did Amit tell you anything else about me, anything more personal?"

She shook her head.

"There's a reason I moved back to the States. While I was in the army I was engaged to Tamar. She was the most beautiful woman in the world. We spent all our free time together. When I was on base, she came to see me. When I had a weekend off, I went to Haifa to see her. And her parents were the most open people I knew. I was already family to them."

It was my turn to stare off. I knew that Ronit was watching me.

"I had just come back from rescuing Laurie. Tamar and I were going to meet in Jerusalem. She was just outside a café when a suicide bomber blew himself up and took the whole café and Tamar with him." I turned to Ronit. "You're stronger than I am. I ran away."

Ronit let a second pass. "You did what you needed to do. And look at where you are now, sitting here in Israel where you can see Jerusalem in the distance."

I looked at her and just shook my head. "Let's go back to town."

At that moment, Ronit's phone rang. She listened for a few seconds and then said, "Did you get the license plate?" Another pause, then, "Thanks." She hung up.

"What happened?"

"The guard we spoke to before, the one at the entrance, thinks he just saw Rabbi Mandel leaving the town in the passenger seat of a car. I have the license plate."

Officer Malkiely called in the number. She put out an alert and got the address for the owner of the car as well. She repeated the address to herself silently. "Let's go."

We crossed to Ronit's car, where she inputted the address into a GPS. In less than two minutes, we were there. The house was on a side street off of the main road at the bottom of a hill. The homes on this block were all built close to each other, with virtually no yard between one house and a neighbor's. The domicile in front of us was two stories, stone of course, with a small plot of grass in front. A short, curving sidewalk led to the white metal front door. There was no screen door.

We rang the bell. Nothing. No one running up or down steps inside, no one saying, "Just a minute." Not a sound.

Was this where the Mandels were staying? Could this be Shelley's family, and the person driving Josh – if it were indeed Josh – was Shelley's brother? Is this where they lived?

I turned around and looked at the front lawn. A well tended flower garden had been planted between the walkway and the one-car driveway on the side. The driveway was empty, just a large slab of new concrete with a basketball pole and backboard at the head. Except for Ronit's Renault, there were no other cars in front of the house.

Ronit rang the bell one more time just to be sure. Nothing.

"What do you think?" she asked.

Instead of answering, I walked over to the front window and peered in. The window had been framed in red metal aluminum trim and the windows were double-pane insulated glass. The lights were off inside, but I could clearly make out a typical living room…couch, a few easy chairs, a coffee table. The room looked well kept.

I stepped back over to Ronit. "No one's here. Unless there's a family room where they're keeping all their toys and kids' belongings, I don't think the Mandels are staying here. Too neat." For some reason I flashed-back to the latest description of where the Mandels had been staying in Williamsport. The last report of the house was that it was very neat.

We meandered back to the car. Ronit turned to me, "It's possible that Rabbi Mandel was just getting a ride into Jerusalem. It's very popular for kids and adults to hitchhike for a ride into town."

I didn't say anything. It was certainly possible. The Mandels could very well be in Efrat, and that fellow in the car may not have been a relative…He might simply have been giving Josh a lift. This could be the home of a random resident of Efrat.

"I'll put someone on the house," Ronit said. "And we'll send officers around to continue checking."

Overhead, I heard the rumble of an aircraft, but when I looked up, I couldn't find it.

"If the Mandels are here," the Shin Bet officer said, "they'll show up. Someone will need to go shopping or want to eat out. And they have to pass the guardhouse one way or the other."

The two of us climbed into the car, and Ronit drove us back into Jerusalem.

24

Katie and Kiffi were taking a break from touring the Old City when I showed up. They were sitting at an outdoor table in the Jewish Quarter rehydrating, not far from a rebuilt domed synagogue – both were nursing cups of iced tea. It was at least 90 degrees in the sun.

"Hey there," I said, approaching their table.

"Hi," Katie said, holding onto her straw hat and looking up at me as I got close. I bent down and gave her a kiss on the lips.

"You ladies seem relaxed." Before taking my own seat I kissed Kiffi on the cheek. "Busy day?"

Kiffi answered: "So far, we did a brief overview of the Four Quarters."

Katie took a pull on her iced tea. "We're going to the *kotel* in a few minutes." The Western Wall. "Want to join us?"

"I'll watch from afar." After Katie had taken her sip, she offered me the cup. I took a sip or two.

"How has your day been?" Kiffi asked.

"There was a Josh sighting. We're checking it out."

"Good," Katie said.

Kiffi looked at me. "So, you're joining us?"

"For a while."

"Then, let's go," Katie ordered. She finished her drink and the three of us stood and headed off across a large plaza in the shadow of the rebuilt domed Hurva Synagogue. We walked down an alleyway, past shops and a few cafés. As the Old City was built on a mountain range, complete with its hills and valleys, the sidewalks, alleys, walkways went up and down following the contour of the landscape. The Western Wall Plaza was at the base of a small valley. Most of the plaza was an open area, unsegregated by gender, but as you got closer to the Western Wall, the prayer sections were physically divided with men on the left and women to the right.

While Katie and Kiffi headed to the women's entrance, I hung back in a shady spot in the back of the general plaza. For a few minutes, I people watched. The large open area in front of me was filled with a conglomeration of humanity. There were many young men dressed in white shirts and black pants, but there were also tourists – both men and women – in T-shirts and shorts, as well as women in long sleeves and long skirts. Almost everyone wore a head covering of some sort, either due to the strong sun or for religious reasons. As I observed the crowd, I could see clusters of tour groups hovering around guides, all describing the history of the area. I was watching a group of Asian tourists, huddled around a man holding a large green umbrella when my phone rang. It was my second phone, the one I used to call Ibrahim.

I took the call. "Yes?"

"Julian Leveque." It was Ibrahim, and that's all he said before hanging up.

Leveque was the name of one of the French contractors he had mentioned last night. Ibrahim must have discovered that Belard was working for him. I couldn't help but wonder if Amit knew that already.

As I thought about all the puzzles pieces of the whole situation, there was still one piece that had yet to be turned over to be seen clearly: Josh's competitor in his Torah rescuing business, Allan Samuels from Charleston, South Carolina. I had never been able to contact him. Last week his secretary told me was in Israel. Now that I was here, it was time to find out where Samuels was so I could pay him a visit. I wanted to see his reaction to Belard's picture and now to Julian Leveque's name.

Using my primary phone, I called the Israeli number I had for

Samuels. He answered on the third ring.

"Mr. Samuels?"

"Yes?"

I was looking out at a group of American middle school kids crowded around a tall, blond guide. The students were all wearing the same style purple school shirt, but I wasn't really concentrating on them. "Hi, your secretary gave me your number. My name is Jerry Horwitz from Temple B'nai Torah outside of Los Angeles. I'm here in Israel on vacation, and back home I'm starting a Torah writing fundraiser for my temple. Since I'm here, I was wondering if I could meet you to discuss your potential involvement."

"Be happy to meet with you," Samuel's voice was a bit raspy. He coughed. "Sorry, I must have picked up something on the plane." He coughed again.

"Where are you staying? I'm moving around the country the next few days, so really, I can come to you."

"Right now I'm in Tzefat up north. Will be here for the next two days, and then I'm going to Haifa."

"Well that's perfect, *I'm* going to be in Tzefat tomorrow." I wasn't, but I would be now.

"Terrific. I'll be here all day."

We then set a time and a place – outside a synagogue where he would be speaking.

"Jerry Horwitz," he repeated the name I had given him.

"That's it. See you tomorrow." I hung up and then absent-mindedly looked over at the group of American middle school kids. The tour guide was pointing to the top of the Western Wall, saying something about the difference in the styles of the stone blocks that made up the wall.

So, we had Josh and Belard, Leveque and Samuels. Those were the pieces, unless I was missing something – which was possible. We still needed to find Josh. Maybe the guy who gave him a ride could fill that in.

The rest of the day went by more slowly than I would have liked. Katie and Kiffi, with me hanging on, did more touring. From the Western Wall, Kiffi took us to the Southern Wall excavations, and then onto the ramparts of the Old City walls. Once we had enough walking and touring, Kiffi parted company, leaving us at Jaffa Gate. I retrieved my car and we went back to our hotel, which, fortunately, wasn't far away. We were both tired and grimy, so Katie and I showered – separately – and then stretched out on her bed. It was terrific to lie down. I put my arm around her and Katie rested her head on my shoulder. At some point Katie's breathing became long and deep, and I realized she had fallen asleep. And then my phone rang.

With my free hand, I grabbed the phone on the nightstand next to my head. It was Amit.

"So you and Ronit have a lead. A license plate."

Katie didn't even stir, so I kept my voice down. "It could just be a guy who took Josh into the city."

"Maybe Rabbi Mandel mentioned where he's staying, and we can find out from the driver."

"Maybe."

"So, Gidon, when was the last time you were on the Gaza border?"

That was out of nowhere. "It's been a few years."

"Be outside your hotel at midnight. Ronit will pick you up."

He hung up.

After a moment: "Seems I have a date tonight," I said out loud.

"That's nice." Katie was awake but hadn't moved.

"It's at midnight."

"Have a good time."

"With Ronit. We may be gone for hours."

"Okay."

"You won't be waiting up, wondering about any hanky-panky?"

"Yes, that's what I'll be doing," she deadpanned, "wondering every minute what you and Ronit might be up to."

"Actually, I'll be wondering."

"What do you mean?"

"I have no idea what it's all about."

"I'll guess you'll find out."

"Guess so." Then, "Do you have plans for tomorrow?"

"Kiffi said something about taking me to Tel Aviv."

"Sounds good. I need to go up north and follow a lead. That guy who is Josh's competition. I want to speak with him. Figured since I'm in the neighborhood, I'll also drop in on Laurie."

"Nate and Rachel will appreciate that."

"Yeah."

"So, Gidon, it's still early." Katie pulled her head back and pushed herself up on her elbows so she was over me. As she looked down into my eyes her hair fell across her neck and face. "You have some time until your date. What do you want to do?"

"What would *you* like to do?"

"I'd like to finish my nap."

25

At 11:55 I was downstairs, watching the traffic on King George Street. While the volume of vehicles had decreased, there were still plenty of cars and trucks on the road, but then that might have been because this was a major crossroads. Both to the right and left were a number of hotels – the Leonardo Plaza to my left, the Dan Panorma and King Solomon to the right – plus there were numerous cafés and eateries in the vicinity as well. Diagonal to where I stood was a dormitory and youth hostel. On its flat roof there was a party in full swing, so naturally kids came to the edge and looked over. As sounds of both Israeli and American rock filtered through the air, I hoped there weren't any guests on the floors proximal to the festivities trying to sleep.

Ronit pulled to the curb on schedule. I climbed in. *"Boker tov,"* I said. Good morning.

"Shalom."

Ronit was dressed in dark pants and a gray Gap hoodie. I was not dissimilarly dressed: black jeans and a black zip up sweatshirt.

As Ronit pulled away, I asked the natural question: "Do you know what this is all about?"

"All Amit said was that we were going to talk to someone who could give us answers."

As she drove, Ronit was leaning heavily on the gas, swerving around any vehicle deemed too slow. She was heading northwest to pick up the highway back toward Tel Aviv. Without taking her eyes off the road she said, "I spoke with the man who gave Josh the ride this morning. Paid him a visit after dinner. Didn't want to wait since our surveillance team said he was home."

"No problem. And?"

"He told us that the rabbi is staying with his wife's brother. We got a name and address."

"Excellent."

"I thought we'd go tomorrow after tonight's meeting. We may have something more to ask Rabbi Mandel."

I nodded. Good thought.

"Besides, this is your case, and you should be there. I wouldn't do that without you."

I looked at Ronit as she concentrated on driving. She had her hair pulled back in a ponytail, revealing a strong jawline. Her head was tilted forward slightly to avoid glare from the rear-view mirror...or maybe it was just a sense of determination.

"How are you going...What route tonight?"

She pulled out behind a double-length tractor-trailer. "Up on Highway 1 to Highway 6 then south and west. Should take about an hour."

I knew the roads. At legal speeds it was more like an hour and a half...and then the Gaza border. Should be interesting.

The drive was very pleasant; we passed Latrun, the site of a Crusader stronghold and more recently the site of a fort first held by the Arabs during the 1948 War and then by the Israelis in the Six Day War. After '67, it became a memorial to fallen Israeli soldiers of the armored brigade.

As the landscape began to flatten, we crossed into the Ayalon Valley, where Joshua defeated the Amorites. It was difficult to picture that ancient battle now, with the lights of modern villages on each side and a brightly lit industrial complex in the distance.

We looped around to Israel's only turnpike, Highway 6, to continue south. Our conversation dropped off, leaving me to watch the road and think about this early morning meeting. Shifting slightly, I felt the Glock clipped near the small of my back. In my right pocket was my three-and-a-half-inch Benchmade knife. Don't leave home without it. At some point, Ronit turned on the radio, and after a search, settled on a jazz station. The darkened landscape went by in a blur.

Seventy minutes after leaving Jerusalem we passed a kibbutz with a long driveway leading to a twelve foot high rolling gate. A single overhead light illuminated a call box near the barrier. A mile further down we passed a lone gas station, ablaze with light. No one was at the pumps. It seemed like we were in the middle of nowhere.

After another half mile, Ronit slowed, then turned right onto an unmarked, barely paved one lane road. Potholes pitted the macadam, bouncing us up and down and side-to-side. There were no lights in any direction, except for our headlamps. The darkness around us was absolute. The Renault's bright white halogen headlights pierced the blackness in front, but there was nothing to see, except for the beaten, rocky road. After another half mile, the single lane rose in a gradual incline. The road peaked without warning and we suddenly came to a guardhouse and a fence blocking the way. Two soldiers in body armor flanked our car. Each guard wore a purple beret and carried a Tavor Assault Rifle; their helmets were within easy reach on their vests. These were Givati infantrymen, assigned to patrol and secure Israel's borders.

The soldier on the left stepped up to Ronit's window, while his partner stood alert off to the front right of the car. He held his weapon ready, left hand on the barrel and his right on the trigger grip. His right index finger was extended across the trigger guard.

Ronit and I took out our identification, and as she handed them to the sentry, I looked beyond the fence to a nondescript one story, sand-colored building with an open dirt area in front. Parked on the left were an armored personnel carrier and two armored jeeps. Off to the right was a grouping of three vehicles: two maroon Toyota sedans with deeply tinted windows and an unmarked medium-sized truck.

The soldier beside Ronit walked around to the guardhouse to a radio unit sitting near a windowsill. He detached the handset and called in the IDs. After reading the names, he looked at us, responded to some questions, then hung up. The sentry, assured we were authorized, nodded to his partner.

The second Givati soldier stepped to the edge of the 10 foot high gate in front of us, fiddled with a lock, and then walked the barrier inward, swinging it open.

"Park wherever you can," the soldier beside us directed. "Someone will meet you."

Ronit slowly pulled toward the building. She took advantage of a space next to the armored jeep, and backed into the spot – always the right move from my perspective. We exited the car, stepping around a series of stacked concrete blocks. The slabs were positioned both to provide cover in a fire-fight and also to serve as obstacles for any vehicles trying to plow headlong into the building. Having been in the army, and having served on similar bases, this was a pretty standard sight.

As we approached the entryway, a young soldier stepped toward us. He was six feet, dark-haired, thin, and couldn't have been more than 20 years old. He wore a small crocheted blue *kippah* and olive fatigues bearing three horizontal stripes on each sleeve above the elbow, indicating he was a *mefaked*, a non-commissioned commander. Even at his young age he was often left in charge of the base.

"Welcome. I'm Dani," he held out his hand, and we each shook it in turn. He smiled warmly. It was a smile that showed even in his eyes. "I hope our road didn't kill your car," he laughed. "Just bill the office."

"Don't worry, I will," Ronit responded, smiling back.

The *mefaked* led us inside. "Your, ah, friends, are already here."

He escorted us past a large common area, and down a narrow, bleak corridor. We weaved our way past a dormitory style room populated with bunk beds – I saw male feet poking out ~~under~~ beneath a blanket on a top bunk – past a room with two soldiers wearing headphones and staring at a monitor, and eventually to a room with a massive door that could have secured a bank vault. We stepped inside a transitional space, then into a small, low-ceilinged, completely blacked out room. The only light inside came from a bank of monitors and radar-like screens.

The tall *mefaked* whispered, "Welcome to the Gaza border."

I looked at the bank of monitors. Some were connected to standard surveillance cameras, while others to night-vision devices. The standard ones – at least those that were active at the moment – showed the guardhouse and the main gate, while another displayed a wide view of the building's parking area. Others, with a green tint, displayed various landscapes and buildings in the distance. Two soldiers – a woman and a man – sat in upholstered chairs in front of the displays.

As my eyes adjusted to the darkness, I realized that above the bank of monitors was a long horizontal window about five inches wide. My guess was that it looked out onto the border. Besides the soldiers in the room, I knew someone else was present. I turned to the right to see Amit and another man standing off in a corner. The other man was of average height with a round face and squinty eyes. He had a medium size belly on him, and wore an open collared, light-colored shirt. The stranger assessed me through his narrow eyes, turned to Amit and nodded.

"Dani," Amit said to the non-com next to us, "we're heading out. I'll call you in about ten minutes."

"Okay," the young soldier replied.

Amit turned to us. "Let's go."

Both Ronit and I nodded, and we followed Amit and the nameless man out of the darkened room. Apparently familiar with the layout of the building, Amit led us confidently through the winding hallways to the entrance. Once outside, we turned left toward the unmarked truck and two maroon Toyotas. Amit, still without an explanation as to what was happening, approached the driver of the truck, who was patiently sitting behind the wheel. The nondescript man had his window lowered and left arm resting on the frame. He turned at Amit's approach. The Shin Bet man said simply, "*Yallah*," Arabic for "Let's go," then turned back toward us. The driver started his motor.

Amit motioned to the closer Toyota. Ronit took shotgun while I slid into the back seat. The stranger with the paunch walked to the second car. Amit, now behind the wheel, looked over at us. "Here, put these on." He handed us each a pair of head-mounted night optical goggles. The Shin Bet man donned his own pair and quickly fastened the securing straps around his head, jaw, and chin. Obviously, he had used his set before and didn't need to make adjustments. It took Ronit and me a few moments. By the time we were set, all three vehicles – the two cars and the truck – had pulled out of the main gate, each without headlights.

We immediately turned left and drove along the border fence's security road. Next to us, and running over to the fence, was a fifteen foot combed dirt track. Patrols at various times would drive along the track and examine it for footprints and disturbances. Sound devices were buried in sensitive locations, and cameras regularly scanned the entire length. We were, no doubt, being watched back in the darkened surveillance room.

I examined the 12-foot high fence on my left. It was not at all like familiar chain-link barriers. This fence seemed much simpler in a way, with just horizontal and vertical wires. There was extra support along the bottom of the fence, however, across the top there was no horizontal rail; the vertical wires stood unsupported the last foot up. Additionally, the horizontal wires were barbed.

We drove in our caravan for about five more minutes. After another mile, the lead car, the one with the narrow-eyed man with the paunch, swung to the right. Amit followed, as did the truck behind us. All three vehicles made a large circle until we arced back to face the fence. Amit turned off the motor.

"Let's go to the truck," he said and stepped out of the car.

In the amplified light of the goggles, we followed Amit. As we approached the truck, cameras and small communication dishes began rising from the roof. The driver, as well as Amit, were obviously familiar with the routine. Within a minute we were all – driver included – inside the body of the truck, goggles removed, watching a bank of four monitors. On the high def screens we could clearly see the border fence and the rolling landscape beyond. The large stretch of no man's land had low scrubs and grass closer to us, with a few two story square buildings clustered in the distance. The truck driver, now positioned in front of a recording studio-like control panel, played with some dials. One of the cameras began zooming in. He centered on a particular square, flat roofed building.

"David, that's one of the rocket locations."

Amit nodded, then turned to us. "We know that Hamas has stored rockets in that house. We know of other locations, too. Many are in people's homes. Makes getting to them very difficult."

The man at the controls made further adjustments and zoomed in on another house. We could see movement in one of the windows. Amit checked his watch, then turned to the man with the paunch who had been with us back at the base. "Call the *mefaked*. Tell him to turn off his cameras for this section."

The man nodded, took out his cell phone, and relayed Amit's message. With the phone still to his ear, the man waited for confirmation. After a moment, he hung up and turned to Amit, "We're okay. They're blacked out."

"Bring him over."

The man dialed another number, waited, and then said to whoever was on the other end, "You're clear. Start heading toward the border. We'll direct you." The man with the paunch, lowered the phone, but kept the line open.

All of us in the surveillance truck watched the center monitor, the one focused on the square shaped house with movement in the window. As we watched, the movement stopped, but then the back door opened. We saw a man – difficult to distinguish how tall – exit the house to his left. He was wearing a light top and dark pants; other details were lost in the distance and the darkness. With the telescopic lens, the man could easily have been a few miles away. We watched as he climbed into a car – it looked like a pick-up – and drove over to a small road. The technician at the control panel adjusted a post-like swivel knob, and the camera followed the pick-up.

As we watched, the vehicle rode along a curving, bumpy road – we could clearly see it bounce up and down as the driver steered toward us. The camera stayed with him, slowly pulling back as the vehicle approached. I looked at the other monitors. There was no movement in any other views; the houses that other cameras were trained on, plus the open fields, were all quiet and motionless.

The pick-up approached a gulley and disappeared for a moment into the depression, but then came out. The driver followed the road to the left. After a moment, the man with the open phone line next to me spoke into his phone.

"That's close enough. Park and get out."

The vehicle stopped and the man in the light colored shirt or jacket exited the vehicle. He was wearing a jacket; we could see it clearly now.

"Walk to your left…"

He did so…

"Now turn right and come straight."

The camera pulled back as the man approached. In the foreground we could see the top of the border fence. The man kept coming.

The only sound in the surveillance truck was the low hum of an air-conditioning unit.

I looked at the other monitors. Nothing had changed. The night, as far as we could tell, was quiet…none of the buildings showed signs of movement. A good sniper, though, would be set up inside, away from a window. Maybe there'd be a reflection off his scope. Maybe not. If he were good, and depending on his equipment, we might not even see a muzzle flash. The fellow crossing no-man's-land wouldn't know what hit him.

The man continued to the fence.

"Disconnect the wires at the post on your left," the man with the phone directed. If it were possible, his eyes narrowed even more as he focused on the monitor.

The man from Gaza disconnected the upper part of the fence, let the matrix of wires hang limply, and climbed over the vertical base supports.

"Okay, let's go," Amit said.

The man with the phone hung up, and he and Amit led us outside. We walked away from the truck to stand next to the two Toyotas. Thirty seconds later, the guest from Gaza came up the small rise from the border fence. As he came closer, I saw that he was smaller than I expected. He was about five-six, skinny, and had a Mahmoud Ahmadinejad look about him. He was wearing a cloth jacket and had a close-cropped salt and pepper beard over a triangular face. A splotch of dark hair had fallen across his forehead. The man tentatively took in each of us, one at a time.

The squinty-eyed man with the paunch, the one who had been on the phone, stepped forward and shook his guest's hand. "Come, let's talk." He led the skinny man to his blacked-out Toyota. He must have been the man's handler.

Amit turned to us. "Stay here. We'll be back in a few minutes."

With that, Amit climbed into the Toyota with the other two. They drove off into the night.

When the dust settled, Ronit and I were left staring at each other. After a long moment, I looked at her. "How 'bout them O's?"

"What?"

"Baltimore joke. The O's…the Orioles??"

She had no idea. We moseyed over to Amit's car, the one we had arrived in.

"So, Officer Malkiely, ever been to a meeting like this before?"

She shook her head. "No. This is a first. I've been to bases like that one," she nodded to where we had been earlier, "but not to something like this. You?"

"The meetings I've been to were more straightforward. There's a place in Gaza City I like that's quite a hotspot."

She looked at me not knowing whether I was serious or not.

After a few moments, I changed the subject: "So we'll talk to Josh and Shelley tomorrow?"

"Yes. See if we can get your list of where they visited on their last trip here."

"Good. Time's going by."

After another moment, I sat down on the ground and leaned against the car. Ronit began to pace.

"Relax. This is their game and they're enjoying it."

She sat down next to me.

We listened to the night. It was very quiet, though off in the distance there was a low rumble of a jet. Given its altitude, there was only a vague sense of where it was.

So, the Gaza border. Not an unfamiliar location to most IDF soldiers. Fact was, beneath the night sky we could have been anywhere. But we weren't. I wondered how long it would be before another round of rockets would be fired from various locations across the way.

I stared into the night for I don't know how many minutes. At some point – it could have been fifteen minutes later – there was the sound of tires crunching on gravel. We both stood to see the other Toyota approach. When it pulled to a stop, Amit and the Ahmadinejad look-alike stepped out.

Amit motioned to the other car. "Let's go into my car and talk."

We took our previous positions in the Toyota with Amit and Ronit in front, while the Gazan joined me in back.

Amit introduced his guest: "This is Harun."

Ronit and I nodded, and I had to smile. In Arabic, "Harun" meant superior.

"Tell my friends about yourself," Amit asked the man next to me.

Harun cleared his throat. He spoke slowly, thinking about what he wanted to say. "I live outside Gaza City with my wife and three children. I am an engineer...but not very busy these days." He smiled a smile that didn't climb to his eyes.

"Tell them what you told me about the foreign investors," Amit prompted.

"In Gaza there are many foreigners looking to make money from Hamas by selling their business services. We have people from France, from the Czech Republic, from Saudi Arabia, from Germany, and other places. Hamas gets its weapons from Iran, as you know, but they still need to provide food, water, clothing, and more to the citizens. That's where these other people try to sell the government their..." he was looking for the right word...

"Products," Amit offered.

"Yes. Products." Harun shifted in the seat.

"Tell us about this man," he held up a picture of Belard.

"I know him as Mr. Roland. He works for one of the French businessmen. Right now I'm not sure which. He once worked for Mr. Gagnon as well as Mr. Leveque. He's their...I don't know how to describe it...if Mr. Gagnon or Mr. Leveque needs something done, Mr. Roland makes sure it happens."

"How do you know these things?" This from Ronit.

"I used to work for both of them. Mr. Gagnon owns a construction company, and..." he shrugged, "I am an engineer.

"And Mr. Leveque is an importer," Ronit continued. "What would an engineer do for him?"

Harun avoided looking at Ronit. "Anything. Errands, computers...I need to earn money for my family."

"Tell me about Leveque, " I said. That was the name Ibrahim had given me as Belard's boss.

"The Hamas leaders love him. As an importer he can get them food, equipment, clothes...anything. He and some of the Hamas people own a big food and electronics store in Gaza City. I'm told he has a suite at a hotel on the coast and a big house outside of the city." Harun paused. "They get the money and the rest of us can't get food to eat or medicine. I know people who come into Israel to be treated."

"What else about Leveque?" I asked.

"He can be a very angry man if he doesn't get what he wants. I've seen this. He just looks at Mr. Roland...Belard...and no one sees the person he's angry with again."

There was knock at Amit's window. He opened the door to see Harun's handler. "Time to go," he said.

With that, the four of us stepped out of the car.

"Anything else you can tell us?" Ronit asked.

"I'm told he keeps a room at a hotel in Jerusalem. But that's just a rumor probably spread by people who want to see him gone."

The handler pulled Harun aside. There was a short conversation out of earshot, and then the handler held out a large manila envelope that was folded in half. Harun took it, then looked back at us and began to head toward the Gaza fence.

As the skinny figure in the light cloth jacket walked down the slope to the border, Amit looked at me. "Why the interest in Leveque particularly?"

"It's a name I came across in my travels."

"Well, this is very interesting."

Both Ronit and I turned to the Shin Bet man.

"Why?"

"Because the phone number you asked me to track down...the one you found on the hit man in your dojo...the number belongs to Julian Leveque. It's his number."

There it was, the connection between the guys after Josh and Leveque. And the Shin Bet man knew. We could have been pursuing Leveque days ago. We could also have narrowed our focus with Josh to find out what their connection was.

I looked at Amit and felt the energy surge up my back and spread across my torso and arms. I locked it all down, but took a step closer to Amit. Out of the corner of my eye, I noticed Ronit had taken a slight step back, probably not even consciously. The Shin Bet man knew, I repeated to myself.

"When were you going to tell me?"

The handler excused himself rather quickly and returned to the truck to direct his informant back across the border.

"I found out today."

That was such bullshit.

"We just started listening in," Amit continued.

"And you didn't tell me because...??"

"Because I wanted to see if his name came up from other sources... to be certain."

"And you're happy now."

He nodded. "Now we'll find out if the rumor about him having a place in Jerusalem is true. It'll give us another place to look."

"You need to check with Dror to see if the police have any unsolved murders lately." I realized I wasn't asking him to speak with the police chief. I was telling him.

"If Leveque and Belard make people disappear there may be other avenues to investigate. I'll call Commander Dror on the way back tonight, and will leave a message if I don't reach him."

"David, this isn't good." I looked hard into his eyes. "You don't treat people you work with this way." After a long, very quiet moment. "Take us back to the base. Ronit needs to drive us to Jerusalem."

He nodded and climbed into his maroon Toyota. Ronit stepped over to me. She lowered her voice: "I thought you were going to kill him."

"I'm more disciplined than that. Just severely hurt him."

The corners of her mouth turned up in an ever-so-slight smile.

I moved slightly closer. "One thing. Check on this Harun guy."

"Don't trust him?"

"No. I don't."

26

The forensic lab at police headquarters was not what I expected. That's not exactly accurate. The *division* of the forensic lab I was in was not what I expected. We had been summoned to the basement of the police building on Haim Bar-Lev Road, specifically to the Toolmarks and Materials Laboratory, because they had relevant information for us. This lab was the location for world renown, cutting edge, forensic identification work, and it was as far away from a Hollywood image as it could get. But it was very Israeli.

I was standing in a cluttered, bright workspace with white walls and a high ceiling. Four desks with computers lined one wall, tall white cabinets covered another, and an exhaust chamber was inset into a third. The fourth wall was a combination of windows and counter space, the latter covered with computers and printers. Miscellaneous white tables jutted out into the room, and papers, notebooks, bins of shoes, and boxes of supplies were stacked wherever there was space. On the wall over the workstations someone had tacked up a poster of a dark-haired, mustached man with piercing dark eyes and a long nose. He was sitting at a desk, and appeared as if he had just looked up when the camera had captured him. The caption read "Edmond Locard" with a quote: "Every contact leaves a trace."

Ronit and I had been joined by Commander Dror, the police chief, and we were all standing in the center of the room, speaking with a woman about forty, whose eyes were bright and wide with excitement. Their slight almond shape hinted at an ancestor more from the East than the West. She was Avital, one of the lead forensic scientists. Following the informality of the country, Avital was dressed not in a lab coat, but in street clothes: a lightweight, flowing black skirt and a white T-shirt under an open, button down lavender blouse. She was holding two blue file folders.

"We've had four unsolved murders in the past three months... one stabbing and three gunshots," Avital reported. "Over that period of time, it's a little unusual, but with the drug traffic and the political tension, it happens from time to time."

"Is this in Jerusalem or the entire country?" I asked.

"All of Israel," Commander Dror answered, signature glasses atop his head. "This lab serves the entire country, even for Shabak. Everything comes through here."

"It's two of the gunshot cases that caught our attention," Avital went on. "In these two cases both victims were killed the same way, plus based on footprints taken at the crime scene, the same two pairs of shoes were at both locations."

Dror took the files from Avital's hands but didn't open them. "Both victims were women. One was twenty-one from Abu Gosh," he named an Arab community outside of Jerusalem, "and one was thirty-two from Rishon LeTzion, outside of Tel Aviv. The woman from Rishon was a glass artist who worked at home, and the woman from Abu Gosh worked as a chambermaid here in Jerusalem."

Avital continued: "Both were shot once in the heart and once in the head. Very professional. We recovered all four bullets. All were .9mm, but the two women were killed by different guns."

"Different shooters," Ronit said.

"Maybe. We can't be sure. The killer could have switched guns."

Dror opened the files in his hand, scanning them. "The artist was discovered in her workshop by a friend," Dror said, "and the Abu Gosh woman was found in the basement stairwell of the hotel where she worked."

"And the only thing that connects them besides how they were killed was the common set of footprints?" I verified.

Avital nodded.

"You can be that sure about the footprints?" Ronit questioned.

Avital smiled. "Here, step up on the table." She pulled a chair closer.

Ronit stepped up on the chair and then put her left shoe down on a nearby white laminate tabletop.

"Now step back."

Ronit came down.

Avital went over to a bin on the floor and pulled out a sheet of paper that was a little longer and wider than a legal size page. She turned the paper over and we could see it was glossy on one side. As we watched, Avital began peeling the glossy side from the paper backing. "Unless you live and work all day in a sterile environment there's dust and dirt everywhere," she explained as she separated the layers. "Outside of such an environment, a thin layer of dirt adheres to the bottom of your shoe. When you then step onto a seemingly clean surface, you transfer that dust and dirt in the pattern of the sole of your shoe."

Avital took the transparent sheet and placed it over where Ronit had stepped.

"We can use an adhesive lifter to pull up the print."

She ran a rubber roller over the sheet and then slowly peeled back the adhesive transparency from the countertop. She held the sheet up so we could see the sole print of Ronit's Oxfords. "Every shoe, unless it's one-of-a-kind custom, is mass produced. Most shoes have distinct sole patterns and all show unique wear. No two people walk the same way or in the exact same places. In two of these murder cases, two pairs of shoes, or two people, were at both scenes. We found one set in the stairwell and the same set in the artist's workshop."

Dror, obviously proud of his scientist, said, "There's more."

"We know the brand of shoes," Avital smiled.

"How?" Ronit asked.

"A team with a copy of the sole patterns spent days at shoe stores," Dror beamed. "It took *days*," he emphasized.

I looked at Avital. "I hope you got overtime." Then after a moment, "So what kind of shoes are these?"

"Both the same brand," the scientist answered. "Calzados Rayfra. Not very common at crime scenes. They're manufactured in a small family factory in the mountains of Spain."

"I had never heard of them," Dror put in, still proud.

"So, what's the connection to our case? Do we know if Belard and Leveque wear these shoes?" Ronit questioned.

Before anyone could answer, a tall, skinny man wearing a plaid shirt and faded black jeans entered the room. He was carrying an unloaded automatic in his right hand. He looked at Avital, who said, "Another minute, Benny." The man checked some papers on a desk, then left the room, still holding onto the gun.

Ronit and I both looked back at the police commander, waiting for an explanation.

"We know these two murders are connected because of how the women were killed plus the shoe prints. We don't know yet if the prints belong to Belard and Leveque, but until last night we didn't even have their names. When David called in the middle of the night he wanted me to see if Leveque had a place in Jerusalem."

I looked at Dror and made the connection. "He keeps a room at the hotel where the chambermaid was killed."

He nodded. "The Leonardo. The one on King George."

Before I could say anything, like there had to be other people with expensive shoes at the hotel, the tall, skinny man holding the automatic walked back in the room. Avital went over to him. "You can put it down now."

The skinny man put down the pistol.

Avital picked up a nearby small spray can and spritzed the palm of the man's hand. In a short while red marks appeared. She looked at me, holding up the can. "It's a highly sensitive reagent for iron. You'll see that the pattern on Benny's hand matches the contact points on the gun."

Dror was back and watching us. "No longer can a suspect claim, 'That's not my gun' if he or she just held it."

Avital pointed over her shoulder to the poster on the wall, the one of Locard. The forensic scientist smiled, "Every contact leaves a trace," she quoted the line from the poster. "If you can get me those shoes, I can put those two men at the scene."

"If I can get that close to those men, you will have more than shoes to examine."

She just looked into my eyes.

"Thanks for your help," was all I said.

"You're welcome." Avital moved off.

I turned to Ronit. "We need to talk to Josh and Shelley. We have some pictures to show them, and we still need to find the commonality."

Ronit looked at the police chief. "We need pictures of the victims when they were alive."

"I'll get them for you." Dror stepped to one of the workstations and picked up the phone.

She turned back to me: "We already have pictures of Leveque and Belard."

I nodded. Before I could say anything else to Ronit, she was on her cell phone, speaking to another Shin Bet officer. As the Mandels were now under surveillance, she wanted someone to keep them at home until we got there. Once she was off the phone, she looked at me, seeing I had an idea.

"About interviewing Josh, he's got to expect that I'm pissed at him, right?"

"Correct."

"Okay, wait a minute."

I picked up my cell phone and called Katie. After a few rings she picked up.

"Hi. Where'd I catch you?"

"In the room. Just got back from breakfast. What's up?"

"Are you still going to Tel Aviv with Kiffi?"

"That was the plan."

"I have a proposition for you, but you can say 'no' if you want."

"Okay."

"We found where Josh and Shelley are staying."

"Great."

"And I'll be going over to speak with them. I figure they'll know I'm upset because they left Williamsport."

"Uh huh. Wait." There was moment's pause. "You want someone to be there to temper the situation."

"That's what I was thinking. Now I know you didn't want to see them when this whole thing started–"

"I'll come with you."

"Are you sure?"

"Yeah, they're good people and you need my help."

"And if they ask about your background?"

"I'll be fine."

"You're sure?"

"Yes."

"Thanks. Pick you up in half an hour?"

"That'll be fine. I'll call Kiffi."

"Thank you," I repeated.

We hung up.

"You want to take Katie to help interview the Mandels?" Ronit asked.

I nodded, not knowing if she were going to object.

"She'll be able to put them at ease."

"I hope so."

"I'll stay here."

"Why?"

"You and Katie should see them. You don't need another Shabak officer there. It'll overwhelm them, plus there's plenty to do. I want to follow-up on Leveque and find out more about the two victims. There's also the man from last night." She meant the informant.

"Thanks. What about Amit? He wants you with me, right?"

"It'll be fine. We'll keep him informed."

I smiled, touched her arm in a gesture of appreciation, and headed out.

27

"In your opinion, what are the reasons people commit murder?" I asked Katie.

We were on our way to interview the Mandels in Efrat, taking the exact same route I had taken yesterday with Ronit, when I brought up the question.

"People kill for money," Katie answered.

"To get it or to keep it," I acknowledged. "The killing could happen as part of a street robbery or as something more grand. What else… another reason why someone would commit murder."

We had just turned on to the Tunnel Road, and as yesterday, the sun was bright and hot, and the landscape to either side was just as sandy and empty, with the exception of the occasional steppe farming.

"For sex," she offered.

"Be more specific."

"A crime of passion. Someone is jealous. Maybe a sexual liaison with one person would jeopardize another."

"'Liason.' I like that. There could be blackmail…"

"And that relates back to money," Katie said. "What about drugs?"

I nodded. "Maybe for an addict to get the drugs, or for a distributor to stay in business."

"Relates to money."

"What about for power?"

"Like in *The Godfather*?" Katie asked. "To keep what you have or to eliminate the competition. Relates to money again."

"I agree." On the dual lane road, I found myself behind a cement truck that was struggling to gain speed. "I've been thinking about this, and I came up with two more." I edged to the left to see if it were safe to pass. I pulled back to the right as there was oncoming traffic. "Think of this part of the world…or Iraq or Afghanistan."

"Religion," Katie said. "Relates to power and to enforce a way of life. Doesn't only happen here. There are people back home who have killed over the abortion issue."

"I agree. I came up with one more. Retribution."

"Pay back? Revenge?"

I nodded. "Or justice. Think Osama bin Laden or drone strikes. Goes along with pre-emptive strikes to prevent further innocent deaths. Targeted assassinations."

"Okay, so how does this relate to what's going on here?"

"If our assumptions are correct, and either Belard or Leveque killed those two women, what could those ladies have possibly done to spark any of the reasons we just mentioned? Take the woman at the hotel."

I edged to the left again, saw that the road both on the other side and in front of the truck was clear, so I pressed on the accelerator.

Katie was about to say something but stopped, as I sped into the oncoming traffic lane. Once we were safely back on our side of the road, she answered my question. "She was a chambermaid. Maybe Leveque or Belard took advantage of her and she fought back. Maybe she saw something in Leveque's room when she was cleaning up." She paused. "Maybe she was blackmailing him."

"It would have to be something really good, and she'd have to be very secure to confront him. No, I think she discovered something in his room like you said, and either Leveque or Belard found out."

"Okay. What about the artist near Tel Aviv?" Katie asked.

"Leveque could have had an affair with her and the relationship went wrong somehow. That's your crime of passion. What about money as a factor?"

"He could have commissioned something from her, and maybe

they were arguing over a price?"

"Difficult to know isn't it? Maybe Ronit will turn up something in her research."

"What if all these murders – the two women here, Mr. Meyers in Rhode Island, and the attack on Josh – are all unrelated…and that Belard and Leveque are just bad men?"

"The timing is too close. They're not a coincidence. They all have something in common relating to Leveque. We need more information."

Our conversation dropped off, as there seemed nothing more to say. We continued on our way, through the tunnels avoiding the Arab villages, driving beside high, bulletproof barriers, and toward the check-point. Katie was looking intently at the security measures.

"All this is really necessary," she said, her tone indicating some uncertainty.

"Between the barriers separating Jewish and Arab areas and these checkpoints, terror attacks inside the population centers have been cut back almost completely."

Katie didn't say anything. She was taking it all in. As we drove through the border-like crossing unfettered, she noted that while we breezed through, a number of cars heading into Jerusalem on the other side were being stopped by soldiers and the drivers questioned.

"So Israelis pass right through," Katie queried, "but Arabs can't?"

"It's a generalization, and profiling is involved, but pretty much. Unfortunately, the sins of a few Palestinians are visited upon their whole community. But the cost of not having this security is too high for the Israelis…bombings, shooting, stabbings. It would be nice if there were another way." All I could think of was stop trying to kill us and these barriers would come down. But I didn't say it.

The turn off for Efrat approached. We passed the guard at the gate and continued on.

"Any idea what you're going to say to Josh?"

"I thought I'd wait to see what he says."

In another five minutes we pulled to the curb in front of a semi-detached house. After grabbing a large gray envelope, we walked up a set of stairs and followed a sidewalk to the front door, which was on the side of the house beneath a young cherry tree. I knocked.

When the door swung open, I saw two people at the entryway. The first was a man with a neatly trimmed blond beard while the second was a fit looking, twentyish security man. I held up my identification for both to see. Without introducing myself by name, I said to the first man, "Shelley's brother?"

He nodded.

"Where are they?"

"In the living room," he motioned to my right.

The entry vestibule led to a hallway that went both right and left. To the left was the kitchen where I caught sight of the Mandel kids at a table. To the right was a dining room and living room. Katie and I stepped to the right and turned a corner to see Josh and Shelley sitting on a couch, sharing a newspaper. Both looked up to see me, and both froze, newspaper in hand. After a moment Josh jumped to his feet.

"Gidon…hi."

"Josh."

"You're in Israel."

"You didn't like Williamsport? Not enough to keep you busy? The Little League Hall of Fame, Susquehanna River activities, Hershey Park not too far away." I meant it to be funny, but it didn't come out the way I expected.

"I…"

Before he got any further, I held out my hand. Josh reluctantly shook it, not sure if my offering were genuine. I looked past him to Shelley, who stood up and was turning slightly red. I smiled and moved closer to her. Tears began welling up in her eyes. "I'm sorry. I'm sorry. I was just so worried for the kids, for us…"

"It's okay. Really." There was no point in beating her – them – up over what was already done. I stepped in and gave her a kiss on the cheek. "I'm glad you're all right."

"You're here in Israel," Josh repeated.

"It's where the trail led, plus you're here." A moment went by. "We need to talk." I introduced Katie: "This is my friend Katie Harris. You actually had invited her that Friday night." They all shook hands.

"It's a good thing you weren't there," Shelley joked.

Katie smiled.

I indicated that they should sit again, and Katie and I pulled up nearby chairs. "Let me tell you what's going on."

I mentioned my trip to Rhode Island, about Mr. Meyers being killed, the Gaza phone number leading to Leveque, and finally the two murdered women. I passed the gray envelope in my hand to Katie who was closer. She took out a stack of pictures; Leveque's was on top. "Does this man look familiar?" Katie asked, holding the French businessman's photo for both Josh and Shelley to see. They took it.

After a moment, "No," Josh shook his head.

Shelley, too, shook her head. "I don't think so."

"What about either of these two women?" Katie continued, showing them the pictures of the two murder victims.

Josh, again, shook his head, but Shelley seemed less certain: "Who are they?"

"One's a chambermaid," I answered, "and one's a glass artist. They were both murdered – possibly by either Leveque or Belard. If you've seen either of them, we need to know where."

Josh and Shelley looked at each other, but before either could answer, raised children's voices came from the kitchen. A moment later there was a dual cry of "Mommy!"

"You guys keep going." Shelley and her brother, who had been standing in the background, walked toward the kitchen.

I continued as Shelley suggested. "So, the pictures? Know either of the women?"

Josh shook his head.

"You're sure?" Katie asked.

Josh nodded. "As far as I can remember."

I was thinking commonalities. If it were "no" to the two women there was one more possibility. "Have you ever been to the Leonardo Plaza Hotel?"

"Sure. Last year, I think. We just walked through the lobby to see what it was like."

"Not on your trip a few months ago?"

"No."

Shelley walked back into the room, explaining the commotion, "Coloring marker conflict." She turned to Josh. "Can I see the pictures again?"

He handed her the stack of photos. Shelley looked at the chambermaid's picture, moved it aside, then looked at the artist's photo. "I know her." She paused. "We saw her at the craft fair in Tel Aviv. She had a booth. We bought some glassware from her."

Josh just shrugged. "Shelley shops and I wander."

"And you never saw Leveque?"

"I don't think so. It's hard to tell." She was still thinking.

"All right, one more thing," I said. "Do you remember that I asked you to make a list of where you went on your last trip here?"

"Done," Shelley said.

"What?"

"Well, mostly done. I felt so guilty about leaving Williamsport, Josh and I worked on it on the plane. I wanted to show it to you as a peace offering in case you were really pissed at us."

"It's on the laptop," Josh added.

"Can you print it out?"

"Sure. Laptop's upstairs," Shelley said.

"Terrific. While you're at it," I fished in my pocket and pulled out a USB drive. "Can you print a file on here called 'Meyers Itinerary?' We'll then be able to compare this one to yours."

"Sure," she took the drive. She turned to her brother.

"Use the printer in my office," he instructed.

Shelley looked at Katie. "Want to keep me company?"

Katie smiled, "Sure," and the two women disappeared around a corner.

I watched them exit, then said to Josh. "Do I need to be concerned?"

"Only if you have something to hide? Have you been bad?"

I beat the crap out of four guys the other night, but that's not what he meant. "I'm always a gentleman."

"How long have you and Katie been together?"

"Maybe six months."

"May it be everything you want."

Whatever that was. "Thanks."

"So, Gidon, tell me the truth, are we safe here?"

"I think so. Leveque is in Gaza and it's unlikely that he knows you're in Israel. Last place he was looking was the States, so probably. I wouldn't get your picture in the paper or on television, though."

"I'll stay away from any political demonstrations," he smiled. He thought for second. "The shul office knows I'm here. I spoke with my secretary."

How likely was it that Belard's men would phone the synagogue office to ask for him? At some point after not finding him, they might call. It was possible that such an inquiry may have already occurred. "Call her, please, and instruct her that if anyone asks for you, just say you're on vacation and she's not at liberty to say where."

"Okay."

"Also find out if anyone has asked for you since you've been gone."

He nodded.

"Allan Samuels." Josh's Torah rescue competition. It was a random mention...as I intended.

"Yes?"

"Anything you want to mention about him?"

"Not really."

"Josh?"

"I've heard he's not a very nice man."

"Can you elaborate?" I looked at him.

"I don't have any first-hand knowledge, so I can't say."

"Josh? I know that he had a problem with you when you got a job and he didn't."

"In Charleston."

I nodded.

"We had some words."

"Any threats made?"

"Not overtly."

"What do you mean?"

"He just said he would not be happy if it ever happened again."

Back in Charleston, the rabbi there alluded to Samuels having connections to less than reputable people. Maybe he had a backer by the name of Leveque. I would have to ask when I saw him later.

"You're going to talk to him?" Josh asked.

"I am."

"Won't that make him more angry at me?"

If he were connected to Leveque, we already had a problem. "I'll keep your name out of the conversation."

As women's voices approached, we saw Katie and Shelley come around the corner. They were standing pretty close together, and looked as if they had shared some secrets. Or maybe I was paranoid.

"Ladies," I looked at them. "Everything okay?"

"Of course," Shelley said. She handed me the USB drive.

"I have both itineraries," Katie held up some papers.

"Josh and I will finish the rest of our notes today," Shelley put in. "We only have the last two days to do."

"You can e-mail them to me." After a moment I headed for the door, and Katie moved next to me. "That's it for now."

"Can't stay for lunch?" Shelley asked.

"Thanks. Appointment to keep. Before I leave though, Josh, I need your cell number."

He gave it to me, and after I put it in my phone I gave them my number.

I looked back at them from the front hallway. "No disappearing on me."

"We won't," Shelley said. "Promise."

Katie and Shelley gave each other a peck on the cheek, and with me wondering what that was all about we walked to the car.

28

As we drove northwest toward the city of Rehovot, I felt the day was full of potential. But that went two ways. I was excited about finding more answers, but slightly anxious about not having enough. While the Mandels were probably safe, I had no illusions that it would last. If Josh's secretary had already revealed he was in Israel, then Belard and his men would be looking for him. Secondly, there was the collaborator from Gaza. While he gave us information on Leveque, we couldn't be certain he wasn't giving Leveque information on us. If so, Josh and his family weren't safe at all.

"We're going to see Laurie?" Katie asked as I drove the back roads to avoid Jerusalem.

"Yup. Be there in about thirty minutes."

Nate and Rachel's daughter had been living in Israel for more than a year now. Last I saw her, which was a number of months ago, she was in a good place…recuperating, teaching kids, had a budding relationship with a young man. Something must have happened since then. Rachel wasn't sure, but Laurie's attitude, or her manner, seemed off to her. She wanted to make sure everything was okay. I did have a special relationship with Laurie, and I trusted that if she were over her head with something, she'd have reached out. If that were the case, she would have been one of my first stops in Israel. I hoped that evaluation was correct.

Laurie lived and worked on a *moshav*, a kibbutz-like community, outside of Rehovot, about fifty minutes northwest of Jerusalem. Early afternoon traffic was light but steady, and before long, we were on the outskirts of town, rumbling over railroad tracks and driving beside fields of sunflowers. As we approached a sign announcing the *moshav*, there was a break in the right-hand field for an access road. We turned onto it, cruising past an open security gate and into the quiet community.

"It wasn't that long ago when this gate would have been closed," I looked at Katie.

"Everyone feels safer these days."

A large, weathered sign made of horizontal wood posts pointed to various streets and important buildings. Without pausing, we continued straight, past a community center. The land was flat and laid out in a grid. Katie observed the community was "tropical-looking." To each side, the roadway edged right up to the front lawns; no curbs or gutters. Cacti and palm trees made up most of the foliage, plus most houses had terra cotta roofs. In a short while, after a few zig-zag turns, we came up on a single story school building set back from the road. As in the past, I parked on the grass near the entrance.

"Laurie doesn't know you're coming, does she?" Katie asked as we got out.

"No."

"Why didn't you call?"

"Didn't want to make a big deal out of this." I came around to her side.

"But you know she's here?"

"She was last time."

We walked past the main entrance toward the other end of the property and the playground. Nothing had changed in the months since I was here. A waist-high chain link fence enclosed a dedicated area of see-saws, a plastic house, tube-like tunnels, swings, and more. As on my last visit, lower school boys and girls climbed ladders, ran across walkways, and generally chased one another from one end of the playground to the other. Two women were standing off to the side, talking as they watched their charges. One teacher was a blonde, about thirty with her hair pinned up. The other woman, perhaps twenty, had white blonde hair, cut short. I recognized the older woman, but not the younger one. Neither was Laurie.

Kate and I stepped inside the gate. Both ladies' posture straightened as they instinctively became more alert.

"*Shalom*. Liat, right?" I addressed the older woman.

"Yes?" She looked at us, trying to see if we were familiar.

"I was here several months ago. I'm a friend of Laurie's." We walked closer.

Liat looked at my face, then, after a few seconds her forehead relaxed and her eyes brightened. "You're...Gidon...Laurie's Gidon."

I smiled. "I am. Is Laurie here?" I looked from Liat to her companion, who had a small gold stud nestled in the curved crease of her nose.

"No. Only in the mornings...she switched to the kindergarten, just for half days."

"So, she's home?

Liat shook her head. "Uncle Phil's."

"A relative's?"

Both women smiled. The younger girl explained, "It's a ranch... further down the road."

"Didn't know about that. She's been there a while?"

"'bout two months," Liat said.

"And you think she's there now?"

"Every afternoon. She finishes here and goes over. It's a short ride. Just go out of the *moshav*, turn right. After a kilometer you'll see the sign."

"*Toda*."

"She'll be excited to see you."

We waved and headed back to the car.

The ranch was indeed not far from the *moshav*. As described, about a kilometer down the road a sign poked out from the corner of the sunflower field: "Uncle Phil's Therapeutic Ranch." Katie and I looked at each other, and I knew my eyebrows had gone up. We were both familiar with these type of innovative, animal therapy places. With the help of social workers and other experts, young and old participants were often able to work through emotional traumas and physical handicaps by taking care of – and interacting with – animals. For example, I knew of a ranch that used horseback riding to help people with cerebral palsy develop a better sense of balance.

We followed signs down a newly paved road and along a fenced-in field to our left. About 50 yards in, a cluster of horses were lazily grazing. To our right was a farmer's field with rows and rows of low, leafy plants.

"Melons," Katie said.

"You can tell?"

"I have knowledge in areas you haven't discovered yet."

"You been holding back on me?"

"You betcha."

The road continued for another quarter mile to empty onto a wide, unpaved parking area with a Parks Service-type office building at its head. I swung around, then backed into a space in front of the building. We stepped out. A pair of young black and white border collies strolled across the lot.

Off to the right of the office, beneath a thatched roof, was a sheltered area presently occupied by a group of young school children. The class was sitting on the ground while a man dressed in jeans and a green T-shirt stood in front, holding a ferret-like animal. The kids were mesmerized as the animal climbed back and forth from one of the man's hands into the other. Katie and I watched for a few moments and then continued to explore. On the other side of the office we stopped by a row of tall cages. In separate habitats, bunnies, raccoons, turtles, and large lizards were either motionless beneath the hot sun, nestled amongst wood shavings, or pacing. To the far side of the cages, alpacas and sheep mingled in a large, grassy pen. A number of young parents and their children were inside, petting the animals under the supervision of staff. It was all very impressive.

We followed a path that led us to an immense expanse behind the office building. Two brown horses were tied to a post on the edge of the field. As we stood beside them, we looked out to see a pair of riders on horses, but closer to the building we saw young men and women – all clad in jeans and the same style green T-shirts – stepping into cages of varying sizes, giving animals food and water. No Laurie. "I don't see her. Maybe she's inside."

The horse to my right eyed me and I scratched the bridge of its nose.

"Check in the office, cowboy?" Katie suggested.

"Reckon so."

We started walking back along the path when "Gidon!" drifted over to us from a distance. We turned toward the voice. As we watched, a woman in a straw cowboy hat rode toward us from the open field.

"Laurie?" Katie asked me, without taking her eyes off the approaching figure.

"Yup. Prepare yourself."

"Gidon, Gidon!!!" She galloped closer, then barely coming to a stop, swung down from the horse and leaped into my arms. "You're back, you're back."

"I'm back, I'm back."

She squeezed me for another second, backed away, then came in for another hug.

"How did you recognize me from out there? You have the eyes of a…" I was going to say sniper, but caught myself… "giraffe. I don't know."

"Are you here by yourself? With my parents? No, you're not by yourself. You have a friend with you. Hi." She peeled off me and extended her hand to Katie. "I'm Laurie."

"Katie," they shook each other's hand.

"I knew you'd come sooner or later. He's my hero, you know.

He rescued me. Middle of the night. Broke in, scooped me up, and brought me back to life."

Katie and I looked at each other. I had never heard Laurie say that so openly and certainly not to someone she had just met.

Laurie pulled away, went back to her horse, grabbed its reins, and gave them to Katie. "Here."

Katie just stood there, reins in hand, not quite sure what to do.

Laurie began to come toward me, then went back to Katie. "Oh, sorry," Laurie took the reins, and then tied the horse to a nearby post. "Where was I?" She looked at me then ran into my arms again. "This is so awesome." Still in my arms, she looked at Katie. "Who are you again?"

"Katie. Gidon's friend from Baltimore."

"Hi. Wait," Laurie looked at Katie. "Are you the chick Gidon mentioned last time he was here?"

Katie turned to me. "I don't know. Am I the chick you mentioned the last time you were here?"

"You are."

"You are *so* lucky," Laurie said. "Gidon's the best. He is so cool. Gunfire all around, screaming, explosions. Doesn't bother him. He'll always keep you safe."

"Of course," I said. Then, "So, aside from having too much caffeine, you seem to be doing great."

"I am *awesome*." She put her arm through mine and began to lead me away. "You stopped off at school, of course, so you know I cut back teaching."

I nodded.

"I'm here every afternoon, helping out with the animals and the children."

"You enjoying it?"

"It's amazing." A second passed. Her pace dropped a notch. "So how long you here?"

"Don't know. Working on something. Came here with Katie. So, fill me in. Last time you told me about a guy. You were excited."

"He cuts right to the chase, doesn't he?" She took a breath, "The guy…yeah, well…that sort of didn't work out. He left."

"His loss."

"Yeah."

Katie and I locked eyes for a second.

"Hey," Katie began, "I want to check out the office. Maybe I can buy something to drink there. You want anything?"

Laurie and I shook our heads.

"Okay."

After Katie left we meandered down a tangential path, past a row of covered enclosures that had a sleeping ibex inside.

"So," I looked at the twenty-one year old who had seen way too much in her life, "you come here to ride?"

"Yeah. I learned back home. People thought it'd be good time for me to get back to it."

We came to a shady area where cut logs had been placed vertically as seats. We took advantage of them.

I looked at Laurie. Beneath her straw cowboy hat, her familiar pixie hairstyle was growing out. The longer hair framed her features beautifully – her high cheekbones still had a touch of red in them – though her face seemed thinner, as if she had dropped some weight.

"It's tough being here sometimes, isn't it?" I said.

"Sometimes."

We both stared off at nothing.

"Do you still have nightmares?" Laurie asked.

"I have the pleasure of nightmares waking me up at night *and* flashbacks during the day." I thought about my soldier, Asaf, being shot in the neck. That nightmare had started again when Belard's man had put a gun to Josh's head. Hadn't had a recurrence recently, though. I wondered if thinking about it would bring it back. "What about you?"

"Yeah. Didn't think they'd last this long. And I still have a problem

315

with rooms and closed doors. I need to see a way out." A moment passed. "Your nightmares. What do you do about them?"

"Accept them."

"Have you ever told anyone, like a doctor?"

No. But that's not what I said. "Sometimes."

I smiled and looked into her eyes. The brightness I had seen in them, the excitement, had dimmed. Looking at her face, I saw that her bangs had grown to cover her entire forehead...but something wasn't right. She was missing...

Laurie let me take off her hat and allowed me to brush her bangs aside. She watched my reaction at seeing that parts of her eyebrows had been unevenly plucked away.

"I did that," she said. "Pulled out the eyebrows...picked at them with my fingers. Couldn't help myself. They said it was stress."

I let her bangs drop and squeezed her hand slightly for a moment. "What's going on?"

"Oh, I had a little meltdown about two months ago. I was at school, and a couple of the little kids got into an argument. I had some trouble dealing with it. The more they yelled at each other the more I cried. I didn't want the kids to fight." She stopped speaking for a few minutes. There was some squawking from birds in a cage not too far away. "Told my counselor. Took a break from work, then we adjusted my schedule. The counselor thought it'd be easier if I were an aide in the kindergarten, plus she wanted me to come here in the afternoons."

"And you've been here for about two months?"

She nodded. "This is a great place."

"It is."

Laurie looked into my eyes, and I saw her become quiet again. "Gidon, can you do something for me?"

"Of course. Anything."

"I want to go back north to where it began."

...To where she and a girlfriend had lingered too late one night... to where they had crossed paths with four terrorists who had slipped across the border...to where they had cut down her friend when she started screaming...to where they had carried Laurie back into Lebanon to be tortured and used as a hostage.

"I want you to take me back north," she repeated.

"In a few days I'll be finished here..."

"Okay. I can wait. But I want to go back."

"I'll take you."

"Just you and me."

"Just you and me."

"And you won't run back to the States? You'll stay longer than last time?"

"I'll stay."

"Promise?"

"Promise." I let more than a few seconds go by. "Now, I want to get your picture for your mom and dad." I straightened her bangs to cover her forehead and returned her straw cowboy hat.

She jumped up and put it back on. "C'mon," she pulled me up. "Let's find Katie and get her picture, too."

She headed toward the office with me in tow.

29

By mid-afternoon Katie and I found ourselves sitting at a rest stop along the highway, having a late lunch. We sat at a small round table toward the back of the food service area, each eating a baguette filled with slices of different types of cheese, tomatoes, onions, cucumbers, and more. While we ate, we both occupied ourselves with a task. I had my laptop open, pulling up images of Allan Samuels, the sketchy Torah rescue man we were on our way to see in Tzefat, and Katie was looking over the print-out of Mrs. Meyers' daily log from their Israel trip.

"What's the story on this man you're going to see?" Katie asked, after swallowing a bite.

The diner where we sat was more of a café, with two young men serving freshly prepared sandwiches, as well as cold and hot drinks and ice cream from behind a small display case. There was a steady flow of motorists coming in for something to eat or just to stretch their legs.

"Samuels," I answered, "does the same sort of work that Josh does in locating and rescuing Torah scrolls from old Jewish communities around the world. For Josh, anyway, it often means going into places where the communities have been destroyed, and locating whatever he can of old prayer books, Torahs, and anyone who remembers the old community. If he can track down a Torah, he brings it back to Baltimore to be repaired, if it's reparable."

I paused to work on an ice coffee slushie, while Katie sipped a mango drink.

"And people hire him to do this?"

"Usually, a congregation in need of a Torah will have a fund-raising event to either buy a scroll or to commission having one written for them. It can probably cost a hundred thousand dollars to write a new Torah, because it's such meticulous, hand-crafted work. If you don't want to go that route, some congregations find it meaningful to bring in a Torah that has survived from a destroyed community, like from the Holocaust. It becomes a memorial to that community. That's where Josh comes in."

"And this guy, Samuels?"

"My impression is that Josh is in it to rescue Torahs, while this guy is in it to make money. It's not a stretch to say he has a problem with Josh because of the competition. In fact, he's threatened Josh, so Samuels and I will need to chat about that."

I looked at the picture of Samuels I had pulled up on the laptop. He appeared to be about forty, balding, with jet black hair on the sides. His face was round, and his eyes – at least in the photo – seemed black and hard, like he was staring down the photographer. I saved the photo for later reference.

Katie and I finished our sandwiches and our drinks, and as we were collecting our trash, Katie indicated a need for the facilities. We disposed of the sandwich wrappings and napkins and then Katie headed off. While she was gone, I smiled at a thought I had been nursing. On the laptop I quickly located an inn near Tzefat I had known about, and hurriedly booked a room. Katie returned a few minutes later, we gathered our personal items and went back to the car.

The drive into the Upper Galilee from where we were would take another hour, and as we moved away from the central part of the country the terrain became increasingly diverse. We drove past flat areas and stretches of farmland, but also, particularly toward the north, into hills and a rising elevation. While Katie continued to read the Meyers daily account, I plugged my phone into a hands-free unit and called Nate. It was still early in Baltimore, and I reached my friend before he had left for work.

"Hey there," I said. "Greetings from the land of the Bible."

"He IS alive," Nate said.

"I am. Yes."

"You weren't on World News, so all must be quiet."

"Quiet, but interesting. Before we talk shop, is Rachel still home?"

"Yeah. I'll put her on."

After a moment, Rachel picked up an extension and I proceeded to tell them about my visit with Laurie. I was mostly straightforward. I said she looked great, had joined a riding club, and was having some ups and downs emotionally. They didn't need the details. Overall, I said, I thought she was doing okay. I told them that she had supportive friends – I did note she was seeing a counselor – and really seemed to be in a good place at the moment. I also mentioned that she and I would get together once this case was over. Rachel couldn't thank me enough. I told them I was e-mailing some pictures of Laurie, so they should check that in a little.

Once Rachel hung up, I brought Nate up to speed. I told him we had found the Mandels – no I didn't yell at them upon our reunion – and that we had a potential connection between Belard, his boss Leveque, and some murders here. We now had to connect the dots to Josh, and hopefully I'd know more after speaking with Samuels tonight. At the end of the conversation, Nate thanked me for checking on Laurie, and then dropped his voice slightly.

"Tell me the truth about Laurie. Is she really doing okay?"

"Yes, she is. As I said, she had some rough moments about two months ago, but she's better now."

"I know that she has to have some crazy shit running around her brain, but she won't talk to us about it. Did she say anything to you?"

"We spoke about some of the stuff we have in common." I didn't want to get specific because I didn't think it was fair to Laurie. On the other hand, Nate was her dad and he was my friend. "I promised her we'd spend time together. And I promise you, I won't leave Israel unless I'm sure she's doing okay."

"Maybe we should just come and visit."

"I think you should. Laurie would love to see you."

"Let me see what I can do on this end to make that happen."

A moment went by.

"Thanks, Gidon."

"Talk to you later, bossman." We hung up.

Katie who had remained silent the entire time we were on speaker, said, "You're a good man," and she leaned over and gave me a kiss.

"Thanks, bosslady. Meanwhile," I nodded to the papers in her hand, "thanks for going over those day-to-day listings." She was trying to find an overlap between the Meyers list and the Mandel list. "Anything of interest? Any commonalties?"

Katie flipped some of the pages. "Not really, just the regular stuff of going touring, restaurants, shopping. The Meyers list is pretty specific. Looks like they had all their receipts and used those to recreate their days."

"And there's nothing that's the same on both lists?"

"Well, maybe they were in the Old City on the same day, but I don't have anything else in common, like a specific tour or a museum visit at the same time, at least for the Mandels."

"Anyone visit the Leonardo Hotel?"

"Wait a minute. I think so." Katie shuffled some pages. After about thirty seconds: "Yeah, the Meyers did. On March 3. They ate dinner at the hotel restaurant."

"Now check for the Mandels on the same date."

She shuffled some pages. "Their list doesn't go that far. They weren't finished making their notes, remember? What's up with the Leonardo? Why that specific hotel? You already asked Josh about it."

"Leveque has a room there, but," I paused, "you wouldn't have known that because you weren't at the forensic lab when we talked about it."

"No."

I shook my head at myself for not remembering that Katie wasn't with us at police headquarters. After a second, my mind went back to Meyers being at the hotel on March 3. I dialed Ronit's number.

"Hey, it's Gidon" I said when she picked up. "What's the date of death for the two women we talked about?"

"One minute." Ronit went off for a few seconds. "The chambermaid was killed on March 5 and the artist on March 4."

"Do you have any video from the Leonardo?"

"The Serious Crime Unit has a copy. The chambermaid is on it, but not the artist. I already asked them to look at it again for Leveque or Belard. There are five or six cameras, so it'll take a while."

"Terrific. Have another date for you. March 3. Mr. Meyers was there on the 3rd."

"Interesting. March 3rd 4th, and 5th. Something was going on. What about Rabbi Mandel?"

"I'm waiting to find out. He says no, though. Meanwhile, any more intel on the collaborator?"

"No. Amit hasn't been available, and I can't seem to find the Gaza man's handler. I'll keep trying."

"Thanks. I'm meeting with the other Torah rescue guy in a little while. I'll let you know what he says and doesn't say."

"Okay."

We hung up.

"You like her," Katie said, looking at me. "Ronit."

"I do. She's very good, and we have some things in common."

"And you just like her."

I smiled. "I do. I also think Amit is being a pain in the ass and not helping her do her job." After another moment. "She'll manage."

∽

We continued northwest into the Upper Galilee, and by now the roadways were either cutting through mountains or winding along a flattened slope. In the distance we could see a hazy Mount Hermon.

We turned off of Route 89 and began the climb up to Tzefat. The city had the distinction of being the highest in the State of Israel. With its isolation up in the mountains, Tzefat had always attracted people, young and old, who were seeking a spiritual meaning to their lives. Additionally, because of its location, artists came here to find inspiration among the high hills, valleys, forests and simply where Heaven touched the Earth.

The main road up into town was a spiral, winding climb. We passed schools, synagogues, a sepulcher or two of famous rabbis' mausoleums, as well as parks, tall housing units, and small markets. The road eventually dead-ended onto a dirt parking lot at the base of the artists' colony. We parked in the shade of an olive tree, and walked up a narrow street that soon branched off into alleys and walkways.

"You've been here before, obviously." Katie said, holding my hand, as I led the way.

"In various capacities. Soldier, shopper, meanderer."

We continued up a slope toward the main alley that had galleries, trinket shops, and small eateries. Though it was almost evening, the alley was still filled with men, women, and families. There was more English spoken here than Hebrew.

"The main tourist area?" Katie asked.

"How could you tell?" I smiled as we passed teenagers, families, and tour guides. "There's more to Tzefat than this, but before we leave this area, I need to make a small purchase." I went over to a display of key chains and necklaces and found an orphaned *kippah* on a table. It was green and white with a Golani Brigade symbol crocheted into the pattern. It wasn't my unit, but it would work. I may soon be poking my head in a synagogue and I'd need a head covering. I paid the vendor, tucked the *kippah* into a pocket, and took Katie's hand once again.

As we walked toward the far end of the alley, I could tell that Katie was trying to take it all in. It was pretty overwhelming, with shop after shop of artwork, Judaic crafts, and religious paraphernalia. At a break between stores we turned a corner and climbed a set of stone stairs bringing us up an additional level of the city. We walked along another alley hemmed in on each side by stone-block buildings that had window frames trimmed in rich turquoise. A number of doors, as well, were painted the same blue-green color. I saw Katie looking at them.

"Keeps away the evil eye," I noted.

The alley branched left and right. We turned left and followed the sidewalk through a decorative gate to a covered courtyard and an entrance to a synagogue.

"This is where Samuels said to meet him. Out here." I recalled the phone conversation we had while Katie and Kiffi were visiting the *kotel* yesterday.

"Where is he now?"

"Inside. He's meeting with congregants, probably about hiring him. Said he'd see me afterwards in…" I looked at my watch…"twenty minutes. I don't want him to see you. Might I suggest that you–"

"Check out the shopping? See if I can find a necklace or a skirt or something. That's so chauvinistic."

"I was going to say stroll through the galleries, but if you want to shop for souvenirs or clothes…"

"I may be able to fit that in, too," she smiled. "Just show me where to go and when to meet you."

I gave Katie directions as well as time and a place for a rendezvous if I couldn't find her.

She walked off, looked back at me over her shoulder, and disappeared around a corner. I stepped into the synagogue.

As I slowly closed the wooden door, I looked around to see a group of men gathered in pews off to the side. To my left, an ancient, gray-haired man hobbled toward me, leaning on a cane. Without saying a word, he held out a cardboard *kippah*. I waved him off, producing my own *kippah*, the one I had just bought. The fellow retreated back the way he had come.

The synagogue was easily several hundred years old. In the center was not only a raised *bima*, but a *bima* "tower" up perhaps eight steps. It dominated the entire room. Around it on the periphery, all the walls, plus the ceiling were white plaster with a large, old chandelier suspended over the center of the room. The ark in front was a worn, dark wood cabinet with a wooden "Ten Commandments" above it.

I sat near the door with a clear view of gathered men. Half a dozen members were seated, facing a man standing in front of them. The fellow making the presentation was clearly Samuels, whose photo I studied earlier. He was taller than I expected and more husky. As the focus of attention, Samuels, cuffs rolled back onto his forearms, was speaking about deadlines and what to expect at each point. After a few moments of watching and listening to his pitch, I stood up and stepped back outside. The ancient man with the cane didn't even look up.

Once back outside, I scanned the area. The modest courtyard was in front of me, then beyond it the decorative gates, and then beyond that the sidewalk which ran both right and left. I stepped to the left of the door, and leaned back against the synagogue wall so I could watch the entrance to the synagogue as well as the pedestrian alleyway. The sun had already passed behind some of the taller structures, bathing the courtyard and the synagogue in muted, indirect light. A light breeze drifted through the air.

After a few minutes, the door to the synagogue opened and a handful of congregants came out. They were bantering back and forth about Samuels' price and his installment schedule. The majority of men wanted to commit, but a few had doubts. In another two minutes the Torah rescue businessman came out. I let him get halfway across the courtyard. "Mr. Samuels?"

He turned. "Mr. Horwitz?" My *nom de guerre* for the meeting.

I nodded.

"You want to discuss a Torah project for your *shul* in Los Angeles?"

I shook my head. "I want to talk about a man named Belard, a man named Leveque, Josh Mandel, and you."

"*Who* are you?" His eyes darted across my face.

"A friend of Rabbi Mandel's."

His eyes, as depicted in his photo online, were indeed hard.

"Fuck off."

Such a nice guy.

Samuels turned to go through the open gate, but I quickly moved in front of him, blocking his way. It wasn't lost on me that he didn't ask, "Belard Who or Leveque Who?"

"We need to talk," I said.

He moved his hand toward my chest to shove me away. At that instant I rotated my torso so he pushed empty space. He lost his balance, moving past me. With one hand I grabbed his collar while simultaneously sweeping out his feet. It took him less than a second to go from vertical to flat on his back. Samuels looked up, not sure what had just happened. His face turned red. He got to his feet and rushed me. I waited until the last moment then stepped to the side. I put out an arm as he went past, grabbing his shoulder, taking him off balance again. His own momentum brought him to the ground once more. He looked up at me for a second time.

"C'mon, there's no point to this," I said.

I let him get up, and saw what was coming. He swung at me with his right fist. I blocked it with my left forearm, and then rotating my hips punched him square in the breastbone. There was a distinctive "whack" at impact, and Samuels collapsed inwards. My punch was purposefully not full force; I wanted him hurt, not hemorrhaging internally.

The big man kept trying to catch his breath, but expanding his ribcage was almost now impossible without pain. I walked him back to sit on a cement bench near the edge of the courtyard.

"Breathe shallow and lower down," I said. "It'll be easier."

He sat and looked at me, completely uncertain. His breath was coming hard now, mouth open and audible.

"You'll be fine. And like I said, we need to talk."

As I leaned over Samuels my back was now to the courtyard entrance. While I watched his face, I felt a movement – something – behind me. I spun, crouching down. Two men had just turned the corner to enter the courtyard. Both were tall and dressed casually. Both had lightweight, light colored jackets. I didn't recognize the man on the left, however I had seen a photo of the man on the right. It had been taken at a Hertz counter. I had also seen him in person, briefly. He had been parked in a maroon Buick outside of the Mandel's house and had just sent two men in to kill Josh.

Belard and I locked eyes for a second. He knew who I was. There was a gun in his hand and he was bringing it up. I dove to the side as he fired two rapid shots. When I hit the ground I rolled and sprang back to my feet. Belard and the other man were gone, rounding the alleyway corner to the left. I ran after them, looking over my shoulder toward Samuels. He was on the ground, blood saturating his chest.

The alley was way too narrow. The tall buildings on either side, made the passageway seem more confined than it was. Shoppers, locals, sightseers were frozen, staring at me as I raced past them. Belard and the other man were up ahead, moving straight, throwing whoever was in their way to the side. One elderly man was thrown into a wall and he fell to the ground. I bent over to see if he were all right, and after confirming that he was – though not spending the time to pick him up – continued on after Belard and his buddy.

My Glock was out now as I turned another corner. Almost immediately a flight of stairs dropped off in front of me. The two men were already at the bottom. I slipped on the first two cement steps, jumped a few feet, caught the edge of another step and regained my footing, running down three stairs at a time. A young couple coming up the steps quickly got out of my way.

I wanted Belard.

At the bottom of the stairs I sprinted to the right, following the two men. I came around a blind corner and knocked over a woman carrying a shopping bag. I shouted back an apology, but kept running. As I looked up, I found myself in the main shopping alleyway. All that was ahead was a mass of people, filling the space between one shop and another and across the width of the walkway. With Belard and his partner plowing through, a number of men and women were already lying in their wake. I moved forward, passing Katie, perhaps, on my right. I wasn't sure and I wasn't looking back.

I grabbed a man wearing a blue baseball cap and shifted him out of the way. He fell into a man next to him, and the two of them knocked over a tall, rotating rack of postcards. Two teenage girls wearing IDF T-shirts saw me, and their eyes went wide. They jumped out of the way. The Glock was still in my hand, with my right index finger outside the trigger guard. I chambered a round as I ran.

Belard was beginning to disappear. If he turned a corner and I couldn't see where, he'd vanish into the alleys or narrow spaces between shops and houses. I glanced off a portly man in a Hawaiian shirt.

The thought that Belard now knew I was in Israel ran through my mind more than once. If he got away it would not be good. Further up the alley, the crowd hadn't thinned; it was becoming more dense. All I could see was a column of people and the stores to either side. The crowd was inadvertently sheltering him.

"Everyone down!" I shouted in English and in Hebrew. "Everyone down. Now!!"

Almost immediately, the crowd in front of me began dropping. Some covered their heads as they huddled on the ground. All these people had gotten out of the way, but now there was no path for me. I had to jump over or sidestep anyone lying or squatting.

Belard, a hundred feet up the alley, was raising his gun. I threw myself to the left into a display of wooden *hamsas*. A gunshot broke off a piece of stone above my head. As I righted myself, I saw Belard approach a corner, his man a step behind him.

Belard made the turn, but his man tripped over a small garbage can or a stool or something, and he went down. I was twenty feet closer by the time he pulled himself up. He managed to round the corner ahead of me. I didn't slow down to make the turn; I continued full speed, knowing that the man might have stopped out of sight to level his gun. That's what I would have done. Didn't matter. I wasn't going to slow down. He'd have to hit a moving target. My intertia in the turn threw me into the opposite wall.

A bullet ricocheted beside me at face level, spraying my cheek with shards of cement. The man was in a doorway, about twenty feet ahead of me, firing. I pushed off the wall, simultaneously launching into a roll toward the other side. I didn't know where the man's bullets went, though I heard some thuds to my left.

I came out of my roll kneeling on one knee. The man had already begun to bolt out of the doorway. My chest was heaving. Holding the Glock in a two-handed grip, I brought my elbows down and locked everything as best I could. I squeezed the trigger twice. The double slam of the .40 shots caught him left of center, catapulting him straight back. He landed on his side and didn't move. I looked beyond him. Belard was not in sight. I ran to the nearest intersection of alleys. Nothing. Stone sidewalks and their centerline depression for gutters ran straight ahead and to the right and left. No one. Not a soul. No one to ask, no one to point me in a direction.

Belard was gone.

30

By the time ambulances and the police arrived, the man in the alleyway, Belard's man, was dead. He was still breathing the last time I checked, but he wasn't fifteen minutes later.

Interesting choice the man had made. If he had stayed in the doorway when I had come around the corner, he might have had me. Adrenaline does interesting things to decision-making. He may have had a shot. Maybe not.

What a mess. Two crime scenes. Before I went to find Katie, whose last image of me may have been my chase through the alley, I drafted some omnipresent soldiers to block off the area where I shot Belard's man, as well as the courtyard where Samuels had been hit. He was dead, too, and I didn't for a second think that Belard was trying to kill me instead of Samuels. Belard had been aiming too high, plus he hadn't known that I was in the country. Now he did. None of this was good. Samuels dead, Belard gone, his man dead, Belard now knowing that I, and perhaps by extension, Josh and his family were here – if he hadn't already known that.

The only positive thing about this evening was that maybe forensics could get a shoeprint of Belard off the ground in the courtyard. That was Ronit's idea when I spoke to her. If they could, then maybe Avital in the lab at police headquarters could match it to the prints at the other murder scenes.

Ronit, though, came up with one major issue to add to the "Not Good" column: "Belard is in Israel and we didn't know that," she said to me.

"Yup."

"He slipped in somehow. That's very disturbing."

"Through Gaza?"

"Most likely."

"Everything okay with the Mandels?" I asked. With Belard around, I had begun worrying.

"No idea. Once we caught up with them, our officers went home." There was a moment of silence over the phone. "Any reason to think that Belard knows where the rabbi is?"

"Not unless Josh told his secretary at home and she told whoever asked. Guess we'll need to find out. I'll ask."

After a moment, Ronit added, "There is one more thing."

"Why did Belard kill Samuels?"

"You thought of that, too?"

"Yup. Add it to the list."

We hung up, and I went off to find Katie. She was calmly talking to a young couple in front of an art gallery, but when she saw me she pulled me into a long hug and a kiss.

"Sorry I couldn't get here sooner," I said a few moments later.

"I knew you were okay."

"Really?"

"I've started assuming that until someone tells me you're hurt or dead, you're okay."

"Really?" I asked again.

"No, but I'm working on it."

I gave *her* a hug and kiss.

We nodded to the couple Katie had been talking to. They wished us well, and moved on.

"So tell me what's going on," Katie said, looping her arm through mine.

"Well, Samuels is dead."

She stopped walking.

"Belard shot him. That's why the chase. And now I have more questions, like what was that all about?" I told her about my brief conversation with Samuels – that he hadn't been surprised when I mentioned Belard, Leveque or Josh.

"What now?" Katie asked.

"Check back with the police. Maybe we can get some clarity."

We walked back to the synagogue courtyard to speak with the newly arrived officers. I introduced myself to the young sergeant major in charge who seemed to be expecting me, and explained what happened. We stood off to the side while officers began going over Samuels' body and examining the scene. Katie kept her back to the lifeless figure the entire time. The officers, for their part, were conscious of the entryway of the courtyard where Belard and his man had stood. Ronit must have called Amit, and Amit must have called Dror, and Dror must have called the Northern District people. By the time my account of the evening had ended, police officers had retrieved Samuels' cell phone and a key card for a nearby hotel. They would head there next. For now, a separate forensics team was pulling footprints from the ground near the gate entryway. It was going to be a long night for all of them.

As for us, I looked at Katie and said, "I don't know about you, but I could go for checking into a nice inn and trying to not think about all this for an evening."

"You don't happen to know of a place nearby?"

"Perhaps."

"Perhaps?"

"Perhaps I know a place that's waiting for us."

"You do?" She smiled and pulled me away...

ॐ

We spent the night at a beautiful two story place in the picturesque town of Rosh Pina, up on the northeast slope of Mount Canaan, overlooking the Hula Valley and the Golan Heights. Unfortunately, my plans for a romantic evening collapsed along with the rest of me in short order. I had enough energy to check the view on the balcony and then shower before hitting the bed. That's really all I remembered… along with a vague recollection of Katie lying on top of me before I passed out. The next thing I knew it was 7:00 in the morning and my phone was ringing. It was Ronit.

"*Boker tov*," she said. "Where are you?"

"I'm in bed," I mumbled. I looked over to see Katie stirring next to me. Light was pouring in from three different windows. "Where are you?"

"At work. I could use your help."

"What's happening?" I moved my tongue around in my mouth so I wouldn't sound like I had been sleeping. Never worked, of course.

"I have all the in-house videos from the Leonardo Hotel on March 3rd when Mr. Meyers was there. There are recordings from six cameras. You're going to help me go through them."

"Not for another couple of hours."

"Are you still up north?"

"Rosh Pina."

"Too bad you won't have enough time to eat in one of their marvelous cafés or walk through the beautiful town."

"You've become pretty bossy, you know."

I could hear her smile.

"I'll give you until 11:30 to get here. I'll meet you in the lobby of your hotel. We can work there. I want to get away from the office. Bring your laptop."

She hung up and I blinked a few times to clear my eyes.

"Ronit?" Katie asked.

"Uh huh. She wants us back in Jerusalem."

"Really?"

Before I could say anything else, Katie moved on top of me under the covers. She wasn't wearing anything.

"This has a familiar feeling to it," I said.

"Like last night before you passed out."

"Well," I looked into her eyes, "I'm awake now."

Katie shifted her hips slightly. "Uh huh. How do I know you won't pass out again?"

I was becoming more awake every second. "Guess I'll have to work on it."

∽

The trip down to Jerusalem took just over two and half hours. Along the way I called Josh to ask two questions. The first was whether he had spoken to his secretary about not telling anyone he was here. He said she hadn't, though there were a few inquiries. It was a short respite, I realized. Belard and Leveque would find out somehow. The second question I asked was really a request that he and Shelley join us at the Prima Kings. There were still some items I wanted to discuss, and now maybe some video to look at, if we found pictures of Belard or Leveque.

Once we got to Jerusalem, we parked two blocks from the hotel on one of the shady side streets, and then went upstairs for a change of clothes. By the time we headed down to the lobby we were both ready for work. Katie insisted on helping, and I welcomed the extra pair of eyes.

The elevators deposited us onto the expansive lounge area of upholstered chairs, love seats, and coffee tables. As the hotel was situated on a corner, large picture windows wrapped the front of the building so we could see King George Street on one side and intersecting Ramban Street on the other. A quick look around revealed a handful of guests in the lobby, all sitting near the front window. In about an hour, lunch would be served. We could hear the clatter of dishes being set out in an adjacent dining area.

Katie and I sat in a pair of armchairs to watch both the foot and vehicle traffic on King George. Before we had a chance to settle in, we could see Josh and Shelley crossing the street and walkiing up to the hotel. In a matter of minutes, they were sitting on a sofa at right angles to us. Both Mandels looked rested and wanted to know if I had made any progress.

Progress? I thought. Samuels is dead. Belard knows they're here. The Frenchman seemed to be able to slip into the country without alerting anyone. There was also are a pair of homicide victims, the two women, who were also connected to the case. On the other hand, maybe something in their lives would turn up a connection. The clues were there; we just weren't seeing them. Personally, I'd settle for killing Belard before more people were killed. We could sort it all out later.

The cars outside our window on King George stopped at the traffic light, and I spotted Ronit's Renault in line. After the light changed, I watched as she turned and pulled to the curb on the intersecting Ramban Street, up a short ways from the hotel entrance. The Shin Bet agent came out of her Renault carrying a laptop case, and walked to the entrance, and stepped briskly into the lobby.

As soon as I saw Ronit approach, I knew something was up. Her auburn hair was atypically disheveled, plus her eyes were full of energy and her cheeks flushed. Ronit turned from me to the Mandels.

"It wasn't you they've been after," she said without preface to Josh. "It was you," she turned to Shelley.

"What are you talking about?" I asked.

"I just saw it on the hotel video ten minutes ago. Leveque was coming out of his room at the Leonardo with the glass artist from the Tel Aviv area. They were very affectionate."

"They were having an affair," I said. "That's what was going on."

"And you," Ronit turned back to Shelley, "were having dinner in the restaurant with a young couple. You weren't there, Rabbi."

"Our cousins from New York. You remember, Josh," Shelley turned to her husband.

"I knew they were in town and that you were going to dinner with them. I didn't know it was at the Leonardo. Why didn't you say something when Gidon asked about going to the hotel?"

"Because," I said, realization dawning, "when we talked about it in Efrat, Shelley had gone out of the room to deal with the kids in the kitchen."

Katie looked at Ronit: "So what's the connection to Leveque?"

"Leveque and the glass artist came down in a service elevator and got out on the ground floor. Shelley had just walked out a stairwell–"

"To go to my car," she was remembering. "I saw this couple under the light just outside the door."

"Leveque and the artist," Ronit confirmed.

"I didn't get a clear look at them."

"But he saw you," I said.

Ronit went on: "He must have killed the woman at some point… we don't know why… and wanted to get rid of anyone who could put them together."

"And Mr. Meyers?" I asked. "He's on video, too."

"He got into the elevator with them earlier in the evening. And the chambermaid must have seen something also." Ronit looked at all of us. "This has nothing to do with rescuing Torahs, or maybe it does. I don't know. Maybe there's another connection to Samuels we're not seeing."

"This is unbelievable," Shelley said.

"I want to show you," Ronit said, putting her laptop case on an upholstered chair near her. "But," she looked in her case, "I left the power cord in my car. I'll be right back."

She turned and headed out the door.

I looked at Shelley. "Don't worry about anything. We're going to take care of you."

After a moment, I followed Ronit out. There were any number of questions I had about timing and who was where. I crossed the lobby, went out the sliding glass doors, and down the short flight of Jerusalem stone steps.

Ronit's Renault was fifty feet up the street. She was opening the passenger side door, when movement across the road caught my attention. On the other side from me I saw a man standing behind a waist-high cement pylon used to prevent cars from running over a curb. He was fairly slight, wearing a cloth jacket, and had a Mahmoud Ahmadinejad look about him. A splotch of dark hair had fallen across his forehead. I knew him. I had watched him cross the Gaza border, and then I sat with him in the back of Amit's car. The informant. Harun.

I looked back toward Ronit. She had just closed her car door. There was a small gym bag near the right back tire. The bag was not Ronit's. I rushed forward.

"Ronit!!!"

The explosion threw me backwards into the side of a metal cage used for bottle recycling, then dropped me to the ground as the compression waved passed. For I don't know how long I was looking down at the pavement. An intense, pervasive high-pitched ringing filled my head, and when I finally looked up – probably after only a few seconds – I couldn't quite see. My vision was blurry, like pieces of whatever was in front of me were not there. I had no idea why I was still alive. I *was* still alive. I could feel my heart beating in my chest and a pounding in my head. Blood was coming out of my nose and running onto my shirt, but I wasn't aware of it. After a few moments, my vision cleared. I picked myself up off the ground to see a mangled green metal drum used for holding old newspapers.

To the right, windows on the first floor of the hotel were blown out. Headlights and taillights on cars across the street flashed as their alarms must have been blaring, but I couldn't hear them. I looked to where the Renault had been. Now it was just a charred shell with black smoke pouring out of it.

And Ronit.

Ronit had been blown twenty feet toward the hotel wall. I slowly walked toward her. Her eyes were open and blood was seeping out of her nose and ears. Her chest was a mass of blood, bone, and tissue. Her legs were bent at impossible angles, and her shoes were no longer on her feet. Her arms, her arms were just not there. I turned away.

I looked up toward the hotel and I saw Katie, Josh, and Shelley standing almost untouched inside the blasted out picture window. They had been shielded by the concrete wall on the side of the hotel. They were just staring at me. I looked back across the street.

Harun, the informant from Gaza, stood up from behind his concrete pylon protection. Why had he hung around? What was that all about? Did he know something about the radius of the blast? Did he want to make sure of something? He looked at me, then raised his eyes toward Katie, Josh, and Shelley. I saw him stare at Shelley. He turned back to me and began to run away from the hotel, down the side street. I started after him. The thought of whether I could or could not run didn't occur to me. I took a step, tripped, stood up, took another step, then continued to put one foot in front of the other. My pace picked up. I wasn't feeling any pain, not in my chest, or in my legs or in my head. I wasn't feeling much of anything except one very basic emotion. I could run that's all that mattered to me.

Harun was fast, but nothing was going to stop me. He started off on the sidewalk, but moved into the street, then back onto the sidewalk. I stayed right with him, following him between cars, dodging metal lampposts, jumping over discarded chairs from a sidewalk café.

He ran through a parking lot, but I followed. He darted up a flight of stairs into the open square between two apartment towers. I was twenty feet behind, but getting closer. He burst through a gate. I was through it before it had a chance to close all the way. He scrambled down a flight of steps and ran across the driveway of an old stone mansion. I jumped the same steps while fixing my eyes on the back of his head. He ran across the front of the mansion, now a Christian study center, toward its far corner. He was angling to disappear around the side, not far from a large planter with a statue of an angel with outstretched wings. I caught him just as he reached the corner, in the shadow of the statue.

I reached for his collar and yanked him to the side. He fell over and rolled a few times. I had no idea if anyone were watching me and I didn't care. He stood up and I kicked him in the gut. He keeled over. I pulled him to his feet – he was heaving, trying to catch is breath – and I punched him square in the face, breaking his nose. He collapsed. I picked him up again and stamped down on his right instep. I didn't have to hear the crack to know I had broken several bones in his ankle. I let him fall again. I picked him up and broke his other ankle. Without hesitation, I grabbed the collar of his jacket and dragged him behind me as I walked off.

It was three blocks back to the hotel, but like everything else, I didn't feel the distance. I passed any number of people and all of them got out of my way. My hearing had started to return, and I could make out sirens in the distance. Approaching the Prima Kings, I walked down the center of the shady street. I passed Ronit's car still billowing black smoke, but dared not look any further to the side.

At the corner, several police cars had pulled up along with three ambulances. People were all over the sidewalk. Officers were talking to people while EMTs began treating men and women and a few children for cuts and shock. They were asking questions, looking in ears and eyes, setting up IV bags, wrapping bandages, securing supine patients to stretchers. I dumped Harun in front of a police officer, who began to ask me some questions. Before he could articulate anything, I simply said, "I'm Shin Bet. He's the bomber. Watch him." With two broken feet and barely able to breathe, I wasn't too concerned he'd take off. Still...

"Gidon!" Katie came over to me, sobbing, and wrapped her arms around me.

"Are you okay?" I asked.

She nodded. "You?"

"I think I have all my parts."

Katie wiped drying blood from my face. I looked behind her to see Josh talking to some cops. He was rubbing the side of his face.

"Josh okay?"

Katie didn't answer. She turned to me. Her mouth was a tight line and her eyes began glistening even more.

"Where's Shelley?" I asked, a cold chill running through me.

"She's gone."

"What do you mean? Dead? She seemed fine when I took off."

"Someone came up to us right after the explosion, punched Josh, pointed a gun at me, and grabbed Shelley. He dragged her to a car and shoved her in."

Without a word, I turned away from Katie and walked back to where I had dumped Harun at the officer's feet. A doctor was about to bend over him.

"Step away," I ordered.

"What?"

I took out my Glock. "Step away."

The doctor backed off. Two officers came over.

"Don't," was all I said. "Turn around if you want."

Under any other conditions I had no doubt the officers would have given me a hard time. Not now.

They looked me, nodded to each other, but didn't turn away.

I bent over the informant. His corneas were glassy, and the skin below each eye was already discolored from his smashed nose. Blood was streaming out of both nostrils.

"Harun, do you hear me?" I slapped his face and his eyes refocused. They went wide when he saw me.

"Where did your men take Mrs. Mandel?"

He didn't answer and I slapped him again.

"I...won't... tell you," he croaked.

"Yeah, you will."

I pressed the Glock against his shoulder and looked into his eyes. Blood continued to run down his face.

"No martyrdom for you. But you'll get to live but with only one arm."

He just looked at me.

I pushed the muzzle of the gun harder into the joint and began to squeeze the trigger. How much distance would the small polymer piece against my forefinger have to travel before the gun fired? .5 inches. 12.5 millimeters. Just another millisecond and it would be there.

"Leveque," Harun whispered.

I didn't move. "What?"

"Leveque. They're taking her to Leveque in Gaza."

31

We didn't have any further information six hours later. But we did six hours after that.

We were in a conference room down the hall from David Amit's office. The Shin Bet man had pulled together quite a group. Police, Army and Naval officers, intelligence people. Monitors displayed a drone's view of an ocean-front mansion while the conference table was filled with similar photos, as well as charts and other miscellaneous documents. Various personnel were huddled in groups, reviewing all the material. Many of the soldiers held lit cigarettes, with thin smoke rising from the ends.

I only knew two people in the room: Amit, and the man who was Harun's handler. While Amit and I sat off in a corner away from the conference table, the handler was sitting at the far end, reviewing his own collection of papers.

"So what's his name?" I asked, staring at the man across the room. "Harun's keeper.

"Shaul."

"The first King of Israel," I noted. "Went a bit crazy. Fell on his own sword in the end."

"You'd like to help our Shaul do the same thing?"

I looked at Amit. He had on his small stylish glasses, but the eyes behind them looked more weary than I remembered. Ronit would still be alive if Shaul had done his job better. And Shelley might be still be standing next to Josh.

I didn't answer the question. Instead: "Do you trust him?"

Amit nodded. "Yes. I do."

I shook my head.

I missed Katie. I missed seeing her, although it had only been a few hours. She was back at the hotel with Josh and some police communications people in case the kidnappers called.

"What the hell is going on?" I asked. "A bomb in downtown Jerusalem? Kidnapping a possible murder witness?"

As we spoke I knew that Israel Air Force planes were bombing the shit out of Hamas locations in Gaza: terrorist strongholds, weapons arsenals, missile locations. Later tonight there'd be another round, but this time with helicopters targeting specific, known terrorists, firing air to surface missiles, blowing up their cars with them inside. Naturally, other Hamas fighters would duck into civilian's houses and fire rockets into Israel, knowing the Israelis wouldn't target them there. The world, with few exceptions, would find a reason to criticize Israel, though the IDF took painstaking efforts to hit only combatants.

Amit caught Shaul's attention across the table and waved him over. He made his way past the soldiers to our side.

"Tell us what you think," Amit said to him. "We have other informants in Gaza," he said. "Reliable sources."

I kept my mouth closed at his mention of "reliable."

Shaul noted my silence and went on, avoiding looking in my direction. "They say there's a power struggle in the Hamas ranks. Belard and Leveque have become very valuable to one of the factions."

"What has this to do with our case?" I asked.

"The bomb, I believe, was Belard's idea to gain credibility."

Amit nodded. "Killing Ronit and setting off a bomb demonstrates he has balls."

"And kidnapping Shelley?"

"A bonus," the handler said. "Because of how we capitulated when they kidnapped Gilad Shalit, kidnapping is now part of the Hamas arsenal."

"Since Shelley is an American," Amit postulated, "Hamas can negotiate for almost anything it wants – release of frozen assets, prisoners in Israeli jails, prisoners in U.S. prisons. Or so they hope."

"Leveque," I noted, "seems to have graduated from worrying about covering his murder of the glass artist."

"Once he rose in Hamas it must not have mattered," Shaul, the handler said. "Now he feels he has protection."

I continued to watch the soldiers and the intelligence people working at the conference table. Shaul went back to his spot across the room.

After a long while, I said: "I miss Ronit."

Amit just nodded.

I began to think about how excited she had been in the hotel lobby just twelve hours ago – her eyes full of energy, the confidence she had.

"Major, we're ready," one of the officers at the table called to me. I put Ronit out of my mind and walked over. Amit followed.

I stood between representatives of two of Israel's most elite special ops units. On my right was a young naval officer, wearing the bat wing and shield insignia of Shayetet 13, Israel's equivalent of the SEALs. To my left was an officer of my old unit, Sayeret Matkal. The only insignia he wore related to his rank, three bars, *Seren*.

"What do you have?" I asked no one in particular.

Oren, the naval commando, answered, pointing to various daylight and night-time photos of a mansion by the sea. "This is Leveque's," he said. "It's about sixteen kilometers south of Gaza City, and as you see, it has a little bit of security."

The mansion was situated rear of center in an immense rectangle of land. The bulk of the property was in front and bordered a narrow street, while the rear property led to a sloping beach and the Mediterranean. The entire estate, with the exception of the sea side, was surrounded by a 15 foot wall. A guardhouse flanked the gated, front entrance to the property. Miscellaneous photos depicted sentries, closed circuit televisions, motion sensors, and more. The night shots showed both front and rear lawns ablaze with light, emanating from fixtures mounted on the house as well as on the perimeter walls. The mansion itself was three stories, with a modest deck off the second floor. Windows on that floor were blacked out in comparison to all the others we could see.

The Matkal officer picked up: "We believe Mrs. Mandel is being held on the second floor, on the right side."

I looked at David Amit skeptically.

"Ever since the name Leveque came up a few nights ago," he said, "we've been watching the house. Drones, undercover agents, and communication intercept teams have all been in position for 48 hours. We also have been watching Leveque's hotel room in Gaza City, as well as his office."

"For two days now?"

"I like to know who we're dealing with."

"And your crew saw Shelley at the mansion."

"One of the teams reported seeing Leveque and Belard taking a woman of Shelley's description from Leveque's hotel to the house."

"Do we know if she is still alive?"

Amit shook his head.

"If she's alive, they'll move her within twenty-four hours," the Matkal officer said. "We have an operational window, and if we wait too long, the opportunity might not come again."

"I know," I said, like it was my call.

In reality, this above all of our heads, and I had no clout here. Shelley was an American citizen. The embassy had already been contacted, but the Israeli military was already planning. They always planned – and practiced. I knew that first hand.

"We can be in and out within forty minutes, depending what we find," Oren, the Shayetet officer noted.

The door to the conference room opened, and in strode a tall officer, perhaps ten years older than me, wearing a colonel's rank on his shoulder. He was a handsome man with a high forehead, short salt and pepper hair, and though I couldn't see them from here, I knew he had cool blue eyes. He was known by all simply as Roey – not by his rank or his last name – and he was my commanding officer a lifetime ago.

We met halfway around the table and gave each other a hug. When we separated, he gave me an affectionate tap on the cheek. "So, I'll give you a hard time later about not calling me. You've been here for several days, I understand."

I smiled. "Sometimes I am not a good person."

He put his arm around my shoulder. "We'll talk later. Meanwhile, *chaverim,*" he took his arm off and addressed the two special operations officers, "continue your briefing."

The Matkal *seren* explained that it would be a joint operation, Matkal and Shayetet. Matkal would come in from the front and sides while Shayetet would come in from the sea. Over the next ten minutes, the officers laid out the details of the assault and rescue. They had a number of scenarios, and this was the one they liked best.

After the briefing, Roey looked at me: "So, Gidon, where will you be? Wet or dry?"

Was I coming in by land or with the naval commandos? "This time, I'll be getting my feet wet, if they'll have me. If all goes according to plan, they'll be first upstairs where they have Shelley. I want to be the first in the room."

Oren, the navy man nodded.

"And if *we* get there first?" the Matkal officer leaned in.

"Then I'll buy *you* the first beer."

The junior officers went back to discuss more details while Amit, my former commander, and I stepped to the side.

"David," the tall officer with steely blue eyes said to Amit, "once this is over, we'll need to talk about how Hamas got her into Gaza in the first place."

There had to be a tunnel that they didn't know about. All Amit said was, "Tomorrow."

"Indeed," my former Matkal boss acknowledged. "Meanwhile, I need to take this plan to my chief and to the Prime Minister. It's their decision." He turned to the pair of special operators leaning over the conference table, "Gentlemen, head back to your units. We may have a go/no go decision by the time you get there."

They began to gather their photos, charts, and drawings. As they did, I looked at Shaul, the informant's handler, who was still on the other side of the room. He had been present during the briefing, and while I wasn't comfortable with that, Amit trusted him. Still, I couldn't help myself. I walked over to him and leaned next to his ear.

"I just want you to know, if you couldn't have guessed, that I am holding you accountable for Ronit and for Shelley. You better pray that we find Shelley in perfect health."

I looked into his eyes and then followed the other military men out of the room.

32

The five of us rose out of the surf into the early morning darkness and stepped onto the edge of the beach. Kneeling in the rocky sand safely beyond the wash of the mansion's lights, we stripped off our swim gear and stowed the equipment subsurface. Less than an hour ago the Prime Minister had given the go order, and none of us had any idea if the U.S. President knew about this operation and if he had signed off on it. It really didn't matter. Not to us. We just wanted to retrieve Shelley before she was harmed any more than she probably had been.

As I worked next to my partner, I said a silent thank you for my basic underwater cross-training. If it had been anything more complicated than a swim from the Zodiak out in the Mediterranean, I probably wouldn't have been on this side of the assault. And, if the Shayetet unit had any misgivings, they kept it to themselves, or at least from me. No one liked a non-team member suddenly inserted into an operation, particularly not one from another service.

We set and checked our com units, put our night vision devices in the stand-by position, checked our weapons, and moved out. Two men peeled off to the left, while Oren, the young naval officer from the briefing, stayed with me along with one other man. Still in darkness, we moved forward, clad in our tactical vests and clutching our M4s. Continuing up the gentle sandy slope, we moved to the edge of the floodlight range. Ahead of us, thirty feet up the beach, sat a rectangular concrete patio, sandwiched between the sand and the backyard. A row of lounge chairs had been left in their last position on the concrete pad, some fully reclined, others with their backs at 45 degrees. It seemed surreal to be on a private, wealthy estate where Leveque lived so well when on either side of the perimeter wall was squalor and dilapidated housing. But that wasn't my issue. I continued to scan the property.

Beyond the patio, the estate's backyard was not green and lush, but carpeted with a field of overgrown, parched, rough grass. The three story mansion lay on the other side. The entire backyard, from the house to the edge of the beach was deserted. There were no sentries back here, though we knew that motion sensors were placed all along the property. Either they had to be pretty sophisticated to distinguish between roving animals and humans, or they had a fair amount of false alarms. We assumed they were sophisticated.

The mansion itself was a mixed European-Middle-Eastern style: boxy, made of stone and cement, sloping roof lines, terraces on the side, ornate railings, and windows flanked by shutters. The back of the mansion had a ground level pair of sliding patio doors and a set of French doors. The second floor, where we hoped Shelley was, had a wide metal deck facing us. Two armed sentries stood close to the guardrail, continually scanning the yard. The three of us paused where floodlight met shadow for a moment, then the man between Oren and me assumed a prone shooter's posture, lining up his M4 on the men on the deck.

We waited.

A number of things were about to happen simultaneously. The Matkal team was infiltrating the front and flanks of the property and would soon take out any sentries in their way. Off on the Israeli side of the Gaza Strip, power was about to be cut to this grid. A Matkal soldier inside the perimeter would sever the power line from the mansion's back up generator, and the man on the ground next to me would take his shot. Oren had overall operational command.

Cutting the power had been his idea, and it had been debated. Sudden power loss was like announcing, "We're coming!" Fortunately,

Amit reasoned, Gaza habitually suffered from intermittent brownouts and blackouts. So, for the last ten hours he had his men cut power to the estate randomly. Hopefully, the terrorists would ready themselves each time for a rescue that never came. The thinking was that over the course of hours, they'd become accustomed to the outages and would settle down. It was not dissimilar to a strategy Joshua used in the Bible, marching his troops around ancient Jericho multiple times over the course of a week, only to have them stand down each time. The residents became desensitized to the troop movement and were unprepared when one of the build-ups led to an actual attack. For us, we just needed those precious minutes to get upstairs before someone executed Shelley.

I looked toward the southern sky. The heavens off to my right were orange, reflecting the fires still burning from when the Air Force attacked multiple buildings earlier that day.

I checked my watch. 4 AM. It would be light in a few hours, but we'd be long gone by then. I breathed evenly.

Any moment...power would be cut, the back up line severed, sharpshooters would shoot, and soldiers would infiltrate the mansion.

Oren rested a hand on the sharpshooter's leg.

We didn't know what waited for us inside, or what the room configurations were. Was Leveque there? Belard? Were there non-combatants in the house? Anyone roaming around? Children? The thought crossed my mind that terrorists and insurgents had already begun using women, not just as shields, but as partners in becoming suicide bombers and guerilla fighters.

Hold on, Shelley.

There was a slight crackle in my left ear, then, "*Lavan* in position." The man at the back-up generator.

"*Zahav.*" A Matkal sharpshooter in front.

"*Shachor.*" The man at the power station.

"*Adom.*" The sharpshooter near me.

Oren looked at me and I nodded ever-so-slightly.

"*Shachor*," he calmly said to the man at the power station, "Now."

In a second, the lights to the entire area died. The mansion was in blackness, both inside and out. Then, for a brief moment, the lights came back on as the generator kicked in. After another second the area went dark again as the generator connection was severed. I also knew that cell phone communications were being disrupted from a truck a block away.

I looked down at Oren's hand that was resting on the sharpshooter's leg. I saw a slight squeeze. His go signal.

The sharpshooter squeezed the trigger of his suppressed M4. At under 100 yards, that's all the firepower he needed. A red splotch appeared on the wall behind the right-hand sentry's head. He collapsed. The other sentry had a chance to look over, but that was all. The sharpshooter caught him just above his ear.

We flipped down our night vision goggles and moved forward at a half run, looking right and left, simultaneously moving our weapons as we scanned the yard. In thirty seconds we were at the back French doors. A one second burst from Oren's suppressed carbine unlocked it. We were joined by the other two team members who had earlier peeled off to the side. The five of us stepped into the kitchen, each one of us sweeping a different zone. No one was inside. We moved fluidly, decisively. I took point. The overwhelming impression I had was one of smell. Rotting garbage. The counters were covered with used dishes, some with dried food on them. The team followed me into the next room and fanned out.

A man carrying an AK-47 appeared on my right. I shot him in the chest at close range. We were in what may have been intended as a family room. It certainly wasn't that now. There was no furniture except for a desk and computer. Nothing on the walls except white paint. Nothing on the floor except a large, worn area rug. There were, however, AK-47's against one wall, plus crates of ammunition. We cleared the room, then kept moving through the opposite door. I heard someone shouting in Arabic ahead of me and then silence. The

Matkal team at work.

I led the way into a larger room. It had the potential to be an office. Like the other room, this one was bare, except for a portrait of Osama bin Laden on one wall and a green and white Hamas flag on another. There was another computer on a desk, and in this room, instead of a stack of AK 47's, there was an open crate of RPG's. The side of the crate was marked in Farsi. As we covered the room, we saw a man in a white shirt and dark pants stirring on the floor near a corner. He looked up when we entered and began to go for a nearby pistol. He was shot in the head.

Another hallway. Clear.

A first floor bedroom without a bed, but with stacks of guns and crates of grenades. The bathroom stank, but was empty.

We came to a wide staircase that ascended to a landing, then climbed right again, onto the second floor. I went up the steps staying to the left side, while the man behind me stayed right. If necessary, one of us could cover the other. I reached the landing and walked up to the second floor. The hallway branched right and left.

Shelley was supposed to be in one of the bedrooms on the right side, which was our left, since we came from the back. Objectively, the sound of our activities from the first floor should not have carried upstairs. There was movement to the right, and we were joined by the Matkal team. We continued down the hall. Matkal took the right side, we took the left.

The first bedroom we entered must have been the master bedroom suite. This room had a bed, a king size one, off to the side and was occupied by a fortyish, bearded man who continued to sleep as we entered the room. We pulled him out of bed. He had been sleeping bare to the waist, wearing white linen bottoms tied in front. I kicked out his knees from behind, putting him on the floor. He fell backwards and was smart enough to stay down and quiet. One of the Shayetet commandos secured the man's hands behind him.

We were about to move into another room, when my earpiece

crackled, "We found the package. Down the hall on the right."

And, what's her condition? Why didn't he say whether she was alive or not? My heart began to sink. We all knew how these things usually went.

I motioned for the rest of the team to continue clearing the house, while I moved down the hall. I walked past the first room on the right. Nothing. I continued to the second room.

Inside, two Matkal officers were standing slightly to the left, looking at the only piece of furniture in the room – an armchair that had a dark-haired woman tied into it by her wrists and ankles. The woman's head had fallen forward against her chest and the back of her hair was matted with blood.

Oh, God.

There was a third Matkal soldier and he was kneeling next to the motionless woman.

We didn't get here soon enough. If I had been smart enough, we wouldn't have needed to be here at all.

The soldier lifted her head. There was some resistance in her neck, but he was able to tilt her head back. Shelley's long, dark wavy hair covered her face. I moved forward and brushed her hair aside, swallowing hard.

Dark, lifeless eyes stared out at nothing. A bullet hole was in the middle of her forehead.

"I'm sorry," the Matkal soldier next to me said. He moved her head slightly, testing her neck's flexibility. "If it matters, she's been dead for hours."

I took a step back. "It's not her."

The soldiers all looked at me.

"It's not Shelley." The woman had Shelley's build and her coloring, particularly from behind, but it wasn't her. After a moment. "That son-of-a-bitch," I said, thinking of Harun. He sent us here.

Oren came into the room. "I heard. It's not her. Who is she??"

"I don't know." Another one of Leveque's witnesses was all I could imagine.

"The house is secure," he then said. "And we've gathered the sleeping beauties in the big room downstairs."

"Good. I've got questions that need answering."

He nodded and led the way.

While I followed Oren down into a large room on the first floor, the power came back on. The Shayetet officer must have given the all clear.

The room with the assembled residents was another no-frills, empty use of space. It had probably been intended as a living room.

Besides me, only three of the commandos were present. The others were either on perimeter, assuring no unwanted guests would pop in, or were gathering the computers and all the documents they could find. Whatever happened now, we had to move quickly. Odds were too great that someone from the neighborhood would stumble onto us and react with gunfire. In a matter of minutes Hamas soldiers would pour into the area.

I looked at the small group of prisoners in the middle of the room. There were five of them in two rows – two women and two men in front; a single male in back. I noted that the man we had found earlier in the master bedroom was in front, second from the right. All were on their knees. All had their hands secured behind them.

I took out my automatic. Every second that passed was a second lost. A fourth commando – the sharpshooter on my team – entered and spoke to Oren: "Kassam rockets in the basement." Kassams, the rockets that Hamas fighters shot into Israel, often from the safe haven of civilian houses.

Oren just nodded.

I would leave him to deal with that. I had another agenda. The group of five people on the floor looked up at me. Some had hatred in their eyes, some had fear. It crossed gender lines. The question was who had what I wanted?

I turned to the man right of center, the man from the master bedroom. Logical choice. He had the most luxurious room. An important man would take a comfortable room. When I looked at him, he couldn't hold my gaze for more than a few seconds. The leader, the man responsible for all the ordnance here after Belard or Leveque left, would be the one with the answers. It wasn't him.

I looked at the remaining people, including the women. I soon fixed on the man in the back row. He had a scruffy, black beard covering a long, sad looking face. He had edged himself behind one of the women, and kept looking down, away from me. There was something about him...about his position in the group. I had been involved in several house searches where a terrorist used an innocent woman or child as cover.

The first man I considered, the one from the master bedroom, was a decoy. This other one was the guy. I went around behind the group, grabbed the man by the collar, and dragged him to the center of the room. I pushed him over with my foot and pointed my gun at his face.

"Where's Belard? Where's the American woman?" I asked.

He shook his head urgently, and muttered in Arabic the equivalent of "Please, please. I don't know anything."

"I don't believe you."

With a slight feeing of déjà vu, I moved the barrel down to the man's right thigh. He squirmed for a second, trying to get away. He wouldn't be able to. "Where's Belard and where's the American woman?"

The man didn't answer; he just pleaded.

"Major," I heard Oren say calmly.

"Where's Belard and where's the American woman?" I repeated, holding the gun steady.

"Don't shoot. Don't shoot!" he screamed.

I thought of Shelley. I thought of the bomb in Jerusalem. I thought of Ronit.

"Major," Oren said, a little more emphatically.

There was only one sound in the large room, and it came from the man pleading. Otherwise, there was complete silence. No one moved: not any of us, not any of the prisoners. All eyes were on me and the gun pointing at the man's thigh. I thought of Harun on the ground outside the Prima Kings, bleeding, and my Glock shoved into his shoulder.

After another long moment when the sequence of events raced through my mind, I lowered the gun. "They're not here," I looked up at the Shayetet officer. "Harun lied. Belard never came to Gaza with Shelley. They never left Jerusalem."

Oren didn't say anything.

"They're down the street from the kidnapping site…in Leveque's hotel room, at the Leonardo."

I turned to the man at my feet. He had gotten quiet. It was all the confirmation I needed.

"He's the boss," I said to Oren, nodding to the man I had been about to shoot. Then into my microphone, "I need a ride to Jerusalem."

"Sixty seconds. The back lawn," I heard a voice in my ear. I recognized my former commander, Roey. "We're bringing an escort."

I turned to Oren and the team, "Sorry, I can't help you clean up."

"Not a problem," the naval special ops man said. "Good luck."

I nodded and hustled out.

Time was critical. If we were to get to Shelley, we had to do it with overwhelming force, yet keep her safe. We could get to her in the hotel room, if necessary. We could get to her in the lobby. We just had to get to her.

"We need eyes on the hotel," I said, running through the kitchen.

"On its way," Roey said. "We'll have intel by the time you arrive."

"Let's hope he's still there with her." I burst through the French doors and out onto the yard.

Interesting move for Belard and Leveque, I thought, staying in Jerusalem. Perhaps they figured that after the bombing they couldn't get into Gaza with Shelley. Maybe they'd trade her for safe passage.

Already I could hear the deep rhythmic concussion of an

approaching heavy helicopter. There was a second sound as well – a faster, higher rotor sound...the escort. Roey was not taking any chances. He was treating this as a hot extract. Hostile forces were definitely in the area, and the transport would draw everyone's attention. If there were other houses with the kind of weapons we had just seen, then all someone had to do was pull out an RPG and aim it at the helo coming in.

In a matter of seconds an Apache attack helicopter flew overhead. It circled the property then took up a position over the beach. I saw lights come on in the neighboring properties. Off in the southern sky the orange glow of burning buildings had subsided. The sky otherwise was dark and would remain so until dawn edged up in forty-five minutes.

Standing on the border of the lawn, I thought of the team inside the house. At this moment they were probably sending photos of their prisoners back for facial recognition. If any came back on our wanted list, he or she would be taking a ride into Israel along with the commandos.

As far as all the weapons we found, there would be no time to get them out. After I left, the naval commandos would depart the way they had come – by water. Another round of helicopters would come in, first for the Matkal team's extract, and then a gunship or two would pulverize the house with Hellfire missiles and Hydra rockets. There was no doubt that the weapons we found would otherwise be used against Israeli soldiers and civilians.

The deep staccato rhythm of a CH-53 Yasur helicopter blocked out all other sound. The big transport moved over the roof of the house and descended in a matter of seconds into the center of the yard. The rotor wash blew back all the shrubs and forced the palm branches on neighboring trees to bend against their will. I ran for the side of the helicopter and the open hatch aft of the cockpit. I crossed the distance to the helo in ten seconds and stepped into the doorway, a pair of powerful hands helping me in. The helicopter rose immediately.

"We'll be in Jerusalem in ten minutes," the IDF officer who had helped me into the aircraft, shouted over the engine noise. I looked into the familiar eyes of my former commander.

"It's five minutes too long. They've been out of communication for almost an hour now." I referenced when cell service had been cut. Would they consider killing their hostage to try to escape untethered?

Roey read my mind: "Hopefully, they're thinking that holding Mrs. Mandel will keep them safe."

I hoped so. That would give us a chance. The CH-53 banked eastward.

While we raced toward Jerusalem we went over several scenarios. Considering Belard and Leveque knew we had to be coming, none of the plans afforded a true element of surprise.

I sat on a bench, Roey opposite me. We looked at each other. My mind wandered as the miles to the capitol city closed. I saw a different hostage scenario in my head – the one in my nightmares when the bomb maker held my soldier at gunpoint...and Asaf being hit in the split second before I fired.

"Mrs. Mandel is alive." Amit's voice broke into my thoughts.

"What?"

"Mrs. Mandel is alive. We placed an electronics surveillance team in the room under Leveque's. Just heard...the three of them are still there. Leveque, Belard, and Mrs. Mandel. Leveque and Belard have been arguing what to do. They're very...anxious."

"Do you have a team next door?"

"No. The rooms on each side are occupied. Too much noise getting them out this time of night. We have men in the lobby and on the roof. We'll cover the other exits as necessary."

"I'll meet you inside the entrance. Have the hotel manager there in case we need directions."

He acknowledged and clicked off.

I closed my eyes. I thought of Josh waiting in a hotel room, Katie by his side, for word on Shelley. I still thought about how I had all this wrong. Shelley, not Josh.

The whine of the engines filled my ears. Below us, I knew the landscape was changing from rolling plains to the foothills of the Judean mountains.

My eyes still closed, I pictured Laurie running toward me and then jumping into my arms at the ranch. I saw Ronit in profile as she drove us to the Gaza border. I saw her sitting with me in Efrat, sipping an ice coffee slushie and telling me about her life.

"We can't come in over the hotel," Roey's voice announced at some point.

I opened my eyes and saw him looking at me.

"I thought about coming in on the roof," he said, "but the sound of the helicopter will panic them."

I nodded, suggesting Independence Park, the large park adjacent to the hotel.

"Still too close, but at least it won't be on top of him."

"One minute," I heard the pilot say. "I can't land. Too many trees."

Roey and I stood up, clasping a grab bar on the bulkhead. My former commander came over and handed me a pair of fast rope gloves. While I put them on, he donned his own pair.

"When was the last time you did this?" I asked.

"Last week," he smiled, his cool blue eyes on me. "You?"

"I was busy last week."

I handed him my M4 and he slipped the sling diagonally across his torso. We pulled open the hatch. Below us, lights of the city passed by. From our height I could see the walls of the Old City illuminated by orange floodlights, and in these pre-dawn hours, a line of traffic approaching Jaffa Gate. We yawed slightly to the right.

"Standby," the pilot's voice in my ear said.

I grabbed a rope secured above me. We came in over the northeastern corner of the rectangular-like park. The Leonardo Plaza Hotel was diagonally across the field on the other side of a line of trees. I glanced at an emblem beside the open hatch – a graphic of a dragon-like bird, wings spread and talons out. The words Nocturnal Birds of Prey Squadron arced around it.

The CH-53 descended rapidly, then paused. I kicked the 90 foot braided rope out into the night. After a second it hit the ground. Holding on, I swung out, grabbed the rope with my boots, then slid down. My gloves smoked as the fibers raced through my hands. I was conscious of the expanse of the park around me, and then I was on the grass. Without waiting for Roey, I ran off toward the line of trees across the park.

The wind rushed past my face. As I crossed the field, I heard the helicopter ascend…and then it was gone. While I ran, I quickly scanned the grass to my right and left. Sprinklers had come on and were watering sections of the lawn near the crest of a small hill. No one was around. I ran across several sidewalks, through a break in the trees, and onto a long driveway. Two white taxis were parked twenty feet from the entrance, their drivers, standing beside their vehicles, awaiting an all-clear. Soldiers in black tactical gear flanked the hotel entrance. One held a door open for me. I entered the lobby with Roey seconds behind. Amit, plus a group of army and Shin Bet personnel, stood in the center of the expansive room. They met us as we came in.

"They're on the 17th floor," Amit immediately said. "1723. We have the key card." He nodded to a young soldier in body armor, with a shaved head and piercing dark eyes who was holding the small plastic rectangle.

A blonde woman in a white shirt and navy skirt stepped forward. The nametag on her blouse gave her name and title: *Manager.* "Take the service elevator," she said. "Use the key card to activate it. When you come out upstairs their room will be on your left as you come out. Now follow me." The woman hustled off and we all sprinted behind her to a hallway at the other end of the lobby. We turned left, ran past several banquet rooms and then stopped in front of an elevator. I pushed the up arrow and the doors slid open. I stepped in along with three soldiers.

As soon as the doors closed, I felt the need to ask no one in particular: "You're Roey's men?"

"Yes," the soldier who had taken the key card answered.

I nodded. Good. They were Matkal and we had similar, if not identical training in many areas.

"Welcome back," the young warrior said.

I didn't respond immediately. He didn't know that I was only "back" to get Shelley…that I was angry that I didn't have the clarity to see the whole picture…that I just needed them to be extraordinary at their jobs for the next five minutes. We were now a team, but they didn't need to know what was running through my mind.

"What's your name?" I asked.

"Sam."

"Sam," I began, as I edged back the slide on my Glock verifying there was a round in the chamber, "when we get to the room, you open the door. I'll be first in."

He nodded as did the other two team members.

"Amit," I said into my mic, "status?" He was in touch with the surveillance team.

"Footsteps walking back and forth," he reported. "They're arguing about Mrs. Mandel."

The floor counter on the display registered 16. I took a few deep breaths.

On 17 the doors separated, and we quickly but silently moved down the hall to the left.

Past a lounge area. Past flowers on a table against a wall. Across a gold carpet. Odd numbered rooms on the right, even numbers on the left. When we passed 1719 there was a single gunshot, coming from a room ahead of us. Shit!

Keep moving, I said to myself. Don't think.

"Gidon," Amit's voice said.

"Not now."

We came to 1723.

"Where inside are they?" I asked.

"Rooms to the left of the entrance," Amit responded.

I didn't have to say anything. Sam inserted the key card. The team lined up behind us. The green LED on the lock came on. We burst into the room. Every light had been turned on. I faced an open, expansive living room containing two sofas and an upholstered chair. A large flat panel TV hung on one wall. The drapes were pulled shut. No one was there. There were two open doorways, one to the right and one to the left. Even though Amit said the trio was to the left, we had to be thorough. Two of the men behind me moved to the right without exchanging a word. Sam and I swept left, my automatic moving with me.

Four gunshots rang out in quick succession from down the hall. We hustled through the narrow passageway. Bathroom on the right. Nothing. Bedroom next on the right. We rushed in, looking for any movement, any presence. I expected to see Belard holding Shelley at gunpoint. Instead, we saw Leveque lying on his back, atop the made-up queen bed. He had a gunshot wound to the chest. Blood was saturating his shirt.

"Leveque is down," I said, and we continued back into the hallway toward the last room straight ahead.

The dead Frenchman accounted for the single gunshot we had heard outside the suite. What about the other four? And where were Belard and Shelley?

The other Matkal men joined us. We entered the master suite. It was empty. King-size bed, TV on the wall, a desk, chair, and computer off to the far side. A small sitting area near the picture windows. A pair of entryways were on our left. Two of the Matkal men took the first left. Sam and I continued to the next opening. Was Belard making a stand with Shelley, or was she already dead?

The doorway led into an alcove and to the connecting doors for the next suite. The inner one had been swung open. The normally closed second door was open, its lock side splintered. The four gunshots.

My earpiece crackled. Amit. "Belard and Mrs. Mandel are in the hallway." He must have been watching a hotel monitor. "They're going back the way you came to the service elevator."

We ran back through Leveque's suite. I pulled open the door to the hallway and looked up the corridor. It was clear. Belard and Shelley had already made the turn to the elevator.

"They just got in the elevator," Amit said, his voice even. "They're coming down. Gidon, go past that elevator. There're two more up the hall. We're sending them to you."

I ran down the hallway.

"He'll go for one of the basement exits," I said. "You have to keep him inside the building."

I ran past the flowers on the table against the wall. I ran past the lounge area.

"Put men in the basement alcove on the inside near the elevator. Let him come out with Shelley. No firefight. Talk to him. Slow him down. I want to get outside."

I reached the passenger elevators, but had to wait. Both cars were two floors below me.

If Belard got to the parking lot, this wasn't going to be good.

"Do you have snipers set?" I asked.

"There's no shot. Too many obstructions outside," I heard Roey say.

The elevator chimed and the doors opened. I ran in and pressed "L." Nothing. The doors didn't close. There was no "Close Door" button.

Sam, the Matkal soldier, rounded the corner and began to step into the elevator car. He was halfway in when I pushed him out. He looked at me, surprised. The doors closed. If he had been caught in the way, the doors would have opened again. There was no time.

The elevator descended. I prayed that an early rising guest on a floor below didn't want to head downstairs. If he stopped the elevator, it was all over.

I looked at my reflection in a mirror on the wall. My face was blackened from camouflage paint and my hair was wet with sweat. The eyes that peered back at me were bloodshot and showed more than a little worry.

The floor counter dropped to 5, then 4...

"They're in the basement," Amit said.

"How do I get to the basement exit when I come out the hotel entrance?"

"*Which* basement exit? There are several."

"The one where Leveque saw Shelley three months ago...the one she came out of for the parking lot." Ronit would have known the answer. She had seen the video.

There was a pause. I heard him ask someone. Then, "We don't know exactly which one."

Shit.

Which door would Shelley have come out of? What had she been doing before going downstairs? What had Ronit said?...Shelley was in the restaurant.

"Where would a guest have gone after coming out of the restaurant?"

There was some discussion off-mic, then Amit: "Come out the lobby and go around to the left. There's a small access road on that side. There's a door right there."

The elevator opened and I ran out across the lobby.

"I'll have men there in thirty seconds," I heard Roey say.

"I'll be there in twenty."

I raced out of the lobby, past the two taxis waiting near the entrance. I tripped, rolled, and sprang to my feet again. The corner of the hotel went by on my left and I saw a narrow access road that led to a door at ground level about 100 feet away. The door didn't have a knob on the outside, but it had a white fluorescent fixture over it. I stepped into the shadow thrown by a large dumpster.

My heart was racing. I was breathing way too heavily for a calm, clear shot. I tried taking long, controlled deep breaths. I looked around. Roey was right. There was no clear shot for a sniper. Too much foliage and cover.

There was a metallic sound coming from the other side of the basement door as a release bar was pushed. A vertical line of light appeared in the entryway as the door opened.

Belard stepped out with a large caliber automatic pressed to the side of Shelley's temple. He was pushing so hard that her head was tilted to the side. She was grimacing in pain. Behind them I saw one of the Matkal men. Shelley and Belard stepped clear of the door.

I took another few deep breaths, prayed it would be enough, then came into the light, gun raised.

Both Belard and Shelley saw me at the same time.

Belard recognized me. It showed in his eyes. There was some surprise there as well.

He stopped pushing Shelley for just a second. "We're leaving," he said. He moved her so she stayed between the two of us.

I didn't respond.

I realized immediately he wasn't going to take his gun off his hostage. There was no way to take a shot. He'd walk with Shelley over to his car.

After another heartbeat, he half-pushed, half-pulled her to his left. I slowly stepped the opposite way.

A team of soldiers approached from the opposite end of the hotel.

How good were Belard's nerves? He had shot Mr. Meyers. The two women here in Israel – the glass artist and the chambermaid. He had shot Samuels right in front of me in Tzefat. Leveque minutes ago – whatever that was about. If Belard couldn't get away, he would shoot Shelley. He knew we realized if we took a shot, he'd likely spasm or twitch or move a fraction of an inch and pull the trigger. He'd be shot, but Shelley would be dead instantly.

As the soldiers came up on Belard's left, he turned his head slightly to see what was happening. I moved another step to the left closer to the building. Shelley was no longer completely shielding him. This had never happened before in my experience with hostages. Shelley was still pulled close – her head was right there – but Belard was exposed just enough.

The angle was right. The time was right. If I could make the shot, Belard's muscles would simply cease functioning.

At this moment, there was no emotion. Just training and desire, and maybe something else. I adjusted my aim, finding the spot just below and behind his ear, and pulled the trigger. The Glock recoiled and the gunshot could be heard clearly throughout the immediate vicinity and beyond. Everything stopped. But Belard crumpled straight to the ground. Not a sound, not a word, not a look. There was just nothing holding him up anymore.

Shelley stood there, unsure of what had happened. She turned to me, opened her mouth, then closed it. There was nothing to say. Tears started coming as a release to her built-up tension. She stayed right where she was and silently sobbed. I went over and put my arms around her. We stood like that for a little while. I didn't know how long. At some point she said something, but her head was still on my chest.

"What?" I asked looking at her.

She pulled back, looked at me, eyes still full of tears, and said softly, "Good shot."

I smiled, said a silent thank you, and kissed the top of her head.

33

Ronit was buried in the late morning in a cemetery just south of Haifa. We were standing under a cloudless sky among a modest group beside an open grave. Ronit's parents were there, as were friends and several co-workers. Amit stood across from me, quiet the entire time. In his clamped down expression, I could tell he was extremely upset. Josh and Shelley were there as well. That was impressive, considering what they, what Shelley, had been through. As for us, Katie and I held hands the entire time, and as Ronit's body was lowered into its final resting place, tears overflowed Katie's eyes and ran down her cheeks.

Ronit's grave was side-by-side her husband's. They had been married six months, Ronit had told me, when Yoav, patrolling with his small army unit, was overwhelmed by a Palestinian mob and beaten to death.

I really liked Ronit. I decided that if Harun the "collaborator" made it out of prison in some insane prisoner swap, I'd find him, whether he was in Gaza or Lebanon or wherever, make sure he saw me, and then kill him.

As mourners shoveled dirt into the grave, I grabbed an available spade and helped. Finally, when it was done, I stood back, sweat running down the side of my face. Ronit was the one who had solved the case. She had called me tenacious, but she was more so. I knew I'd see her face and hear her voice for quite a while.

Once the service was over, we walked back to the car without talking to anyone. Katie and I barely spoke to each other during the entire funeral. Fortunately, as it was Friday, we had the weekend to regroup, at least physically. By the time we returned to Jerusalem, many of the shops had closed, either out of respect for or in preparation of the coming *shabbat*. Over the next twenty-four hours, Katie and I slept, held each other, and walked the streets both ancient and new.

Our hotel had boarded up the shattered windows with plastic panels. Glass had been swept up from the sidewalk, and the burned out skeletons of cars had been towed. Whether it was a miracle or the small amount of explosive used, only Ronit had been killed.

Every moment Katie and I were together, I'd watch her, knowing what images were in her mind. I knew what Katie saw after the bomb went off, as well as the sight of me with the bloody Harun. Katie, too, had a relationship with Ronit, plus she saw up close what Josh had gone through when Shelley had been taken. And there had to be an image of Shelley at the hands of the killers.

On Saturday afternoon when we walked through the neighborhood of Yemin Moshe near the famous Montefiore windmill, Katie stopped and spontaneously asked, "How can people do this to other people?" I shrugged weakly, as my answers in these still-raw hours ran the gamut from philosophical to religious to politically incorrect. Some responses should be left unspoken.

Later, I saw Katie sitting in a chair in our room, book in her lap, and tears silently running down her face. When Sunday came, I wanted her to have a change of scenery. We drove to Tel Aviv, walked along the hotel-beach promenade, looked at men and women in bathing suits that were flattering on some and less so on others; we ate at trendy restaurants, and took in Old Jaffa in the evening. On Monday, Katie wanted to go to Yad Vashem, the Holocaust museum and research center, not to go through the tour, but to start checking the archives. With Kiffi's help she began the process. Katie wanted to see if there were any record of her family – not about her grandfather who was an opportunist at people's mortal expense, but about her great uncle who had smuggled food to people at the cost of his own life.

While she began her research, I headed down to Beersheva where the family of my soldier friend Asaf had their home. I hadn't spent much time with them since he had been killed, and it was long overdue.

I also spent some time with Josh and Shelley. They were both doing okay. Shelley really seemed fine, certainly by all appearances. Josh didn't want to leave her side. They, embarrassingly, couldn't thank me enough, which was ironic because I felt if I had been smarter, so much of the pain would have been avoided.

I spoke with Jon in Baltimore, updating him. "That was *you!?*" he exclaimed when he heard on international news about a hostage rescue and that the kidnapper had been killed. Actually, I just said I had been involved, but he made the leap. He also said, that I'd "have to tell him all about it," but we both knew I wouldn't. All my students were doing fine, though at this point I felt they were more his students. I received a call from the member of Josh's synagogue who had "hired" me. After my offer to return the balance of his expense money, he told me to keep it. Expecting that, I knew I'd donate it somewhere, perhaps to that therapeutic ranch where Laurie was working.

I reached Nate at home to update him on how everything had been resolved. Naturally, he said, "So, you couldn't just let them handle it."

Over the course of the week, Amit and I met along with Roey to debrief. I was feeling better about Amit. I still didn't trust him entirely when it came to revealing all the information, but I knew I could count on him when I needed to. As we discussed the mission in Gaza, it turned out that two of the five people the team had interviewed – one man and one woman – were wanted for terrorism by the Israelis. They joined the Matkal team, along with the body of the woman we had discovered, in the air evac from the mansion. Amit, Roey, and I also talked about the choices that were made at the Leonardo Plaza. For instance, why have Leveque's room in Gaza under surveillance, but not the one here? If a team had been in place locally, they would have seen or heard that Leveque and Belard had Shelley in Jerusalem, a few blocks from the bombing. Also, why the decision not to put coverage on each exit of the hotel, and be satisfied with poor sniper coverage?"

In the end, none of us knew why Belard killed Leveque. All surveillance could provide was that after an argument where the two men had resolved to take Shelley in their escape, Belard turned on Leveque and shot him. We could only speculate.

Tangential to all of this, there were still questions about Allan Samuels, Josh's competition. From financial papers in his hotel room, he appeared to be blackmailing Leveque. Shin Bet, the FBI, and Interpol would have to dig more.

Finally, Amit, Roey, and I talked about inter-agency and cross army cooperation. At some point, I turned to my former Matkal boss and told him I owed his men a beer, since they got to the hostage in Gaza first.

For Katie and me, the week moved along. On the Thursday after Ronit's funeral, we were eating dinner in a dairy restaurant off of Jaffa Road when Katie started a conversation I was somewhat anticipating.

"I'd like to go home next week," she said.

I looked up from my meal, but didn't say anything.

"I have to get back to school and I need to sort through the last week."

I nodded. "What about your research into your great uncle? You're just getting started."

"It'll be there." She put down a forkful of tortellini. "What are your thoughts?"

After a moment, "I'd like to show you the country a little more. Spend a few days in the south. Spend time in the north. Really, just get away together."

"You're not ready to come back," Katie said.

"I promised I'd spend time with Laurie."

Katie didn't say anything for a few moments. Then, "How long do you think you'll stay?"

"A few weeks."

She looked into my eyes. "I just want to be in my own house with my own routine. I'll miss you."

When we returned to the hotel we booked Katie on a flight to Baltimore for Sunday night. A few hours later as we got ready for bed, she presented me with a gift-wrapped package. "It's really not for tonight. More something for the morning."

I opened the wrapping to find 3 packages of Uno brand boxers. I looked at Katie, confused.

"On our first day here you made a specific stop to buy local clothes. You didn't want to be wearing American styles."

"Yeah," I smiled, not sure where this was going.

"And when I asked about your underwear, you indicated that you didn't need to go that far."

"Uh huh."

"Well, I thought to be truly authentic, you'd need something other than what you usually wear."

"Where did you buy these?"

"The *shuk*."

It would have been interesting to see the look on the shop owner's face where she made the purchase. I held up each cellophane package. One underwear pattern was called "paintball," and looked like splotches of green paint on a black background. One was "stealth grey" – Katie said for creeping around at night in my underwear – and one was blue and white horizontal stripes, because those were the colors and pattern – sort-of – of the Israeli flag.

"You'll have to wear them while I'm gone so you'll think of me."

"That's never a challenge and it's always a pleasure." I smiled and kissed her.

We spent the next two days, enjoying each other's company. Instead of staying in Jerusalem, we went back up to Rosh Pina for the time that we didn't have after Samuels was killed in Tzefat. We strolled through the town, perused the art galleries, and generally just enjoyed the quiet and the mountain air.

When Sunday evening came, Katie and I were melancholy over not staying together. I knew she needed to go back to Baltimore for the distance and to process everything, and I needed to spend time with Laurie, as promised. Though I didn't tell Katie, I also wanted to spend time with Ronit's family. I wanted to hear more about Ronit, plus I wanted to give them my impressions of her.

I stayed with Katie as she went through the check-in process at Ben Gurion Airport...the questions from the security personnel, the baggage screening, and the counter check-in. I couldn't follow her past the metal detectors – though with my Shin Bet identification I probably could've gotten through – so we said good-bye on the shopping concourse. We gave each other a kiss and a long hug. As she turned toward security, I headed out to keep a promise to Nate and Rachel's daughter.

ACKNOWLEDGMENTS

Confluence is work of fiction. While many of the locations are represented accurately, some, however, have been altered to fit the needs of particular scenes.

One setting that is pulled from reality is the Toolmarks and Materials Laboratory, Division of Identification of Forensic Science at Israel Police headquarters in Jerusalem. My sincere thanks goes to Superintendent Sarena Wiesner and to the Division's collective scientists for an in-depth look at the groundbreaking forensic work they do. They, indeed, bring to the fore Edmond Locard's axiom: "Every contact leaves a trace."

Many thanks to tour educator extraordinaire Judy Auerbach for sharing her knowledge on locations, roadways, and general atmosphere of specific areas in Israel. To Eli and to Sam, thanks for putting up with my incessant questions; your answers have helped lend verisimilitude to the story.

A special thank you goes to Albert Aboulafia for his "medical consults," and to Becky Schwartz for her quick once-over of the manuscript. Finally, at Apprentice House, Dr. Kevin Atticks and Drew Peters have earned my sincere gratitude for their advice, direction, and dedicated work on the book.

Thank you, all.

ABOUT THE AUTHOR

In addition to *Confluence*, Stephen J. Gordon is the author of *In the Name of God*, Gidon Aronson's debut thriller. Mr. Gordon's other writing credits include a memoir for *Good Housekeeping* and television series work for Maryland Public Television. His feature film script *Rapid Eye Movement* was accepted by the Independent Feature Film Market in New York. Mr. Gordon lives in Baltimore.

Apprentice House is the country's only campus-based, student-staffed book publishing company. Directed by professors and industry professionals, it is a nonprofit activity of the Communication Department at Loyola University Maryland.

Using state-of-the-art technology and an experiential learning model of education, Apprentice House publishes books in untraditional ways. This dual responsibility as publishers and educators creates an unprecedented collaborative environment among faculty and students, while teaching tomorrow's editors, designers, and marketers.

Outside of class, progress on book projects is carried forth by the AH Book Publishing Club, a co-curricular campus organization supported by Loyola University Maryland's Office of Student Activities.

Eclectic and provocative, Apprentice House titles intend to entertain as well as spark dialogue on a variety of topics. Financial contributions to sustain the press's work are welcomed. Contributions are tax deductible to the fullest extent allowed by the IRS.

To learn more about Apprentice House books or to obtain submission guidelines, please visit www.apprenticehouse.com.

Apprentice House
Communication Department
Loyola University Maryland
4501 N. Charles Street
Baltimore, MD 21210
Ph: 410-617-5265 •F ax: 410-617-2198
info@apprenticehouse.com
www.apprenticehouse.com

CPSIA information can be obtained at www.ICGtesting.com
Printed in the USA
BVOW070343290113

311834BV00001B/3/P